EVERY THOUGHT

LOVE BETWEEN THE LYRICS

SALLY O'KEEF

To Reagan and Brooklyn.

CHAPTER ONE

NOTHING SAID "FRESH START" on a Friday morning like a spray tan, a smile, and my feet in these four-inch heels, silently begging for mercy. Oh, how I'd missed the record industry. But here I was, ready to hop back into the fire as a judge on *Singing Sensation*, the reality TV competition I'd won six seasons ago.

I stared at the fabric-covered extra skin bursting from the top of the belt cinched around my waist and sucked in my stomach. *Note to self: Less Pop-Tarts, more protein.* If only Axl didn't love them so much. Great, I was blaming an almost four-year-old for my pastry addiction.

Sebastian, *Singing Sensation's* sadistic stylist—say that five times fast—clucked his tongue and twirled his finger in that uppity French way of his. Fabian, my personal stylist, stood behind him, hands on hips, glaring at the older man's back.

I only had to deal with Sebastian and his snide comments for a few months. Show up, judge the singers, dodge Sebastian, and voila! I'd get my own talk show! And Axl would get a mom who had time to make him a decent meal and put him to bed each night.

Sebastian sighed. "Turn."

Like a skin-tight, leather-wearing puppet on his string—I waddled in a slow circle. When this was over and I had my own talk show, I'd bring *my* stylist with me.

"Oh, I must have gotten your measurements wrong; it doesn't fit quite right."

Fabian growled.

What made Sebastian the way he was? Probably heartbreak. It ruined the best of us. I avoided my reflection in the mirror, unwilling to see the trainwreck Evan had left behind.

"Maybe we add a jacket to cover the not-so-desirable parts?" Sebastian suggested.

My cheeks flamed, and I bit my tongue. If I snapped back, I'd be labeled "difficult" again. I met Vince's gaze in the mirror. At six-four and 240 pounds, my security guard was an imposing figure. To me, he just looked like a big salt-and-pepper teddy bear, but Sebastian shot him a nervous glance. Vince's jaw ticked, and his nostrils flared. He was supposed to protect me from physical threats, so this was definitely outside his job description, but I could tell he was itching to turn Sebastian into French toast.

The *not-so-desirable parts*. Ugh. "I had a baby." My smile strangled each word. This man had obliterated my self-esteem when I won the show. Now, I was back. Lucky me.

Sebastian shook his head, like me having a baby was tantamount to Brittney eloping with a backup dancer. "Zat was four years ago, yes?"

Fabian stepped between Sebastian and me. "She doesn't need a jacket. She needs clothes that fit her right." He dove into the clothing rack, his growls getting louder with each item he flipped through.

Then he turned his accusing gaze on Sebastian. "Why are none of these her size?"

"Zey are." He came over and searched a few items, then pulled out a jacket. "Here!"

I widened my eyes at Fabian and pictured shaking Sebastian until his dark wig went flying from his bald head. There had to be a song in that somewhere. What rhymed with bald? Crawled.

Sprawled. Hauled? Installed... Yeah, bald wasn't the best word to rhyme. Grumpy. Dumpy. Frumpy.

I chuckled, and Sebastian's gaze shot up to me. "Vwat is funny?"

I shrugged and bit my lip to keep from smiling.

He huffed and stomped his foot inside his pilgrim-style shoes. *This* was why I couldn't trust him to dress me. He came straight from the 1780s. But if I wanted my talk show, if I wanted to be the emotionally available mother Axl needed, I had to just grin and bear it.

With jerky movements, Sebastian reached out and grabbed my belt. "Try zis." He tightened it another notch. "Perfect."

Yup, breathing was officially out, and stuffed sausages were in.

Sebastian stomped from the room, huffing like a bull.

Fabian shook his head and took off the belt. "Let's get you something wider."

He'd just buckled a thick black belt around my waist when Colby, my best friend Dylan's younger brother and Axl's nanny, burst through the door, his face red, his breaths labored. "Is Axl in here?"

Axl.

Vince was on his feet and out the door in a split second.

My heart rate surged, and my stomach dropped to my toes. "He escaped?" I stopped myself before I tacked on *again*. That kid was going to be the death of me! I rushed out the door, Colby on my heels.

"We were in your dressing room. I turned around for thirty seconds, I swear, and the next thing I know, he's gone."

It was going to be okay. The location was secure. Security knew to keep him inside, but that didn't stop all the what-ifs from parading around in my mind.

Voices echoed down the long hallway. Black-and-white posters of smiling celebrities lined the walls, and my shoes clacked on the thin red carpet that covered the cement floor.

"Go check my dressing room again. I'll look this way."

Fabian rushed from the fitting room. "What can I do?"

"Check the emergency exit and the back alley," I tossed over my shoulder.

What kind of mother couldn't keep track of her son? *This* was why I needed a change of career. I couldn't keep hauling Axl around like a carry-on bag.

I half-jogged half-wobbled my way down the hall to the metal double doors that led into the full auditorium. Two bulky men stood there with their arms folded over their chests.

"Have you seen a little boy? This tall. Dark, shaggy hair, blue eyes." I put a hand at my hip level to show Axl's height as I unstrapped my shoes and kicked them off. The bigger of the two pointed to the hallway that led to the stage doors.

I ran down the hallway where he'd indicated. As I passed the staff room, a familiar giggle met my ears. I skidded to a stop and turned back to the room. Axl, dark hair mussed, a red cape tied around his neck, and his teddy bear under one arm, stood in the center of a crowd of stage assistants like a king holding court.

I pressed my hand to my pounding heart and released a relieved breath.

Vince rushed in seconds after me and immediately radioed that we'd found him.

"Axl, you rascal," I said as I scooped him up and pressed a kiss to his soft cheek. He stared back at me with Evan's eyes, and it took me a second to see Axl again instead of the man who'd broken my heart. I let out a shaky breath, part relief, part fear. "You scared Mommy."

He picked at the red sequins at my collarbone. "You're gonna be on TV, wight, Mom?"

"Right, buddy."

"And you're gonna judge the singers, wight, Mom?"

"Right, buddy." I smiled and snuggled him closer. "Say bye to your new friends."

"Bye, pwepope!"

A chorus of "Bye, Axl" followed us out of the room.

Vince escorted us down the hallway toward my dressing

room. A faint mix of cigarette smoke and weed drifted through the hall. Typical—exactly what I wanted Axl to avoid. Some things in this business never changed.

As we passed the security guards, Axl waved to them too. "Bye, pwepope!"

Thank you, I mouthed and nodded to my discarded shoes. Vince picked them up.

When we entered the dressing room, Colby was pacing the floor in front of the dressing screen, tugging at his sandy-blond hair.

"Axl! You scared me, little guy." Colby pulled Axl from my arms and hugged him tight. "You can't run off like that."

What was I thinking when I asked Colby to be his nanny? A baby watching a baby.

Then Axl put a chubby hand on each of Colby's cheeks and held it until Colby looked at him. "Sorry, Unca BB."

Love.

That was what I was thinking. Colby loved Axl and vice versa. Warmth bloomed in my chest and a soft smile spread across my face. Axl was without a doubt the best thing I'd ever done. I couldn't imagine my life without him. Even if Evan had broken me, I couldn't regret my time with him, because it'd given me Axl.

Vince cleared his throat. "They're asking for you."

I gave Axl one last kiss and checked myself in the mirror. It would do.

Outside, a man was waiting with a mic pack and an earpiece.

I squinted at him, my memory pulling me back to what felt like a thousand years ago.

I made up a song about him the season I won *Singing Sensation*. Gus, the sound guy. "Gus, right?"

"Good memory." He smiled, his attention on the mic pack. "Say something for me?"

I sang a few bars of "November Rain," a Guns N' Roses song and Axl's lullaby.

"Beautiful," he said, giving me a thumbs up. "You're good."

As I followed him down the corridor, a director's voice

crackled through Gus's radio. "Okay, take Jenny to the side of the stage. She'll enter in front of the curtains."

He gestured me toward the hallway. A camera crew waited at the far end, and Jaryce, the show's host, strode toward me with his trademark smile and a suit so bright it could stop traffic. He held his arms open, and I stepped into them.

"Jenny! It's so good to see you again!" he said in my ear.

"You too." He was the only redeeming part of this show.

"You have a little something..." He pointed at his own collarbone, and I glanced down and saw a partially eaten Cheerio clinging to my sequins. Jaryce was a gem. I wiped it off.

"Kids," I said in explanation.

He grinned. "Ready?"

I gave myself another quick once-over and nodded. "Ready."

The red lights on the camera indicated we were already rolling, so I forced myself to smile. The director motioned for us to walk, and the cameraman walked backward in front of us, capturing everything.

"Are you excited to find out who the other judge is?" Jaryce prompted.

I glanced at him. "I'm ecstatic." *Focus on walking, Jenny.* I was rusty at walking in heels after so long away.

"Any guesses?" Amusement flashed in his eyes.

Oh, he was loving this. The question was a trap. Anything I said could be used to create drama later. "I'm just excited to find the next *Singing Sensation.*"

It was exactly the soundbite they wanted. The red lights turned off and the cameraman gave me a thumbs up.

I followed Jaryce up the stairs to the stage. The crew blocked the curtains covering the stage, but parted to let Jaryce through, and a director led me to a spot to the side where I'd enter. Loud chatter came from the other side of the curtain, where the audience waited.

This was it. The first step to a solid future, and as long as the other judge wasn't a total d-bag, I was home free.

Jaryce's voice came through the speakers, and the audience quieted, then cheered.

"Hello everybody! Welcome to *Singing Sensation* season fifteen. We're coming to you from Friction Theater in Los Angeles. Let's meet this season's judges!

"You all know Kimball Stone, executive director for *Singing Sensation* and CEO of Titan Records."

The crowd went crazy, and I watched on a small screen backstage as Kimball stood on the judges' dais, a spotlight on him as he waved to the crowd.

"You're next," the director said.

My heart pounded. It didn't matter how many times I got in front of a crowd, my heart always decided to run a marathon.

"Our second judge won season nine of *Singing Sensation*. Her last album went double platinum, a first for a *Singing Sensation* alumnus. Please give a warm welcome to Jenny Gentry!"

The crowd went wild, and the director pulled back the curtain enough for me to step through. The lights blinded me. I waved in the direction of the crowd. *Left, right, left, right. Don't trip.*

"Smile," a voice said through my earpiece.

I did.

Jaryce met me at the walkway that went between the stage and the judges' dais. He kissed my extended hand, then air-kissed my cheeks. I returned the gesture.

Kimball met me part way along the catwalk to the dais and took my hand. Same smug smirk, same salt-and-pepper hair.

"Cut!" the director called. The crowd quieted as a group of assistants swarmed. Kelsey scurried over and powdered my nose and forehead.

"You're doing great," she whispered.

"Thanks."

As everyone cleared away, a director sent me to stand by Jaryce.

"When we say action, just wait for Kimball to come get your hand and lead you over the walkway."

Oh, goodie. Forced chivalry.

I waited like a damsel in distress for my monochromatic knight in black chinos.

They told the crowd to cheer again and called action.

I smiled as Kimball came over and took my hand. I'd written a song about "Kimball, the greedy capitalist" the year I won *Singing Sensation*. I'd have to fish it out of my notebooks, but I seemed to remember it included something about money clenched in his fists. It was a good one. We settled into the soft chairs behind the white kidney-shaped table. The chair to my right was empty.

Jaryce stepped forward, mic in hand. "Are you ready to meet the third judge?"

Kimball and I exchanged bright, fake grins as the audience whooped and hollered.

The curtain drew back.

The cameras turned toward me. Even Kimball's eyes gleamed with anticipation.

Then came the sound of drumsticks striking out a rhythm—one I knew too well.

The hairs on the back of my neck stood up.

The stage lights came on.

No.

They wouldn't.

They didn't.

But they did.

Evan Black, my ex-boyfriend, my son's father, and the man who had shattered my heart, strutted onto the stage.

CHAPTER TWO

I'D FACED SOLD-OUT CROWDS, hostile interviews,

and cocaine withdrawals—but nothing prepared me for Jenny Gentry in a red dress.

Time slowed, and I stumbled over my lyrics. Her dark hair seemed to glisten under the spotlight. Her smile sent a jolt of longing through me, and those piercing green eyes. They saw into my soul.

The music seemed too loud for the moment. Instead of drums, there should've been a string quartet. Or a flute. Hell, I'd settle for a piano. Anything to keep me suspended in this magic bubble. I gripped the microphone tighter as I sang the first chorus, my bandmates in position behind me.

Then reality set in. I'd be around her for the next few months. Nearly nonstop. My mouth went dry, and my whole body screamed that I needed to get away. I'd fought hard to stay clean, and Jenny was a complication I couldn't afford. I shoved my hand in my pocket and clutched my eleven-month sobriety medallion like a lifeline. The cold metal dug into my hand and reminded me exactly what I'd survived.

Jenny was a professional, so her expression froze in a smile, but behind those eyes, I could see the fear. The tightening around her mouth. The way her throat worked as she swallowed. Our gazes locked as I sang, and I saw something I couldn't quite name in her eyes. Distrust? Skepticism?

She must've read every headline from the last four years, the ones that painted me as a cautionary tale. Of course, the paparazzi stopped reporting on me as soon as I got my life together—sober rock stars didn't sell gossip rags.

My stomach sank. What must she think of me? Drug addict. Alcoholic. Walking disaster. Not that she was wrong.

We do recover, I thought sarcastically, repeating the oft-used Narcotics Anonymous phrase as I replaced my noisy thoughts with the sound of the fans cheering.

They were what mattered. What I was doing this all for. A solo career. The last notes of my song bled into silence, and then the deafening roar of the crowd took over.

A cameraman moved in from my left, trying to catch my reaction, but I couldn't tear my gaze away from Jenny's. I knew the drill—they thrived on drama, on and off the stage—but this was more than I'd bargained for. How had I not seen it coming?

"Cut!" the director called, and a makeup person rushed over and patted Jenny's nose with powder.

Static replaced the crowd's cheers.

My body froze, doing nothing but drawing in air—guess we knew what I did in a fight-or-flight situation... I froze. Blink, and the whole scene might shatter. I'd find myself in the Parkland house with the guys, high as a kite. Like the last year had never happened. Or worse, that I'd relapsed. Again.

THE DIRECTOR CALLED for another take, telling Jenny and I to meet each other on the catwalk and embrace. I muttered a few choice words but nodded. The scene was deja vu—our chemistry on full display when every nerve in me screamed to run.

Jenny's face paled, and I forced my eyes away from her.

The director stepped off camera, the stage lights flared to life, and he called, "Action!"

The final notes of my song hummed through the speakers as the lights dimmed. The crowd cheered. Jenny looked directly into my eyes. A thrill shot through me at the sight of her smile, and for a fleeting second, I almost let myself believe it was real—the smile, the spark, the excitement. *It doesn't matter. She doesn't love you—she can't.*

She ran across the catwalk, but my feet stayed rooted to the floor. I had just enough presence of mind to open my arms before she threw herself into them.

The scent of her floral shampoo punched me in the face, and memories came rushing back: meeting her in this same building when she hit the top ten, our coaching sessions, the chemistry we had to ignore because of our contracts. Then, after she won the show, our first real date. Our first kiss. Our relationship played out in stanzas behind my closed eyes, each moment looping like a song I never wanted to end—until that final discordant note. When she ripped it all away.

I squeezed the medallion tighter, letting the sting remind me of everything she'd put me through—remind me why I should let her go and refuse to look at her again. It took everything I had not to turn and run off the stage. Give up the contract. Tell Kimball to take his drama and stick it where the sun don't shine.

"Cut!" the director shouted.

Jenny pushed my arms off her and took a step back, fire flashing in her green eyes. How long had I stood there holding her? Too long, apparently.

"Take it from when Jenny gets to the stage," the director barked. He waved one of the cameramen to the front of the stage and another to take position behind us.

I took the time to study her. Time had been kind. Her face was a little rounder, her body curvier—healthier than I'd ever seen her. More beautiful than the fading version of her I'd been carrying around in my memories. Even with the tension tightening her eyes, she smiled up at me, and that smile hit my chest like something I'd been missing the past four years. *Stop it!*

"Action!"

The crowd cheered, Jenny leapt into my arms, and I held her like an addict clutching their next hit. *Maybe that's what I am.*

"Cut!" the director shouted.

Jenny's smile vanished.

The director scowled at me. "You're holding her for too long, Evan. Make it quicker. We want *friendly*. That's what we're selling."

"Can't you just cut to a different angle when the hug's long enough?" Jenny grumbled.

Maybe I made them shoot a few more takes because I wanted to keep holding her. Maybe it was me trying to test my resolve. See how close I could get to the edge without tumbling over. Run through the storm like a buffalo. And maybe I just liked to get under her skin like she'd been under mine for the past four years.

When the director finally called it—apparently satisfied that we'd hugged each other into oblivion—he told us to take a ten-minute break. Jenny stalked down the hallway like she was auditioning for a horror movie. It wasn't that I was *trying* to follow, but my room just happened to be down the same corridor. Pure coincidence. Bad luck. Story of my life.

She spun on me at her door, eyes narrowed like she was about to set me on fire.

"You screwed up the shot on purpose," she accused.

Maybe I had. Maybe I just liked watching the vein in her forehead pop. "Sorry. It won't happen again," I said, all contrition and zero sincerity. Pissing her off made it easier to keep my distance.

The door opened, and a little boy snuck out and turned, immediately stopping and shouting, "Mommy!"

I froze. This was her son—the reason she'd left. Mini-Jenny, minus the ability to glare daggers. The pain hit hard, like it always did. She'd wanted a kid so badly she'd gone and had one less than a year after dumping me. Efficient, really. Like ordering express shipping on heartbreak.

When Jenny saw him, her face softened. "Axl, you rascal. Are you sneaking out again?"

He giggled.

She tickled his tummy and opened the door, ushering him back inside. "Colby, did you know Axl was running away again?" she called into the room, then closed it on my face.

I didn't know what I expected. Maybe some sort of actual reunion. A real hug. A catch-up session. But all I got instead was a silent accusation, which made no sense. She broke up with me, not the other way around.

I didn't need these games.

Made it maybe twenty feet down the hall before it hit me—heat, need, that gnawing itch under my skin. The craving.

The scent of weed got stronger the closer I got to my dressing room. Dammit. My band was still in there. If I went in right now... I couldn't trust myself not to participate.

The guys would hand it over with smiles, like I was the prodigal screw-up finally coming home. Jenny, the memories, the knife in my chest at seeing her and her revenge baby—obliterated in a heartbeat.

The drugs would smother me sweetly, wrap me in nothingness, hold me down until I begged to stay.

STOP!

I pressed my head against the cool steel of my dressing room door. Metal over madness. One breath. Then another, pretending the chill could freeze it out of me.

Do you want to end up dead like your birth mom? That thought slammed into me like a two-by-four. One slip—one second of letting go—and I'd be right there, another casualty.

After a few steadying breaths, I strode down the hallway, away from temptation. At the end, I opened what appeared to be a janitorial closet. I stepped into the dark closet and pulled the door closed. The sharp tang of cleaners cleared my head. I pulled out my phone and texted my sponsor.

Me: Just had a moment. I wanted it so bad.

Kellan: Don't forget to check in with your emotions. Try to figure out what caused it. Do you need me to come get you?

> Me: No. I think I'm good. You know how I took this gig on Singing Sensation? Jenny's the other judge. She brought her revenge baby with her.

> Kellan: Gentry? Seriously? Ouch.

This job was supposed to be my clean break from the band, my step toward being less of a walking train wreck. A respectable gig, cameras and all. All I had to do was treat Jenny like I'd treat any other recording artist: polite, professional, and distant. Easy.

> Kellan: There's a meeting tonight. Can you be there?

We fly to Denver tomorrow morning at the most ungodly hour.

> Me: I'll be there.

Jenny hadn't made the official list of people I'd harmed back in my addict days, but I had to be honest—I hadn't done her any favors either. The way she looked at me when the directors made us hug? Yeah, Exhibit A. Plus, Aiden had been dropping hints that I needed to call her for about a year, and something about the tone of his voice made me think I'd done something I didn't remember.

The kid thing had blindsided me. We'd been together for almost two years, perfectly content in our mutual "kids? Hell no" pact.

And then, out of nowhere, she wanted a baby.

One minute we were on the same page. The next, we weren't even reading the same damn book.

Still, I was determined to shove our messy past into the rearview where it belonged. We might never braid friendship bracelets together, but cordial? I could fake cordial.

Caring had cost me before. Jenny had cost me before. And I was too damn smart to buy the same lie twice.

Love wasn't safe. Love expected things. Love looked you in the eye and decided you weren't enough.

But fans?

Fans were different.

They didn't see a mess. They saw what I showed them—the lyrics, the grin, the performance. They loved the highlight reel, not the person behind it. And that was fine by me.

Their love came in applause and streaming numbers. Predictable. Controlled. Conditional, sure—but at least the conditions were clear.

Jenny had loved the man. They loved the myth. And between them, only one of them hadn't walked away.

So I wrote another verse. Another song.

And told myself it was enough.

CHAPTER THREE

I'D SPENT the last ninety minutes in a grueling interview with country singer Jo Pierson, the other coach for season 9 of *Singing Sensation.* Breaking down our top picks, explaining who we thought would win and why. And I was pumped to meet the group of ten contestants we'd be dividing and coaching through the season.

The director stopped us outside the conference room doors. "We'll just wait for the cue. One of the contestants is taking a bathroom break, then we'll go."

That sounded like the best idea. "I'm going to do that too. I'll be back."

I grabbed the cigarettes from my duffle bag and headed out to the gated parking lot. As I opened the door, I struck my lighter.

"Don't light that!" a feminine voice said, making my heart stutter.

I looked down at her, sitting on the cement parking block, and raised an eyebrow. Then I pocketed my lighter and pulled the ciggy from my mouth as I plopped down on the block beside her.

She looked up at me with sea-green eyes; she had a cute pixie-like nose and apple-red cheeks. Her long, dark hair had been curled into loose waves, and she wore tight jeans and a tighter green T-shirt. My breath caught. She was stunning.

Her name had completely escaped me, despite watching hours of the auditions to see who I'd be coaching.

"Sorry. I just don't want it to affect… Never mind, it's stupid."

I dropped the cigarette on the ground and went to crush it with my boot out of habit.

She gasped. "Don't litter."

I paused, boot mid-air, looked back at her, at the lashes framing her eyes, at the light dusting of freckles across the bridge of that pixie nose. She might be a sprite. Or an illusion. I had the strangest urge to reach out and see if she was real.

"What's your name?" I found my voice.

She cocked her head, and the movement sent the magical scent of her shampoo drifting through the air like an enchantment. "You're Evan Black," she said, instead of answering my question.

I nodded. Slow—mentally and physically.

"Those things're bad for your health." She pointed to the cigarette still on the ground beneath my hovering boot. Then she reached out and snagged it from the ground, along with the pack in my hand, her fingers brushing mine and sending my heart skittering from my chest to my stomach.

"Hey!" I protested weakly. I found that I didn't actually mind.

She stood and tossed them into the garbage can outside the studio door, dusted her hands. "There're people who like your music and prefer you don't destroy your voice."

I stared at the column of her neck, at her lush lips, the way they curled around the words she spoke.

"Are you one of those people?" I asked and held my breath.

She shrugged. "You're talented."

That didn't answer the question. In fact, she hadn't answered any of my questions. I stood, almost in a trance. I towered over her.

I watched her eyes widen, watched her straighten to her full height as if challenging me, watched her gaze take in my broad shoulders, my T-shirt, then her gaze brushed over my face like a caress. My lips, my eyes, my nose, my hair. My jaw. One side of my mouth tipped up in a smile, and I heard her intake of breath, soft and sweet.

I stepped closer. Couldn't help myself. But I didn't touch. She had an innocence about her that warned me away. Like she thought she was more street savvy than she was. If I touched her —as much as I wanted to—it would be a breach of contract, and I couldn't protect her from Kimball.

I dropped my hand that had drifted toward her of its own accord. "Tell me your name."

She swallowed. I followed the movement with my gaze, wishing I could brush my thumb over that spot on her neck, feel the softness of her skin.

"Jenny."

Then I remembered. "Jenny Gentry from Montana. You sing pop."

She held my gaze and nodded. "I sing pop," she confirmed, a blush staining her cheeks.

I put a hand out between us. "Nice to meet you."

She looked down at my hand and finally smiled. My heart thundered in my chest.

"Thanks for the most interesting smoke break of my life."

She laughed, shook my hand.

Every single thing out of her mouth had surprised me.

Something told me that Jenny Gentry had grit, and I admired the hell out of grit.

CHAPTER FOUR

MY HEART HAD BEEN REPLACED by a jagged shard of glass, and all I could think about was getting as far away from here as possible. Each heartbeat hurt more than the last.

Of all the shady, underhanded, weaselly things to do, Kimball pulls this? Despicable. *Ratings are more important than your comfort.* I couldn't count the number of times he'd said that to me when I was a contestant. I growled low in my throat, my hands shaking.

It wasn't that I followed Evan's life after our breakup, but he was my son's father—and my best friend married his best friend—so I got updates. Videos leaked of him high and drunk nearly every weekend...slowly deteriorating, his cheeks becoming sunken, his eyes losing their spark. And I had been the catalyst. The last straw of his self-control.

Eventually, the updates from Aiden had stopped. Evan had cut off communication with him. I had cried for him. Mourned the man he was and the life he could've had. Mourned the father Axl would never know.

Now, I was in my own personal hell. What if Evan found out? It would destroy him. He never wanted to be a dad, so after he flatly refused to reconsider kids, I did the only thing I could to protect the life already growing inside me.

I left.

My eyes burned and my feet ached. I took a deep breath and pushed off the closed bathroom door that I'd been leaning against. It would be okay.

I video-called Dylan.

She answered, her blonde hair in a messy bun on top of her head. Aiden's head over her shoulder.

"Jenny!"

I went straight to interrogation. "If I find out you knew Evan was the other judge, our friendship is over."

She gasped and glanced over her shoulder at a very guilty-looking Aiden.

"You knew!" I accused.

"Let's not pretend you don't keep secrets," he said.

He had a point. Dylan had finally broken down and told Aiden who Axl's father was after I called her to rant about Evan being a deadbeat no-good father. Aiden then called Evan and asked what was going on with me and the baby; Evan didn't seem to know what Aiden was talking about. That was the first clue I had that Evan didn't remember the phone call the day after Axl's birth. He didn't remember calling me a liar, a cheater, calling me names, telling me he had a vasectomy. It hurt. So, I'd sworn Aiden to secrecy. He was less than thrilled with that prospect. But a year later, when Evan was basically killing himself with drugs, I pointed out how smart I was for keeping it from him.

"Don't forget our deal," Aiden said.

I clenched my jaw and forced a smile. "What deal?" Did that sound innocent enough? Probably not.

He took the phone from Dylan. "When he's sober for a year, you promised to tell him 'bout Axl. June 13th was his relapse date."

And Axl's birthday, and Dylan and Aiden's anniversary. What a coincidence.

He raised his eyebrows, meeting my gaze through the phone. "So June 14th will be a year."

"He relapsed for one day?"

A nod.

"That's a month away." It felt too soon. I wasn't ready. What if he wanted custody? What if the courts forced Axl to go to his house on the weekends? How was I supposed to give him the stability he needed and be the mom he wanted if he was living outside of my home fifty percent of the time? And how could I trust that Evan would take care of him properly? Keep him safe from...the kinds of stuff rock stars were known for.

"If you don't tell him, Jenny, I will. I can't keep lyin' to him."

My throat tightened, and I nodded. "If he makes it a year, I'll tell him. But you have to let me do it my own way." I had to be sure he wasn't going to relapse again. I had to protect Axl above all else, even above stupid promises I never thought I'd have to keep.

A vice clamped around my heart at the thought of splitting Axl's time with anyone. I was the one who stayed up with him through sleepless nights. The one who sang to him when he was sick. I was the one who he came to when he bonked his head or skinned his knee. Taking that from me would rip my heart from my chest.

Then I remembered the hug on the stage earlier. "He smelled like weed and cigarettes!"

A massive sigh blew through me before my breath caught. Did that mean he'd relapsed again? Did he know I was the other judge before going into today? Had I caused that? Was I really that hard to be around?

"Was his band there?" Aiden asked, voice flat.

Ah. I saw where he was going with this. "Yeah."

He stared at me like he was staring at a stupid person after stating the obvious.

I unclenched my jaw and said lightly, "I'll allow that it might not have been him." Then tacked on, "I guess."

Dylan cackled in the background.

Aiden went into another room, and her laughter was muffled. "Hey, can you do me a huge favor?"

"I thought I already was."

His lips thinned and he stared at me again.

"Fine. What?"

"You know better than anyone how lonely this business can be. Even when you're surrounded by people. Don't let him get in his head."

"Break's almost up," Vince called through the door.

"I've gotta go."

He kept on staring.

"Promise me, Jenny."

I could've pointed out that I hadn't kept my last promise, or at least hadn't intended to, but I didn't. "What if he doesn't want to talk to me?" That was probably the lamest question I'd ever asked. He'd stood outside my door after the break, waiting for me to talk to him. To say something. To introduce Axl, but I hadn't.

His eyebrow lifted. More staring.

"Fine. I'll be nice..." *Ish*. Even if talking to him hurt. Even if seeing him again nearly overwhelmed me with guilt.

"Just look out for him, please?"

I sighed. "I will."

Dylan wrestled the phone back from Aiden and blew me a kiss. "I love you, bestie!"

"Love you too."

"Tell him soon!" Aiden shouted as I ended the call.

Gah! Why had I made that deal? I'd checked with a lawyer to make sure I couldn't get in trouble for keeping Axl's existence from Evan, and he advised me to tell Evan. I did. But I couldn't help that he didn't remember it. I couldn't be blamed for him being too drunk or high or whatever to remember he had fathered a child and accused me of being a despicable cheater who couldn't keep her legs closed.

And I was positive the Evan that broke my heart and turned to drugs would be petty enough to make me split weekends. His lawyers would make sure of it.

I rebuckled the belt and took another peek in the mirror. *You're a professional. You've got this. You didn't do anything wrong.*

As I entered the theater, Vince walked me past the front row of auditioners, keeping them at bay with a glare and a few sharp words. He took the seat closest to the judges' dais and folded his arms over his chest.

Evan and Kimball sat at either end of the table, and I took the spot in the middle.

I eyed Evan, then leaned closer, trying to catch a whiff of the smoke I'd smelled earlier. Surprisingly, it was gone.

He caught me sniffing.

"Hi," I said. Lame. Guilty.

"Well, hello."

"How's things?" Oh my gosh, could I please come up with something to say that didn't sound so...LAME?!

His half smile slid across his face like a breeze, softening his features and making my heart do stupid things in my chest. *It's the cameras. I always get nervous before a show.*

"Things're good. You?"

"Yeah. Good. Same here."

The director counted down to recording as Evan and I stared at each other, something weird pulsing in the air between us. And I noticed his eyes. Those blue eyes that could be as clear as a Montana lake or as tumultuous as a Tennessee storm.

They had their spark back.

CHAPTER FIVE

AFTER FILMING, my assistant, Javi, waited for me in my dressing room, lounging like he owned the place. His dark hair was longer than mine by an inch, and he used to pull it back into a man bun until we started calling him Gomez Addams.

Mirrors covered the right wall of the dressing room, and I ducked behind the dressing screen to the left of King Javi's chaise and tugged my shirt off. "Do you think *Singing Sensation*'d let me out of my contract?" I checked my watch. The band would be waiting for me at the studio.

"So, I take it that it didn't go well?" Javi's Puerto Rican accent was a little stronger than usual. Or maybe it felt that way because I couldn't read his lips when I was mid-wardrobe change.

"I just can't believe Jenny's the other judge. Plus, she's glaring daggers at me like *I'm* the one who broke her heart instead of the other way around." I yanked my own T-shirt on and wrestled my arms through the holes.

"Yeah. About that... I've been thinking that this might be good healing. I'm sure Kellan would agree with me. Maybe you need to make amends."

"Did you miss the part where I said I didn't break her heart? I wasn't with her anymore when I started using. What would I even make amends for?"

"I'm sure you'll think of something."

I glared. His dark eyes held my stare without flinching.

"Fine," he said lightly, pulling his phone from his pocket. "I'll contact Gil and tell him you want out of your contract. I'm sure he'll be happy you're turning down the solo career too."

Damn. The solo contract.

I narrowed my eyes. "I know what you're doing. Reverse psychology won't work on me. I'm not two." Except it was going to work, because I needed that solo contract.

"Don't be a cow, man. Be a buffalo. Charge into the storm."

"You and that damn buffalo."

Cows ran from a storm, causing them to be in it for longer, while buffalo charged into the storm, facing it head-on, which actually minimized their time in the chaos. I'd made the mistake of telling Javi about the analogy after one particularly poignant NA meeting. He'd used it to motivate me ever since.

"So you're saying I should stick around, so I can actually get my solo career and face my past with Jenny." At some point, I'd slid my hand into my pocket and was currently squeezing my sobriety medallion.

"You're the one who always talks about closure and healing, *amigo*."

He had me there. There were several people in my past that I still needed to find my peace with. I conceded his point with a nod. "Fair enough."

He smiled, his white teeth flashing against his bronze skin. "I knew you'd see it my way."

I grunted.

If I had to stay, at least I'd get the chance to figure out what happened between Jenny and me. Maybe get some of the healing my heart and sobriety demanded. After I figured out what went wrong, I could keep it from happening again. Or fix it. I pulled my hand from my pocket and traced the indents from my coin in my palm.

Javi tilted his head, lips pursed like he was about to give a TED Talk on my mental health.

"Quit psychoanalyzing me. I'm fine."

I *was* fine. I had beaten the addiction, fought off the cravings, and each time I did, I felt a little less like a walking disaster. Seeing Jenny again hurt like hell, but I wouldn't let it derail me… more than it already had.

"Glad to hear it. You need me to play moderator at the writing session?"

The studio was supposed to be neutral ground—a safe zone away from drugs, alcohol, and the Parkland house chaos. I was meeting with the guys to work on our next album. A project that might never happen if they didn't get their act together.

Back when Jenny and I first started dating, I'd lived with them. Bad idea. And I liked her more than I liked living with them. So six months into our relationship, I'd bought another house and moved closer to the studio and to her, carved out my own space, and now it made staying clean feel a little less like a punishment. Less temptation, more breathing room, and a chance to keep my life from imploding.

The night of Aiden and Dylan's wedding, my foster mom died in a car accident. I'd already been a mess from seeing Jenny at the wedding. By the reception, I'd been almost too drunk to give the best man speech. Then, as I was getting back to the hotel, I got the call about my mom. The pain had been unbearable, and I just wanted to stop thinking about it. I wanted to rewind time and be there with her. Tell her I loved her again, but she was gone in the most horrific and painful way imaginable. My body shook, and my insides had felt simultaneously too empty and too full.

My band had come to the wedding, so that night, after the news came in, I went to their suite and sat next to Beckett, taking the joint from his fingers. I could still hear my internal debate. Could feel the rough paper squeezed between my fingers.

The band erupted like I'd just signed over my soul. Cheers, high-fives, probably a marching band somewhere in the background. They'd won. The high-and-mighty Evan Black had fallen.

And I'd escaped the pain, the misery, and hadn't looked back.

"Evan?"

I blinked, shaking off the haze. "Sorry. What did you ask me?"

"Do you need me to moderate at the studio?"

"No, I'll be okay. Do I have anything else tonight?" Besides the meeting I'd already committed to.

"Nope."

"Good. Want to come with me to a meeting tonight?" Recovery 101: surround yourself with people who actually gave a damn about your goals. I was asking him as a friend, not as his boss, though sometimes the lines blurred.

"If you need me there, I'm there." No hesitation. I loved this guy.

"But...?" I prompted, looking down at the pants they'd put me in. Would they miss them if I decided to keep them? Probably not. I stuffed my feet into my shoes.

Javi wore the dark puppy-dog look he always got when he didn't want to disappoint.

"But...I have a date tonight that I'd rather not cancel."

"Have fun." I bent down to tie the laces of my combat boots.

"You sure you don't need me?"

"Kellan will be there." I switched boots and looked up just in time to see the tension drain from his shoulders. Relief in HD.

He straightened quickly and sent me an unapologetic grin. "See you tomorrow then?"

I waved him toward the door. "See ya tomorrow."

My mind went back to Jenny and my problem with her. I'd just treat her like I would any other judge. Well, not like Kimball. I'd be nicer to her than I was to Kimball.

We pulled into the studio's gated parking lot. I scanned for the band's cars. Nada. Ghost town.

"Just wait here," my head security guard, Ryan, said. "I'll check if anyone is actually alive in there."

I hopped out behind him and jogged to the entrance. He shot me an annoyed look over his shoulder.

Checked in at the front desk with the secretary. No one. Literally no one was here. Checked my watch. Five minutes late. Maybe they'd bother showing up before the apocalypse.

I made my way to the conference room we'd reserved and snagged a cracker from the spread Javi had arranged. The guy was the best. Then I grabbed a couple of chips, dunked them in dip, and slumped into a chair with a stack of paper. Ryan came in a few minutes later, after doing whatever it was security people did to keep me from getting shot or mobbed by rabid fans.

"You good?"

I nodded.

"I'll be at the front desk if you need me."

"Cool."

Jenny and I were supposed to do a duet at the *Singing Sensation* finale. I had a few minutes before the guys arrived, so I put pen to paper, hoping for inspiration.

After what felt like eternity, pen poised over a blank sheet, I stood and paced the length of the conference table.

Nothing.

Not a single lyric for the duet with Jenny. Not a line for the songs we'd need for the upcoming album—or my solo album, which would hopefully be coming out instead of the album with the band—not that they knew that yet.

Zilch.

I wasn't one of those purists who had to write their own lyrics, like my buddy Aiden. But I knew the songs landed better when I actually *felt* them. Usually, in a slump, I'd dive into a pile of demos until one struck a chord.

That sounded exhausting. And depressing. And I really didn't feel like it.

Because I was a masochist, I hooked up my phone to the speakers and played "November Rain." Jenny's version. Before Jenny and I had even started dating, I'd suggested she sing it.

She'd released it as a single before her debut album, and I'd listened to it on repeat so many times it probably qualified as a minor obsession.

The first two verses had been what really made me push it.

That, and her voice was built to sing a broken-down version of the song. Right after the breakup, it felt like an anthem to my heartache, but hearing it now, all I felt was strength. I'd moved past it. Transcended any need I had for validation from a woman.

Finally, the door opened and Ryan and Reese, Ryan's brother and another security guard, slipped in.

I checked my watch. Thirty minutes solo. The band wasn't coming. Jimmy, the rhythm guitarist, was the only one likely to answer, so I called him. Silence. Nolan, lead guitar? Nope. Beckett, on bass? Nada. Derek, the drummer? Zippity doo dah.

I stood, stretched, and left the blank sheet on the table. "Let's just swing by the house to check on them."

I hated going back there. Hated the smells. Hated the sounds. Hated the way every little thing could trigger a craving. Just thinking about it made me want a cigarette—or three. But no. Not today. I was committed to healing. To health. Giving in to the little things only made saying no to the big things harder.

"Either of you have a piece of gum?" I patted my pockets and found my empty pack. Ryan produced a stick of spearmint from his pocket. Instant relief. Addicted to gum? Far better than the alternative.

Back in the car, Reese drove us to the Parkland house. The front lawn looked halfway decent, thanks to Carl—adoptive dad and accountant—who'd hired a landscaper long before I moved out. Inside? Significantly worse.

There wasn't a cloud of smoke like I'd expected when I opened the door, but the stench of stale cigarettes hit me in the face and lingered in my mouth. Nausea churned, and I breathed shallowly as I stepped past an overturned trash bag that had been left by the front door.

Shoes were scattered across the entryway, one of them in a dried pile of vomit.

"This is disgusting," Ryan said from behind me, hand clamped over his nose.

No argument there. I nodded and picked my way through the

entryway, eyes watering. We were gonna have a talk about a mandatory cleaning lady once a week. Music blared from somewhere in the back, and I followed it to the backyard.

There they were. The guys, lounging by the pool, and Beckett's girlfriend stretched out on a floating flamingo in the middle of the pool, bikini and sunglasses in full effect.

As I switched off the music, all five pairs of eyes snapped to me. "Did you guys forget that we had a writing session scheduled today?"

Beckett scowled at me. "You can't force creativity. We can't just write on command. Besides, we came to your gig this morning. None of us feel like writing after spending the day listening to how great you are. The only good part about it is that it'll help the band's name recognition."

My gut twisted at his words. His hostility had always been simmering, but now, sober and in the light of day, it was plain as day. I'd tried to chalk it up to personality quirks before. Nope. Just pure, unadulterated resentment. And when he found out I was leaving the band... I could almost guarantee Beckett would go out of his way to drag my name through the mud.

I sighed and glanced at the others for backup. They nodded as if Beckett had just dropped a golden nugget of wisdom.

"How do you guys think we wrote when we were first starting out? We *scheduled* writing sessions." Sure, sometimes inspiration struck from out of nowhere, but nothing was stopping them from scribbling ideas down and bringing them to me when we actually sat down together. It wasn't rocket science.

"Just piss off. We're busy," Beckett shot back, then walked past me, shoulder-checking me in the process.

Real mature.

Ryan shoved him and growled something so low I couldn't hear it.

Weren't we just a masterclass in band camaraderie?

Kellan met me at the church entrance where the Narcotics Anonymous meetings were held, nudged me like we were sneaking into a movie, and steered me through the doors.

Reese stood sentry outside, arms crossed, and Ryan already waited inside.

I didn't usually talk at these meetings. Just sat at the back and listened. Other people's stories helped. No one warned you before you started using that you'd trade in pretty much everything you cared about for that next hit. That nothing else would matter. I got "lucky"—if you could call it that. My drug era only lasted a couple of years. I managed to find my rock bottom fast. Overachiever points.

The person leading the meeting asked each person who felt comfortable to stand and introduce themselves. I muttered, "Skip."

Kellan popped up instead, giving the awkward three-fingered wave. "I'm Kellan Daniels, former LAPD. Lost my job and nearly lost my life to drugs. I've been clean for six years. This is my friend Noah. He's been clean for almost one year."

Noah. My birth name. The alias I wore like a mask when I didn't want *Evan Black* recognized in places like this.

Kellan sat. The next person introduced themselves.

The metal doors banged open, and a large redheaded mountain of a man with a massive beard and full-sleeve tattoos strode in. Kellan gasped.

"Friend of yours?"

He nodded. "A brother, really. Never thought I'd see him in a meeting like this."

When his turn came, he stood. "I'm Declan Murphy. Ever'one calls me Murph or Murphy," he said, a thick Irish brogue filling the room. "I been clean for three days." Then he sat.

I watched him, curious how he knew my sponsor.

Midway through the meeting, Murphy noticed Kellan and stood, his metal chair scraping across the hardwood floor. He walked over to us as the speaker was talking about his own rock-bottom moment.

He shook Kellan's hand and took the seat on the other side of him.

I turned my attention back to the speaker and his story. He talked about his own *why*.

After the meeting, the Irishman spared me only a quick glance and a: "Big fan o' yer music." Then he turned to Kellan and swallowed the older man in a hug. "How's it going, Daniels?" His Irish accent was so thick I had to mentally add subtitles.

The two men slapped each other's backs so hard they were sure to leave bruises.

"Murph, it's good to see you." Kellan officially introduced us. "Declan Murphy, this is Evan Black. Evan, this is Murph. We were on the force together."

"A cop."

"Ex." Murphy rubbed the back of his neck. "Ex-cop."

Kellan gripped his shoulder. "They kicked you out?"

"Last week," Murphy rasped. "Officially, I'm medically retired."

Kellan nodded as if no other explanation were needed. "Need to talk about it?"

Murphy nodded.

Kellan looked to me as if he was asking for a hall pass.

I stuck out a hand. We did the half-handshake, half-hug, two-pat-on-the-back move. "See ya around, man. Thanks for being there. Good luck with your recovery, Murphy." It didn't feel like I'd earned the privilege of calling him Murph like Kellan had.

"Thanks," Murphy said.

"Any time. And I mean it." Kellan held my gaze until I nodded.

The two of them disappeared deeper into the building, while I took off through the door Reese held open.

As we wove through the thick L.A. traffic back to my place, my thoughts strayed to Jenny. Did I have something to make amends for? No. But, I could be nicer to her, and maybe she'd be kind enough to give me a clue as to what I'd done to earn the ire she so vehemently wielded like a weapon toward me.

Tomorrow's goal: Use my irresistible charm to get on Jenny's good side.

THE SECOND DAY of the L.A. auditions, the name of the game was avoidance.

Stay as far away from Evan as possible and speak to him only when necessary. Easy peasy. My assistant, Alli, sat on the chaise lounge against the wall while Lindsay, my makeup artist, and Kelsey, my hairstylist, chattered about their nights.

"How was your night, Jenny, what did you do?" Kelsey asked.

"I did a video walkthrough of a house with my realtor."

"Oh! How was it?" Lindsay massaged moisturizer into my skin.

"Meh." Since coming back to L.A., I'd been trying to find a house that we could turn into a home. So far, we'd had no luck.

My mind flashed to the disastrous meal I'd made last night. "Then I made dinner..." I avoided mentioning that I'd burned the chicken parmesan and overcooked the pasta. "And put Axl to bed." I loved reading to him every night, which was the benefit of not touring so much. These little snippets of time would have to do until I had my talk show.

"Sounds like a good night," Lindsay said.

"It was."

"How is it seeing Evan again?" Kelsey parted my hair, spritzed it, and wrapped a section around a curling wand.

My face must not have used my inside voice, because Lindsay burst out laughing. "That bad?"

Kelsey released the hair she'd been curling and sectioned out another piece. She met my eyes in the mirror after she had the curling wand set. "He's very handsome though. You can't complain about getting to sit next to that all day. I powdered his nose between takes yesterday and he flashed that dimple at me. I don't know how anyone resists the dimple."

I rolled my eyes. "Yeah, that dimple has probably ensnared many a woman."

There was a time I considered writing a song about his dimple. I just couldn't get past the word pimple, which was the only word I could think of to rhyme with it. There had to be other words, but my brain couldn't come up with any.

Simple!

There. I'd done it. Songwriting could commence. Later.

An ode to Evan Black's dimple—seems easy, but it's not so simple.

Enough, Jenny. Quit thinking about his dimple.

Sebastian and Fabian finally agreed on an outfit—high-waisted black jean skirt and a flowy orange top—and sent me out to the wolves—err, judges.

Like yesterday, we were in front of a live audience. Jaryce introduced us one by one, and I took my spot between the two men.

"You look really nice today," Evan whispered between takes. I could hear the smile in his voice, smell the cedar and vanilla of his cologne. Feel the weight of his gaze on the side of my face.

I avoided looking at his dimple and gave him a polite smile. Professional even. "Thanks."

"I was thinking we should go for lunch today. Catch up a little."

Nope. I'd rather alphabetize my sock drawer by emotional-damage level. I tsked a little sarcastically. "Sorry, we're not allowed to leave the venue."

Gio's voice came over the speakers. "Evan, Jenny, if you're ready. We're ready to start filming again."

I snapped my mouth closed and scooted my chair deeper beneath the table. Sipping my coffee, I tried to look innocent.

Jaryce introduced the next singer.

"What about coffee?" Evan whispered.

Without looking at him, I lifted my cup and took another swallow.

He retreated.

From then on, every single break we had, Evan was there. Inviting me for a writing session, trying to take me to dinner, wanting to "catch up," asking me stupid questions like, "How's Axl?"

My one- to two-word answers didn't seem to deter him from trying to talk to me. At all.

He followed me through the line at the dinner buffet. "What'd you think of that last girl? She had pipes, am I right?"

I pressed my lips together. He knew I liked talking about music and singers, but he wasn't going to get any extra words out of me. Why was he following me? He needed to take a hint.

He stabbed a couple olives with a fork and tried to shake them one-handed onto his plate. One flew off and hit my leg. I pointed to the not-burnt shredded chicken a couple dishes ahead of where I was and said to the woman in front of me, "Mind if I sneak ahead?"

She smiled warmly. "Not at all."

But even that didn't deter Evan. He just spoke over her. "That guy who sang 'True Living, Living True' had a decent voice, but it felt too thin for the song. He needs something else, or he needs to learn how to use his diaphragm."

That didn't require a response, so I ignored him and added chicken to my plate.

As I approached the mac and cheese, which looked and

smelled amazing, I reached for it, then pulled my hand back. Sebastian was getting in my head, and I hated it. Was I fat? No. Did I have fat? Yes. Was not eating mac and cheese going to get rid of my fat? I didn't know, but I wasn't going to risk it.

"You still playing the guitar?" Evan asked, his voice right by my ear. I startled and closed my eyes, resigning myself to my fate. I glanced back at the lady who'd let me cut. She had a sly smile on her lips and didn't meet my gaze.

Evan stared at me, waiting for my response.

"Yes." That was all he was getting. How was I supposed to keep my distance when he and his dimple followed me around like a lost puppy all day?

He leaned over the table as I spooned green salad onto my plate, farther and farther over until I looked up at him. "Have you given Axl an ax yet?"

"Nope." I picked up the fat-free dressing and spread it over the greens.

Evan scooped a big portion of mac and cheese onto his plate, emptying the metal pan. My stomach growled and my drool glands activated at the thought of the mac and cheese. It was all gone. No getting any now.

"You should get him one." He mimed playing an air guitar. "You'd be surprised at how quickly kids pick this stuff up. I was seven when I started."

This I knew. I nodded along, disinterested.

"Mommy!" Axl crowed and ran toward me, wrapping his arms around my leg. He looked up at me with those devastating blue eyes. "Hi, Mom."

My stomach jolted, and I looked at Evan.

"Hi, buddy. Did you get dinner?" I glanced at Colby, who had followed him into the room.

"Not yet." Colby answered for him, prying him from my leg and picking him up. "We're just about to get in line. He just woke up from his N-A-P."

I moved down the line and skipped the rolls.

"I want mac and cheese," Axl said.

Colby looked up and down the buffet line until he saw the empty tray.

"It's all gone, little guy. Let's find something else."

His chin quivered, and he said, "Okay."

Evan frowned and looked at the mac and cheese piled on his plate. "You can have mine."

Axl's gaze darted to Evan's plate and lit up. "Mac and cheese!"

He squirmed until Colby put him on his feet, then he grabbed Colby's hand and dragged him to the start of the buffet to grab a plate.

I moved to the drinks and grabbed a bottle of water, then strode to a table that had been marked as reserved. Evan jogged to keep up.

Colby showed up a few seconds after we'd sat down with a plate. Axl carried a spoon.

He climbed up on the seat beside Evan and took a bite of his mac and cheese. Evan laughed, that dimple flashing, and Axl grinned at me, sauce on his cheek right where he had a matching dimple.

"Ope," Colby said, taking Axl's spoon and using it to bulldoze the mac and cheese from Evan's plate to his. "Let's just move this onto your plate."

My heart ached, and anger surged. I looked away.

This could've been us. This could've been the last four years. Axl eating off Evan's plate. Axl looking up at his dad with those identical blue eyes. Laughing, teasing, having fun. I didn't know if I was more mad at Evan for taking that from us, or at the drugs. Definitely Evan. And it didn't make a whole lot of sense. But when the man you were in love with called you a liar and a cheater, even if he didn't remember it, it still hurt.

I stood, my appetite gone. "I'll be in my dressing room." I gave Colby a meaningful look, and he scrambled to gather Axl and his plate.

CHAPTER SEVEN

AXL HADN'T SLEPT all week, which meant the dark bags under my eyes were extra prominent on Friday morning at four a.m. Colby and I had napped in shifts all week, and when Axl started running a fever early this morning, instead of being at the airport with me, he and Vince had stayed home to take Axl to the doctor to check for an ear infection. I'd tried to postpone the trip, but Vince assured me they would take care of Axl and keep me in the loop.

Reese, one of Evan's security guys, had stepped in to fill the void of protection. He was an inch or two shorter than Vince, but what he lacked in height, he made up for in size. The brothers—Ryan and Reese—were practically identical. Square jaws, classically good looks, dark hair and eyes, muscles that had their own gravitational pull. Mid-thirties. I needed to hire a second security guard. It was too hard for one security guard to keep track of Axl *and* me. Back when Evan and I were dating, Vince had become really close with Reese and Ryan. I trusted both of them implicitly, which was how we found ourselves here.

When I got onto the airplane, Evan was already there, knuckles white, breath shallow. I tried to give him an indifferent nod when I passed, friendly and distant, but he didn't even open his eyes.

"Is he not taking beta blockers?" I asked Reese when we got out of earshot.

Reese shook his head. "He won't take anything that could alter his mood. He's nervous that it'll lead to bigger slips."

"I see." He was taking his recovery seriously; I couldn't help but be impressed. I took my seat in the next compartment, but I could still see through the doorway to where Evan sat. He tried to breathe, but it sounded like he'd just run a marathon and was having an asthma attack. "Is he okay?"

"Should be." Reese had taken the seat beside me and leaned over to look at him. He chuckled.

I swatted his arm. "You shouldn't laugh," I said through a laugh. "He's terrified."

As soon as we were at the venue in Denver, Lindsay and Kelsey descended on me. Both were short women, like me. Kelsey was busty with blonde hair and the personality of an overly excited puppy. Lindsay had curly brown hair and was more like a fox: observant and clever. Fabian was missing this stop on the tour— wasn't sure if he said family emergency or fashion emergency— but he told me he'd approved all the outfits Sebastian showed him.

In my dressing room, Lindsay started with a mask to try to reduce the Chanel-sized bags under my eyes while Kelsey worked her magic on my locks.

As I processed, Sebastian brought a rack of clothes into my room. "I have the perfect outfit for you." He shuffled through the clothes for a second, then pulled a white leather bodysuit off the rack. "Feast your eyes on this."

I laughed to cover my discomfort. "Are you out of your mind?" I'd look like the Michelin Man. There was no way Fabian had given him the stamp of approval.

"Vwat's wrong vith it?" He held it away from him, studying it.

"Umm. First of all, the zipper probably won't go up. Secondly, it'll show every single imperfection on my body."

"You'll be sitting—"

I threw my hands in the air. "Exactly, my muffin top will burst over the top of it."

"Two words. Shape. Wear." He held his hands out and spread them like a rainbow with each word.

"I'm not wearing a girdle, Sebastian. Plus, shapewear is one word." I looked to Lindsay and Kelsey to back me up. "Help a girl out."

Lindsay shrugged. "You'd probably look good in it."

Kelsey spoke around a bobby pin. "You never know till you try."

He held up his hand. "I vant you to try it on, and if you don't look fabulous, I won't say another vword about it."

If he wanted me to squeeze my butt into that, I would, just to get him to shut up.

Kelsey pinned a curl in place and sprayed it with a generous amount of hairspray.

Lindsay pulled the mask off and wiped my face with a warm washcloth. "Your eyes look much better."

"Thanks."

When they finished my hair and makeup, I stretched like an Olympic athlete getting ready to run a marathon, making Sebastian roll his eyes and Lindsay and Kelsey giggle. "Let's do this. Do I need butter or something to slide it on?"

Sebastian scoffed.

"I was serious," I deadpanned, holding back a smile.

Putting it on took all four of us about ten minutes of rolling, pulling, grunting, nipping, and tucking. When I had it on but unzipped, I pursed my lips and looked in the full-length mirror.

I was a campfire away from making the world's biggest s'more, but would Sebastian change his mind? No, because he didn't want to admit he was wrong.

"Just help me zip it," he said.

We had it at my bra line when someone knocked on my door.

"It's stuck," Sebastian said. "I think it caught on the lace of your bra."

"Get the door, I'll work with it." I turned to the mirror and started fiddling with the zipper, gently trying to untangle it without ripping my underwear.

If I could just... I stuck my tongue out and teased the zipper down a couple of notches.

"It's for you," Sebastian said.

Evan stood in the doorway with a coffee cup in hand, body frozen, mouth hanging open.

My skin heated under his intense gaze, and a quick slideshow of times he'd looked at me played in my mind. I put a stop to it and cleared my throat. "My face is up here." My voice cracked like a whip, a little grumpier than I intended, but no worse than he deserved.

I glanced down at myself, at every imperfection amplified in this skin-tight monstrosity. My cheeks flamed.

Evan snapped his mouth closed and shook his head like he had water in his ears, then stepped into the room, holding the cup in his outstretched hand. "I got you a coffee."

He said it so softly, so sweetly, that my breath caught.

A rich scent wafted from the cup. I looked at the order scrawled on the side and confirmed he remembered my favorite drink. After all this time. A pain started somewhere in my chest and radiated outward. I swallowed hard and tore my gaze from him.

But how dare he think he could come in here with a coffee like it would fix everything? Like it would unbreak my heart, unbreak me—our family. I took the cup from his hand, walked over to the trash can, and unceremoniously dropped it in. "Get. Out."

His mouth worked, but no sounds came out. I pushed his shoulder, and he let me shove him out the door, then I closed it on his face.

Lindsay whistled and placed a hand on my back. "Dang. That was brutal."

"He looked so sad," Kelsey said. "Like you killed his puppy."

Angry tears burned the back of my eyes, and I blinked them away.

Lindsay put a hand on my shoulder, gently turning me toward her. "Are you okay?"

My emotions were all over the place. I clenched my jaw. Damn him. It shouldn't hurt to see him anymore. I nodded. "Yes."

No.

"I think it's safe to say that Evan liked the outfit," Kelsey said, fiddling with the zipper until it was all the way up.

Lindsay hushed her but said in a soft tone, "You do look really good."

I avoided the mirror. If they thought I looked good, I'd trust their judgment, but I couldn't bear to see myself.

Freaking Evan. Did he think a coffee would fix things between us? No chance of that happening.

He could never be the stable father Axl needed. A nagging voice in the back of my head said there was more to it than that, but I shut that voice up real quick.

Sebastian gave me one more finishing touch—a gold necklace that draped down and encircled my waist—then left the dressing room.

About twenty minutes later, an announcement came over the speaker in the corner of the room as Lindsay spritzed me with setting spray and Kelsey finger-combed through my curls.

"Judges, we'll need you ready in about fifteen minutes."

"Ladies?" I said as they worked on finishing touches.

They both focused on their respective tasks, but Lindsay glanced at me to let me know she was listening.

"How long have you been in the showbiz industry?" I asked.

Lindsay spread lip stain over my lips. "Six years."

Kelsey came around and sat in a director's chair, her work done. "Four years."

"What's the most messed up thing you've ever seen behind the scenes?"

Kelsey's gaze cut to mine, and her eyebrows shot up. Her eyes darkened. "I don't think I'm allowed to say. Non-disclosures and all that."

I nodded and looked at Lindsay.

She pointed at Kelsey with her makeup brush. "What she said, but it hasn't all been sunshine and rainbows."

The music industry, the entertainment industry in general, was disgusting to women. Sebastian had been responsible for at least four eating disorders in my season alone. Something had to change. When I landed my own talk show, would I have enough influence to spark that change?

"Let's just say that it's a doggy dog world," Kelsey said, nodding sagely. Her heavily made-up eyes held my gaze.

"It's a dog-eat-dog world," I echoed.

A mischievous smile stole across Kelsey's face. "Evan's reaction to you in that romper... I think he's still in love with you."

I shook my head, but my stomach flipped against my will. "He's not." And I needed to do everything in my power to keep it that way.

Someone knocked at the door, then Reese cracked it open. "Hey, Jen? Kimball Stone's out here. Wants a word with you."

"Send him in."

Reese opened the door and gestured for Kimball to enter. Kimball stared at Lindsay and Kelsey until they scampered away.

"I'll just be outside the door."

Kimball cut right to the chase. "No more of the silent treatment that you gave Evan in L.A. We're selling friendship and friendly, flirty banter. If you can't follow directions and follow your contract, we'll have to find a replacement. I don't want to do that, Jenny. I don't. You're my favorite Double S winner. I want to see you succeed, but ratings are more important than your comfort."

I clenched my teeth. Would he really release me from my contract?

"Can you do it?" he asked. "Can you put aside your feelings and do what needs to be done for the ratings?"

No. If he was asking me to *flirt* with Evan, no. "You want me to flirt? I can't do it."

"No. No, that would be crazy. And immoral for me to suggest it. I want you to be friendly. That's it. Professional, but with an air of camaraderie."

I gave him a flat stare.

"This is a request, Jenny. From a friend. But if you can't comply, it'll be a demand from your boss. Or a breach of contract."

I couldn't lose this contract, or my chance for my own talk show. But could I allow myself to be that close to Evan? There was no other option. "Okay."

JENNY HAD no idea how stunning she was, and how seeing her in that jumper made my heart do somersaults. I shuffled around my dressing room like a man three sheets to the wind.

Javi lay on the chaise and tossed a lacrosse ball against the wall next to the door, catching it over and over.

"Hey, *amigo*. How did Jenny like her coffee?"

I intercepted the ball and squeezed it in my palm. "She didn't."

"What do you mean?" He sat up and held his hand open.

I spun the ball in my hand, knuckles white. "She threw it away." I chucked the ball against the wall, it bounced, hit the ceiling, and Javi caught it before it knocked into the opposite wall. "This is stupid. Why am I even trying? She wants nothing to do with me." I pointed at him. "This is your fault, you know. This whole thing was your idea."

A slow smile crept across his face. "She threw it away? That's great news."

I cocked my head and stared at him. "How do you figure?"

He stood and smacked the back of his hand against my shoulder. "Don't you see? If she didn't like you, she wouldn't have thrown the coffee away. She *likes* you."

"This isn't kindergarten, Javi."

He tossed the ball in the air, and I caught it.

"Listen to me. A woman who is over you? She gives the coffee away. A woman who doesn't care? She drinks it. A woman who is still in love with you but trying to convince herself she isn't? She sends a message. She doesn't trust herself to stay away, so she has to make it look like she hates you so you keep your distance. This is good news." He waggled his dark eyebrows and looked at me expectantly. "Eh? Eh?"

A begrudging smile lifted one corner of my mouth. Not that I thought he was right, but he was such an idiot that I couldn't help but be amused. Could he be right? Could throwing the coffee away mean that Jenny didn't trust herself around me? The other side of my mouth lifted.

"Now you're seeing it Javi's way." He snatched the ball from my hands. "Keep up the good work. You'll win her over in no time."

Win her over. Was that what I wanted? There was a tiny part of me, in the recesses of my mind, that kept reminding me that if she got too close, she wouldn't like what she found. I wasn't the same person I'd been back when we were dating. I had a past before, but now... Now I had a closet overflowing with skeletons, a luggage set full of baggage, and a heart being held together with duct tape.

CHAPTER NINE

ON THE SECOND day of Denver auditions, the theme music for *Singing Sensation* played over the speakers, and Jaryce hyped up the crowd.

"Here we are, Denver. Season 15! Are you guys ready to sing?"

The crowd screamed.

"Okay, let's get this party started! Any words of advice from our judges?"

It was agreed I would go first and Kimball would go last.

I stared at the camera with the red light and said, "Sing like you're in your shower and no one's listening."

After the crowd settled, Evan said, "Leave it all on the stage. Show us your very best or you might not get a second chance." His blue eyes found mine and held them, like his words had double meaning.

He was right. He wouldn't get another chance. He'd already screwed up the last one I'd given him.

Kimball said, "I'm never wrong. If I tell you not to sing something, listen to me."

The crowd laughed.

I grinned at Kimball and stuck out my tongue.

Career suicide, Kimball had called my song choice for the finale. After I won, he privately admitted that I was right, and this was the one time he'd ever been wrong. But he loved to remind me that he was in charge. *I know, Kimball.*

"Good luck," he said.

As the first contestant walked onto the stage, Kimball leaned over and whispered, "Remember, professional camaraderie."

I pressed my lips together and gave the subtlest of nods. I knew Kimball wanted what was best for me, but I hated that he always forced compliance.

"What's your name and where're you from?" Evan asked.

I barely registered the kid's words, too lost in my own thoughts. How was I supposed to act like nothing was wrong when it felt like everything was? Seeing Evan hurt. A lot. And the fact that he was oblivious to the pain he caused me—well, that pissed me off even more. To top it all off, Axl had an ear infection. The doctor wanted him to wait a full week to fly out, so he wouldn't be joining me on the road until we hit New York.

The contestant's song started, and I had to force myself to focus on him. The tone of his voice built on the lyrics, and I found myself forgetting my worries and enjoying the music.

When he was done, he held the mic at his side and looked at us expectantly.

"You're up, Miss Gentry," the voice said in my earpiece.

"You have a unique quality to your voice that I found myself getting lost in. It's a definite yes from me." I gave a thumbs up.

Evan shifted beside me, and I could feel his gaze on the side of my face. I glanced over, and as soon as I did, he looked away.

"I thought you were really good. I want to hear you do something a little grittier. Grungier. I liked it. I say yes."

Kimball nodded thoughtfully and stared at him until the contestant put the mic to his lips and said, "Kimball?"

"You know, Oliver, I like you. I do. I think you've got potential. I'd love to see you in the live shows."

The crowd roared as Oliver leapt up and down on the stage.

Kimball leaned over and whispered, "We need better banter between takes."

I took a sip of my coffee to avoid responding. Speaking of coffee, maybe throwing Evan's coffee away yesterday was an overreaction, but it didn't feel like it. It felt warranted. I was already unhappy with myself after trying to squeeze into that stupid outfit—*don't ask me what we did when I had to pee*—and in came Evan. I wanted to feel my best, show him my best self, so he could see what he'd stupidly given up. And he stared at me like a starving man staring at the last piece of bacon.

Kimball signaled his assistant, and I knew Gio would chase down Oliver and give him the whole spiel. *All hail the mighty Kimball. Obey him and all your wildest dreams will come true.*

Yeah, at what personal cost?

I was sounding a little ungrateful. Kimball really had done so much for me, for my career. He'd championed me and made sure I had all the best advice. And he'd stuck up for me with Sebastian. But that didn't make him any easier to stomach.

AFTER FILMING, Evan followed me to my dressing room. Reese and Ryan trailed a little behind us. I opened the door and tried to slam it on his face, but he put his foot in the crack.

Alli sat at the vanity and grinned at Evan as I brushed past her and went behind a changing screen to rid myself of today's "outfit"—Fabian couldn't get back soon enough.

"Do you want to get together tonight to work on the duet?"

I was already pulling pins from my hair. Oh, that felt so much better. The headache forming behind my eyes eased.

"Is that a yes?" he asked.

Out of nowhere, Alli said, "Kimball said they want you guys to film a writing session. With Axl gone, tonight is a good night."

I sighed and pulled my sundress over my head. My makeup was already done. "Fine."

"Great. We'll get Chinese and write some words. My room or yours?"

We'd be surrounded by film crew, which would add an extra layer of protection.

"I don't care," I called over the dressing screen.

"Sweet. I'll have them set up in my hotel room. See ya at seven?"

I sighed and looked at the time. An hour.

"Great."

After he left, Alli said, "You can come out from behind the screen now. They're gone."

I trudged out from behind it and collapsed on an oversized leather chair. "I'm annoyed."

"Why?"

"Why did it have to be Evan?" I whined.

Alli stood and tucked the chair back in the vanity. She met my gaze in the mirror. "I think if you gave him a chance, you'd find he's not the same man who hurt you before. I was talking to Javi during filming, and he seems to think Evan has turned a new leaf. That this is the time that sobriety sticks."

I blew out a breath. Not that I wanted him to relapse, because that would make me an awful person, but it sure would take some pressure off me if he just smoked a doobie. "He said some really awful things to me after I had Axl. I don't know how I'm just supposed to forget that."

"Not to be a stickler or anything, but you said some pretty mean things to me when you were recovering from childbirth."

I rolled my eyes and uncrossed my legs. "That was different. I was in pain."

She faced me fully, crossed her arms, and folded her fist under her chin. "I'll wait while you think that one through."

The implication being that Evan was in pain. Telling him that Axl was his son caused him pain? That was even worse. "I stand by my previous statement."

She sighed and shook her head. "You would. I'll tell Reese to get the car."

When she was gone, I stared at myself in the mirror, examining the shadows under my eyes. In my eyes. In my heart.

The cameras would be there, which meant Kimball would expect me to be cordial when the last thing I was feeling was cordial. He'd want "banter."

Which meant I would have to give it to him.

And I'd have to be careful to keep the barriers around my heart up.

evan

THE HOTEL ROOM smelled like soy sauce and orange peel, the kind of sharp-sweet that clung to your clothes afterward. Takeout containers were spread across the small round table like we'd given up pretending this was dinner and not a truce. We got enough for the camera crew to indulge too, so now white rice was everywhere, along with chopsticks stacked in paper sleeves.

The camera guy adjusted his lens for the third time, pretending not to listen. The sound tech hovered by the door, all of them trying to look casual while absolutely not being casual. A red light blinked on the camera, steady and patient.

Jenny perched on the couch, a notebook balanced on one knee, one foot tucked under her, the other bouncing. She smiled when the camera swung her way—bright, easy, the smile she used when she wanted to look like nothing could touch her.

"Okay," she said, clapping once. "Songwriting. Very organic. Very late-night tortured artists. Everyone comfortable?"

I was on the chair across from her, guitar resting against my knee. "I'm comfortable."

She tilted her head. "That wasn't a question for you. You're always comfortable. You thrive in chaos."

"That's not true," I said. "I thrive in mild inconvenience."

She laughed. It sounded real enough. If I hadn't known her, I might've believed it.

She nudged one of the cartons on the coffee table between us with her foot. "You're gonna regret that General Tso's. It's like eating regret with a side of self-loathing."

"I regret nothing." I took another bite to prove it.

The camera zoomed slightly, catching the grease shine on the carton, the way my fingers were already sticky. Jenny noticed and leaned forward, stage-whispering, "This is riveting television."

"For you, maybe," I said. "People love watching me make bad decisions."

She grinned, quick and sharp, then dropped her gaze to the notebook. The grin slipped as soon as the camera panned away.

There it was. The line between Jenny-for-show and Jenny-when-she-thought-no-one-was-looking. Incidentally, I was regretting those words.

I cleared my throat and adjusted the guitar. "So, lyrics."

"Right." She twirled the pen between her fingers. "Because we're very serious about that."

"You're the one who said words first this time."

"I said *eventually*," she corrected. "You're the melody guy. I just...annotate."

"Annotate. Is that what we're calling it now?"

She shrugged. "I don't want to step on your process."

"My process is mostly staring at the wall until something hurts enough to write it down."

She looked up, eyes flicking to mine, then away. "Well. Lucky wall."

I played a soft progression, something I'd been carrying around for weeks. It filled the space between us, gentle but insistent. Jenny's leg stopped bouncing.

She listened. Really listened. That part of her couldn't fake it.

"That's pretty."

"Pretty's a start. What does it make you think of?"

She smirked. "Besides late-night infomercials and emotional vulnerability?"

I waited.

She sighed and looked at the ceiling. "Fine. It sounds like not being able to shut your brain up."

I nodded. "Yeah."

"Like every thought is…" She waved the pen vaguely. "Loud. Crowded. Annoying."

"Like a bad roommate."

She laughed and added, "Like a bad roommate who keeps leaving emotional dishes in the sink."

I smiled. "That's a line."

She froze. Just for a second.

Then she laughed again, a little too fast.

"Don't get excited. I didn't say it was a *good* line."

"You didn't say it wasn't," she said lightly. She looked down. Scribbled something in the notebook. "You're impossible."

"You've known that."

She glanced at the camera, then back at me. "People are going to think we're having fun."

"Aren't we?"

Her pen stilled. "We're working."

"Those things don't have to be mutually exclusive."

She met my eyes, really met them this time, and for a moment the room felt smaller. Quieter. Like the camera crew had dissolved into static.

Then she broke it. "Careful. That almost sounded like a life philosophy."

I chuckled. "I'm full of surprises."

"Mm. That's one word for it." There was that sardonic bite I knew and loved.

I played the progression again, slower this time. Let it breathe. "You said 'every thought' like it meant something."

She stiffened, just a hair. "It's a common phrase."

"Sure. So is 'I'm fine.' Doesn't mean it's true."

She snorted. "Wow. You get deep after bedtime."

"I had Chinese food. It unlocked a new level."

She smiled despite herself. "That's alarming."

"Talk to me. For the song."

She exhaled, long and slow. "Every thought...is like... It's like they line up. Waiting their turn. And you think you've dealt with one, but it just circles back."

"Circles back?"

"Yeah. Because unresolved things are rude like that."

I nodded, fingers moving instinctively on the strings. "What happens when they come back?"

She hesitated. The forced banter tried to rise again—I could see it—but this time it didn't quite make it.

"They hurt," she said quietly. Then louder, with a shrug, said, "But that's art, right? Pain, drama, blah, blah, blah."

I didn't let her off the hook. "Who are the thoughts about?"

She smiled for the camera, fake. "You, obviously."

The crew laughed. I didn't.

I leaned forward, forgetting about the notes, leaning my elbow on my knee, guitar balanced against me. "Jenny."

She met my gaze, and the smile faded. "Evan."

"I don't need details." I felt like I'd finally gained an inch. "I'm not asking you to relive anything. I just—" I searched for the right words. "I want to write it right."

She studied me, measuring. Deciding how much she trusted me. Or didn't. "Then write it like...loving someone doesn't turn off when things go wrong."

My chest tightened. "It doesn't."

"No, it doesn't."

Silence stretched between us, heavy and real. The camera caught it all. I didn't care.

I played again, and this time the melody shifted, deepened. She started writing, fast now, pen flying. No jokes. No performances.

After a minute, she looked up. "I hate that this is good."

I smiled. "You hate a lot of accurate things."

She rolled her eyes, but her smile was different now. Tired. Honest. "Don't get used to this."

"I won't. But I'll remember it."

She held my gaze for a second longer than necessary, then looked back down at the page. "Okay. Let's call it 'Every Thought.'"

I nodded. "Yeah. That fits."

I didn't say what I was really thinking—that every thought I had seemed to circle back to her too. That I'd spend however long it took earning the right to hear the rest of the story.

For now, the song was enough.

She stood abruptly. "I've gotta go." And she walked out, leaving the crew and I staring after her in confusion.

CHAPTER ELEVEN

BRIGHT AND EARLY THE next morning, I dragged Reese out of bed and up a mountain. Granted, it was more of a foothill, but I needed to climb. Needed to feel my muscles burning to expel the aching in my chest. I'd been way too vulnerable last night. Said way too much. That's why I'd fled from his room last night. How could I let him reopen my heart after all the effort I'd put into closing it?

When Evan and I broke up, I was still completely in love with him. The pain had dulled with time and distance, but it hadn't gone away completely. What did that mean?

Reese kept on my heels the duration of the hike, his breaths labored.

"You need to work on your cardio," I teased him.

"No kidding. Luckily, Evan doesn't do much mountain climbing."

I stopped at an overlook and stood, facing the city. I inhaled a deep breath, then let it out slowly, focusing on relaxing my muscles and clearing my mind.

Then I found a stump and sat, watching the shadows shorten as the sun rose higher in the sky.

What was I going to do? I couldn't stay away from him while

making it look like we were friends for the cameras. It was exhausting. I could try treating him like I did Vince and Colby: like a brother. An annoying little brother who wouldn't leave me alone.

I wasn't sleeping well either. Being so far away from Axl was hard. I missed him. Colby had called me last night to video chat, and I'd missed it because I was with Evan. My eyes unexpectedly stung, and I blinked before anything could come of it. He'd wanted me and I hadn't been there. I couldn't do our nightly routine, tuck him in, sing him "November Rain."

"Ready to head back?" Reese asked.

I pulled my baseball hat low over my eyes and stood, stretched. "Yeah."

We started down the trail. "You okay if we are with Evan today?"

"No." I stepped over a fallen log. If he was trying to push us together, I wouldn't be happy. I'd have to find a new security guard to finish out the week.

"You don't have to talk to him at all. It's just that Ryan has been talking to a girl in Boulder, and he wants to go see her while we're here. Evan told him he could before we knew that you'd need me."

That sounded plausible. I sighed. "I could, like, be in the adjoining room. Would that be close enough?"

"Door open?" he asked.

I had plenty to keep me busy. "As long as Evan stays out."

"I can't control what he does, but I'll encourage him to leave you alone."

That was as good as I could hope for. "Fine."

He sent a voice text to Ryan as we descended, telling him he was good and we'd be back in about an hour.

I USED my keycard to open my hotel room and nearly screamed when I saw a young man standing in my suite. He wore a tuxedo and had a wheeled cart with an espresso machine and other coffee-making gadgets.

"What's this? Who are you?" My gaze jumped to Alli, who was enjoying a coffee on the couch in the living area.

"I'm Travis. I'm a barista." His voice shook with nerves. "Evan Black hired me to follow you around and make as many coffees as you want. He said your favorite was a venti toffee nut latte with an extra shot of espresso."

"Are you kidding me?" I glanced over my shoulder at the closed door. If Vince were here, he never would've gone for this. Evan knew that and was pushing his luck.

"If I were you, I'd just take advantage," Alli murmured.

"I wish I were kidding you," Travis answered sincerely. The guy looked absolutely mortified.

"How much is he paying you?" I asked, thinking I'd just pay him slightly more to go away.

He swallowed and his chin quivered. "He is paying me to ask you if you want a coffee every ten minutes, and I get a thousand-dollar bonus for every coffee you order."

"Why do you need a thousand dollars?" Besides the obvious reason that people wanted money, I had a feeling Travis was motivated for other reasons. It was the chin wobble that gave it away.

"My big brother was in an accident. He's paralyzed, and insurance won't pay for the house renovations we need to make it wheelchair accessible."

Alli's eyes widened. Mine burned with unshed tears. It was awful.

"Alli, would you be so kind as to fetch Reese and have him meet me downstairs? Travis and I are going on a little field trip." I turned to the barista, with his shaggy hair and drooping shoulders. If he was eighteen, it was just barely. "Follow me, Travis."

In the hotel lobby, a couple people did a double take, then stared openly.

I led Travis out the automatic doors and across the busy street. I texted Alli.

> Me: We're gonna need a lot more coffee and supplies. Can you get on that ASAP? I don't care what you have to do. Take the card and make it happen.

When I went into the hotel and asked to borrow their power and an extension cord, the receptionist was happy to help in exchange for a picture, an autograph, and a coffee. I made a post on my social media, advertising free coffee outside the hotel and started calling to passersby that there was free coffee.

Alli played crowd control and requested a delivery order for coffee supplies.

My phone buzzed with a text from Evan.

> Heartbreaker: Where are you? Reese is freaking out.

> Me: We're across the street.

Oops.

I pocketed my phone and took the next order. Each person told me what they wanted, and I relayed it to Travis, keeping a running total for Evan.

Reese sprinted out of the hotel and across the street like a stunt double in an action movie. "What are you doing?"

"Just costing Evan a little money," I said lightly.

Speak of the devil, Evan and Javi joined us a short time later.

"What's going on?" Evan asked as I added a tally to my list.

"We're earning money for Travis's family's house renovations. So far, Evan has donated"—I did a quick count—"fifteen thousand dollars." I sent him a triumphant smile.

Evan's mouth dropped open, and Travis's hands shook as he made a black coffee for the man beside me.

"That's not—" Evan started.

"You promised Travis a thousand-dollar bonus for every coffee I ordered. You didn't say I had to drink it."

Javi guffawed. "She got you, *amigo!*"

A line had formed. People took pictures, Reese's face was red, and he sent Javi inside the hotel to get their crowd control equipment. Within ten minutes, we had the line roped off against the building. A car pulled up, and Alli rushed to help unload all the supplies.

"Evan, be a dear and go see if the hotel has a table we can borrow for all these extra supplies." I grinned at him and gave him a little push toward the door.

The police and news showed up a short while later, and the whole thing turned into a spectacle—though I can't say Reese was upset for the extra security. I told Alli to find out who I needed to pay for it, just so there weren't upset taxpayers.

"You could just go down the line and offer everyone five hundred dollars to get out of line," Javi suggested. "It'd save you a ton of money."

I smacked Javi's arm and turned a stern look on Evan. "Don't you dare. This is for a good cause."

"Oh?" Evan asked.

I explained Travis's predicament.

Evan metaphorically rolled up his sleeves and worked as Travis's assistant, making coffee, warming milk, using the frother. Anything Travis needed, Evan, Javi, or Alli was there to provide.

There was something insanely attractive about a man who knew how to work hard. Who took direction, even if he was used to making all the decisions. Evan didn't complain once.

Channel 7 News asked for a live interview with Evan and me during their ten o'clock segment that night. I looked like hell. I didn't have makeup on and was still wearing the clothes I'd had on this morning when I dragged Reese hiking. When Fabian saw this, he wouldn't say anything, but he'd give me that disapproving look; he'd pinch his lips together and narrow his eyes.

We'd been standing for almost twelve hours, and we'd decided we were cutting everyone off at midnight. Alli had made two more orders for cups and other supplies.

Some of the police officers who'd spent the morning with us had stayed to provide extra security after their shift, and a small group of baristas, eager for their fifteen minutes of fame, showed up and were helping fulfill all the orders. Everything was running smoothly as Evan and I stepped aside with the reporter and camera crew.

"Tell us, Evan," the woman said, "how did this impromptu fundraiser for a local teenager and his family come about?"

Evan grinned and rubbed the back of his neck. "I've been buying Jenny coffee for days, and she keeps refusing to drink it. So, I hired Travis to follow her around all day and ask her if he could make her a coffee. I figured this was the best way to get her to accept. Annoy her until she relented."

The reporter's eyes sparked with amusement. She turned to me.

"Then what happened, Jenny?"

"Travis told me he was getting a thousand-dollar bonus for every coffee I ordered." I shrugged. "When he told me about his brother, that's when an idea struck. Evan didn't say I had to *drink* the coffee, just order it."

The reporter laughed and looked at the camera. "So you came out here in front of the Hilton and started giving away free coffee?"

She put the microphone back in my face. "That about sums it up."

Evan said, "And we have some good news."

The reporter swung the microphone his way.

"So far, we've donated over three hundred thousand dollars." The people closest to us who could hear the interview cheered. "But that's not all. Because Jenny Gentry is such a kindhearted soul, she's agreed to match my donation."

I stared at him incredulously, but he knew exactly what he was doing. The crowd roared. I laughed, not at all surprised he'd sprung it on me. And truthfully, delighted he'd thought to.

Evan spoke over the cacophony, taking the microphone from the reporter's hand. "That means we've raised over six hundred thousand dollars. We'll be here until midnight, so come by and see us."

The light on the camera blinked off, and the reporter thanked us for our time. I sauntered over to a grinning Evan and shook my head. "Touché," I said.

I went over and ordered a coffee for myself. Poor Travis was running ragged, even with all the extra help around him, but his smile never wavered. As I took the first sip, I savored the rich flavor on my tongue. It wasn't my regular drink order, because we were just serving what we had on hand, but it was enough. I let my eyelids drop as I cradled the thick paper cup in my hand.

The weight of someone's gaze was heavy on my back. I turned and found Evan watching me with an amused expression on his face. "Enjoying your coffee?"

"Immensely."

That didn't mean I had to drink every coffee he put in my face, but I could appreciate being outsmarted. He'd won this round. I'd just have to win the next one. And make sure I didn't lose my head in the process.

CHAPTER TWELVE

MY FEET ACHED the next morning. Standing on cement for hours had a way of really reminding you of your age. I wasn't getting any younger. But my diligence had paid off. While simultaneously costing me over a quarter of a million dollars. But Jenny drank a coffee that I paid for! I just had to keep being persistent.

Much to Jenny's dismay, the two of us did the radio morning show circuit the last three days we were in Denver—together. Some we did from the hotel room, and others we went into the studio. I brought her a coffee every single morning. I'd had to get Javi to convince Alli to let me fill that role.

We boarded the plane to New York on Thursday morning.

My stomach was the embodiment of static electricity. Nerves buzzed through me, crackling, popping, and overwhelmingly loud.

I stood on the tarmac, the sun not quite peeking over the horizon. My feet were planted firmly on the ground as I stared up into the plane's door.

"Why didn't we take a bus?" I asked. "There's plenty of time between audition cities, isn't there?" There had to be. The crew drove the equipment from city to city.

Ryan and Reese stood behind me, both waiting to see if I'd

board the plane willingly, or if they'd have to carry me on in a straitjacket. Javi, Alli, and Jenny had already walked onto the plane like it was nothing.

My phone vibrated in my pocket, and I looked at the caller ID. It was, like, three a.m. in L.A., so why was Kellan calling me?

"Hello?"

"Hey, man. I texted Javi, and he said you were about to get on an airplane. Do you have a second?"

I stepped away from the stairs, and Ryan and Reese groaned. I chuckled. "Yeah, everything okay?"

"Remember Murph? You met him at the NA meeting a couple weeks back."

"Yeah."

He let out a heavy breath. "I have a huge favor to ask you. We need to get him out of L.A. Get him away from temptation. He's looking for a job. Is there any chance you can bring him on your security team? He's vetted."

I ran a hand through my hair and turned, making eye contact with Ryan. "I'm okay with it, but I need you to talk to Ryan to make sure he's good with it. He gets the final say."

"I understand, and I appreciate this so much. Is he there now?"

"Yup. Here he is." I held my phone out to Ryan.

His brows furrowed, but he took it from my hands. "Hello?"

I watched him carefully, remembering the Irishman and how I had a hard time understanding him. That wouldn't be a problem, right?

Ryan nodded as Kellan spoke. "So, he's two weeks clean right now?" Ryan's gaze shot to me. "And you trust him?"

I couldn't hear Kellan's side of the conversion, but he was doing a lot more talking than Ryan was.

"I think it would be good for him too." Another look at me. "Can I talk to him?"

Ryan changed to a video call and wandered out of earshot.

Reese pointed to the airplane. "Should we just rip the bandage off?"

I sighed and trudged to the stairs like a prisoner headed for the gallows. The closer I got to the airplane, the more my stomach vibrated with nervous energy. Would it really be that bad to take a beta blocker? This feeling would still be there, but it would be underwater. Muted.

Nope.

That was the slippery slope of addiction. I felt around in my pockets until I found a pack of gum and unceremoniously popped a stick in my mouth, then I mounted the steps.

Jenny was in the deepest compartment sleeping, so I took the one beside hers.

"Awesome. Have Kellan arrange it with Javi. I'll look forward to meeting you in New York." Ryan's words preceded him into the compartment, and his gaze immediately found Reese. "I think we'll need to do combined security. I just hired Murphy. Vince was talking to me a couple weeks ago about hiring another security guard to help keep track of Axl, but I think it'll be better for Murphy to be with Evan." Then his gaze found me. "How do you feel about being his nightly check in?"

"As in, for his sobriety?"

Ryan nodded. "He needs someone who cares about keeping him clean. You need accountability. It'll be good for both of you."

That almost sounded like Kellan speaking through Ryan. "Okay."

Ryan tossed me my phone and sat beside Reese. "If we combine security, and the four of us cover Evan, Jenny, and Axl, I'd feel a lot better. I'll talk to Vince about it when we see them later today. Maybe they can get Murphy on the same flight with Axl, Vince, and the kid."

It was funny that Ryan called the manny "the kid" and not Axl, who was actually a kid.

The pilot came over the speakers, and I was re-reminded that we were about to turn into human cannonballs.

Wonderful.

I threw a second piece of gum in my mouth and tried to breathe. The plane taxied down the runway, and I gripped the arms of my seat, my eyes screwed shut, my breaths labored. How could anyone sleep through this? My stomach climbed into my throat, my heart hid behind my ribcage, my bladder decided it was terrified and needed to be emptied.

Sweat covered me from head to toe. I chomped my gum as if chewing loud enough could drown out the anxiety thundering through me.

And within eighty-five terrifying minutes, we were finally in the air. It was probably more like seconds, but it felt like minutes.

My body cautiously relaxed. Ryan and Reese both hunkered down into the cots. I stayed belted into my seat, but as much as I tried to trick my mind into thinking we were safely on the ground, it wouldn't allow me to drift off.

Instead, my thoughts turned to Jenny, like they always seemed to do.

She would hate that we were stuck together for security reasons, but I didn't mind it. I was making progress with the coffee. I just had to keep going. I sent Javi a text, asking him to order Jenny a coffee and have it at the airport when we got there. Maybe one of the show's drivers could make a detour before they picked us up.

We had a fuller schedule in New York. A live TV interview, among other things. And Axl would be there. We'd have to try to get another writing session in. She'd refused to do another one after our last attempt.

But she wouldn't really have a choice. I was desperate to see what she'd written, but she'd taken her notebook with her. Maybe I could convince her to do a writing session tonight and take a peek.

THAT AFTERNOON, I tracked Colby's location from the airport to the hotel. When they were in the building, I waited for Axl outside the elevator bank on my floor.

The doors slid open, and a redheaded mountain with tattoo sleeves stood in front of the doors, a dubious look on his face. I flinched back, regretting my hasty decision to ditch Reese in the room.

Axl plowed around him, his little legs pumping as he squealed, and threw himself at me. "Mommy!" I knelt and enveloped him in a hug.

Vince clapped the man on the back, and the three men exited the elevator together.

I buried my head in Axl's hair, inhaling that scent that was all baby shampoo and little boy. "Hey, buddy. I missed you."

He pulled back and picked at the neckline of my shirt. "We went on a big pwane, and I saw wots of pwepope. And Unca BB and Vince came. And Murph. This is Murph." Axl pointed at the man with the tattoo sleeves.

"Nice ta meet ya, Miss Gentry." And wow did he have an accent. Oh, the ladies would love him. He gave a slight wave, his hands clamped in front of him, his shoulders slumped like he was trying to look less imposing than he was.

I lifted Axl and propped him on my knee. "Nice to meet you, Murph."

Vince gave me a look, widening his eyes to try to communicate silently. "He's the new addition to our joint security detail."

"Joint?"

Vince nodded. "Yeah. We're borrowing Reese, but figured it would be easier for all of us to keep track of everyone if we combined forces for the duration."

I opened my mouth to tell them what a terrible idea that was, but Vince's look cut me off. Obviously there was a reason, and he'd tell me what that reason was when we were in private. "That sounds...wonderful."

"Let's get out of the hall, shall we?" Vince pointed toward the suites.

Axl wrapped his arms and legs around me as I carried him into the room.

A short time later, Evan arrived, and the living area in my suite was full of men, and Alli.

Axl dragged his Slash bear behind him as he made the rounds, talking to each person.

When Evan saw the bear, he stopped mid-sentence and widened his eyes. He looked for me until our gazes locked. He pointed to the bear and raised a brow. I gave a single nod. Yes, it was the bear Evan had specially made for me forever ago. And no, I didn't want to talk about why I'd given it to my son. It was an Axl Rose teddy bear that we'd named Slash.

Evan joined me in the kitchen area. He put a hand on the counter beside me, leaning against it. "Tonight, I think we should do a writing session."

I almost laughed at him. "Sorry, I've got plans." Alli had gone shopping so that I could try my hand at another recipe. I glanced around the kitchen instinctively. I'd been bringing some basic kitchen gadgets with me: a couple of hot plates, since most hotels didn't have stoves, and pots and pans.

"All night? We really do need to put more words on paper."

"Yeah. I have a date. I probably won't be available until morn-ing." No need to tell him the date was with a four-year-old.

I took some satisfaction in the way his eyes widened and his jaw clenched. The way his knuckles went white on the counter.

"Okay, tomorrow then."

I nodded noncommittally. "I'll have my people contact your people."

His lips twitched. "They already did. Your people didn't mention a date tonight. In fact, your people said you were free after you put Axl to bed. What time should I be here for dinner?"

My gaze cut to Alli, who was laughing at something Javi said. "Your people are infiltrating my people!"

Evan shrugged, unrepentant. "Not intentionally, but it is a nice side benefit."

"She's fired." I said it without any bite.

Evan laughed, a deep rich sound that I pretended I didn't like. "How many times have you fired her over the years?"

"More than I can count."

"Seven p.m.?"

"It might be inedible." That was not me deterring him. That was me being honest. I'd made some pretty bad food over the past several months.

"I'll eat before I come." He winked.

I couldn't help but smile. "Bring me some too, just in case."

He saluted and walked away.

Had I just invited Evan to join us for dinner? I hadn't. He'd invited himself, but I hadn't said no. I swallowed, ignoring the voice in the back of my mind that told me I was playing a dangerous game.

evan

I BROUGHT my writing notebook with me to dinner and placed it on the coffee table. Jenny stood at the counter, chopping vegetables and putting them in a bowl.

"How can I help?" I washed my hands in the sink next to her.

"I need to get the chicken on. Do you know how to work a hot plate?"

"Nope."

"K. Take over cutting the vegetables. See how big they are? Try to make them all that size." She handed me the knife and fiddled with the hot plate on the island across from me.

I started chopping zucchini. "What are we having?" I glanced over my shoulder as she put a skillet on the hot plate and turned it on.

A canvas bag stood on the counter beside her, and she pulled oil out and put a few splashes on the warming pan, then she opened the fridge and retrieved a plastic-covered bowl filled with marinating chicken.

I couldn't help it. I was impressed.

Axl came running out of the hallway full-throttle. He leaped onto the couch, then bounced a few times before jumping off and rushing into the kitchen.

He hugged Jenny's legs, and she hugged him back, one-handed, as she tried to put chicken into the pan.

He came to me next. "Hi, Van."

"Hi, Ax-O."

He laughed. "It's Ax-O."

"That's what I said."

Jenny put the bowl in the sink and swatted me with the back of her hand. "It's Axl, right?" She directed her question at him.

"Yeah!"

She leaned into me and murmured, "We try not to baby talk around him so he hears the correct way to say his words."

"Ah." I cut the last of the bell peppers and added them to the bowl with the onions and zucchini. "Axl, do you like music?"

"Yes! I sing wots! Wike Mom."

I put the bowl next to Jenny on the counter. "Need anything else?"

She shook her head, and I walked over to the couch that faced the kitchen and took a seat. From this vantage, I could see into the open adjoining hotel room, to Vince and Murphy, deep in conversation.

Axl came and jumped on the couch beside me, literally, like a trampoline. When he lost his balance, I caught him before he went head-first into the glass coffee table.

He giggled.

I set him on the couch beside me.

Jenny watched us from the kitchen while pretending not to.

"Did you go on a pwane?"

I nodded. "Yes, did you?"

He climbed on my lap and grabbed my face, forcing me to look at him. "Yeah. We went up in the sky a wot, and I waved at the pwepope. And with Murph."

I needed a decoder ring or the Rosetta stone just to under-stand this kid sometimes. His hands on my face made my words come out muffled. "Oh, yeah?"

"Yeah, and we fwew in the cwouds. Wike a waimbow." He released me so he could arc his hand through the air.

I caught "rainbow."

"Did you see a leprechaun?" I grabbed him under his armpits and put him on the floor in front of me. Kids had no grasp of personal space, and it made me laugh.

His little brow furrowed.

"With a pot of gold at the end of the rainbow?" I clarified, my forearms on my knees so I was closer to his level.

He grabbed my face again, his little eyes wide, like his brain was going faster than his mouth could form words. "And we saw airpwanes too. And caws. And a twain."

"A train?"

"And it had a caboose!"

I started to smell something bitter, and I looked up to find Jenny staring at us. The pan in front of her had smoke coming off it.

"How's that chicken coming?" I asked.

She blinked and threw her attention to the food in front of her. She stirred it and said something under her breath I couldn't hear.

I joined her in the kitchen. "May I?" Taking the spatula from her hand, I stirred the chicken. There were a couple spots that were blackened, but the rest was fine. The bitter smell had been the garlic, and there wasn't much we could do about that. I spooned the burned pieces from the pan and onto a paper towel, then I dumped the vegetables in and turned the hot plate down.

She put the lid on the pan and shook her head. "Why don't you go get yourself some dinner. Axl and I will eat this."

"It's fine. I'm happy to eat your cooking. It smells good."

"Just go." She pushed my shoulder, and I resisted only a minute until I met her gaze and saw the look in her eyes. The defeat, the wounded pride.

"But we need to write."

Jenny shook her head, her mouth pulled into a thin line. "I can't write tonight."

I knew that look. This was the same Jenny I'd seen in the parking lot the day we'd met. The one who took the cigarettes from my hand and threw them in the garbage. She wouldn't relent. "Are you sure?"

She continued staring, the resolve behind her eyes like steel.

I took a step backward, toward the door. "Do you want me to get you anything?"

"No."

CHAPTER FIFTEEN

THEY MADE Evan and me ride in the limousine together to auditions Saturday morning. It felt like punishment for barely speaking two words to him the day before. The truth was I was a little bit scared after seeing him and Axl interact together. Dinner on Thursday night had freaked me out. Not the dinner itself, but how normal it felt. How well I worked in the kitchen with Evan by my side. How he swooped in to help save the meal. And it was delicious, even after I'd burned it. I almost regretted kicking him out. Almost.

As we traveled to the venue, the silence stretched between us like a rubber band. I glanced around the limo, desperate for something to puncture the weird tension. Vince had the partition up between the driver and passenger compartments. My gaze snagged on Evan's bare ankles between his ripped jeans and his snake-print loafers, and I laughed.

"What?" Evan followed my gaze to his feet and crossed his ankles as a blush stole across his cheeks.

"I see you still forget to pack socks." We'd been on dozens of trips together over our relationship, and I'd taken to packing extra socks for him after he'd borrowed mine one too many times.

He rubbed the back of his neck and grinned. "Yeah, and Ryan and Reese don't share like you used to."

"To be fair, you do stink them up."

"Do not!"

"Do too."

I laughed and, for a moment, something easy passed between us—warm and familiar. Like we hadn't lost anything at all.

They took us back to hair and makeup, and I was dressed in a casual outfit in record time—thank heavens Fabian was back. Apparently, we were doing crowd work this morning. Gus put a mic pack in my waistband, and I fished it through the back of my blouse before clipping the mic to my collar.

When they ushered me back into the limo, Evan was already inside, still sockless.

"Now you're just messing with me."

That crooked grin that used to make my heart stutter made an appearance. "Maybe."

I turned my head away to hide my smile.

The driver pulled the limo around to the front of the venue like we were just arriving, then Vince opened the door.

A huge line of auditioners wrapped around the block. We stopped at the end of the line, and a director and a couple of cameramen met us there.

"We're going to get a few shots of you two working the crowd. Just go down the line and talk to people. Individually, if you would."

Evan gestured for me to go first.

I looked at the producer and raised an eyebrow. "Do you have people in mind?"

He shook his head. "Go with your gut."

I smiled and waved at the line of contestants, keeping a five-foot gap between myself and the barricade that kept us apart. I posed for some selfies, watched some kids breakdance, and listened to tons of people trying to catch my ear with their music. Some played the guitar, harmonica, tambourine, bongos, and— my favorite—the accordion.

From the corner of my eye, I watched Evan interact with people. He laughed and joked, then took a quick accordion lesson from the same kid I'd listened to. Evan really was charismatic. It made me remember what drew me to him in the first place. Evan had this way of leaning into life, like standing still was a personal offense. He wanted to learn things, try things, go places—preferably all at once. Adventure wasn't a bonus feature for him. It was the point.

A pang of longing hit me hard in the chest, but I shoved it down. This was for Axl. He needed stability. People he could rely on. Evan wanted a solo career. He'd be going on tours, gone eight to nine months out of the year. That was the opposite of stable. Axl and I didn't need someone to ruin our routine and leave us when things got too hard. He'd left once, and he'd do it again. He didn't even put up a fight last night when I'd asked him to leave.

"You okay, Miss Gentry?" the director whispered.

I blinked my eyes back into focus and plastered a smile to my face. "Never better." I just needed to keep my mind from wandering back to where it wanted to go.

I posed for a picture with an overly flirtatious man and prayed he wouldn't have a good voice, so I didn't have to deal with him anymore.

When I was finished, I stood in the shade of a tree next to the entrance and watched Evan talking to a girl in a wheelchair. He crouched down to her level and put his hand on the armrest. She blushed and smiled, but I wasn't close enough to hear their conversation. I noticed the Irishman and Ryan standing a discreet distance away, their heads on a swivel, ready for danger. As I looked around, I found Vince doing the same. He inclined his head but otherwise didn't show any sign of emotion. Reese would come later, with Axl and Colby.

My gaze wandered back to Evan—it was the charisma, I swear. I didn't have the same charm he did. The way with people. Axl had inherited that trait from his dad, and perhaps I didn't mind it like I might've a week ago.

And that kinda scared me.

CHAPTER SIXTEEN

DURING OUR LUNCH BREAK, I found Javi sprawled out on the chaise lounge in my dressing room like he owned the place. I ducked behind the screen and yanked off my shirt—whether they wanted a wardrobe change or not, they were getting one. I was hot as anything.

And I couldn't keep Jenny out of my head.

She'd asked me to leave last night without even trying to write.

And then this morning with the socks...

She'd been so normal. Like whatever had passed between us could be folded up and put away.

Maybe I was overthinking it. Hell yes, I was.

I glanced around the dressing room, all blacks and reds. Probably supposed to be regal, but it felt more like a brothel.

Sebastian'd left a garment bag on my dressing screen. I changed quickly—black ripped jeans, combat boots, gray Metallica T-shirt, leather vest. Typical Evan Black. Armor.

When I was done, they escorted me to the judges' stand. Murphy sat on one side of it and Ryan stood by the door, scanning the crowd like someone might rush the stage for murder or memorabilia. Coin toss.

Kimball was already seated, dark clothes, dark mood—predictable as gravity.

Jenny walked in a few minutes later—she'd had a costume change too.

Hot pink mini dress. White feather boa. The room tilted.

I stood and offered her my hand. She looked at it, stepped up on her own, then caught herself and took it.

Willingly.

My heart kicked hard against my ribs. For a second, I thought about tightening my grip. Just enough to feel if she'd pull away.

I didn't.

"Thanks," she whispered, and then took her seat between Kimball and me.

"You look lovely," Kimball told her.

Something ugly twisted in my gut. I swallowed it down.

Javi appeared with a sponsor cup and handed it to me. I set it in front of Jenny without comment.

She blew on the lid and took a sip, eyes closing in quiet bliss.

The producers hyped the crowd. The cameras rolled.

I watched Jenny like if I stared hard enough, she might crack open and spill the truth.

Jaryce shouted from behind the curtain, "Season fifteen, are we ready?"

The crowd screamed. I cheered, hollow.

The first contestant came out. Kimball handled introductions. Names blurred. Voices stacked. I scribbled notes in the provided notebook, then along the margin. Without meaning to, a melody started to take shape.

"Ask his name," my earpiece said.

Dammit.

I leaned into the mic. "What's your name and where're you from?"

I finally looked up. The guy had been taking selfies with Jenny this morning. The green monster stirred.

"I'm Troy Maddox from the Jersey Shore. Home of the yachts,

the shots, and the vocal chops!" He raised his hands theatrically, and the crowd cheered.

Of course you were.

"What are you singing?" Kimball asked.

"I'm singing 'Midnight Confetti' with my own twist."

He was good. Too good.

Jenny laughed, soft, breathy. Her foot tapped. She mouthed the chorus with him.

Something dark and hot uncoiled in my chest.

"Evan," my earpiece warned.

I focused on the stage. "You've got a helluva voice, Jersey Shore. Congratulations."

The crowd cheered.

Jenny leaned toward me. "Did you even hear his audition?"

I picked up her coffee cup and took a sip. "Of course I did."

She thwacked my arm and took her cup back. "Liar."

"How did it go?" Javi asked later, accent thicker than usual.

"How do you think?" I tugged my shirt on. "Where's Ryan?"

"With Reese. Murphy's got you."

I reached into my pocket and closed my fingers around my sobriety medallion. It felt heavier than it should have. Everything did when Jenny was nearby.

"You sure you're okay? With her?"

"Quit psychoanalyzing me. I'm fine."

I wasn't lying. I'd beaten the addiction. Most days. But June 13th was getting closer, and pain *always* got louder near that date.

Fans waited by the car. I signed, smiled, and posed.

At one point, Murphy said a little loudly, "Hey, give him a bit of space."

Several of my female fans turned to him with new interest, whispering things like, "Did you hear his accent?" and "Oh my gosh, I wanna have his Scottish babies."

To which Murphy replied, "I'm Irish," and they swooned.

I laughed despite myself.

On the ride to the hotel, the migraine hit.

I'd spent the entire day holding everything in. Turned out my body didn't appreciate the effort.

Pain bloomed, rhythmic and brutal, like a jackhammer behind my eyes.

Javi handed me my triptan. The car went quiet.

At the hotel, I pulled on a hoodie and sunglasses and let my guys steer me through the lobby—*Weekend at Bernie's*: rock star edition.

As I lay in the dark later, my thoughts slid back to Jenny in that pink dress. The heels she'd traded for flip-flops the second she could. I replayed the breakup again, trying to find the logic.

She'd been angry. Emotional. No room for reason.

At least that was how it felt at the time.

Sleep took me fast.

THE NEXT MORNING, Javi brought me ginger tea and another triptan —the only real medication I allowed myself.

"What time is it?"

"Nine. You can stay in bed all day."

I took the mug, grateful for the heat. "I'm gonna go back to sleep."

CHAPTER SEVENTEEN

I'D SPENT yesterday shopping for Axl's birthday, then at a Dior photo shoot. I still had a hard time believing that people would buy something just because I was associated with it. But my agent had worked hard to line this up. He called it part of my comeback. I couldn't even remember the name of the perfume—it was supposed to be my signature scent. They'd been sending me samples to try for months until they got the formula right. It did smell good though, so I didn't feel bad endorsing it.

The photo shoot boosted my confidence beyond probably what the acceptable levels were. The photographer kept telling me how beautiful I was. Kept tossing out words like "perfection" and "exquisite." So this morning, going into our interview with *The Morning Exchange*, I was feeling like hot stuff.

The soft lavender jeans hugged my curves and swallowed the extra chub around my waist. America wouldn't know what hit 'em.

When I was dressed, Fabian bid me *adieu*, Lindsay touched up my makeup, and Kelsey gave my hair a quick pat and spritz. "You look beautiful," she said.

Alli came in and grinned. "I just saw Evan. You sure you don't want to take another crack at that? Boy is fine."

I laughed and pretended to smooth my lip gloss in the mirror to avoid looking at her. Just because we were getting along didn't mean that I wanted to try another relationship. I was being nice for three reasons. One, I'd destroyed his life and maybe a teensy part of me wanted to help him get back on track. Two, Aiden asked me to keep an eye on Evan in exchange for him lying for me. And three, there was no three. That was it. Guilt and more guilt. No other reason.

"No comment?" she asked.

I shot her a flat look. "Nope."

Her grin grew. "They're ready for you."

Evan and Gio, Kimball's evil minion, met me right outside the trailer. I could've gone the rest of my life without seeing that little weasel again, with his hair plugs that were a shade too dark for the natural hair growing in a Friar Tuck around the bottom of his hairline.

Evan, as always, looked impeccable with his ripped jeans and a deep blue shirt that brought out his eyes. A day's worth of stubble decorated his jaw, which ticked as Gio handed each of us a flash card with approved topics on it.

"Just a couple of notes."

"What does that mean?" I asked.

He snatched the notecard from my hand and shoved it in my face, as if I hadn't already glanced at it. "Stick to the script. Don't give too much away. That sort of thing."

I heard a very distinct growl from Vince behind me. Gio flinched.

"What could there possibly be to give away?" Evan sniped as he pulled Gio's disrespectful hand from in front of my face. "And don't do that. It's rude."

Gio huffed. "I'm also supposed to remind you that you're a brand. We're selling you as friends. Kimball doesn't care how you actually feel about each other, but you need to pretend you're best friends for the cameras."

Evan held the notecard out to me.

I took it and ripped it in half. "We'll take that under advisement."

Gio's nostrils flared. "Your jobs depend on it. No one, and I mean no one, is irreplaceable."

Evan angled himself between me and Gio. "Even you."

I could feel the tension rolling off the three large men around me.

"I'll be watching." With a final huff, Gio stalked away.

Trailers blocked us from the view of the morning show, which was already in full swing.

It was just cool enough to be comfortable outside—luckily it hadn't heated up enough to reek of hot garbage yet. The scent of roasted coffee permeated the air.

"Find that coffee," I whispered to Alli. She saluted and peeled away from the group. I was surprised I'd beat Evan to the punch.

A sound engineer found us and mic'd Evan and me up.

Like a hot beverage ninja, Javi showed up and handed me a cup of coffee. Evan smirked.

"Thanks." I took a grudging sip and handed the cup back to Javi.

The live audience's chatter nearly drowned out the instructions the director gave us, but once we were settled into chairs on the stage beside our two hosts, a director called, "Ten seconds!"

I exhaled and pressed a hand to my stomach, then fluffed out my flowy blouse.

"Stop fidgeting," Evan murmured. "You look beautiful."

Teagan straightened her shoulders, and words appeared on the teleprompter. She said, "Welcome back to *The Morning Exchange* with Teagan and Isaac. With us this morning are *Singing Sensation* judges Evan Black and Jenny Gentry."

The audience gave a loud cheer as Evan and I waved to the cameras.

"So, Jenny and Evan, what can you tell us about this season of *Singing Sensation*?"

We'd filmed six episodes. "Almost nothing. They gave us a list of phrases we're allowed to say."

Evan laughed. "Mine just says 'It's going to be amazing.' I'm using it wisely."

"I got 'Expect the unexpected.' We're basically spies."

The audience laughed, and my stomach settled a little. I could do this. Evan's presence was oddly calming.

"What makes this season different from other seasons?" Isaac asked.

Evan chimed in, "There's a twist!"

"He's not allowed to say what it is." I was enjoying myself immensely. And we were making it up as we went along. No teleprompter for us. I glanced over and noticed there were words for us on the teleprompter, but we'd promptly ignored them. No pun intended.

"I'm not even sure *I* know what it is," Evan said.

I grabbed his arm and looked at Isaac and Teagan conspiratorially. "That's how tight the secrecy is." When did his biceps get so big? That was a question for another time. Or the subject of a song that needed to be written. *No, Jenny, you can't write a song about Evan's biceps.*

Teagan's mouth ticked up in a smile that could only be described as seductive. "You two look comfortable together."

I glanced at Evan, who was leaning back as best he could in his stool, and said, "That's because we rehearsed sitting next to each other."

Evan fake yawned and rested his hand on the back of my seat. "We're naturals."

Heat crawled up my cheeks. "Very natural."

"Should we give you two a moment?" Isaac asked with a chuckle.

Teagan's smile faltered, and she read the next question from the teleprompter. "If you could describe the show in one word, what would it be?"

I said, "Hopeful."

And at the same time Evan said, "Bold."

"Bold?" I challenged.

He shrugged. "I panicked. It sounded good."

Play it up for the cameras, Jenny. "Boldly hopeful."

Evan's eyes lingered on me, a half-smile pulling at the corner of his mouth. I got lost in those eyes. Forgot where I was. Why this was a bad idea. Why I needed to keep my distance. Axl. I needed to make sure Evan was in a good place before I told him about Axl. So we could flirt, we could talk and get to know each other, but at the end of the day, being stuck with Evan as a judge was a blessing. I had an opportunity to see him in a way I wouldn't have otherwise. And make sure he was worthy of our little boy.

The silence stretched for too long.

Isaac cleared his throat and said, "I like it."

"Jenny, Evan, how has it been working with Kimball Stone again?" Teagan asked.

"He always knows exactly what he wants," Evan said.

I laughed. That was an understatement. "And he knows it three business days before the rest of us do."

"He calls it 'vision.' We call it 'Kimball Standard Time.'"

I was doing so much laughing that I nearly convinced *myself* that we were best friends. "It's a different time zone entirely."

The producer pointed to a ticking clock that showed the next commercial break would be in thirty seconds.

"Last question," Isaac said. "What's the biggest thing you're taking away from this experience so far?"

I glanced at Evan, then out at the crew. Alli stood there with my coffee order, Javi beside her with my other coffee. "That team-work matters."

Evan grinned. "And that coffee drives 90% of television."

I laughed a very unladylike snort. "Is that your profound takeaway?"

"I'm being honest!"

Isaac cut off my response with, "Honesty is profound in its own way. Coming up after the break, we're joined by the New York City Animal Shelter with this week's Fur-Ever Home."

The cameras cut. Isaac hugged me, and Teagan took her time hugging Evan. Lots of time.

I finally gave up and walked off set without him. Alli handed me my *real* coffee.

"Thank you."

I glanced over my shoulder and noticed Evan had moved to the second set where they were filling a pen with puppies.

"Evan Black covered in puppies. Is there anything better?" Alli asked, her voice exaggeratedly dreamy.

Maybe Axl would like a puppy. He would be beside himself with excitement right now if he were here. Good thing he wasn't. But after this was all over, and I had my talk show and was all settled into a beautiful house with a decked-out kitchen and a treehouse for Axl, there was no reason I couldn't get him a dog.

I took another sip of coffee and let the warmth seep into my extremities.

Vince handed me a wide hat and led me to the SUV a couple blocks away, then opened the door.

Reese sat in the driver's seat and turned as I entered. "We're heading straight for the airport. Next stop: Nashville."

CHAPTER EIGHTEEN

I COULDN'T STOP THINKING about Jenny. And maybe
I didn't want to.

Things between us had seemed, dare I say it, easy. Friendly.
Fun. But the problem with that was the conversation we'd had
with Gio beforehand. What was fake and what wasn't? Jenny was
a damn good performer. Her music videos had proved that again
and again. She could take on a role without flinching—and be
believable at it.

As we drove to the airport after our foray on the morning talk
show, I kept replaying our banter in my mind. Replaying the way
her cheeks had turned pink when I'd put my arm behind her. The
way she'd smiled when she grabbed my arm.

That was the Jenny I knew. The Jenny I'd missed. My throat
tightened, and my knee started to bounce. Could you fake a
blush?

"You alright, *amigo*?" Javi asked from the seat beside me.

"*Sí.*" That wasn't the full truth. Something was off, but I
didn't know what it was until the airplane came into view.

Ah, yes. Catapulting through the air at a million miles an hour
and praying to gravity or science or God that I landed safely on

the opposite side. Being in the air wasn't so bad, but taking off and landing? Terrifying.

Javi put his hand over mine, and I realized I'd had a small piece of paper that I'd torn into a thousand pieces. "Oops. Was this something important?"

He laughed. "No. It was Teagan Devereau's phone number. Probably best that you tore it up."

Ryan and Murphy laughed from the front seat.

"Where and how did I get it?"

Javi waggled his eyebrows. "She slipped it in your pocket when you were holding a puppy."

Hmm. "Well, that's disturbing."

"Even more disturbin' is tha' I didna see it 'appen." Murphy tore into a protein bar wrapper with his teeth and took a massive bite.

"I did," Ryan said from the driver's seat.

And he didn't protect me. The nerve. I chuckled. "It's taken care of now."

We stopped on the tarmac. I squeezed my hands into fists to keep them from shaking. "You coming, boss?" Murphy said, door open, brows raised.

Sliding out of the SUV, I looked up at the plane and let out a trembling breath. Now or never.

I'd take never.

Murphy stood silently beside me, chewing his protein bar, as Ryan opened the back of the SUV to let some crew take my bags. I slipped my hand in my pocket and squeezed my sobriety medallion.

Javi waited at the foot of the stairs.

The mouth of the private jet gaped open, ready to eat me alive and spit me out once it had masticated me around in its maw for a few hours. Yippy.

"We going in or nah?" Murphy asked.

"I guess so." With another sigh, I trudged up the stairs, each step a feat in bravery. At least for me. Murphy, Ryan, and Javi marched behind me, my own personal executioners.

We were halfway up the steps when I heard giggling inside the airplane and stopped. "Is Axl in there?" No one had told me we were sharing a flight with him. I mean, I guess it should have been obvious. But I hadn't realized it until now.

A Ryan-sounding growl came from behind me. "Yeah."

My heart, which had already been pounding, decided to work double time. Not only was I terrified of flying, but I had to pretend I was chill so I didn't scare the kid. That I didn't want to wrap myself in a bubble and kiss the ground when we landed. That I wasn't mentally checking the emergency exits and wondering where I could find the parachutes in case of an emergency.

I swept into the plane with twenty percent false bravado and eighty percent dread. Jenny was in one of the rear private compartments with her giggling son, and I sighed in relief that I didn't have to face him again. My emotions were all over the place. One minute, I was excited to see her, and the next, I was aching from the reminder that she'd chosen to leave me. And I was a jerk of the highest order for looking at her little boy and feeling betrayed. The kid hadn't done anything, and he was cute enough, but it was as if she'd chosen him over me.

I plopped into one of the leather seats in the main compartment, and Javi took the seat across the table facing me. Murphy and Ryan took the seats on the other side of the plane, directly across from us.

"We should play poker or something," Javi suggested, pulling a deck of face cards from his Mary Poppins bag.

Ryan shook his head and rolled his eyes. "Did your mother drop you on your head when you were a baby?"

Javi looked at me guiltily. "Sorry, *amigo*. I wasn't thinking."

"It's fine." They were as worried as I was about me doing anything addictive. I pulled my sobriety medallion from my pocket and squeezed it. "But I'm up for some cards." It would be a good distraction.

And that was how I found myself surviving takeoff while winning a very intense game of War.

CHAPTER NINETEEN

THE DAY after *The Morning Exchange* interview, as we'd gathered in my suite to figure out the day's schedule, my dad called. "Hello?"

The room went silent, and most everyone filed into the adjoining room to give me privacy.

"Hey, pumpkin. How are things? I saw you're being a judge on that singing competition. Congratulations." I tried to turn the volume down before Evan overheard it, but I could tell by the tightening of his eyes that he had. Of course he hadn't left to give me privacy.

"Thanks, Dad." The fact that my dad hadn't opened with a request for money was a step in the right direction. "Things are good. Axl is learning his letters. It's so cute."

"That's great! Can Grandpa say hi to him?"

"He's still asleep."

"Oh." Disappointment was evident in his voice. "Okay, well, that's not why I called anyway."

"What can I do for you?" I tried to keep my voice low so Evan couldn't hear the conversation, but he went still. Nosy butthead was listening anyway.

"That judging gig must pay a pretty penny."

There it is. I gritted my teeth. "Not really. I'm doing it for the publicity." My dad didn't need to know that eight figures were involved. He seemed to get more needy when he knew how much money I made.

Evan leaned closer, meeting my gaze. His mouth was pulled into a firm line and his jaw ticked.

"Well, the reason I'm calling is 'cause the oven we got for the restaurant is starting to have problems. It sure would be nice to get a new one. Last time we bought used to save some money, but the chef's been complaining that it's not holding temp."

Of course. "I'll talk to my accountant." I mouthed, *He wants money.*

Evan reached his hand out for the phone, and I turned my body away from him.

"Jenny, you're the boss, not your accountant. You tell him where to send money and he does it. Not the other way around."

"I know, Dad, but I invest my money, so I don't just have cash sitting around; that's how it works."

"That's what this is. An *investment.*"

Yeah, an investment that I hadn't seen a single penny from.

Evan held out his hand more insistently.

"Listen, Dad, I have to go."

Before my dad could make a second appeal, Evan took the phone from my hands and hit the End button, then handed it back to me. "Problem solved. I can't believe he's still hitting you up for cash every chance he gets."

I wanted to argue, but he was right.

The phone rang in my hand, but I silenced it. Then, because I couldn't help myself, I texted my accountant to ask if there was money for a stove. He promised he'd research it and do the right thing.

"You're hopeless," Evan said, reading over my shoulder.

"Probably."

Dad was right, in that it was an investment. And I'd continue to invest as long as it kept him away from the sports betting. But it was also an investment in me. In my peace. If I could give him something positive to focus his attention on, something to generate an income without my constant intervention, I could worry less about the next time he popped into my life, asking for a few thousand dollars. Or a few hundred thousand dollars.

Our last stop of the auditions loop was in Phoenix, where Saguaro & Sage was located. Maybe I'd stop by and surprise him.

Evan's phone pinged from his pocket, and he pulled it out.

It was my turn to be nosy.

"Whatcha looking at?" I leaned over until his screen was visible. He had an auction site up with an autographed guitar. The pop-up on the screen said he'd been outbid. "Extending your collection?"

He looked up at me. A shadow passed behind his eyes, and he put the phone back in his pocket. "No."

My brow furrowed. "Why are you lying to me?"

"I'm not."

Did he think I was stupid? Blind? "I just saw you on an auction site." This was the dumbest hill for him to die on.

He stood and crossed to the adjoining door, looked back at me, then went into the other room.

I still remember the day he told me about his guitar collection. We'd been dating for about seven months, and we were sitting in his music room. His collection dominated one wall. I inspected each one—twelve in total—and he walked a step behind, telling me about them.

"That's a 1958 Les Paul 'Burst." He pointed to a beautiful cherry sunburst finish. "Only 434 of them were made that year, and each one faded a little differently. This is one of my favorite guitars. That one"—he nodded to the next one in line—"is a 1961 Fender Stratocaster with an Olympic White body and a rosewood neck. It's the guitar I bought myself after our first album dropped."

The next guitar was an acoustic, which was more up my alley.

"That's a 1946 Martin D-28. The back and sides are solid

Brazilian rosewood. And this is the last year Martin used herring-bone purfling."

"Purfling?" It wasn't a term I was familiar with.

"That little line of inlay along the edge there. This guitar is more than an instrument. It's a piece of American music history." He smiled and lovingly traced a hand over the glass case.

"You're going to love this next one."

I gasped as I saw the signature. "Is that Slash?"

"Yup. This is a 59 Les Paul Standard with a Tobacco 'Burst finish, signed by the man himself." He looked like he might pop from pride. Down the line we went. A Gretsch 6120 signed by Brian Setzer from the Stray Cats, a Pearly Gates signed by Billy Gibbons of ZZ Top, a Frankenstein-style Strat played by Lindsay Ray Vaughn, Stratocaster played by Jimi Hendrix, the Black Strat signed by David Gilmour of Pink Floyd, a "Blackie" replica signed by Eric Clapton, and a Franken Strat with a red body, black stripes, and a single humbucker like the one Eddie Van Halen played.

One more guitar hung at the very end. Well used and dinged up. A little smaller than the others, like it belonged to a child.

It had called to me, beckoning me to come closer, and I obeyed. It was an old acoustic guitar, cheaply made. The name "Noah" was carved on the body, beneath the bridge.

"Who's Noah?" My gaze traced the scratch marks.

Evan was quiet for so long that I turned to make sure he hadn't zoned out. His eyes had a faraway look, and my curiosity burned, but he looked so uncomfortable, so I gave him the out he needed.

"It's okay. You don't have to tell me."

He cleared his throat and put his hand on the clear case. As if it were the most precious guitar in his collection, he unlocked the case and pulled it off the wall with reverent movements. "I want to," he rasped.

It took him another few moments to start speaking, and in that time, he led me to the couch, where I sat, waiting with nervous anticipation.

"This guitar solidified my belief in Santa," he said.

Not where I thought this was going...

I grinned and waved my hand for him to keep going.

"My mom—my birth mom—was an addict. From the time I was old enough to go to school, I had to fend for myself. Her thinking was that if I was old enough to go to school, I was old enough to make my own meals. I was seven when she started dating Gary. He had his own kids and wasn't as deep into drugs as my mom. He made sure that she applied for free breakfasts and lunches at the school. It's the first time I remember having enough food to eat."

My smile drooped, and my stomach swirled uneasily. My upbringing had been rough because of my mom's mental health issues, but she still made sure I was taken care of.

He wouldn't look at me as he continued. "They broke up after a huge fight a couple of days before Christmas. I cried more than she did. He was the only one who really cared what happened to me. Christmas morning, this guitar was left on our front porch with a bow and tag just for me. 'From: Santa,' it said. But now, looking back, I'm sure Gary bought it for me. He was a good guy."

I put a comforting hand on Evan's back and sat silently. How could she treat him so poorly?

"My mom said Santa never brought me presents because I hadn't been good enough. This was the first Christmas that Santa had brought me anything. And I knew that there was no way my mom could afford a brand-new guitar, so that ruled her out. The only logical explanation in my seven-year-old mind was that Santa was real."

I scooted behind him on the couch, one leg on either side of him and my forehead leaning into his back as I wrapped my arms around his torso. I didn't know which of us needed the hug more, but it soothed me to do something.

"Anyway, I taught myself to play on this guitar. For four years, this guitar was my best friend. I took it with me everywhere. One night, I caught my mom in my room with the case in her hands. She said we were broke and she needed to sell it so we could afford to keep the lights on. I cried and begged her—" His voice broke, and the tears I'd been holding at bay trailed down my cheeks. My chin trembled, and I pulled him tighter, as if I could hold him together, protect him from this memory.

"She slapped me and told me to shut up. She went off about how ungrateful I was, how she had been putting up with me for eleven years, and I needed to be more appreciative. I cried myself to sleep, because she wasn't just selling an instrument, she was selling my coping mechanism. She was selling the only thing I had cared for. My best friend.

"I could play songs on the guitar that encapsulated every emotion I didn't dare speak. The next morning, she was asleep on the couch, and I searched everywhere for the guitar. I found it tucked in the top of her closet and quietly snuck it down and took it with me to school.

"When I got home that afternoon, I hid the guitar in the shed in our backyard to keep it safe from her and went inside. I didn't know if she'd even remember taking it the night before, because she often said things and didn't remember it the next day. I found her on the couch in the same spot I'd left her that morning. I touched her arm to wake her up, and it was cold."

A chill went through me, and Evan's body shook. I scooched from behind him and stood, then stepped between his legs as he sat on the couch, the guitar between us. His head rested on my stomach, and I gently combed through his hair. How horrible for him. What kind of mother would treat her child like that?

An addict.

"Who's Noah?" I asked.

"That's my birth name. Noah Butte. After I aged out of the foster system, I legally changed it to Evan Black. I wanted to leave behind Noah and become something better. A phoenix, if you will." He set the guitar aside and wrapped his arms around my legs, pulling me to him.

"So, there's my messed-up life. That's why I don't want kids— a predisposition for addiction. That's also why I'll never touch drugs."

My chest ached at the memory.

That's also why I'll never touch drugs.

But he had.

And now he was doing everything in his power to dig his way out. But that didn't explain why he wouldn't tell me about the auction site. The guitar.

It was weird, and I wanted to force the issue. Make him tell me, but it wasn't my job to protect him anymore. If he was hiding something, I wouldn't get involved—unless it could potentially hurt Axl.

CHAPTER TWENTY

NASHVILLE.

Damn Nashville.

I simultaneously loved and hated it here. I spent the first day in Jenny's hotel room until she'd seen the auction site, then I'd retreated to my room. I stared at my phone for hours, debating whether I should buy a guitar. Whether I could trust myself again. Then I decided that I could if I made it out of Nashville alive.

Ryan, Reese, or Murphy checked on me every hour or so, just to make sure I was okay and to bring me food, but they mostly stayed in their adjoining room.

The quiet gave my brain too much room to wander.

My adoptive dad. My late adoptive mom. Nashville. The house.

If I didn't stop by, Carl would be hurt. But if I did... If I walked into that house without Tracy in it... It'd all become real.

For years, I'd kept the illusion alive: that she was still there, still just a phone call away.

Going home would shatter that, and I wasn't sure I could survive the fallout sober.

If I slipped, I'd lose everything again. I'd be *that* guy—the addict, the disappointment, the screwup who ruined everything good.

I couldn't go back there. Not again.

It would kill me.

Literally.

We do recover. Yeah, unless we don't.

If I'd done the math and realized I'd be in Nashville on the day Tracy died, I probably wouldn't have taken this gig. Just my luck. June 13th had been the sun I'd orbited around for four years. The day that changed everything.

Plus, I'd been the worst son on the planet, walking out before Tracy's casket had been lowered into the ground. Not looking back. Not calling. Not even checking in to make sure Carl was okay.

Maybe if I patched things up with Carl, I'd be strong enough to stay clean tomorrow. Maybe that was the missing component. I hadn't made amends. Carl had lost two people that day. His wife... and his son. Me. The kid he took a chance on, the one he plucked from the foster program and took into his home.

I rolled out of bed and trudged to the bathroom, turning on the water as hot as I could stand it.

"That you, Evan?" Ryan called.

"Who else would it be?" Okay, I was letting my grumpiness permeate other aspects of my life. "The pope?"

"My nana," Murphy called. They were in the main living area, so I peeked my head out.

"Yo."

"Coffee?" Javi asked, standing and moving to the kitchenette.

"Maybe we could get some on the way to Carl's house."

Javi froze and turned, his mouth gaping. Ryan stared at me, wide-eyed. Murphy had no idea how important this was, so he just raised one red brow.

"For real?" Javi asked.

I nodded. "It's time."

How did you face a man you'd abandoned? How did you apologize for it? How did you make it all right? You didn't. You just showed up and hoped he opened the door.

As it turned out, we didn't stop for coffee on the way. Ryan probably thought if we did, I would bolt. Maybe he was right. The closer we got to Carl's house, the more my hands shook and my brain screamed at me to run away.

Murphy's hand landed on my shoulder from the back seat. A silent *you got this, boss.* Someone must've filled him in during my shower.

I let out a shaky breath. He'd probably tell us to take a hike. And honestly? I couldn't blame him.

Ryan stopped the car in front of his house.

Murphy opened my door and motioned me out like we were about to breach a cartel compound.

I still remembered the first time I'd seen Carl and Tracy's house. I'd felt almost exactly like this. Unsure. Terrified. A whole swarm of what-ifs buzzing in my head. I'd had a garbage bag over my shoulder and an attitude for armor. Back then, it was a dare. *Go on, try to love me.*

My throat burned.

I walked up to the porch. The white paint on the trim was peeling. The flowerpots on either side of the door were full of dead plants. I raised my hand to knock and heard footsteps behind me. Murphy crossed his arms and gave me a nod like, *do it before you chicken out.*

I knocked.

My stomach churned. What if he didn't want to see me? What if he shut the door in my face?

Then the door opened.

He saw my face—and his just crumpled. He pulled me into him, sobbing, and I broke too.

"My son," he whispered over and over.

It was a full-circle moment, a reversal of the old days. His shoulders shook against mine. He felt smaller now, fragile. Now, I was holding him up as much as he was holding me. My ribs ached with the strain of holding back the storm that had been building around my heart since the funeral. My fingers wrapped themselves around Carl's loose shirt, as if I could hold this moment together by sheer force.

But he still drew away, his cheeks shining with tears.

"Are you hungry?"

He ushered us inside, his hand clamped around my arm like if he let go, I'd disappear.

I was an asshole.

A lucky, sobbing asshole.

We hugged again. Then stood there awkwardly in the entry.

"I'm so sorry," I said.

It didn't even scratch the surface. Sorry for Tracy. Sorry for disappearing. Sorry for staining his name with my mess.

"All is forgiven. You're home."

Somewhere I had a list of amends to make, but right now all I could do was breathe.

The sage-green paint Tracy had painted over the ugly yellow I told her looked like dog vomit still colored the entryway. The rug under my feet was new, but the wood floor still creaked under my feet as I followed him into the living room. Papers were left in piles on the old piano where I'd learned to pluck out my first tune. Carl never liked having to stuff everything into his old filing cabinet in the office upstairs. Without Tracy, I guessed the papers never made their way to a folder, and without me, the piano no longer needed to be cleared.

I used to sit there for hours with my mom—until I'd gotten good enough that she said I'd surpassed her. A better son would've called more. Checked in. Not let things fall apart like this.

"Dad."

It was the first time I'd said it without the word *foster* or *adopted.*

Because he was my dad. He was the man who taught me how to be one. The man who loved me when no one else could. Took me too many years to figure that out.

My instincts screamed *get out of here*, but my instincts were usually wrong.

"Have you visited your mom yet?" he asked, referring to Tracy.

I shook my head. "I'm here for the rest of the week. I'll get there."

He nodded toward Murphy. "Who's this?"

"This is Declan Murphy. One of my security guys."

Alarm flashed in his eyes. "Where's Ryan?"

"He's outside."

"You need *two* security guys? What's going on? You have a stalker? Death threats?" He yanked the curtain back and peeked out the window like we were in a spy movie.

I chuckled. "No, nothing like that. I just—"

"Evan's helping me with my recovery," Murphy cut in.

Carl's voice broke. "Are you still...?"

"Yeah. Still clean."

A silent tear trailed down his cheek as he nodded, mouth pressed together to hold back a sob. "I knew you could do it," he rasped.

My chest squeezed. "Thanks."

Time would tell.

I cracked open the front door and waved everyone inside.

While they said their hellos, I went upstairs. The hallway was a shrine—the only photo of my birth mom with me as a baby hung on the wall next to my senior portrait. A snapshot of Aiden and I in the parking lot at The Bluebird Cafe. Tracy and me in front of a baseball diamond when I was fifteen. Tracy and Carl in front of a sailboat at the marina. Memories assaulted me on every side.

My room was untouched. One of my old guitars sat in its stand by the bed. I picked it up, tuned it, and started playing, trying hard to find the melody from the song I'd written on the plane.

"I've missed the sound of that," my dad said from the doorway, leaning on the jamb.

I lifted the guitar. "Mind if I take this with me?"

"The guitar?"

"Yeah. I played this in the Bluebird when I got my first contract. It's not music history—but it's mine." The photo in the hallway was taken shortly after.

"The case should still be in your closet." He sat beside me. "I've missed you. I hope this means you won't be using Javi as your messenger boy anymore?"

My throat went tight. "I'll try."

"Good," he said, words strained.

I laid the guitar on the bed and toured the rest of the house. When I got to the backyard, I couldn't sit by any longer.

"What's going on?" I asked my dad.

He rubbed the back of his neck and shrugged. "Been busy."

Javi had hired him to be my accountant two years ago, when I'd been trying to pull myself out of my addiction.

"What happened to the yard?"

He kicked at the dead flower pot on the back patio and looked out at the weed-filled, overgrown yard.

My mom had taken so much pride in her garden. It was dead now.

"Just had other things to worry about."

"Like what?"

He shrugged. "Bills."

"What bills?" Why hadn't he asked me for help? Or had he? Then it hit me. "Aren't you taking a salary from me?"

His faded gray eyes met mine briefly before he looked back at the ground. "Just enough to get by."

This was not getting by. "Dad. Why didn't you give yourself a raise? Take more money. You're in charge of my finances."

"Didn't reckon I should. Felt wrong to." His voice caught. "I'm your dad."

"You're a professional accountant. Starting today, I'm doubling your salary, and I'm going to make sure you get back pay too." I really was the worst kind of human. I'd used him. Not appreciated him. Ignored him. My chin trembled, and I pulled him into a hug. "I'm so sorry," I whispered. "For everything."

We spent the rest of the day clearing the living room, sorting through bills, making piles to keep or toss.

Each unpaid bill was like a punch to the gut that made me realize how much I'd dropped the ball. *Never again,* I vowed.

When I came across a picture on the piano, my throat went tight. It was my mom and dad with Jenny and me. We were at the marina and had a passerby take several pictures of us. He'd told us to smile and say cheese, and my mom had blurted out, "All right now, y'all, scoot in. We're taking a picture, not measuring for caskets." The guy taking the photo had just held down the button and captured my mom and Jenny mid-laugh, bent at the waist, looking at each other, arms linked like best friends. Dad and I made eye contact over their heads, big smiles on both our faces. We'd gotten some good posed photos, but that had been Mom's favorite. And here it sat, a relic from another time.

THE NEXT MORNING, I woke the guys up early. "Rise and shine, ladies. Today we're doing manual labor. Refinishing the deck, repainting the trim. The rock-star life."

Today was *the* day. June 13th. And I was determined to keep myself busy so I didn't have a second to think about the date. To dwell on the loss. I was a new man. I was better than my addiction, and dammit, I was going to win.

We sanded Dad's house until our arms ached while Javi made a hardware-store run. It was probably a three-day job, but we were going to knock out what we could.

After staring at the contact on my phone for what felt like an hour, I rang up Sam, my high school friend who had jumped right into the family carpet cleaning business the day after graduation. Him and his wife, Lindy, popped out of a cleaning van in the driveway not twenty minutes after my phone call.

Sam's crooked grin stretched across his face. "Hey, superstar. Long time no see." I couldn't help but hug him and Lindy before giving them the grand tour of the house. Dad's cheeks were a bit pink by the end of it, but Sam just grinned like he was skipping around at Disneyland.

Lindy pulled a pair of rubber gloves from the back pocket of her jeans. "We'll have this place shining in no time."

By sunset, every muscle I had was screaming. We'd finished the trim, cleared the yard, and primed the porch. My hands were a patchwork of paint and blisters. I shoved the last piece of gum in my mouth and tossed the empty wrapper in the big dumpster we'd had the city bring.

I was scrubbing paint from my arms with the backyard hose when my dad came out in a nice suit with a bouquet of flowers.

I dried my hands on my jeans, looking back at the house. The sun hung low in the sky. There wasn't much else we could do today. And I was tired enough that I'd fall asleep as soon as my head hit the pillow.

Dad turned off the hose. "Reckon y'oughta head out. I can handle the rest. I'll hire it out."

"You've got the money now." I'd put Javi on bill duty today, calling on each of Dad's bills and paying them. "But I don't wanna leave you with the work half done. We'll be back tomorrow." Even if my hands were blistered and my whole body ached.

I took in his suit again, and it hit me where he was headed. To visit Mom. I'd not only distracted myself today, I'd prevented Dad from visiting his dead wife's grave.

He slapped me on the back. "See ya tomorrow then."

The words were on the tip of my tongue. The offer to go with him to Tracy's grave. I opened my mouth to say them, but I was already so raw from my visit with Carl; I didn't know if I could face Tracy too. Would it be too much?

I went to hug him, then held my hand out for a handshake instead, so I didn't get his clothes dirty. "I'll be back tomorrow."

CHAPTER TWENTY-ONE

AXL'S BIRTHDAY had been a huge success. We'd invited all his "pwepope" for cake and ice cream in a rented conference room —I'd even decorated it myself. Well, with Alli's help. And now, as I closed the door to Axl's bedroom and tiptoed away, I worried about Evan.

This was the night Aiden had specifically asked me to watch Evan. He'd texted me about a dozen times to tell me to check on him and to tell me that Evan wasn't responding. He also insisted I ask Evan if he'd had a chance to visit Tracy's grave yet, and he begged me to encourage him to go. As much as I wanted to help Evan stay sober, Axl was my baby and it was his birthday. Eventually, I'd told Aiden to pay attention to his wife. It was their fourth anniversary! I hadn't heard from him again after that.

I'd invited Evan to the party, then texted him several times throughout the day, and I'd gotten no response. Reese said Ryan wasn't answering his phone either.

I stared at the leftover cake on the hotel suite's kitchen counter. One day, I'd make birthday cakes from scratch, but on the road like this, bakery cake had to do.

Reese popped through the adjoining hotel room door. "Ryan texted me. They got back a half hour ago."

"Where were they?"

Reese pried the clear plastic lid from the cake and searched the drawers until he found a fork.

"Hold on. Let me get a piece out for Evan."

I cut a square for him and put it on a paper plate. An icebreaker. A peace offering. Call it what you would.

"They were at his dad's house doing yardwork and painting all day."

Something loosened in my chest. Carl was good people. "I see."

He paused with his fork above the cake. "I'm good to dig in?"

"Yep."

I went into my room and snagged the gift bag from my dresser, then grabbed a plastic fork and started toward the door.

"Wait! You're going now?"

I waved him off. "Yeah. It's across the hall. I'll be fine."

"Vince might kill me if you go without me."

"He's asleep."

I left him in the suite and knocked on Evan's door. Evan answered in a black T-shirt that clung to him, a pair of gray sweats, bare feet, and wet hair. His eyes were wild, like he'd seen something that terrified him.

What was going on? I tried to see behind him, but he shifted to block my view of the room. He shook his hair out of his eyes and gripped the door so tight, his knuckles were white.

"I brought you cake." I lifted it like an offering. "And a present."

He still didn't say anything, but he released his hold on the door.

"Are you okay?"

His adam's apple bobbed and his jaw worked. The hair on my arms stood on end.

"You're freaking me out. What's going on? Do you have a dead body in there?" I made another attempt to see around him.

He blocked me.

"Evan?"

He looked at me, his stormy eyes lost at sea.

"I'm coming in." I took a step toward him, but he didn't move. I put my hand on his chest, and his heart thundered beneath my touch. Gently, I scooted him away from the door and into the room.

An open bottle of whiskey from the minibar sat on the table. I crossed the room, leaving him by the door, put the cake and gift bag down beside the bottle, and picked it up. It was still full.

"What's going on?" He was freaking me out.

He closed the door and slid to the floor, his shoulders shaking, and buried his head in his hands.

I strode to him and knelt in front of him, using his knees to balance.

"Talk to me, Evan." I felt helpless. I had no idea how to navigate this. Someone else needed to help. I went to stand, and he grabbed my hands.

"Stay," he rasped.

I sank onto the floor in front of him. He didn't release my hands. His shook.

"Stay," he repeated.

"Okay."

Evan still didn't talk, just clung to my hands like they were the only thing standing between him and something awful. Probably that alcohol. Did he not drink anymore? That surprised me more than him not doing drugs. Evan and alcohol were best buddies. I felt like I needed more information.

Evan climbed to his feet and walked to the table. He picked up the whiskey and walked it to the sink, then dumped it down. He dropped the bottle in the trash, then gripped the edge of the sink, shoulders hunched, head hanging low.

I was so bad at this stuff. What did you even say to a person who you'd just stopped from relapsing? "I'm proud of you."

"Wanna go on a field trip?"

I refocused on him, still at the sink. "Where?"

He turned and the edge had left his eyes. "The cemetery."

evan

WE DROVE to the cemetery in silence. Ryan and Reese sat in the front, and I clung to Jenny's hand in the back seat.

When we stopped, Jenny said gently, "You go. I'll be here when you get back." She gave my hand a squeeze.

I met Ryan's eyes in the rearview mirror, and he nodded. The two of us trudged through the graveyard until we got to her marker. Ryan did a quick circle of the area, then gave me the all clear, stepping a few dozen feet away to give me privacy.

The grass crunched under my boots like it was scolding me. *Late again, Evan.* Yeah, well. Story of my life.

I stopped in front of her headstone. A fresh bouquet of daisies sat in the built-in vase, remnants of Dad's visit.

Tracy Jane Black—Mom. The only person who ever looked at a teenager with nicotine breath and a bad attitude and thought, *Yep, I'll take that one.*

Even now, in the thick summer heat, the stone looked too clean. Too still. Too final.

"Hey," I said quietly. My voice sounded rough, like my voice box was made of sandpaper. "I forgot flowers. They'd just melt in this heat anyway."

I tried to smirk, but it felt flimsy. Wilted around the edges.

Sweat slid down my spine, even though a breeze had picked up. My hands still throbbed from sanding the porch and gripping the paintbrush handle. Blisters tugged when I curled my fingers. "We started some work on the house today. Yours and Dad's. My guys and I sanded down the porch and cleaned out the backyard. I have someone else doing the inside. I'm sorry I let it get this out of control."

A warm gust swept through the cemetery, carrying the scent of cut grass and over-watered flowers. It didn't answer me, but it felt like she was listening.

"It hurt," I said, voice low. "Everything hurts. My hands look like I tried to arm wrestle a belt sander. My back keeps locking up. And Dad and I talked. I know. You were waiting for it forever. I couldn't face him."

I swallowed, my throat tight. The heat didn't help. "I wanted to get high today. Really wanted to. Thought about it way more than I want to admit. That deep craving that lives in your bones and won't shut up."

I rubbed my thumb over a blister. It burned. "But I didn't. First time in four years I wasn't drunk or high on this day. You'd... probably like that."

I blew out a shaky breath that felt thick in my chest. "Jenny's here," I added. I looked until I found her, outside the car and standing by a grave. "Not close. Just over there by that miserable angel statue. Seriously, whoever designed it needs therapy. But she came. I know how much you loved her. I found that picture today of the four of us at the marina. We're not there, but we're doing better."

I felt the corner of my mouth twitch. "You'd like this new version of her. She laughs at me like you used to—like she's in on a joke I haven't figured out yet. And she saved me today. Showed up before I made a mistake. Before the cravings tipped over into something I wouldn't come back from. She didn't even say much. Just...sat with me. And it was enough."

My eyes burned.

"I'm trying, Mom," I whispered. "I know I haven't lived up to the Black name. I know I ran. I missed your burial. And I haven't talked to Dad in years. I disappointed you more times than I can count."

I let out a shaky laugh. "If there was a punch card for 'Evan Messes Up,' you would've gotten the freebie."

Cicadas screamed in the trees, filling the silence.

"I miss you. And I'm sorry. For all of it. For the years I've wasted. For how much it took for me to get here. For almost screwing up today."

My breath left me slowly, the kind of exhale that hurt and helped at the same time. "I'm gonna try again tomorrow. And the day after that. And the one after that. One second at a time. I love you." I'd never said that enough when she was alive.

My chin trembled as I turned toward Jenny, shoving my blistered hands in my pockets. The summer night pressed close, hot and buzzing, but it didn't feel as suffocating as before.

I missed my mom fiercely.

CHAPTER TWENTY-THREE

"COME AGAIN?" I asked Reese.

"Yeah, today is the anniversary of his mom's death."

How had I missed that it was the same day? Tears pricked my eyes. He gained a son and lost a mother.

Should I tell him about Axl? Maybe knowing would help him with his sobriety. Or maybe it would shove him right over the edge of the cliff and off the wagon—especially since he was feeling so weak. He'd nearly relapsed today. If I hadn't been there, he would have.

Aiden would understand if I decided to wait. There was nothing to be gained at this point by telling him. It was for his own protection. And Axl's. Today would be the worst day for him to find out.

I'd forgotten how deafening the cicadas in the South were as I paced in front of a mourning angel.

"How'd you get him to come here?" Reese asked. "Ryan said he hasn't been to visit his mom's grave. Ever."

"It was his idea."

Reese's eyebrows shot up, nearly disappearing beneath his shaggy brown hair. He and Ryan looked nearly identical, despite Reese being a couple years younger.

"That's awesome. It's been hard on Ryan to watch him go through this."

My heart broke for Evan. For all he'd been through.

Footsteps crunched on the gravel, and I spun to see Evan approaching.

He wrapped his arms around me, tucking me against him and cocooning me in his larger frame.

I held him.

Let him cry.

Lyrics played in the back of my mind.

You've got shadows stitched in your skin,
But I've seen the fight you're carrying within.

I've been broken by your fall,
Built my walls, made them tall.
But I see you trying to climb,
And it stirs something deep inside.

I still had my guard up, still had to protect my family. My heart. But I couldn't help but be moved by seeing Evan's change. "She'd be so proud of you."

He shook his head—I felt it against the top of my head. I imagined all his stumbles, the way he must've been replaying them in his mind.

"Look how far you've come, Evan."

He sucked in a breath, another, trying to regain control of his emotions.

I pulled back, put a hand on either side of his face, forcing him to look at me—a very Axl move. The soft glow of the street lamp illuminated one side of his face. "She would be so proud of you," I repeated. I put every ounce of sincerity behind those words.

He tried to shake his head again, but I held it firm.

"You know how I know?"

His adam's apple bobbed. His gaze bore into mine. "How?" I

heard the vulnerability behind that single word. The hope he so desperately clung to.

"Because if Axl had been through what you've been through, and he came out the other side clean, I would be so proud of him." My voice broke.

A sob tore through him, and he pulled me to his chest again.

My dad had struggled with his own addiction for years. Not drugs, gambling. If he could overcome it and make something of his life, so could Evan.

We got into the SUV and drove in silence to the hotel. It wasn't the charged silence of the ride to the cemetery; it was peaceful. Comfortable.

Reese escorted us in while Ryan parked the car—the poor guy was exhausted, apparently they'd worked themselves to the bone today.

In the elevator, Evan grabbed my hand again. "Thank you for tonight. For rescuing me."

I swallowed and nodded. "Of course. That's what friends are for." I stared straight ahead, ignoring the scorching heat of his gaze on my face.

We arrived at our floor and waited for Reese to give us the go ahead.

"Come."

Reese walked ahead of us and opened my hotel room door. He went in and held the door open for me.

Evan paused at the door and felt his pockets. "I forgot my key."

Reese waved us in. "You can hang out in here until Ryan gets upstairs. It's not safe to just be out in the hallway."

Evan put a hand on the small of my back and followed me into the room. Reese wasted no time scooping up the remainder of the partially eaten cake and taking it into the adjoining room. "I'll be in here. Holler if you need me."

The suite had a dining area and kitchen directly straight when you entered the room, and a living area to the left. Between the two, a hallway led deeper into the suite and split off to two bedrooms. One for me and Axl and one for Colby.

Evan wandered to the couch and sprawled across it. I went to the loveseat that formed an L around the coffee table and sat. I yawned.

"You tired?"

I nodded. "Aren't you? It's nearly midnight."

"My adrenaline is probably pretty high right now. I'll crash later." He snagged the remote off the coffee table. "Wanna watch a movie?"

I stood and made my way into the kitchenette. "Do you want coffee?" I definitely needed some caffeine if I was going to stay awake for a movie. If Evan had another moment of weakness, I didn't want to be asleep if he needed me.

He hesitated. I'd forgotten he was so picky about his coffee.

"I brought it with me. It's that blend I use that you like. It's good. Want me to make you a cup?"

"Do ogres have layers?"

"Some of you may die," I quoted in my best Lord Farquaad accent, "but that's a sacrifice *I* am willing to make."

"Good memory," Evan mused. He turned on the TV and burst out laughing. *Shrek* was on.

I grinned as I got the coffee pod from a container on the counter. *Shrek* was one of Axl's favorite movies, and even though I'd watched it more times than I could count, I enjoyed it every time.

There was a knock on the door, and I peeked through the peephole, then opened the door. "Can you let me in the room, then take the key?"

"Of course."

I made sure I had my own key, then slipped into Evan's room and grabbed the cake and gift bag. Ryan stopped me on the way out and put something in my hand.

I looked down at it and my breath caught. It was a one-year sobriety coin.

"It's official at midnight. Will you give it to him?"

My throat closed as I pocketed the coin. "Of course I will."

Ryan watched until I was safely back in my own room.

I set the cake and gift bag on the couch at his feet.

When the coffee was ready, I brought it to the coffee table and set his mug beside him. He sat up and patted the couch beside him. I only hesitated a moment before I took it.

I snagged the gift bag and handed it to him.

The way he looked at me would've made a lesser woman faint. "You got me a present?"

I shrugged, trying to ignore the intensity in his eyes. "I saw them when I was shopping for Axl's birthday."

He ripped the tissue paper from the top and peered inside, letting out a delighted laugh. It was the most genuine happiness I'd seen from him. Ever.

"You got me socks?"

He dumped them onto his lap and lifted each pair individually. "Guns N' Roses socks? I can't believe they make these!" Each pair was a different album, even our much-debated albums of 1993 and 2008.

He found the "Spaghetti Incident" album-themed socks and tossed them on my lap with an "Ew."

I laughed and stuffed it into the bag. "You need all of them." I'd even bought him two "Appetite for Destruction" pairs so he had seven.

He kicked his shoes off and put on a pair, lifting his feet and wriggling his toes. "They're comfy." He put an arm around my shoulder and pulled me against his side. He placed a kiss on top of my head. "Thank you."

I grabbed two forks and we shared the last piece of Axl's birthday cake.

At midnight, I paused the movie and stood.

He looked at me with sleepy eyes.

I dug into my pocket and pulled out the coin, holding it in my fist.

"Ryan gave me this for you."

I opened my palm.

He looked down at the coin, and his chin trembled, his eyes filling with tears. He stood and scooped me into a hug, lifting me off the ground, our bodies pressed tight, the only sound between us his shaky breaths.

When he put me down, he rubbed the tears from his eyes with one hand and reached into his pocket with the other. He pulled out the other coin and held it up. "Trade me?" His voice was rough with emotion.

I shook my head. "No. You earned both of these. You keep them."

He nodded, his lips pressed together to suppress a sob. I placed the coin into his hand. "Congratulations. You made it."

He sniffed and nodded again.

THE NEXT MORNING, someone knocked on the door and woke me. I was slumped against a warm shoulder, a blanket over me, a kink in my neck and back. Evan didn't move, so I tiptoed over to the door, peeked through the peephole, sighed heavily, and opened it.

Kimball stood there, neat and tidy. He strode in without waiting for an invitation. I opened my mouth to protest, but he cut me off before I could.

"I wanted to check how your progress is going for the duet for the fina—" His gaze caught Evan asleep on the couch, then jumped to me and my mussed hair. I hadn't even bothered to clean off my makeup before falling asleep last night. It must've looked bad.

"Well, isn't this cozy?"

"What were you asking me about the duet?" I tried to redirect him to keep him from getting the wrong idea.

He blinked and brought his attention to me. "Your song for the finale. What do you have so far? I'd love to hear it."

"What?" It was too early to process his words. I needed more caffeine before I should be expected to have adult conversations.

"You and Evan? The duet for the finale. The two guest judges always do a duet."

Of course. I'd been purposely avoiding writing it after the last disastrous incident. "We haven't had much time to work on it. We planned to spend some time together writing it this week." Which was a lie, but Kimball didn't need to know that.

"Okay. I'll look forward to hearing it then." He headed back toward the door, closing it softly behind him.

Evan's eyes popped open immediately.

"You were awake that whole time?!" I accused.

A crooked grin stole across his features. "Who me? Would I pretend to be asleep so I didn't have to lick Kimball Stone's boots? Never. Good job getting rid of him, by the way. We should probably write that song sooner than later."

"I'll be sure to include a line about how you betrayed me to my enemies."

He laughed and stood, gathering his socks and putting them into the gift bag.

I walked him to the door, and he pressed a kiss to my forehead, one that made my stomach flip and my knees weak.

"See ya later."

"See ya."

CHAPTER TWENTY-FOUR

I TOOK a few minutes to gather myself in the bathroom. Stared at myself in the mirror. Looked into my clear eyes. *I'm proud of you*, I told my reflection. I did it. I looked down at the two medallions in my hand. *I did it!* I made it to a year. I couldn't have done it without Jenny's help last night. She really had caught me before I fell.

When I came out, Jenny held my keycard pinched between her fingers. I walked up to her and ran a hand through my disheveled hair. "Guess I should get back."

"Guess so."

She stood straight and looked up at me with those green eyes. I went to grab the card, and she pulled it away, a challenge in her eyes and a smile on her lips. "You gonna be okay?"

I swallowed and stepped closer to her, invading any private bubble she had. "Yeah." I tucked a strand of hair behind her ear, fully expecting her to pull away, but she didn't. She'd seen me at my worst, at my lowest, and she'd pulled me out.

Even if I wanted something more with Jenny, even if I longed to close the last few inches between us and bring my lips to hers, I could never be worthy of her. She could never really love someone who was so screwed up.

I stepped back and dropped my hand. "Do you have plans today?"

She rocked back on her heels and looked away from me. "Just hanging out with Axl."

"Would you wanna— Never mind."

She looked back up. "What?"

"We're painting my dad's porch today, doing some yard work, cleaning out the house. I was just gonna see if you guys wanted to come along. We were gonna leave around nine."

"She'd love to." The man nanny came wandering in, shirtless and in pajama pants. Kid looked like he hit the gym. I glanced at Jenny to see if she was checking him out, but she seemed wholly unaffected.

He stretched and grabbed a mug from the cabinet. "I'll come along and keep an eye on the rascally rabbit."

Jenny widened her eyes at him, her jaw clenched. So...that was a no. Okay then.

"It was stupid. It's fine. Enjoy your family day." I plucked the keycard from Jenny's fingers and went to the door.

"No. I want to. It's just, I don't want Axl to be in the way."

He wouldn't be.

"It's okay. Seriously." I opened the door and stepped through the hall, letting myself into my room before she could come up with another lame excuse.

I'D FOUND a ton of my old clothes at my dad's house, so after my shower, I dressed in something easy I could change out of when we got there. Ryan, Javi, and Murphy were ready to go, and when we stepped out into the hall, a group of people waited for us. But my eyes went to Jenny, her hair in a messy bun, wearing jeans, a T-shirt, and a pair of sneakers.

"You okay if we tag along?"

You sure you want to? "Yeah."

Reese and Ryan went to get the cars. Vince and Murphy escorted us down to the parking lot. In the lobby, people who were checking in or leaving the hotel stopped us for pictures and autographs. Javi came through with the Sharpies.

Jenny signed more autographs than I did, and I happily stood by her side as she chatted with her fans. When we finally got out of there an hour later, Jenny's smile was a little less vibrant.

"You doing okay?"

"I'm an extroverted introvert. That just drained my social battery."

I smirked.

"I'm an energy vampire. I feed on it. There's seriously nothing like it."

We drove separately to my dad's house, and when we arrived, Axl, in what I was starting to see was his way, walked around chattering about everything.

"That's a fwower pot, wight, Mom?"

"Right, buddy."

I grinned and walked up the steps to the front door. My dad opened it before I could knock.

"Evan! You brought someone." He had eyes only for Jenny, a warm smile on his face as he pushed past me and walked down the stairs toward her.

"Carl," Jenny said, opening her arms.

He picked her up in a bear hug. She laughed.

"I have missed you," he said. "Introduce me to this little boy of yours."

Axl stood behind her, watching the interaction with his wide blue eyes.

My dad knelt in front of him. "What's your name?" He looked at me, then back at Axl, his adam's apple bobbing.

"Ax-O Gentry. What's yours?"

He cleared his throat. "I'm Carl Black." He held out his hand and took Axl's, jiggling it, making his whole-body wiggle with the movement. Axl giggled, and after my dad let go, Axl held out his hand and grabbed my dad's.

"Again."

He jiggled it again.

Jenny watched on with a sweet smile on her face.

"You're in trouble, *amigo,*" Javi murmured.

I elbowed him.

For the next hour while I painted the deck, Axl followed Jenny around, peppering her with question after question, each one ending in "wight, Mom?"

My dad went over to them with a small paintbrush that was perfect for Axl's tiny hands. "Want to help me paint the deck?"

Axl's eyes lit up. "Can I?" He directed the question at Jenny.

She sent a questioning look to my dad, who nodded.

"Sure, buddy."

My dad scooped Axl up and took him over to the far side of the deck—smart of him to not let the kid play Picasso where it'd be super visible.

Javi gave me a none-too-gentle shove to Jenny's side. I stumbled to a stop beside her, and she looked up at me from where she was weeding the flower patch in front of the porch.

"You okay?" she asked.

I tried to play it off smooth, but I'd basically kicked dust into her face; there was really no recovering from that. Javi and Murphy guffawed from where they were standing—Murphy throwing yard debris into a huge dumpster and Javi "supervising."

"Need help?" I asked.

She looked down the line of weed-free flowers, then to the tiny patch left. "I think I've got it." She smirked.

My face flamed, and I rubbed the back of my neck. "Okay. Cool." Seriously, James Bond would be jealous of my suave moves. Why was I feeling so off-balance around her? Not anyone else, just Jenny.

I looked around for something else to do and found myself wandering over to where Axl and my dad were painting the deck.

Axl's clothes had white paint on them, his face, his hair, his shoes. He dipped the inch-wide paintbrush into the can of paint, dripped it across the flowers, and slopped it onto the latticework that prevented cats and other critters from making a home under the deck.

"Good job, Axl. You're such a good helper." My dad smoothed the paint across the deck. This must've been their routine.

"Room for one more?" I asked, selecting a paintbrush from the bucket next to them. My hands hurt just wrapping them around the handle.

"Sure, Evan." My dad grinned and continued to stroke the paint across the lattice.

"Sure, Van," Axl parroted. "He can paint wiff us, wight, Caw?"

"Right, Axl."

Axl grabbed my finger and pulled me over to the paint can. "You dip it in, wike this, ven you put it on the wood and paint." He smashed the brush onto the lattice, flattening the bristles and completely ruining the brush.

I looked at my dad to see his reaction, but he just smiled.

Okay then.

Following Axl's directions, I dipped the tip of the brush in the paint, then took over the spot he'd abandoned, spreading the glops of paint he'd left behind.

Under his breath, my dad asked, "Are you sure Axl isn't yours? He looks just like you."

I looked back at Axl, who was painting a dandelion white. Didn't really wanna get into this with him, but it was better we put this to bed before his hopes got too high. "I had a vasectomy seven years ago, Dad. He's not mine."

Like I'd predicted, disappointment washed over his face. "I didn't know that."

"Yeah, I didn't really advertise it. I didn't want to disappoint you guys. I know you wanted grandkids. It's just not in the cards for me. Whether addiction is nurture or nature, I don't think it's a good idea for me to reproduce."

"You could get a reversal. Or do what your mom and I did. Adopt." His gaze went to Axl, and I read the longing there.

If you'd asked me a month ago about having kids, I would've

said hell no, but with Axl nearby, that answer had changed to a soft no.

CHAPTER TWENTY-FIVE

DAY one of the Nashville auditions was straight fire. Felt like we sent half the city through to the next round.

Jenny looked at me differently now—in a good way. Like she saw me again. Not just the washed-up junkie who'd torched his life, but an actual person worth knowing.

During our lunch break, I caught my reflection in the mirror. Looked into my own eyes until I recognized the guy staring back at me. The old Evan. The one who had all the answers, the one who believed in himself—and in love.

I turned to leave just as a shadow fell across the door. Jenny stood there with her hand raised like she'd been about to knock.

"Hey," she said.

"Hi."

She'd seen me so low. I wasn't sure what to do with myself around her now.

"Did you need something?"

She flinched.

Nice one, idiot. Way to sound like HR.

"Um. No. I just came to check on you."

Warmth spread through my limbs, quiet and certain. "We're friends, right?"

Her expression tightened, but she nodded. "We are."

That was more than I deserved.

Javi came jogging up with her coffee order in hand, looking confused at which one of us to hand the drink to.

"I had Javi grab you a cup of coffee."

That softened her. "Thanks." She took the cup, checked the label, sipped. "Delicious."

Every time she smiled at me, I wanted to tell her I didn't want to be *just* friends. I wanted the real thing. Her laughter. Her chaos. Her heart.

"Thanks for helping me the other night." I stepped closer. Close enough to see the brown flecks in her eyes. Close enough to remember how her nose crinkled when she laughed—the same nose she used to hate. I'd told her a hundred times it was perfect. Still was.

After the cemetery and yesterday, it felt like things between us had shifted. She'd seen how ugly my life was, and she hadn't run. She knew what a risk I was, knew what a terrible son I'd been. And she still looked up at me with that softness in her eyes.

Her coffee cup stood between us like a shield—too much space for my liking. I wanted her in my arms again. Her floral shampoo, that hint of vanilla perfume. It was all muscle memory now.

A PA popped into the corridor. "Oh."

I looked up but didn't step away.

"They need you both on set," she said.

Jenny's hand brushed mine. "We'll be right there."

I swallowed hard as I stared into those inviting green eyes. So much had changed the past couple of days, and the air became charged between us.

She lowered her coffee cup, just slightly.

I could see the hunger in her eyes. If I leaned forward, I knew she'd let me kiss her.

Her gaze traced my lips, and I closed the distance. Our foreheads brushed, and she lifted her chin toward me. Then she was gone. She ducked beneath my arm and escaped down the hallway. She was to the auditorium doors before I even lifted my head.

Heat climbed the back of my neck, and I tried to take a deep breath, the cold air hitting the back of my throat. I watched the door close behind her retreating back. I'd completely misread the situation. I leaned an elbow on the wall and hung my head. That had been a mistake. I'd obviously mistaken her help through the night for something more. I needed to apologize to her, promise to not try to kiss her again. She knew as well as I did that I didn't deserve her.

CHAPTER TWENTY-SIX

KISSING EVAN YESTERDAY would've been a disaster. Even if I wanted to.

Kelsey, Lindsay, and I were alone in my hotel room as they prepped me for the day.

"Let me get this straight," Kelsey said, my hair gripped in her hands. "Evan Black had you *pinned against a wall, tried to kiss you,* and you ducked under his arm and ran away?"

Lindsay and I laughed, even though I knew it wasn't funny— well, maybe a little funny.

"Yep."

"Why?" Kelsey asked. "I would've kissed him if he'd done that to me. I've always wanted a man to pin me—"

"Kels, focus," Lindsay interrupted. "But yes, Jenny, inquiring minds need to know. Why didn't you kiss him?"

"Is he a bad kisser?" Kelsey asked, brushing through my hair. "Ew. I once dated the hottest guy and he seriously gave the sloppiest kisses. Total turn off."

My cheeks heated. "No, he's definitely not a bad kisser. I wanted to kiss him. I really did."

Lindsay pulled my eye masks off. "But...?"

I shrugged. "I have my reasons..."

Kelsey ran the brush through a tangle a little too hard. "Oops," she said lightly.

Lindsay shook her head. "We've signed NDAs, remember?"

I only had to consider it a moment before the whole story came tumbling out of my mouth. Every detail. From Evan being Axl's dad, to the promise I'd made to Aiden to tell Evan the truth. I told them about the night of Axl's birthday, staying up with Evan, cuddling on the couch. Giving him the sobriety medallion. They gasped in all the right places, putting hands over their hearts or mouths.

At the end of the story, it was like a weight had been lifted from my chest.

"Oh my gosh, it's so romantic!" Kelsey fanned herself with one hand.

Lindsay shook her head and started moisturizing my face. "No. Don't you see? She has to protect Axl. Kissing Evan is like a conflict of interest."

I found myself nodding along. "That's exactly how I feel. How am I supposed to make the right decisions for Axl if my brain's all cloudy from kissing Evan?"

Kelsey started the first curl. "I still think it's romantic. It's your second-chance romance!"

Evan and I shared a limo to the venue in Nashville. The ride was silent, the air thick with tension. Guilt gnawed at me. He was wearing the socks I gave him—at least he wasn't so angry that he wouldn't accept my gift.

"I need to apologize," he said.

At the same time, I said, "I owe you an explanation."

"No, you don't," we both said, and laughed nervously.

"Please." Evan angled his legs toward me. "Let me apologize. I was in a really vulnerable spot the other day, and I misinterpreted your help for something else. I never should have tried to kiss you. It won't happen again." The earnestness in his gaze hurt my chest.

I should've been happy. Relieved even. I nodded. "Thank you." But inside I was a torrent of conflicting emotions.

I had to remember Axl. He was my main motivator. The reason I was doing this. When the time was right, I would tell Evan everything. And then maybe he would understand why I had kept Axl away like I had.

When we pulled up to the venue, the directors waited with cameras ready. Like always, when we exited a car, the crowd cheered as soon as they saw us. I took a second to compose myself, rubbing my hand on my too-short skirt. Evan and I waved at the contestants and fans as they wired us for sound.

Gus handed me an earpiece. "You know the drill."

I forced a grin. "How could I forget?"

While they wired Evan, I searched the crowd for something to distract me from the flashes of his abs I was catching as they tucked the receiver in his waistband. My gaze landed on a head of curly red hair. Freckles dotted her nose and cheeks, and her green eyes were almost the same shade as mine. I pointed her out to the director, and he nodded, then approached her while I watched, instructing the contestants in the background to "act natural."

I walked to the edge of the barricades and pointed to her. She smiled as she approached the rope.

"What's your name?" I asked her.

The cameraman got really close.

"Maisie Grace," she said. A tattered guitar case rested against her jean skirt-clad thigh, and her cowboy boots were well-loved. I put her at about eighteen. She sported a button-up plaid shirt with the ends tied above her belly button. She reminded me a little of me—only five inches taller and before I got swept up in the Hollywood scene.

My smile widened. "How long have you been singing, Maisie?" She was a country girl through and through, and I was here for it. If she could sing, she would definitely go far.

"Since I was old enough to walk. My daddy's a pastor, so I've been singin' in the church choir all my life."

"Does he support your dreams to be a singer?"

Her cheeks turned crimson, making her freckles stand out even more. She shook her head. "I mean, he doesn't *not* support it, but he thinks I'm volunteerin' at the animal shelter today." She looked directly at the camera and clasped her hands in a praying motion. "Love you, Daddy and Mama."

Poor girl. Hopefully she didn't get in trouble for lying.

"Well, good luck to you."

Maisie inclined her head and stepped back into line with her guitar.

I meandered the crowd, but Evan captured my attention. He just had this personality that drew people in. He knelt at the ropes and played a card game with a couple of teenagers waiting in line. They couldn't have been much older than sixteen—the youngest the show allowed.

They laughed as Evan put a card on top, and the crowd erupted in cheers around them. As I got closer, I saw what they were playing: War. He'd just flipped a joker on top of the other kid's ace.

These moments with Evan, when he let his guard down, when he just allowed himself to have fun and not worry about everything else—like our coffee fundraiser at the hotel in Denver— were beautiful. And dangerous. I turned away from the scene as my eyes burned. If I kept watching, I might cry, and that was not what I wanted. Maybe I was lying to myself, or grasping at straws, or both. But I needed to remember who Evan was a year ago. As we got closer, it was easy to forget that he was—*is*—an addict. In recovery, sure, but could he actually put the past behind him for good? Could he see past his own hurt to heal himself?

Inside the venue, Kelsey touched up my hair while Lindsay powdered the sweat from my nose and forehead. I exhaled as my mind worked a mile a minute to decipher my emotions.

The PA poked her head in and gave us a ten-minute warning.

"What if Aiden tells Evan before I get a chance?" I asked my gossip group.

"Just keep biting your time," Kelsey said.

Did she… "What?"

"Biding your time," Lindsay said, shrugging. "Be patient. You said Aiden agreed that telling him on the anniversary of his mom's death could've been disastrous, but he gave you what? Another couple of weeks? He wouldn't go back on that."

I shook my hands out and exhaled another breath. "What if I tell him about Axl and he doesn't stay clean?"

Lindsay looked me in the eyes. "Jenny, you can't control what other people do. You can only control yourself. If he doesn't stay clean, then that's on him. It's not your fault."

Wasn't it? If I'd told him about Axl before his mom died, would he have been holding his son that night? Would he have been with me? Axl and I could have been enough to keep him clean if I'd given him the option… But I hadn't. I could've held his hand through his pain like he would've done for me. If I'd told him earlier, I could've saved us both years of heartache and pain.

Cowboy boots tapped across the stage. A familiar, smiling face stepped up to the mic.

Kimball leaned forward. "What's your name?"

"Maisie Grace."

She looked at me and I winked. Maisie brushed her curly red hair from her face and adjusted her guitar.

"That's a very unique name."

She had that fire in her eyes, that hunger to prove herself.

"Yeah, my dad's a pastor. His favorite song is Amazing Grace." Her cheeks turned red.

"What are you singing for us today?"

Maisie adjusted the second mic to her guitar's height. "I'm going to be singing *The Fire that Stayed* by Jolene Mae Carter."

"And I take it you'll be playing it on the guitar too?"

She nodded.

"Off you go then."

As the first notes rang out across the silent theater, chills rose on my arms. Maisie nailed the first verse, and I prayed Kimball wouldn't stop her before the chorus.

"You were the spark I never planned,
The heat I held with open hands.
Years have gone, but I still ache—
You're the fire that stayed."

That twang! The smoky way her voice wrapped around the words. It left me nearly speechless. Top that with the lyrics, and my entire throat was about ready to collapse. My thoughts flashed to Evan—I couldn't help it. I'd tried to put that darned fire out, but he was like a trick birthday candle. He kept relighting after I blew him from my mind.

When she finished, Kimball got to his feet and gave her a standing ovation. My body rose of its own accord, and soon the entire audience had joined us.

"You go first," the voice in my earpiece said.

As I sat, I adjusted my mic and my outfit while I waited for the crowd to quiet down. "First of all, your voice is incredible. Your pitch and tone. You have this"—I rubbed my fingers together to try to find the textured word I wanted—"shadowed quality that I find enchanting."

Kimball made a sound of question, so I explained.

"Like, not quite dark but holding secrets. I think you are exactly what this show needs. I say yes!"

The audience applauded.

Kimball sat back with a cocky smile on his face. "You know…" He shook his head and wiped his hand across his mouth. "If I were a betting man, I would place a wager that you win this season."

The other hopeful contestants went crazy behind us.

Maisie put her hands on her cheeks and took a couple of steps back from the microphone. The crowd continued to clap, and she waved, stepped forward, and said, "Thank you all so much!"

As she was exiting the stage, Kimball's assistant Gio approached the judges' stand.

Oh no. Been there, done that. Had the T-shirt. I didn't want

Maisie to go through the same thing I had. I'd been borderline anorexic when I was competing.

I grabbed Kimball's arm. "Leave her alone. She's not some Country Girl Barbie you can dress up and turn into Malibu Barbie. She's a person."

Annoyance flashed in Kimball's eyes. "I've been in this business decades longer than you, Jenny. Trust me. What I'm doing will only help her. She needs the audience's votes to win the show, which means I need to make her more marketable. And you would see that if you would just open your eyes." He finished giving Gio directions, and his assistant disappeared out a door beside the stage.

Dang it.

Maybe he was right. But I wasn't here to play industry games. I was here to do my job, protect my son, and keep my head down. No distractions. No side projects. Just focus.

CHAPTER TWENTY-SEVEN

THE MORNING after we wrapped filming in Nashville, I stood on the tarmac looking up at the plane.

A little hand wrapped around my finger. "C'mon, Van. We going on the pwane. And it goes up in the aiw, wight, Mom?"

"Right, Axl," Jenny said, holding his other hand. She nodded toward the plane, a little bit of a challenge. "You getting on, 'Van'?"

Axl pulled me forward, completely unaware that my stomach was in knots or that my head swam just thinking about the upcoming takeoff and landing. He took the first step so calmly, so surely, that a little bit of his confidence seeped into me. Ignorance was, as they said, bliss.

He took three steps before I had to take the first one to keep up with him. He stopped and looked back at my feet still on the tarmac. "You just put you foot up, wike this. Bam!" And he raised his little foot in the air, wobbled, then stepped up, turned around, and waited for me to do the same.

I stepped. He added the "Bam!" sound effect.

The next few steps, I took with him as he "bammed" the rest of the way.

Jenny stood behind me, her soft laugh filling the air. I glanced back at her. She raised her hands in an "I'm innocent" gesture. "I didn't say anything."

"You didn't have to."

"C'mon, Van!" Axl yelled from the top. "Hi, Mom!"

Someone really ought to teach him about the dangers of flying. Or falling, as it were.

"Hey, buddy."

"I did it by mysewf. You didn't hoed my hand."

Jenny smiled at him and said, "You're such a big boy."

"I'm all growed up." He jumped in the air to add a little height to his small frame.

"Van is scared," Jenny told him over my head.

I turned back and muttered, "I'm right here."

She smirked. "You're scared," she told me quieter.

I wished she were wrong. My heart was fluttering in my chest like a dying bird.

"Hoed Van's hand!" Axl suggested. He descended the stairs a few steps, until he could reach me, grabbed my hand, and pulled me forward. Jenny put her hands on my lower back and pushed me from behind.

"Oh, this is lovely. I'm being kidnapped by a toddler and the Keebler Elf."

Jenny laughed and pinched my side. As far as kidnappings went, this one actually wasn't so bad. I reached my hand back that wasn't being jerked forward by the toddler and grabbed Jenny's. She only fought me for a second, and I was convinced it was just for show. She linked our fingers together, and my stomach flipped.

When we got into the plane, Axl said, "See? It's fun." He towed me into one of the private compartments where his car seat was already strapped in, then he climbed on the seat beside it and traversed to his.

"Sit by me, Van."

Sweat beaded on my brow, and I did my best to wipe it away as discreetly as possible. Jenny took the rear-facing seat across a small table from us and buckled in.

"How come you have wat-o on you fo-head?"

"I'm hot," I said, closing my eyes.

The engines started. I buckled my seatbelt, doing my best to hide how my insides were trying to become my outsides. I'd heard somewhere that remaining calm in stressful situations helped kids stay calm too. Maybe the reverse was true though. Maybe Axl staying calm while I was over here with a mild panic attack would help me calm down.

My knees bounced beneath the table, and Jenny grabbed my hands. "Hey," she whispered.

I opened my eyes.

"Try to envision yourself somewhere else. Where's your happy place? Where brings you the most joy?"

That file in my mental filing cabinet was empty. Everywhere I'd ever loved had been tainted by something. Death, heartache, drugs. "I don't have one."

Her eyes widened. "Okay." She looked around the room as if searching her own mental filing cabinet. "Let's go to mine."

How was that supposed to work?

"Close your eyes and picture yourself on a wide green lawn. There are mature trees. One of them has a treehouse with a rope swing. A bridge going to another tree with wide ropes and planks."

"Like a pirate?" I asked, trying to envision it.

She laughed. "No, not like a pirate. Planks of wood."

"A pirate ship would be cooler."

"Yeah!" Axl agreed. "A piwate ship."

I allowed myself to picture this big yard with lots of grass, mature trees with a pirate ship-themed tree house—Axl and I were totally on the same page.

"The house is white. It has two stories with a wrap-around porch. There is a bed of wildflowers planted all the way around it, and they're in full bloom. Pinks, whites, yellows, reds, purples. Colors everywhere."

I added this house to my landscape, liking the way it was turning out. Of course, Jenny was sitting on the steps coming off the back porch, and she had a book in her hand. Her feet were bare. Axl squealed from the pirate playhouse.

"There's a porch swing that rocks in the summer breeze. Planters with flowing flowers are attached to the railing around the porch. And French doors open up to a beautiful modern kitchen. There's a big table for friends and family. A kitchen that I'm going to learn to not burn things in one day." There was humor in her voice. She squeezed my hands.

I laughed, trying to picture this. Me sitting at this table, Jenny with an apron on, bustling about the kitchen. The aroma of fresh bread and something warm and spice-filled permeated the air. Axl sneaking a cookie from the counter.

"What else?" I asked.

She hummed as she thought. "A family room with big comfy couches. The kind you sit on and your feet dangle in the air because they're so deep. Very inappropriate for company, but excellent for that homey feel. And lots of throw pillows.

"Big picture windows and high ceilings. Room for a giant Christmas tree in the living room. Fireplaces. Everywhere."

I chuckled, picturing a fireplace in the middle of the kitchen.

"Axl's room is zoo themed, with a mural painted on the wall. Life-sized stuffed animals. An elephant that is a slide."

"The trunk?" I asked.

"Yeah!" Axl cheered. "The twunk is a slide. And giwaffes as big as mountains!"

I pictured a little area with stuffed monkeys swinging from vines and monkey bars across the ceiling over a foam pit. It was rad.

"Evan?" Jenny said.

I peeked open an eye. We were in the air.

She released my hands.

Holy cow. It worked. We'd taken off, and I didn't even feel it.

"Thank you." I relaxed into my chair and closed my eyes, going back to Jenny's happy place, adding my own details. A music room with every instrument I was ever interested in learning. Definitely an accordion.

And the more I thought about it, the more I wanted it to be real. A home to share with Jenny. Even living with the kid didn't scare me anymore. But they deserved better than me. Than a man who almost overdosed the same time every year. A man who'd screwed up his life to the point that he hadn't spoken to the only father he'd ever known for four years.

I reached into my pocket and found my sobriety medallion. The one Jenny had given me. The one I had almost not earned. I opened my eyes. Jenny was watching me. As soon as our gazes met, she looked away. I peeked at Axl—asleep.

"Can I ask you a question?" I leaned my elbows on the table between us.

She copied my movements, a smile playing across her beautiful face. "Sure."

"What did I do wrong? Back before."

Those words closed her off faster than my mouth at a sobriety meeting. "I'm not talking about this right now."

So there was something. My stomach tightened, and I watched her. Watched her walls go up. Watched her close in on herself, folding her arms and shifting away from me.

A sinking feeling weighed heavy on my heart. "Jenny, part of my NA is to make amends. I know I did something. Just tell me so I can make it right."

Her gaze shot to me, then to Axl. She whispered—maybe it could be considered a whisper. It was part whisper, part shout. "Have you ever stopped to think that maybe *I* don't want to dredge up the past? We were in a good place. Why did you have to go and ruin it?"

She leaned forward, like she might get up and storm out, then her gaze caught on Axl and she glared at me instead.

"Can you just give me a hint?"

Her eyes that had been so calm a few seconds ago went wild. "A hint? You want a hint? I called you because—" She slammed her mouth closed and covered it with her hands, her eyes filling with tears. She shook her head, a muffled whimper slipping out.

I wanted to wrap my arms around her, tell her to keep going, try to piece the puzzle together and make things right. I stood and knelt beside her.

She turned away from me. "Just go," she squeaked out.

And so I did.

In the next compartment, a migraine started to throb behind my eyes. Kill me now.

CHAPTER TWENTY-EIGHT

I'D ALMOST TOLD HIM. The words were in my mouth. They were a split second from spilling off my tongue, and I'd chickened out.

What if he realized what I already had? That if I'd told him back then, the past four years of his life would've been different. We could've been together. A family. And he wouldn't have turned to drugs. He wouldn't have burned his life to the ground.

I thought back to that moment. When I found out I was pregnant.

I'D GONE into the cruise ship bathroom and locked the door behind me. My hands shook as I pulled the pregnancy test from the package. I couldn't be pregnant. I was on birth control. Could you get pregnant if you missed two days of the pill in a row? I was throwing up, my boobs were sore, and I was late. Google said it was the only logical conclusion.

A baby would ruin my life. Ruin my relationship with Evan. Ruin my career. Plus, we'd both agreed that we didn't want kids. No—that was too mild. We were both adamant that we'd never have kids. There were too many precursors for addiction and mental health problems in our collective DNA, and any child we had would be destined to be a hoarder or an addict.

But deep in my gut, I feared the worst.

I peed on the stick and put it on the counter. I read the directions again as I waited for the results.

A wave of nausea hit me, and I threw up in the toilet, tears blurring my vision.

Evan knocked on the door. "Everything okay, Jenny Rose? Do you need anything?"

"No," I croaked. I wiped my mouth on a towel. I couldn't bring myself to look at the test. Had it been three minutes?

I felt like I was going to throw up again. The anticipation was killing me. What if it said I was pregnant? Would Evan understand? Would he stick around? Would he leave me? I couldn't have an abortion. Wouldn't. Would he want me to?

I put a hand on my stomach. Was there, even now, a tiny life growing inside me? I couldn't take it anymore, and I looked at the test. There was a plus sign.

Pregnant.

I let out a shaky breath. Maybe I could convince Evan that this would be okay? Maybe he would stick around. He'd be a good dad. I could feel it.

But deep down, I knew. This was the beginning of the end.

His birth mom had ruined any happiness he might have found in being a father.

I stuffed the pregnancy test back in the box, folded up the directions and put them in with it, then I shoved everything back in my purse.

What did I do now?

Evan knocked on the door again. "Jenny Rose? Are you okay?"

I shook my head, fisted my hand against my mouth to hold back a sob. I needed the comfort he could give me, but would he withhold it if he knew? I stared at the door handle. As soon as I twisted that knob, our relationship was over.

My heart broke in half.

I couldn't let him see me like this. Couldn't let him see me falling apart. He would know something was wrong. I had to convince him that he wanted kids without telling him I was pregnant.

I splashed some water on my face, exhaled a breath, then opened the door.

Evan folded me into his embrace and wiped the tears from my face as I looked up at him. There was such tenderness in his eyes that would all go away as soon as he found out I was pregnant.

"Talk to me," he said.

I shook my head. "Later. For now, I just want you to hold me."

He led me to the bed, helped me peel off my jeans, then pulled me onto the bed beside him, his hand resting on my hip, his lips at my hairline where he intermittently placed soft kisses.

We watched some shoot-'em-up movie that I didn't pay much attention to, but near the end, as the heroine told the hero she was pregnant, I saw my opportunity.

I rolled onto my stomach, our sides pressed together, and propped my head on my hands.

"I've been thinking..."

Evan smiled a soft smile, full of warmth. "I love your brain. Tell me."

"I think you'd be a really good dad."

His smile froze on his face, and a door slammed closed behind his eyes. He tilted his head. "What makes you say that?"

"Well, for one, Tracy and Carl are good parents. I think you've probably learned a lot from them..."

His brow furrowed.

"And I watched you interact with a young fan at the airport."

"Jenny Rose." His tone had that condescending quality that he rarely if ever used on me.

"Is it too late to just say instinct?" I hadn't given this enough thought. "Seriously though. I was just thinking about our future, and I think we'd make really cute babies." I watched my fingers trace a path over the patch of skin above his heart. He stiffened. I glanced at his face.

He wasn't smiling.

He propped himself up on his elbows, pulling away from me. "Why are you bringing this up? I thought we were on the same page. We both know that our kids would be screwed up from the start. Maybe we could talk about adoption in ten or fifteen years if we're still together."

I bristled. *If we're still together.* I pushed the dig aside—we both knew the mortality rate for celebrity relationships was high. But we were the exception—weren't we?

"I know, but they wouldn't look like you." I brushed a lock of hair from his forehead. "Will you at least think about it?"

He shifted, and I lifted my head. He slid off the bed and paced back and forth. "No. I won't. Jenny, why are you—? Is my love not enough?"

"That's not it at all…" I rolled onto my back, staring at him.

He shook his head and snatched his T-shirt from the floor, then tugged it over his head.

"Don't go," I begged. "Let's talk this through."

"There's nothing to talk about." He shoved his feet into his sandals, then he left.

TELLING him then might not have ended well, but he'd surprised me in the past. Maybe he would've surprised me again. If I'd told him, he might've changed his tune because he wanted to keep me. I would never know now.

All there was to do at this point was to press forward and keep my distance from Evan so he didn't keep asking questions and pushing for answers I wasn't ready to give.

CHAPTER TWENTY-NINE

EVAN WAS SUPPOSED to be here any minute to work on the song for the finale. Kimball had been breathing down our necks to get something on paper and start practicing. I didn't know why he had his knickers in a twist. We still had plenty of time between when they started airing the auditions to when the live shows started.

I was hoping to write today without revealing too much. The last time I'd sat with my notebook and written down lyrics, the truth came out of my pen before I could warn it to stop. Evan would never see those lyrics. They would die with me. Things between us had been so good lately that it scared me. I needed to remember all the reasons why being with him was a bad idea.

But he'd hurdled that one year mark with only a small stumble, and that, more than anything, terrified me. Whether the stumbling or the hurdling scared me more—I wasn't sure. But now, I had to tell him about Axl. I'd made a promise.

I sat on the couch with a pad of paper and scribbled some lyrics.

I've been broken by your fall,
Built my walls, made them tall.

But I see you try to return,
It makes something deep in me burn.

This wretched pen! Why won't it just lie to me? I thought about throwing it across the room. Thought about snapping it in half. What would be the point? Emotional distance was the name of the game, which meant when we were writing, I needed to be smarter. As stupid as it sounded, I got up and walked to the TV stand, finding a pad of paper and a hotel pen. I traded.

Maybe this pen would work better.

A knock sounded on the door.

Vince got to his feet with a grunt, and I held back the half-hearted insult about his age.

I sat back on the couch and turned the page of my notebook and waited as Vince opened the door for Evan.

Evan came in holding his own notebook. We nodded to each other, and he took the recliner across from the coffee table.

He ran a hand through his hair, mussing it up even more. I tracked the movement, watching the flex of his bicep, the veins on his forearms. What was wrong with me? *Enough!*

"I wrote some lyrics, but I kinda feel like an as—"

"Language!" At least he'd given me something else to focus on. Something to get mad at him for. I looked behind me at the closed door, then back at him. "There are little ears around."

"—a jerk," he finished.

"That's okay. Let me see them." I held my hand out and wiggled my fingers until he handed me his notebook. Did friends notice how good their friends smelled?

His lyrics were good. Really good. And quite pointed. More ammunition. More armor. More distance. I tried to ignore the sting. This was what I wanted. Distance. And he'd given it to me on a silver platter. "Have you been working on a melody for this?"

He reached for the notebook, and I handed it back.

Evan cleared his throat and hummed for a second, then sang the lyrics in his gritty tenor voice.

> *"You wanna throw stones wrapped in music*
> *and rhyme,*
> *What you have left, well, it ain't worth a dime.*
> *Call me the villain—you know it's not true,*
> *But don't play the victim when the failure was*
> *you."*

And when he hit the chorus, I was blown away. And more than a little shaken. He went high with the chorus. More emotionally raw.

> *"So write me a song if it helps you sleep,*
> *You can't escape the secrets you keep.*
> *Paint me cold in your bitter song,*
> *But girl, you don't get to say I was wrong,*
> *When you're the one who ran all along."*

When he finished, I took his notebook, trying to contain the tremor in my hands, and copied the lyrics. Why was it so hard for me to hear that? I wasn't in the wrong. He was. "If you haven't already, write that melody down so we have it. I'm going to work on a counterpoint verse."

It took about an hour of stops and starts, but I finally had it. I looked up at Evan, who was just staring at me with a faraway look in his eyes.

"Want to hear what I have?"

His eyes focused, and he nodded.

> *"You built your escape with words left unsaid,*
> *Turned every promise to ashes instead.*
> *Call me the villain, but you drew the line—*
> *Don't paint me a monster for wanting what's*
> *mine."*

He wouldn't understand that last line, but it made tears sting my eyes. I would choose Axl every time. He was the biggest blessing in my life. I would break my heart again and again to protect him.

Evan shook his head.

"What?"

"I just forgot how talented you are."

My stomach flipped, and my cheeks burned with the compliment. "Thank you." *I'd* forgotten how much I enjoyed working with him. Watching the way he stuck his tongue out when he wrote music. How he hummed quietly to himself and tried a hundred different melodies before he found the one he liked.

"We need a bridge." I handed him my notebook, and he jotted down the lyrics I'd written.

While I waited, I got us both a cup of coffee, and we spent the next hour scribbling, tearing out pages, and rewriting.

Finally, I had something I was happy with. "I think I have it."

"I have something too. You go first."

> *"Music can't fade the scars we've made,*
> *Can't drown out love with the notes you*
> > *played.*
> *Your melody breaks, it can't make me stay—*
> *'Cause I've already walked away."*

He stared at me a second, but his gaze felt unfocused, like he was looking through me. "Read it again," he said.

I couldn't read mine again right now, or my emotions might crack through my shields. "Let's hear yours."

He stared at me a second longer, then looked down at his notebook.

> *"Cold strings hum to fill the abyss,*
> *What I don't remember, I'll never miss.*
> *I breathe in chords of what we lost,*
> *Repelling painful silence, whatever the cost."*

My breath froze in my lungs as his words swirled in my mind.

It was so good. But the second line more than anything had goosebumps rising on my arms. He wouldn't miss what he didn't remember. I wish I could forget what he had. "Wow," I whispered.

"Want to do two bridges? Or want to use it as a counterpoint?" He spoke so lightly, like his words hadn't just punched me in the heart and squeezed. "Let's sing it through and decide."

I swallowed and shook my head, trying to find the strength to even sing my part.

We spent the next half hour playing with the melody, then sang them separately and together.

When we finished, I couldn't even find my voice to tell him.

"Definitely two bridges, one by each of us." Evan wrote my bridge in his notebook, and I did the same for his, taking the time to compose myself. "People are going to really feel this song. I can tell."

People. If this song ever left this room, it would cost me something I couldn't afford to lose. If Evan ever understood the lyrics, if someone correctly interpreted them, he would see far more than I wanted him to.

And after he found out Axl was his? Would he even be willing to sing this song with me?

Writing with him brought back so many memories, but I forced them away. There was so much hurt and pain in each of our songs. So much that we'd left unspoken. And I wasn't ready to unravel my feelings. It was much easier to hide them in a song and hope they were obscure enough to not reveal too much.

CHAPTER THIRTY

JENNY SAID Axl hadn't been sleeping well, which explained the small, rumpled figure standing in the hallway like a ghost who'd taken a wrong turn on his way to the afterlife.

"Mom?" he said, voice thin and cracked with sleep.

Axl shuffled into the room, dragging his teddy bear by one arm. He walked straight to Jenny—then saw me.

And changed course.

My heart did that stupid thing where it forgot how to beat like a normal organ. Great. Cool.

He veered like a heat-seeking missile and reached up with one hand. "Hold you."

Jenny frowned, the tiniest crease forming between her brows. "C'mere, sweetheart."

Axl didn't even look at her.

"Hold you, Van."

I glanced at Jenny, silently screaming *help*. She shrugged. Actual shrug. Like this was a normal thing that happened every day. Toddlers casually choosing emotionally complicated men with a history of bad decisions.

"Mommy will hold you," Jenny said, stepping forward and picking him up as he squirmed.

He dive-bombed sideways, committing fully to the betrayal. Jenny made a soft *oof* sound as I caught him on instinct.

And just like that, he was in my lap.

He curled into me like he'd been doing it his whole life, tucked his face into my chest, and pulled his bear onto his own lap. One arm wrapped around the bear, the other clutching my shirt like I might disappear if he loosened his grip.

My chest squeezed so hard it actually hurt.

I froze.

Every alarm I'd ever installed in my brain started blaring at once. *Do not move. Do not breathe. Do not do anything that might make this more real.*

Axl sighed, a soft little sound, and went boneless against me.

I mouthed *What do I do?* at Jenny.

She crossed the room and turned off the overhead light, leaving us in the soft glow of the lamp, then sat on the coffee table in front of me, eyes gentle, mouth tipped into a soft smile. "He hasn't been sleeping well."

That was it. No warning. No instructions. No *do not get attached* disclaimer.

Axl's fingers tightened in my shirt, knuckles white even in sleep. I could feel the steady rise and fall of his breathing, the warmth of him, the complete trust.

This wasn't hypothetical. This wasn't symbolic.

This was a small human choosing me.

And the worst part—the part I couldn't outrun or joke my way around? Was how right it felt.

Not exciting. Not overwhelming.

Natural.

Like the day in the airplane, where he'd towed me up the steps behind him. Like when I'd shared my mac and cheese, because my instincts pulled me toward him.

I'd just sit here for a minute. Just until his breathing was evened out a little more. Just until it was polite to move him.

The minute stretched.

Jenny watched us, her expression unreadable. Not angry. Careful.

I knew that look. I'd seen it in mirrors. It was the look people got when they were assessing damage before it happened. I should've handed him back then. I knew that. I knew all the rules. I'd spent a year learning how to live by them.

But Axl shifted, burrowed closer, and let out another sleepy sigh like I'd fixed something without even trying.

Something in me cracked.

Not loudly. Not dramatically.

Just enough to let the truth in.

I didn't want to give him back.

That realization hit harder than any craving ever had, because this wasn't about wanting something destructive.

This was about wanting something good.

Something I wasn't allowed to want.

I'd come into tonight with a clear plan. Write the song. Keep my distance. Prove I could be stable, safe, evolved. The guy who didn't reach for things that weren't his.

The guy who understood boundaries.

But sitting there with Axl asleep on my chest, I understood something new and deeply inconvenient.

Proximity wasn't neutral.

Being near Jenny's life—really near it—wasn't something I could compartmentalize my way through. It wasn't a harmless overlap. It was a door cracked open just enough to show me what I was missing.

And now that I'd seen it, I couldn't unsee it.

Eventually, gently, I shifted. Axl stirred, whined softly, his fingers tightening again like he was afraid I'd vanish.

My throat burned.

I handed him back to Jenny anyway.

Because wanting wasn't the same thing as choosing.

And choosing right still cost me something.

As Jenny carried him down the hall, his head lolling against her shoulder, I sat there alone with the echo of his weight still pressed into my chest.

I'd thought my goal was simple: stay steady, stay safe, don't want too much.

I was wrong.

That wasn't a goal. That was a shield.

And shields didn't work when the thing you were protecting yourself from was the truth.

If I was going to keep being here—really here—I was going to have to be all in with Jenny *and* Axl...or walk away entirely.

Because pretending this didn't matter?

That was no longer an option.

CHAPTER THIRTY-ONE

I TOLD myself I'd expected it—the way Axl went to Evan like gravity had made a decision without consulting me—but the truth was it rattled me anyway. I'd crafted this lie in my mind where time had smoothed the edges instead of sharpening them. Watching Axl melt into Evan's arms tore a hole straight through that logic.

For a moment, a dangerous, flickering moment, I'd thought about telling Evan as I'd carried Axl down the hall and back to his bed that night.

But once again, I'd chickened out.

Now, on the second day of Phoenix auditions, with hair, makeup, and wardrobe, I put on my armor. My resolve. But honestly, it was weak. Weaker than I needed it to be. Every moment spent with Evan was a moment my heart couldn't afford. Because it was turning into goo every time Evan was around.

No matter how many times I tried to pretend I wasn't affected.

Yesterday, during lunch, he had Javi bring in mac and cheese specifically for Axl. I hadn't even thought to do that. And of course, he'd gotten me coffee both days. He'd followed up with Carl to make sure the kid from Nashville got his funds to start the renovation on his family's house—any extra was to go to help with medical bills and other things to help with his recovery.

It was like Evan knew exactly what to do to ease my fears about getting too close to him.

AFTER FILMING, I tried to get ahold of my dad, but he didn't answer. Evan sent a note to my dressing room, asking me if I wanted to go to dinner, then get in a writing session before our flight back to L.A. tomorrow.

I sent Vince back to the hotel with Axl and Colby and had Alli take my reply to Evan, suggesting we go to Saguaro & Sage, my dad's restaurant—mine too, technically.

I hadn't seen my dad in months, nor had I seen the restaurant. Just pictures of it after the designer finished. But that was over a year ago. Dad had been bugging me to come down and film a few promos for it, but the timing never worked out.

If he could get a cameraman down there tonight, maybe Evan and I could both be in a commercial. Dad would love that. He already had the scripts—he'd sent them to me for approval.

I checked my hair in the mirror, tweaked some curls, adjusted the girls so they looked better, and reapplied my lipstick... I pressed a hand to my fluttering stomach. This was a business dinner, nothing more.

When I was ready, I opened the door, and Evan stood there in a pair of slacks and a maroon button-up shirt. He tugged at the collar.

I laughed.

He looked me up and down. "Wow. You look fantastic." He offered me his elbow and escorted me out the back entrance to the waiting car. Ryan held the door, and the Irishman sat in the back seat behind Reese.

Evan handed me into the car and got in beside me. I was sandwiched between him and the Irishman.

"I've never been to Saguaro & Sage. I tried to call my dad, but I assume he's busy at the restaurant tonight."

"Sounds good. We'll surprise him."

Dad would love it. I was excited to see how the whole venture was going, especially after I bought him that new oven.

When we pulled up, there was a line of people seated outside the restaurant, waiting to get in.

My dad must be so happy with how successful it was.

We dropped the Irishman off to see if he could get us a table and waited a discreet distance away for him to reappear.

"It smells so good," I said. "My dad calls it Midwestern haute cuisine."

They had a mix of American, Mexican, and local fare. A cactus ice cream, prickly pear glazed scallops, and a Sonoran Cobb salad my dad once bragged about.

The Irishman waved us down. He was nodding as we pulled up to the curb. "They can get you in."

Evan got out and helped me slide out as elegantly as possible. As people started recognizing us, a commotion started at the entrance. People took pictures, asked for autographs, screamed our names.

Evan took my hand and waved as he pulled me along behind him. He loved signing autographs and interacting with fans, so together we spent a few minutes interacting with fans.

The manager met us at the door and smiled. "Miss Gentry, Mr. Black, we are so glad to have you as our guests tonight."

"Is my dad here?" I asked.

His smile froze on his face. "David?"

I nodded.

"He sold the restaurant about six months ago..."

THE FLOOR DROPPED out from beneath my feet. I must've misheard him. I stopped walking in the middle of the restaurant, surrounded by people and tables. "Sorry, what?"

Evan put a hand over mine on his elbow. Pulled me closer.

"If you'll follow me..." The manager tried to get us to walk deeper into the restaurant. When I didn't move, he stopped and shuffled back to us. "He's still involved. Just a few weeks ago, he had a new stove brought in, but he sold the restaurant. We have a new owner."

My appetite vanished.

Evan put an arm around my waist. I leaned into his strength.

He'd lied to me?

Scammed me?

My stomach churned with betrayal. "On second thought, we're going to go pay him a visit." I forced a smile and turned. Evan kept me on my feet as I nearly fell over.

We stumbled back to the car, the Irishman meeting us at the door and keeping the line of fans at bay.

Ryan pulled up a few seconds later.

Once we were all back in the car, he started driving. "What's going on?"

The shock had turned to anger. "We're going to pay my dad a visit... Assuming I still have his correct address."

"Jenny's dad sold the restaurant about six months ago. Without talking to her, apparently."

I balled my hands into fists. How dare he lie to me. I grabbed my phone and texted my accountant.

> Me: How long ago did my dad ask for money for a new stove for the restaurant? And did we buy him a new stove or just send him the cash?

As I waited for his reply, I stared past Evan out the window. His hand traced comforting circles on my shoulder. He sat silently, either stewing or waiting for me to give him more details.

> Mike: I purchased a stove and had it delivered directly to Saguaro & Sage. The delivery was completed two weeks ago. We paid a removal fee for the old stove as well. The total was $32,167.47. Do you need more information?

> Me: Can you tell me if there's been any record of my dad selling the restaurant?

> Mike: He's not allowed to sell the restaurant without our approval.

Well, he did.

We turned onto his street.

It was a nice neighborhood with stucco homes. I'd bought this for him too. If he'd sold this house, I was going to kill him.

> Me: Dig into his financials for me, would ya? I need to know what kind of debt he has.

> Mike: You got it. How soon do you need it?

> Me: Right now.

We parked on the road next to the house and got out.

What if my dad moved? What if he sold the house without talking to me?

My hands shook with a mix of anger and betrayal. He couldn't do that, right?

Evan grabbed my hand and squeezed. "It's okay. I'm here."

I took a breath, letting his words wash over me. Evan was here. He was steady. He would get me through this.

Ryan and the Irishman flanked us on the way to the door. My whole body trembled. Fight or flight had kicked in.

At the door, I looked at them. "Don't say anything. I want to see how he responds."

I knocked.

Twenty-three seconds later, Dad opened the door.

He winced. "Hey, pumpkin."

Don't 'hey pumpkin' me! "What's going on?" I tried, and failed, to keep my anger at bay.

"What do you mean?" He glanced over his shoulder into the house but kept the door mostly closed.

"I stopped at Saguaro & Sage to see you. They told me you sold the restaurant six months ago, but last month, I paid for a new stove to be installed—to the tune of thirty-two thousand dollars. So, I repeat: What's going on?"

The mechanical whirl of the garage door opening sounded.

My dad's eyes flashed with panic, and he stepped aside, gesturing for us to enter. "Why don't you come in?"

My guard went up. Something was off. The Irishman put a hand on my elbow to hold me back.

Masked gunmen charged out of the garage and rushed to a car parked across the street. I screamed. Evan's body wrapped around me, and he backed me against the house. Ryan and the Irishman both covered us.

Tires squealed, metal crunched. A couple of gunshots sounded. I flinched, my ears ringing, my body frozen. I couldn't see anything. Evan breathed heavily against me, his body shaking. Did someone get shot?

"Evan?"

"It's all right." He loosened his grip, and I looked around him. Our car had been sideswiped with Reese inside. No!

Ryan tore toward the accident, but the Irishman held me back. He angled himself between Evan, me, the driveway, and my dad. The truck peeled off down the road.

Evan's hands shook as he tucked the hair away from my face, studied me for injury. "Are you okay?" His hands were so gentle as they ran down my bare arms, leaving a trail of goosebumps in their wake.

"Reese!" Ryan screamed. He rushed to the vehicle and pulled his brother out. Reese seemed to be okay.

Evan touched my cheek. "Jenny?"

I buried my head in his chest. Clung to him. He murmured softly against my hair, "I've got you. You're safe."

Ryan thundered up the porch. Before he could take a swing at my dad, the Irishman stopped him.

"Who was that?" Ryan demanded. "What are you involved in?"

I stepped out of Evan's embrace but kept his hand in mine. Reese limped over, cradling his left arm to his body.

My dad's gaze skated around the people in the circle nervously, but he didn't offer an explanation.

"Do you have any idea how lucky you are that your daughter wasn't in that vehicle?" Ryan shouted, pointing at the car.

My dad looked at me as if seeing me for the first time. As if realizing how much trouble he was in. My hands shook, and my insides bubbled.

The SUV's side was destroyed, the tire and wheel totally obliterated, and there were holes in the driver's side door where the bullets had pierced. What if we'd come a few minutes later? Or earlier?

"Reese, are you okay?" I asked.

He nodded. "Just banged up."

I pushed past the Irishman and put a hand on my dad's chest, backing him into the side of the house.

"What the actual hell, Dad?"

"Jenny, please—"

"First, I showed up at your restaurant to surprise you, only to discover you *sold out* without telling me. Then, I came here and your buddies—*armed, might I add*—just shot up my car and ran. You better have some good answers right this second, or so help me, I will drop the thirty-thousand-dollar oven you just scammed me out of on top of your stupid, lying head."

"Those men weren't my friends," he stammered. "I've been meaning to tell you about all the developments—"

"When? Six months ago when you sold? Right after the oven was delivered? When, Dad? Hmm?"

The porch light on the house next door lit up.

Evan's hand slid along my lower back. "Perhaps we can finish this conversation later. Ryan, where's Vince?"

"He's fifteen minutes out," Ryan said.

The Irishman put a forearm against my dad's chest and pushed him into the house. We all followed, and Ryan closed the door and locked it behind us. I was still struggling to wrap my mind around what had happened.

Reese dropped onto the couch, wheezing in pain. There was no blood, but I'd be willing to bet he'd be bruised tomorrow.

Ryan closed the blinds, then went to the garage and closed it. "How much danger is your daughter in?" he called on his way back through the kitchen to the living room.

Ryan cursed and brought in a letter. Handed it to Evan.

I read it over his shoulder.

It was a half-written ransom note. Addressed to me. For the return of my dad.

Evan stalked to where the Irishman held my dad. Grabbed the front of his shirt. "What the hell is this?" He held up the paper.

My dad shook his head. "They were going to kidnap me. You showed up in the nick of time." Something about his demeanor read false to me. He was too calm. Too collected.

Sirens cut through the neighborhood. One of the neighbors must've called the police.

The ringing in my ears intensified. My fingers went numb. I

couldn't catch my breath. What did this all mean? What was happening?

The media were going to have a field day with this one.

My gut told me to investigate, but my head told me to protect myself until I had the facts. I needed to compartmentalize. I forced my focus away from my dad and put it on Evan, at least internally.

When the gunmen ran out, Evan had wrapped me in his arms. He'd protected me without regard to his own safety. His own hands had been shaking, but he'd brushed my hair from my face as he looked me over for injuries. And being in his arms, I'd felt so safe. So cherished.

And I was tired of fighting my feelings, especially after finding out my own father had been likely scamming me this whole time. I was exhausted from trying to push him away. Right now, as everything fell down around me, all I wanted was to curl into him and hold on until it stopped hurting.

CHAPTER THIRTY-THREE

THE ONLY REASON I wasn't beating David Gentry to a bloody pulp was because I didn't want to deal with the cops. For Jenny's sake, I wanted to believe him. To believe that he was innocent in all this, but it didn't feel right.

I made a mental note to call Kellan, see if he could get to the bottom of this through his connections in the P.I. world.

The police pounded on the door.

Ryan let them in.

When they saw Jenny and me in the room, they paused. "We got a call about a disturbance."

"I called that in." Ryan went full diplomatic mode, calm as ever. "We came to visit Miss Gentry's father. When we knocked, three armed men ran out of the garage and got into an SUV parked kitty-corner to the house. They rammed our SUV on their way out and sped off before we got a good look at any of them. There are dash cams on the SUV, so we might be able to pull plates."

I put the ransom note on the coffee table. "We found this in the kitchen." I held Jenny's hand, angling myself between her and her father. I had zero right to hold her like this, but after everything, I wanted to assure myself she was safe. She clung to me. I tried to ignore how much I wanted this to be it. I tried to tell my heart that she was vulnerable and just needed to feel comfort. My heart didn't listen. It wanted more. I kissed the top of Jenny's head and stroked my thumb back and forth across her knuckles.

"They were going to kidnap me and hold me for ransom until Jenny paid it."

The second officer cleared his throat and did that cop walk—chin up, chest out, hand on his gun like he was auditioning for the part of Stereotypical Cop #1 in a movie. He picked up the note and read it.

The cop took Jenny's dad into the kitchen to question him, but my attention was only for the woman beside me.

Her phone buzzed. She pulled it from her back pocket to check it, and I leaned close enough to read over her shoulder.

> Mike: I don't know how he's done it, but he has a reverse mortgage on the house—it has a $750k mortgage on it now. He's on the title, but so are you, so they technically shouldn't be able to do that without your signature.

Jenny turned off the phone and tucked it back into her pocket. She made a soft sound in the back of her throat that sounded a lot like a strangled sob. Her chin trembled. I felt so helpless.

Freaking Dave Gentry. The man was human garbage in a pressed shirt. Jenny didn't deserve a father like him. Silent tears tracked down her cheeks, and she wiped them away like she was embarrassed to be feeling anything. I gently took her hand and placed a kiss on her palm. Then I wiped her tears before wrapping my arms around her and tucking her into my chest. "It sucks now, but I'm going to make this okay." It was a vow I had no right to make, but dammit if I wasn't more serious about that than anything in my life.

Vince appeared in the open doorway, knocking out of habit.

The remaining cop stiffened.

"I'm Miss Gentry's bodyguard," he said smoothly. "I'm here to pick her up." His gaze caught on us, and his brow rose.

Jenny released my hand, stood, chin high, spine as straight as a ruler. "Officer, please keep me updated."

She walked out like a queen who'd just been betrayed by her court.

Vince handed the officers his card. "If you have questions for Miss Gentry, feel free to reach out."

Ryan offered his card too. "Tow truck's on the way for the SUV."

I went to follow her out when one of the cops stopped me.

"Evan Black," the first officer said. "Any chance I can get a picture with you? My teenagers will never believe this."

Even though I wanted to comfort Jenny, I hated leaving a fan empty-handed. I posed with him for a selfie, then stepped into the kitchen and shot a glare at Dave. "Do not contact her again."

"I didn't do anything—"

Murphy's growl cut off anything Dave was going to say.

At least he was smart enough to be afraid.

Murphy shook hands with the cops on the way out.

When we got to the car, Jenny was furiously scribbling in her notebook.

I slid in beside her and scrolled on my phone, totally *not* reading her lyrics over her shoulder.

> *You were a wildfire, gone in a flash,*
> *Left me standing in the ash.*
> *I swore an oath, vowed we were through,*
> *But I can't claim my heart back from you.*

She snapped the notebook shut, and I looked at my phone like I hadn't just read something that cracked me wide open. *Was that about me?*

My heart stuttered like it wasn't sure if it was allowed to hope. I tried to shut it down, tried to remind myself why it was a bad idea to fall again—but then she slipped her hand into mine, and the whole argument went straight to hell.

She was looking to me for comfort, for safety. Could I be that for her? Could I stay sober and be the man she needed me to be? I desperately wanted to be.

Vince drove us back to the hotel. I didn't want to let her out of my sight.

"Do you want to write tonight?" I asked.

She shook her head. "But I don't want to be alone either. Do you want to watch a movie or something? *Midnight City Lights*?" She waggled her brows. "I think after tonight, I need to laugh."

And just like that, my brain rewound to a memory from five years ago.

Jenny was curled up on my couch like she belonged there, knees to her chest, hair in a messy knot, giving me a side-eye that said she regretted every choice that had led her to me. The movie title flashed across the screen: *Midnight City Lights*.

"Seriously?" she asked, deadpan.

"What? It's a cult classic," I said, digging into my carton of lo mein.

"It looks like something you'd find in the bargain bin at CVS."

"Exactly," I said. "Only the finest cinema for my guests."

She threw a popcorn kernel at me, missed, then laughed so hard she nearly missed when the hero delivered his line—something about destiny and neon skylines. I grinned, chewing slower than necessary just to annoy her. "That's poetry, Jenny. You should be taking notes."

"Poetry?" She snorted. "It's a car commercial with dialogue."

I smirked. "Don't knock it. Some people have been deeply moved by Toyotas."

The movie rolled on, all bad synth music and worse acting, and Jenny inched closer—probably for warmth. I decided to take it personally. She leaned against my arm like it was no big deal. But I noticed. Hell, I noticed so hard the movie disappeared.

• • •

IN THE PASSING street lights as we pulled into the hotel, I squeezed her hand. "That's my favorite movie."

But I couldn't forget that Jenny was a package deal. Instant family—just add Dad. And even if I thought Axl was the coolest kid I'd ever been around, I wasn't cut out for a responsibility like that.

CHAPTER THIRTY-FOUR

IN THE PAST FIVE WEEKS, I felt like I'd lived. Felt like I'd seen what life could be like with Evan by my side. I was still trying to process what'd happened in Phoenix. Had my dad been about to be kidnapped? Had we foiled the kidnappers' plans by showing up when we did? Or was he in on the plan? Staging a kidnapping to scam me out of more money...

I had a sinking feeling that he was gambling again. Especially after finding out about the reverse mortgage and that he'd sold the restaurant to a third party. I just didn't understand why he'd do that now. Hadn't I done everything he'd asked? Gone out of my way to help him when he needed it? Why had he betrayed me? Again.

With those thoughts swirling in my mind and feeling more vulnerable than I ever had, I fell asleep beside Evan on the couch in my hotel suite. My head on his chest, our feet folded over each other on the coffee table. Maybe I was using him for comfort. Maybe I just needed to feel like someone wouldn't betray me. He'd been so sweet last night after we got back to the hotel, holding me while I cried until I'd fallen asleep.

When I woke up the next morning. I was in the same spot, but

Axl's head rested on Evan's leg, and his tiny hand was wrapped around Evan's finger.

My heart gave a squeeze.

Our family.

I had tried to push the thought aside for weeks. Axl had an inexplicable connection to Evan. It terrified and excited me in equal measure. Because maybe Evan wouldn't mind so much when he found out that Axl was his.

I disentangled myself from Evan's limbs. His breathing changed, but he settled back in quickly. I stretched, my back twinging from sitting up all night.

My notebook poked out of my bag near the door. I sneaked over and grabbed it, then stared at Axl and Evan for a few moments as I contemplated what to write.

My heart was full.

I flipped open to the song I'd been writing about Evan. I had a couple of verses and a pre-chorus, but I hadn't decided on the chorus yet.

I tapped my pen against my lip as I thought about what word encapsulated Evan.

Reborn.

Remade.

Then it hit me.

Redemption.

I scrawled the word on the page, and lyrics soon followed.

> *Redemption—*
> *It's more than an apology.*
> *It's the road you walk, the man you choose*
> *to be.*
> *Redemption—*
> *It's the fire that purges your soul.*
> *It leads you home and restores you to whole.*

I read it a few times, then started making small tweaks... I gasped. It could be the final chorus.

Redemption—
It's letting the past fade away,
It lets in the love that compels you to stay.
Redemption—
It's a grace that finds you when you roam,
And maybe, just maybe...it leads you home.

I snapped a picture of Axl and Evan, then texted it to him.

Evan stirred again, then mumbled, "Jenny Rose."

It was clear as day and took me back in time to the first time he'd used my middle name.

We were discussing songs I could sing for the finale, and he suggested "November Rain" by Guns N' Roses. He played a few lines on the piano and looked up at me. "Do you know Guns N' Roses?"

Did I ever. I slid my shoe off my foot and showed him my tattoo. "I also have several vintage shirts. And my middle name is Rose."

Evan's eyebrows shot up. He laughed and lifted his shirt sleeve, revealing his tattoo. I knew it was there, but it was fun to see it. "Is your middle name after Axl Rose?"

"I wish. My mom just liked it, but I always told people in high school it was."

He grinned. "I'm gonna call you that from now on."

And he did. He called me Jenny Rose in private until we broke each other's hearts.

I hadn't heard it from him since, until now.

I picked up my pen and started writing the bridge.

Don't tell me with words, don't beg me to
    believe,
Show me with the life you choose to lead.
Every scar can turn into a prayer,
If you prove there's love still living there.
Then the final pre-chorus.
Every sinner's got a song to sing,

And yours a hymn of reckoning.

I swallowed the lump in my throat and tucked the notebook back into my bag.

That song might never see the light of day. I might never record it, but it needed to exist for Evan's sake.

Eventually, the suite stirred, and people rushed around, packing last-minute items and getting ready for the final flight of the season.

Evan woke up and looked down at Axl on his lap. I watched from a distance as he uncurled Axl's fingers from around his, then gently lifted his head and shifted from beneath him. Axl stirred, and Evan combed his fingers through Axl's hair until he settled.

It was such a *dad* thing to do.

And that terrified me.

Evan seemed to be making excellent progress with his sobriety, but I was scared to let him back into our lives... More than he already was.

He spotted me and smiled, making my heart do something I didn't want to examine. Then he walked over and hugged me, natural as can be. I leaned into him, inhaling the scent of his cologne. "Is that nutmeg?" I asked.

A laugh rumbled through his chest. "Yes. And cedar."

I nodded against him. "It smells good."

"Glad you like it. I had fun watching the movie with you last night."

I pulled back and looked up at him. "Me too."

He kept his hands around my waist, our bodies pressed together. "Some people think destiny's written in the stars," he quoted, taking on the cheesy voice from the movie, "but I see mine burning in the neon skies—louder, brighter, impossible to ignore."

I laughed and hugged him one final time. Then he left to go to his own suite.

Alli came out of the back room, dressed, hair and makeup done, ready for a day of travel.

"Do I have anything tonight?"

She pulled up my calendar. "Nothing tonight. Friday, you and Evan have *Closing Time with Jack Holloway*."

Ah, yes. The late-night talk show.

The flight was only about an hour and a half. There were always cameras everywhere, so I'd better get ready.

When I went into the bathroom and looked in the mirror, I winced. My mascara had done the raccoon thing it always did when I forgot to take it off before bed. The bags under my eyes looked less pronounced, oddly enough. Probably because I slept better last night than I had in a long time.

And yet, when Evan had held me, he looked at me like the most beautiful woman in the world. Like his feelings were written in the neon sky... Louder, brighter, impossible to ignore.

I shook my head and got in the shower.

Wishful thinking.

evan

WE'D each had to give a statement, and I was watching my phone like a man possessed for updates from either the news or Kellan.

I'd spent so much time around Jenny in the last month that the next two days felt like detox all over again.

Not from drugs, from her.

Everywhere I went, she was still there. Her laugh echoed in my head, the smell of her shampoo clung to my clothes. It was pathetic. I was like Pavlov's dog, waiting for my next hit of Jenny Rose.

I pulled out my phone and sent her a text.

> Me: Should we coordinate our outfits for the show tonight?

> Jenny Rose: Sebastian is coming over to dress me. I have no idea what I'll be wearing.

> Me: Knowing him, probably something exciting.

To say the least. Not that I was complaining about the tight clothes he put her in, but she was always tugging at her hem or trying to hide her stomach when the cameras came out. It made me want to strangle Sebastian with one of his own silk scarves. The guy was cruel. Fabian at least let her breathe. Sebastian was a diva who dressed like a disco ball.

Two hours before we had to leave for *Closing Time*, a package arrived at my house. Inside: a pair of skinny snake-print pants that would've fit me—if I were made of pipe cleaners. I tried. Got them halfway up my thighs before I nearly dislocated a hip.

The shirt though—vintage Guns N' Roses T-shirt, faded gray, with a skeleton in a top hat—was perfect.

I texted Fabian a pic of the shirt and a few pairs of jeans.

> Me: Which ones with this shirt?

> Fabian: The dark faded blue on the right, pair it with ur black combat boots and the leather cuffs from the Vogue shoot. No necklace. Let the shirt do the talking.

> Fabian: When u have it all on, send a pic and I'll tell u if u should pair it with that black leather vest u wore to auditions in Nashville, just for formality. U'll know if it's too casual.

I threw on the outfit with the Guns N' Roses socks Jenny had bought me—my favorite subtle rebellion against the stylists of the world, and sent him photos, vest on and off.

> Fabian: DEFINITELY keep the vest. Don't button it.

> Me: Thanks, Fabian! You're the best.

> Fabian: I know.

I wasn't nervous about the show. Talk shows were just another type of performance—smile, hit your marks, don't curse on national TV. But I was jittery. The kind of restless energy I used to drown in a bottle. Seeing Jenny again would fix it. Or make it worse. Hard to tell.

· · ·

WHEN WE GOT to the venue later that night, I left my dressing room door cracked open, an invitation for Jenny she didn't know I was offering.

Didn't see her until we were waiting backstage with a director. She walked up, all legs and nerves, and looked me over.

"Why do you get to dress normal?" she complained. "I'm over here in a dress that looks like a bag of popcorn threw up."

She wasn't wrong. I shrugged. "The pants didn't fit, so I texted Fabian. He saved me."

"Why didn't I think of that?"

I laughed. "I dunno. He's your stylist."

Gio appeared out of nowhere—because of course he did—holding two earpieces like we were about to join a secret mission.

The director frowned.

"This is in your contract," Gio said. "You have to wear these while filming."

Jenny growled. "We're not filming *Singing Sensation*."

"The contract states *for the duration of the filming*, not just the show itself."

I raised an eyebrow. "So...what? You want me to wear it in the shower too?"

Gio didn't even blink. "Don't be ridiculous. After your performance on the morning show in New York, you're lucky we're letting you go on at all. Can you two follow a script at all?"

I was being ridiculous?

Kimball Stone was the one trying to bug our lives like we were his personal sitcom.

To make Gio go away, I took the earpiece. "Fine."

Jenny shot me a look that said, *Traitor*.

I raised a brow. *Trust me.*

Gio strutted off, and the director immediately held out his hand. I happily dropped it into his palm. Jenny followed.

"They're introducing you," the director said, yanking the curtain open.

The crowd roared, the lights hit us, and for a second the adrenaline almost felt like the old high.

Jack Holloway met us at center stage, grinning like he'd just scored front-row tickets to our drama. He kissed Jenny on the cheek. I told myself not to react. My fists clenched anyway.

Jenny sat closest to him, and I took the seat beside her.

"Jenny, Evan, welcome. *Singing Sensation,* season fifteen. That's huge."

Jenny's laugh came out polished and sweet. She was good at this. "Right? We're both honored to be part of the show."

Jack turned to me. "Evan, did you know Jenny was going to be the other judge?"

I raised an eyebrow. "No. Kimball Stone kept that one locked up tight."

"We have a clip here, don't we, Danny? Let's roll it."

The screen behind him flickered to life. My song. Jenny's pale face. The crowd lost it. Jenny grinned and put a hand on my knee. The clips switched to our hug—the *very* long hug. The audience cheered. Jenny squirmed in my arms on screen; I looked like a man possessed. Which, in fairness, I kind of had been.

Jack smirked. "So things were a little shaky when you started?"

Jenny handled it with her perfect PR smile. "That's a safe assumption. But Evan's a professional. We've fallen into a routine —a good friendship."

I smiled, but the word *friendship* landed like a gut punch.

"Evan, we've gotten some photos that might need an explanation..."

Oh, great.

My brain was still stuck on the word. *Friendship.*

The first photo was of us under the streetlight, my face in her hair. The night we visited Tracy's grave. Jenny spoke before I could. "That was at his mom's grave. He needed a friend."

The crowd "awwed." I wanted to disappear.

And then the Phoenix shot came up. A neighbor had captured me on the porch, my body shielding her from the gunmen as they ran out.

Jenny spoke again. "There was an incident while we were

filming in Phoenix. Evan didn't know if it was over. He was protecting me."

That was not entirely true, but I could see why she left out all the details.

Jack perked up. "Can you tell us more?"

"Unfortunately, it's an ongoing investigation."

"Oh! Sounds serious!" Jack looked at the cameras. "We have to take a break, but when we come back, Jenny and Evan will join us for a special edition of *Confess or Mess*!"

The audience roared. The lights cut to commercial. Jenny's hand brushed mine as we reached for our mugs, and I told myself it didn't mean anything.

It probably didn't.

But I wanted it to.

CHAPTER THIRTY-SIX

I WAS ALMOST gleeful at the thought of ruining this dress. In *Confess or Mess*, the contestants stood inside an inflatable kiddie pool with a bucket of goop hanging above their head. Jack would ask a question, and we had the choice to either confess or get gooped.

The stage crew brought out the equipment, and I took my high heels off—didn't want to ruin those.

Evan leaned in and whispered in my ear, "I'm really bummed this T-shirt is going to get ruined."

Without thinking, I said, "Just take it off."

He shot me a look, then peeled off his vest and handed it to me. He pulled off the T-shirt, took the vest back from my frozen fingers, and put it back on. The women in the audience went crazy. He tossed it toward the back of the stage.

I froze, the image of Evan's sculpted body branding itself into my brain for future reference. He had definitely been hitting the gym. His chest was well defined, and his abs—oh, his abs. I tried to stop myself from swallowing my tongue.

"You guys ready?" Jack asked.

We nodded—me a little dazedly.

The directors gave us a quick countdown.

"Welcome back to *Closing Time with Jack Holloway*. We're here with Jenny Gentry and Evan Black, and we're about to play a special edition of *Confess or Mess!*"

Evan and I stood at the base of a kiddie pool, ready to get in when we were told to.

"We have a little curveball for our contestants tonight though."

My gaze whipped to Jack. *Curveball?* He pointed to the TV screen that had the logo for *Confess or Mess*. A red line dragged across the word "Mess," and below it, in what looked like lipstick, the word "Kiss" scrawled across the screen.

My stomach flipped. My mouth dropped open. What was going on?

Jack explained the rules to the audience.

Evan reached over and nudged my mouth closed with his forefinger. I laughed, incredulous. I met his gaze.

It'll be okay, his eyes told me.

I'm freaked out, my eyes said back.

He gave a subtle nod.

"Are you ready for your first question, Evan?"

Evan sent me a panicked look that made the crowd laugh. He was so good at this. I was still defensive after having to explain all the pictures of us. Kimball probably leaked them for ratings.

"What's the most embarrassing thing you've done on stage?"

A softball question. Okay, if they were all like this, I could do it.

Evan laughed. "On my very first tour, we were performing at an amphitheater in Idaho, and I forgot an entire verse of 'Doubts Fly,' so I made up an entire verse about toaster pastries. Afterwards, the guys thought it was so funny that we recorded it as a secret track on our album."

The audience guffawed. I grinned.

Jack shook his head. "That's where that verse came from?"

"Yeah. All because I forgot the words."

When the applause died down, Jack turned his attention to me.

I tried to discreetly let out a breath, but of course the mic caught it.

"Jenny, your question. What's the pettiest reason you've turned down a collaboration?"

I stood like a deer in the headlights, my mind refusing to produce anything more than the word "umm."

"That's a hard one." Evan came to my rescue. He widened his eyes at me, like I was supposed to read the person's name in his face.

I was good, but not *that* good.

He leaned into me and mouthed, *Sheena Renfro.*

I hadn't told him about that, so he must've been keeping tabs on me through Dylan and Aiden. *So much for the best friend vault.* But I didn't have room to talk; I'd kept tabs on him too.

"Oh! Sudden inspiration has struck," I said stiltedly. I grinned as the audience chuckled. "A singer tried to steal my best friend's boyfriend. Then, like a year later, her agent reached out to try to arrange a collaboration. I politely declined."

"Will you say who?" Jack asked lightly.

The audience laughed and jeered.

"No, I will not," I replied, matching his tone.

"Next question!"

Evan and I switched places.

"Evan, who's the one person in the industry you'll never work with again?"

Evan glanced back at me. *Help.*

"Do I have to name names?"

Jack turned to the audience. "What do you think? Do you want him to name names?"

The crowd roared in affirmation.

Dang it.

My stomach swooped, because I knew he wouldn't. It wasn't his style.

He shook his head. "Kiss."

When he turned to me, there was something soft in his eyes that took my breath. He cupped my face with his left hand and put his right on my hip. He dipped his head. I leaned into him, my hand on his bare abs. Went up on my tiptoes. My eyes fluttered closed.

Our lips met, and the noise from the crowd dulled. All that existed were his lips and mine. He pulled away too soon, and I stood there, relishing the sensation.

I was in so much trouble.

The roar of the crowd had me dropping back onto my heels. I tried to play it off by winking at Jack. He laughed.

"Jenny, ready for your question?"

I nodded.

"Last one. What's the biggest lie you've told to your manager?"

Obviously this was designed to make us kiss again, but I had the perfect answer.

I cleared my throat and waited for the audience to quiet.

"After *Couple's Cruise*, I told my manager that I never wanted to see Evan Black again."

Evan's gaze captured mine, and that devastating crooked grin that I loved so much made an appearance, dimples and all. My stomach flipped.

Even though it cost me to speak the lie back then, the truth felt like freedom now. Evan was and had always been a person I was drawn to. He and Axl seemed to get along. Now, all I had to do was convince him that he would be a good father before I finally told him the truth about his son.

evan

BEING BACK in L.A. was like waking up from a dream and realizing that the life you'd been living wasn't real. It had been two days, but her words kept looping through my head, giving me something I didn't trust myself to believe in.

Hope.

That was a dangerous drug.

I pulled out my notebook and found the song I had started writing on the flight to Phoenix.

> *I've weathered storms day after day,*
> *'Til your light showed me the way.*
> *You raised me up when I was falling down.*
> *Giving hope when I thought I'd drown.*

I stared at the words. Did I even deserve to sing them?

Then I did something reckless. I invited Jenny over to my place for dinner.

My old guitar arrived from Nashville this morning, so I carried it into the music room and leaned it against the wall, where it could breathe again.

I'd given Ryan and Murphy the night off.

Javi had brought takeout earlier and bailed.

So it was just me.

And Jenny.

Which was probably why I was pacing the entryway like an idiot waiting for his prom date.

When she knocked, I exhaled. Tried to look casual. Failed.

She came in with Vince shadowing her like a watchdog.

"Your guys are gone for the night?" he asked.

"Yeah," I said. "We'll call you when she's ready to come out."

He shook my hand. "Lock the door as soon as I leave."

"Yes, sir."

Jenny pushed him toward the door with a grin. "Thanks, Vince."

When it shut and locked behind him, she turned to me, eyes sparking. "So, what's the plan? When's the last time someone humbled you at pool?"

Something about her like this, playful, unguarded, made me feel lighter than I had in months.

"Murphy's actually pretty good."

"Really?" She rocked on her heels, her hands behind her back, feigning innocence.

"Yeah, but if you're dying to lose, I can show you what I've been working on the last four years." I tossed the challenge over my shoulder.

She laughed, following me toward the kitchen as I grabbed the takeout and two bottles of water.

"Oh, you're on."

We headed for the game room, but she paused at the music room doorway.

"Where are your guitars?" She stepped inside before I could stop her.

I froze. Not where I thought tonight was going. Not what I was ready to explain. But maybe it was time.

"They're...gone," I said finally.

She frowned at the empty cases. "But you loved them so much." She walked the wall and stopped at the final case, the only remaining guitar from my old collection. "You still have your original guitar."

"Yeah." My throat tightened. "I do."

She snatched the takeout from my hands and plopped onto the couch like she was settling in for story time. "I have all the time you need. Tell me what happened. Were you robbed?"

In a way, yeah. By something that didn't need a ski mask.

"You remember when I told you about my first guitar?"

She nodded, poking at noodles with her fork. "Yeah. You said it was the only thing that saved you when you were a kid."

"It saved me again."

She stilled, waiting.

I took a breath. "You saw the tabloids. The drugs. The mess. You know that part."

She nodded.

"I tried rehab a few times. I wasn't ready. Most people have to hit rock bottom before they really *want* to climb out."

Her brows pinched together like she wasn't sure where I was going.

I rubbed a hand over the scruff on my jaw. "Sorry. This is hard. I don't want you to look at me differently, but I think you should know."

Jenny stilled.

"The first time I went to rehab, I was a mess. I had been an addict for about eight months. Five days. I got five days in before I washed out. Checked out. Slipped right back into that life. Fired Javi, told Ryan and Reese to go find someone to protect who wasn't trying to kill himself."

Her lips pressed together. Pain shone in her eyes. I pressed forward.

"Then, one year in, I called Javi and told him I wanted to get clean. He told me if I wanted him to come back to work for me, I had to give my dad power of attorney over my finances."

Her eyes widened.

Part of me wanted to hold this back from her. Let her see the best in me, but she deserved the truth. "At the time I thought he'd lost his mind. But he was right. I was burning through everything —cash, career, relationships. Snorting, drinking, smoking, repeating. Heroin and whiskey at night, cocaine in the morning so I could stay upright. A full-time job killing myself."

I rubbed the back of my neck, embarrassed by how easy it still was to list it all.

"The second time I washed out of rehab, my dad cut me off. I had to start selling things to feed the habit. He made sure all my bills were paid, groceries delivered, but I couldn't touch a cent. So I started selling my guitars. One by one. Over a million dollars in wood and strings. Gone."

I swallowed hard. "Then I got down to the last one. The Noah guitar."

I could still remember the feel of it in my hands—rough fretboard, the letters carved by a little boy who thought music could fix everything.

"I took it out of the case and sat there, just...holding it."

And I remembered *her*. My birth mom. I remembered her taking it to sell for drug money. I remembered how I felt as I watched her walk away. Defeated. Lost. Thinking I'd never see it again. Thinking if I didn't have my guitar, I might as well not exist.

"And I realized if I sold it, that was it. That was the line. I wouldn't come back from that."

The memory hit me like a withdrawal. Hot. Nauseating. Finding her cold body after school.

"I was just like her," I said quietly. "That's what gutted me. I had turned into the thing I hated most. My rock bottom was the moment I thought about selling the only thing that ever saved me. I knew if I did, I'd die. And no one would care."

Like I hadn't cared when she'd died. I had been relieved. That I didn't have to compete with the drugs for her attention. That she hadn't sold the only thing that'd ever truly been mine.

Jenny set her food on the coffee table, untouched. Then she was in front of me, her arms around my waist.

"For what it's worth," she whispered, voice shaking, "I would've cared."

I wrapped my arms around her and breathed her in. Felt the strength of her, holding me together. This is what I wanted, where I belonged.

I swallowed down the lump in my throat as an uncomfortable truth echoed in my mind. I didn't deserve it.

After all I'd done, I could never deserve this woman in my arms or fit into the perfect life she'd created with her little boy. While it was fun to pretend, that was all it would ever be. Me, pretending I fit into a world I had no business wanting.

I brushed the hair from her forehead, looking into her soulful green eyes as she gazed up at me. Man, she was beautiful.

Her smile turned mischievous. "Ready to get your butt kicked at pool?"

When we finally said good night, I let her lead. If she wanted to kiss me, I would do it, but I'd promised her I wouldn't try it again.

CHAPTER THIRTY-EIGHT

THIS MORNING, we were filming promos and commentary on auditions. Fabian had the audacity to be in Paris for the five weeks before the live shows, so Monday morning, when I showed up to the theater, Lindsay, Kelsey, and Sebastian waited for me.

Kelsey did the finishing touches on my hair as she and Lindsay chatted about their weekends.

"How was your weekend, Jenny? Do anything fun?"

I couldn't bring myself to tell them about Evan's story. About how he'd hit rock bottom and clawed his way back out. About how I'd fallen a little bit more for him as he told me his story. How proud I was of him for all he'd overcome.

I went home last night, closed myself in my room, and smiled so big and for so long that my face hurt. I felt like I finally understood Evan, what he'd been through, and all he'd overcome to get where he was, and it put my mind at ease just a little.

We'd played pool, brushing past each other, touching whenever we could, talking like nothing had changed. Then we'd had a good writing session, but for some reason, Evan didn't try to kiss me. Even when I'd been clearly hinting that I'd welcome it. It was killing me.

"I worked on the duet with Evan. It was good. We've got a good start."

As they finished up, Sebastian put his phone down and looked down his long, crooked nose at me, extending something in his hand. Someone must've punched him at one point—not that I blamed them one bit.

"I've got an option from Fabian, but I don't zink it vill fit."

Kelsey finished winding the cords on her curling irons and Lindsay packed the last of her makeup.

"Good luck," Lindsay whispered.

They gave me one last apprehensive look as they left me in the shark-infested waters. I waved, then turned my attention to the Frenchman.

I glared and took the garment bag from Sebastian's outstretched hand. Behind the dressing screen, I couldn't help but notice the scale. Who'd put it there? Fabian would never. It had to be Sebastian. Just out of curiosity, I peeled my clothes off and stepped onto it. My eyes widened at the number. I'd gained fifteen pounds over the past five weeks!

My reflection showed the extra around my waist, maybe my thighs. I shook my head and unzipped the garment bag, pulling out the low-cut yellow dress.

I tried stepping into it, but it wouldn't slide over my hips. I changed tactics and slid it over my head, inching it down until it was over my butt. How had I let this happen? Sure, I'd been a little lax with my diet and exercise, but it hadn't been *that* bad, had it?

The last thing I wanted to do was tell Sebastian he was right, but there was no way I was going in public in this. I looked like an overstuffed banana.

"It doesn't fit," I said over the dressing screen, my jaw clenched, cheeks burning.

Sebastian made a soft sound that I interpreted as a French "No duh."

I let out a breath and hiked up the hem to get it back over my head. Nope. There was no way I was doing this alone. I tried until I heard the seam ripping. I would never live this down.

With my tail between my legs, and my dress stuck over my shoulders, arms trapped above my head, view tunneled to the ceiling, I relented. "I'm going to need help getting this off."

Fabian must've been giving me bigger sizes as the auditions progressed. And now that I was in Sebastian's sinister hands, he wasn't going to let me ignore the truth. But he said Fabian had left the dress for me. Unless he'd lied to prove a point?

"Bend," Sebastian said.

I hinged my waist until I saw him through the top of the dress. He grabbed the hem and pulled as I backed away from him, until the dress released me from its hold.

I stood in front of Sebastian in my bra and panties, my extra weight on display for him to see. I expected a snide remark from him. Some dig at my body, but instead, he turned and walked out from behind the dressing screen.

"I vill get you somezing bigger."

This humiliation would never happen again. I didn't care what I had to do; I was going to lose weight. I had a nutritionist that helped me after I had Axl. She'd probably be happy to help again. I just dreaded the cleanses, the liquid diet. But I didn't want to start the live shows looking like this.

Sebastian came back in with a pair of high-waisted gray slacks and a ruched turquoise blouse. This was more my style anyway. I'd have to tell Fabian the dress didn't fit. Maybe he'd help me line up more outfits while he was away.

"Remember, better body, better life." The mantra made my teeth clench. I couldn't count the number of times he'd said that during Season 9.

"Thanks," I managed without pummeling him.

We paired the outfit with black platforms that gave me an extra three inches.

"I vill send in hair to touch up." Sebastian left.

Kelsey peeked her head in. "Everything okay? I hear we might've had a hair emergency."

She looked at me with her wide blue eyes. "Oh. What'd you do?"

I exhaled as discreetly as possible, trying to force the embarrassment to drain from me with the air. It didn't work. "Wardrobe malfunction." More like body malfunction.

"We'll get you all fixed up." She plugged in her curling iron and started pulling the pins from my hair.

As we waited on the stage for Kimball and Jaryce to start filming, Evan put my regular coffee order in front of me. I wrapped my fingers around the cup and held it, an internal battle raging. I leaned back in my director's chair and stared at it on the small cocktail table.

"What's wrong?" Evan asked.

I slid it away from me. "I'm not feeling it today."

He stepped closer, his eyes full of concern. He invaded my personal space, his cedar scent cocooning me in a bubble of Evan. In that charming way of his, he put the back of his hand on my head to feel my temperature. "Jenny isn't 'feeling' coffee? Are you okay? Have you been replaced by body snatchers?"

I tried to play it off, to match his energy, but my frustration came through the cracks. "Stop. I'm just not in the mood for coffee."

Which was the biggest lie. The more I smelled the rich, warm aroma, the harder it was to not take the cup back and drink the entire thing. The combination of Evan's cologne and the coffee were what I imagined heaven smelled like.

The production crew moved about, doing production crew stuff. I leaned back again, putting distance between me and the two intoxicating scents.

Evan took the hint and sat in the chair next to me, leaving the one on my other side for Kimball. "Oh, I was gonna tell you, I hired a P.I. to take a peek at what your dad was up to. I hope that's okay?"

I nodded, my hands aching to take the coffee. "That's great." My mouth watered. I needed an alternative. Immediately. I ignored the way my stomach knotted when my dad was mentioned and tried to push it away.

Why couldn't I just be one of those girls who thought nothing tasted as good as skinny felt? Those girls had never had a venti toffee nut latte. Obviously.

The stage doors opened. Kimball and Jaryce walked in.

Jaryce was in a jogging suit, obviously behind the camera today instead of in front of it. Most of these comments would be voiceovers, but not all, unfortunately.

The format was basically Kimball, Evan, and me on the stage, watching the auditions on the big screen, then talking about the auditions and making predictions that would be recorded and aired with select performers. The ones we thought would have a big impact on the show. We'd done interviews after each day of auditions, but it was fun to look back and refresh our memories on the performances.

The first episode started. They had some voiceover work from other interviews, but they'd added the contestant's intro packages for those Kimball had deemed "noteworthy."

Jaryce asked questions, and we answered them. And I accidentally sipped some of the coffee when I wasn't thinking.

We recorded multiple takes, the director or Kimball asking us to say something multiple times, until we were finally finished with the first episode.

Before I could get out the door, Kimball said, "How's the song coming? I'd love to hear what you have."

Evan and I exchanged a look. I hated disappointing people, and I think Evan knew that, because he was the one who spoke up. "We were planning to really put in some work on that tonight. Can we touch base next week?"

Kimball's lips thinned, but he nodded. "Of course. I look forward to it."

"Thanks, Kimball." Evan took my hand and led me off the stage.

Jaryce caught my eye and looked at our joined hands, then raised a brow. I shrugged.

CHAPTER THIRTY-NINE

KIMBALL HAD ASKED me to perform a song for the first live show next month. Like a mini concert for the remaining contestants. So the next day, before we started filming, I was doing a test run.

Javi opened the door just as I adjusted my collar in the mirror.

"Sound check," he said, nodding toward Gus, the sound guy, standing behind him.

I gave my reflection a final once-over. "You good to get me Jenny's coffee order?"

Javi grinned. "You got it, *amigo*."

Gus wired me up, then I grabbed my guitar and headed for the stage.

The crew had taken over the breakroom, the low buzz of chatter and silverware echoing down the hall. I waved as I passed.

When I stepped through the side door to the stage, a sharp squeal of feedback cut through the air. I winced, instinctively rubbing my temple.

Then I saw him.

Axl stood in the middle of the stage, the lights bouncing off his hair like a halo. He was dragging the mic stand down to his level, little fingers gripping the pole like a climber scaling a mountain. My lips curved into a smile.

"Hewwo?" he said into the mic, his voice echoing, high and curious. "Ho-wee cow, ho-wee cow!" He giggled.

My chest went soft. Where the hell was the manny? This kid had more escapes under his belt than Houdini.

Axl cleared his throat, then sang, a little off key, "When I wook into your eyes, I can see a wove restwained…"

I froze. That song.

Jenny's song.

I slipped my strap over my shoulder and stepped quietly onto the stage.

"Darlin' when I hoed you, don't you know I fee-o the same," he continued, dead serious now.

The same arrangement I'd helped Jenny with for the *Singing Sensation* finale.

I hit the next chord, slow and easy.

Axl turned, eyes wide. My heart did a full somersault. He had the same crinkles at the corners of his eyes when he smiled as Jenny. I nodded him on.

"Yeah," I sang, picking up the next line.

Axl laughed, and I crouched beside him, my guitar humming against my chest. "It's your line," I whispered. "You're the star."

He jumped right back in, brave as anything. I took harmony.

"Nothin' lasts forever. And we both know love can change."

The words hit harder than I wanted them to. Once, it was Jenny singing about loss. Now it was her son, this small, earnest mirror of her, singing with me about the same damn thing.

"And it's hard to hold a candle in the cold November rain."

He finished with a flourish, then threw his little hand up for a high five. I met it midair.

Before I could set my guitar down, he dropped the mic and launched himself at me.

I caught him easily. His tiny arms clamped around my neck, his hair brushing my cheek. He smelled like baby shampoo and sugar—warm, simple things.

Home, if home didn't hurt.

I closed my eyes and let the moment breathe. I'd never pictured myself as the father type. I'd barely figured out being a human type. But this kid—this fearless, singing, pure-hearted tornado was burrowing in deep.

"If I ever have a kid," I muttered into his hair, "they better be just like you." I couldn't believe those words left my lips. That Axl had me even considering fatherhood was a miracle in itself. Would I be a good father? Hell no. But Jenny was a wonderful mother. Could she pick up my slack?

I set him down gently. "Have you eaten breakfast yet, little dude?"

He shook his head.

"You hungry?"

He nodded, solemn, like we were negotiating a treaty.

Gus appeared to take my guitar. "Sound okay?"

"Yeah, perfect." I reached for Axl's hand. His palm was small, sticky, trusting. "Let's go feed you before you eat a mic cable."

We made it three steps before he stopped dead.

"What's up, little man?"

"I weft Slash." He pointed toward the mic stand, where his teddy bear was facedown like a fallen soldier.

I let go of his hand, and he stomped across the stage to retrieve it, triumphant as he held it high.

"Good to go?" I asked when he rejoined me.

He raised the bear, gave me a thumbs-up that nearly cost Slash an arm.

"Excellent," I said, scooping him up. "Rock stars need their fuel."

We were halfway down the hall when the manny came barreling toward us, pale and panting.

"Oh, thank heavens!" Colby reached for Axl, but Axl tucked his head into my shoulder and popped his thumb in his mouth.

Something loosened in my chest—some small, locked door I hadn't realized was still shut. I held him a little tighter.

Colby frowned but fell in step beside me. "He was asleep in

Jenny's dressing room. I went to the bathroom and grabbed a plate of food. When I got back, he was missing. I about had a heart attack."

"Where's Jenny?" I asked.

"Arguing with Sebastian in wardrobe, I imagine."

"Hmm." I shifted Axl higher and carried him into the break room.

The buffet was a junk food dream—waffles, pastries, pancakes. All carbs and regret.

"What are we eating, dude?"

He pointed at everything Jenny would probably file under "never." I filled the plate anyway. Colby gave me a look like *you're a dead man walking*, then carried the evidence for me.

Axl dragged me to an empty table. I straddled the bench, helped him up beside me, and swiped a sausage off his plate.

"Balance," I said, biting into it.

He copied me, biting into his own sausage link with a grin.

Then someone tapped my shoulder.

I looked up, still chewing. Jenny stood there, unreadable.

"Uh-oh," I said, swallowing the rest of the sausage. "I'm in trouble..." I sing-songed the last word, and Axl giggled beside me.

CHAPTER FORTY

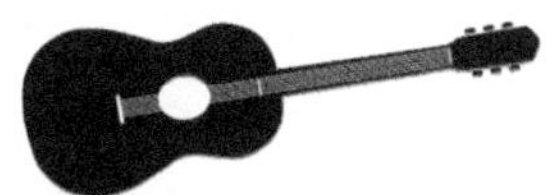

MY EMOTIONS WERE all over the place. I'd just finished arguing with Sebastian about my outfit for the day, and I was exhausted. Plus, I'd started a drink cleanse today at Sloan's orders —my nutritionist. My nerves were frayed.

Then I'd entered the auditorium and saw Axl on the stage trying to get the mic down. I pulled my phone out and hit record.

My smile was nearly painful as I watched him sing the first line to my version of "November Rain." Then Evan came out with his guitar, and I nearly burst. When Evan harmonized with Axl and sang the rest of the song, tears ran freely down my cheeks. Good thing it was dark in the theater, so I was able to watch unnoticed.

Then Axl had thrown himself into Evan's arms, and my heart almost broke.

The more they interacted, the deeper their bond became, and the harder it made keeping the secret. I would tell Evan eventually, but things were going so well that I didn't want to screw it up.

I sat in the darkened theater long after they'd left, just wondering how Evan felt about it all. And trying to figure out what I was going to do about it.

. . .

EVAN STOOD and popped the rest of the sausage in his mouth.

"Can I talk to you for a minute?" I nodded toward the door, and Evan tugged on an imaginary collar, gulped exaggeratedly, then saluted Axl and Colby.

"Farewell, my fellow soldiers."

I hid my smile and rolled my eyes.

My life was words. Songs. Music. But for the life of me, I had no idea how to broach the topic. I led him into my dressing room and closed the door behind us and locked it.

Evan raised an eyebrow but otherwise didn't say anything.

I pulled my phone from my pocket, unlocked it, cued up the video, and handed it to him.

He watched the whole thing, his cheeks pink, his lips curving into a soft smile.

When it finished, he handed the phone back to me. "Will you send that to me?"

I tossed the phone onto the padded chair beside my dressing screen, then turned back to Evan. My hands shook. My whole body felt like it was going to ignite.

"I'm mad at you," I said.

That eyebrow rose again. "Oh? What did I do this time?"

Made me question my decisions. I pushed him, but he barely took a step back. My throat burned.

"You're so good with Axl."

He smirked. "So you're mad at me because your kid sees how amazing I am?"

I shoved him again, but this time he caught my hand and held it to his chest. His heart hammered against my palm, and the words died in my throat.

He took a step closer, so close I could smell the cedar and nutmeg of his cologne. His tongue traced a soft path across his bottom lip, and his gaze traveled my face, eyes, cheeks, mouth.

I swallowed.

Opened my mouth.

Closed it.

He took another step, his blue eyes alight with a passion I hadn't seen in ages.

I tilted my head back, daring him to make the first move. *Kiss me, Evan.*

We'd kissed on *Closing Time,* but it didn't count, because it was forced and in front of a studio audience.

His hand that wasn't holding mine to his chest came up, and his thumb traced a trail down my jaw. Across my chin, to my lips.

My stomach swooped, and my heart beat in tandem with his.

He tilted my head up, and his eyes slipped closed. I drew up on my tiptoes.

Someone knocked on the door.

Evan paused, his lips a breath away from mine, and cursed.

"Language," I whispered, but disappointment filled my soul.

He cupped the back of my neck and dropped his forehead to mine.

They knocked again.

"Don't move." Evan reluctantly released me and walked to the door.

He opened it with a growl.

Javi stood there with a coffee cup in his hands. He looked over Evan's shoulder and caught sight of me.

I probably looked dazed, my eyes unfocused and my mouth open in anticipation.

He winced and handed Evan the drink. "Here's Jenny's coffee order."

Evan took it from him and turned to me, a tortured expression on his face.

"They're asking for you in the auditorium too," Javi said.

I tried to force a smile, to pretend that the interruption didn't bother me. But I longed to feel his lips on mine. His heart beneath my hand, the smell of his cologne as he filled my senses.

Evan held the cup out, his blue eyes an ocean of longing. "This is for you."

I took it from him. Our fingers brushed.

"Rain check," he rasped and gave me one last lingering look, then left the room.

I cradled the cup to my chest, then flopped back onto a chair. I let out a long breath and placed the coffee on the table beside me untouched.

Warmth spread from my toes and throughout my body.

No one had ever made me feel as loved as Evan did. Did he love me? I stood and walked to the door, ready to throw it open and chase him down. Just as I reached for the handle, the door burst open.

Evan's gaze locked on me, and his urgent expression had my skin prickling. In two seconds, I was in his arms.

Our lips crashed together.

It was like coming home.

Like we had both grown so much, yet simultaneously like nothing had changed at all.

His breaths were heavy, his lips turning gentle as he carried me to the chair.

He broke the kiss and set me on my feet, his hands cradling my face. He placed a soft kiss to my lips, my chin, my nose, my forehead, each eyelid.

"Jenny Rose." He said my name like a prayer, a plea.

I curled my hands into his shirt and pulled him closer. Closer.

His arms wrapped around me, and he smiled before capturing my mouth with his again.

CHAPTER FORTY-ONE

MY PULSE WAS STILL TRYING to settle from kissing Jenny. My lips still tingled, and my brain hadn't quite caught up. What was I thinking? That was the worst idea. But I couldn't have stopped myself if I'd tried—which, to be clear, I hadn't. Jenny deserved so much more than me and my issues.

I did a couple of quick run-throughs of my song before Kimball, Jenny, and Jaryce joined me on stage to film the commentary on the next episode.

Jenny carried a cup that wasn't the coffee I'd gotten her, and as soon as she put it down, I picked it up and took a sip.

"Wai—"

"Blech!" Immediate regret. It tasted like dirt and green. "What is that?"

"It's a cleanse," she said, taking the cup from my hand and forcing a couple of swallows down.

"Mmm." She tried to smile, but it didn't reach her eyes.

"Why the hell are you drinking a cleanse? That's disgusting. It tastes like what I'd drink if I hated myself."

"Pretty much," she murmured.

She took another drink, and I watched the lines at her eyes deepen as she swallowed. Yeah, she hated it. I didn't get it.

. . .

THAT NIGHT, I went to Jenny's to work on our song. She told me to show up at 8, but I was driving myself crazy sitting at home alone, so I had Ryan drop me off at 7:30. I had to see her.

Vince showed me into her makeshift music room. "She's in the middle of her bedtime routine with Axl. She'll be in when she's done."

I made myself comfortable at the baby grand piano that faced the window on one side of the room, playing the accompaniment I'd written to go with our song. The one we were supposed to be writing.

Four guitar stands stood against one wall and just above them hung a case with a signed guitar. It was the guitar I'd gotten for Jenny for our one-year anniversary. It was almost identical to the one I'd had on my wall before I'd sold them off.

Not only did she still have it, she displayed it.

A couple of padded chairs stood on either corner of that wall, perfect for playing the guitar.

Her notebook sat open on the piano's music stand. The word "pre-chorus" was written at the top of an open page, with the lyrics:

> *How long will your memory haunt me?*
> *The pain of your absence is taking its toll.*
> *Will I find a way to break free,*
> *From the image of you that's burned into my*
> *soul?*

I read it again and again as I looped the chords. She needed to find a way to break free. The kiss this morning was stupid. Because it made it that much harder to stay away from her. I was an idiot. It never should have happened. But as much as I wanted to regret it, as much as I *should* regret it, I couldn't. It was... Everything. And dammit, that scared me.

I played around with the words, singing a melody to the accompaniment as I played it.

Then I started writing a verse to go with it.

We fit together, like mountain and sky,
But our love held a poison we tried to deny.
At first truly happy, then merely brave faces,
Our paths took us both to such different places.

I was singing it with the accompaniment when Jenny came in. "What's that?" she asked.

I stopped playing and spun on the piano bench until I faced her. "I saw your pre-chorus, so I just wrote a verse to go with it."

She sat beside me. Close. Too close. I could smell the floral scent of her perfume, the peachy scent of her shampoo. Could feel the heat of her body with mine. Wanted to feel it more while simultaneously trying to force myself to inch away.

"This is a good verse. Is this, like, the life of our relationship? This is the first time we were together."

She said it like a statement. A fact. So I didn't correct her. Instead, I nodded.

"This is good! I wrote a second verse the first time we wrote together. We might need to tweak it a little to match this one, but we can make the second verse about being apart."

She picked up her notebook and studied the words I'd written as she made some changes to her own lyrics.

I watched her, mesmerized by the smile on her face, the way she chewed on the end of the pen as she thought. The way she hummed without realizing she was doing it.

Finally, she said, "I've got it. Ready?"

I smiled, unable to help myself. "Ready."

"I've buried us in a place deep below,
A spot in my memory where I never go.
Yet, every day you're escaping, it seems,

*Pulling me back to us in my thoughts and my
dreams."*

I played a few chords, and she scooted closer, until our sides were pressed together and her head was on my shoulder. We'd sat by the piano like this so many times before. I used to keep playing and lean over to kiss her head. I didn't do that now. Couldn't bring myself to. It was a slippery slope that I would gladly slip-and-slide down if I wasn't careful. She deserved the white picket fence with a Clark Kent kind of guy. A clean-cut superhero who wouldn't let her down. Because I inevitably would.

I scooted away just a little, forcing her to lift her head. I didn't look up to see the hurt in her eyes. But I could feel it as she picked up her pen and started working on the next verse.

"The sound of your voice draws me nearer to you," she said.

I swallowed, guilt eating me up. I'd led her on when I needed to put distance between us.

"We're both stronger now for the hurt we've been through." I supplied the next line and started playing the accompaniment.

She sang it softly, the words squeezing my heart.

*"Every step, every breath, every glance,
Every thought tells me, 'Take one more
chance.'"*

She ended in a whisper, her gaze scalding the side of my face. Should I pull away from her? Should I tell her that I wasn't the man for her? *Yes.* But she stood and crossed the room, selected an acoustic guitar, and sat in one of the chairs before I could say anything.

These feelings sounded like a problem for future Evan.

CHAPTER FORTY-TWO

THE WEEKS FLEW by and our routine persisted—I tried to keep my distance, and Jenny made it nearly impossible. I'd even participated in Axl's bedtime routine a few times. That one was my own fault though. My house was starting to feel empty compared to hers.

When we finally got to the live shows, I stood on stage, ready to open the show with my own song.

"I'm gonna do something a little different today," I said into the mic. My voice came out steadier than I felt. I strummed a slow chord on my acoustic.

The audience cheered.

"I've been working on a song for a few days," I said. "It's called 'Hope.' And I *hope*"—I smirked at the word—"you don't mind if I keep the lyrics in front of me. It's that new."

I waited for the hush to fall, the hum of the lights settling into the quiet. Then I started.

> *"I've weathered storms day after day,*
> *'Til your light showed me the way.*
> *You raised me up when I was falling down,*
> *Giving home when I thought I'd drown."*

The first verse came easy, like the guitar already knew the chords. My throat tightened when I hit the next line.

> *"But even in the dark, I found a spark,*
> *A fragile flame that pulled me back."*

I grinned at the crowd. "Now, pretend there's backup singers here doing the '*Hope—*' part, yeah?"
Laughter rolled back at me, soft and warm.

> *"It's a whisper that strengthens my soul,*
> *A steady hand when I lose control."*

I let the chords loop under me, breathing between them. "Here too, '*Hope—*'"

> *"It's the anchor when the storm won't cease,*
> *My only lasting peace."*

I could feel it. The song landing. Not just with them. With me.

> *"I've broken trust, I've burned my name,*
> *Built my house on shifting blame.*
> *But the ruins taught me how to see,*
> *That the wreckage could still carry me."*

I sang the chorus again, then went into the bridge.

> *"Whispered words, strong as a shout,*
> *It's the quiet that drowns out the doubt.*
> *Thin as a thread, though strong as rope,*
> *Hope... My hope."*

My voice cracked halfway through, but I didn't fix it. I let it stay human. Raw.

I looked up. "You guys know what to do, let's hear it! '*Hope—*'"

The audience answered, one note strong enough to lift the roof.

> "*It's a whisper that strengthens my soul,*
> *A steady hand when I lose control.*"

I pointed at them. "*Hope—*"

> "*It's the anchor when the storm won't cease,*
> *My only lasting peace...*
> *My only lasting peace.*"

The applause hit like a surf—loud, relentless, beautiful.

Jaryce strutted onstage in something that might've once been a suit before the glitter ate it. "Let's hear it for your judge, Evan Black!"

A stagehand relieved me of my guitar. I stepped off the stage and joined Jenny and Kimball at the judges' table. My heartbeat was still synced with the crowd's clapping.

Jenny grabbed my hand, squeezed. "That was wonderful."

The tabletop was a mess of contestant photos, names scrawled in Sharpie. Reality resumed.

"Who's up, Kimball?" Jaryce asked.

Kimball flipped two photos. "Darnell Jacobson and Stevie White."

And just like that, we were in the grind. Sixty-second songs, fast decisions, people's dreams hanging on our nods. Necessary, but it still scraped something inside me every time a hopeful voice cracked.

Between contestants, I reached for Jenny's cup and took a swig. Immediate ick.

"Ew!" I sputtered, handing it back. "Where's the latte Javi brought you?"

She swatted my arm. "It's my lunch."

"Are you still drinking those? Why does it taste like rabbit food?"

She smirked. "Just...cleansing myself."

"Of joy?"

She took another sip, eye twitching. "Yum."

I laughed. "Yeah, totally believable. You need your taste buds checked."

She tried to glare, failed, and laughed with me.

When filming wrapped, I was in my dressing room halfway through packing up when Jenny came in carrying a guitar case like it was the crown jewels.

"I got you something," she said, eyes bright. "Sit. Sit."

I dropped onto the chaise. She set the case on my lap, hands fidgeting like she couldn't wait.

I unlatched the buckles and lifted the lid.

My breath caught. A 59 Les Paul Standard, Tobacco 'Burst finish, signed by Slash himself.

Chills erupted over my body. Words wouldn't form.

"I—uh—you got me one signed by Slash when I was first starting out," she said quickly. "It just felt right that you had one too. For...starting over."

My throat closed. I blinked hard, tears burning behind my eyes. I stood, pulled her in, held her tight. She laughed against my neck, half-sniffling.

I hadn't rebuilt my guitar collection because I was scared to. Scared I'd relapse, pawn them, destroy them. That part of me was still fragile.

But Jenny giving me this—it said she wasn't scared. She believed I wouldn't fall.

"Thank you, Jenny Rose," I said into her hair.

When I let her go, she wiped at her cheeks, embarrassed. "I was worried I got it wrong. I wanted to get you more than one, but that was all I could find on such short notice. It's probably not the exact one, but it's close."

"It's perfect," I said, and I meant it.

Later, at home, I placed it in an empty display case.

A start.

Then I grabbed my Sharpie, pulled out my old guitar from Nashville, and scrawled my name across the body. It wasn't about ego—it was about claiming it. Declaring I was still here.

I placed it in the case next to Noah's guitar.

Three guitars. Nine empty cases left.

But for the first time, the emptiness didn't scare me.

It looked like room to grow.

The start of a new era.

A new Evan.

And even though I'd told myself to stay away from Jenny, from that dangerous hope she stirred in me, I couldn't help but be drawn in.

I was starting to question if it was even worth staying away.

CHAPTER FORTY-THREE

AFTER TWO EPISODES of vicious cuts, we finally had our top 20!

This week was blind head-to-head competition. The judges wore blindfolds and gave their feedback before seeing the competitors. It was the battle of the genres too. They were going up against someone in their same genre or the closest thing to it —singing the same song.

I put a hand to my growling stomach and stepped behind the dressing screen and onto the scale. The green drinks were working! I was down twelve pounds.

Sebastian dressed me in full Effie Trinket attire: a mauve dress with massive puff sleeves and a pencil skirt, and a scarf that looked like I was being attacked by a colorful vampiric gremlin. Fabian had extended his stay and, according to Sebastian, was in touch with him about wardrobe choices. The skirt definitely felt Fabian, maybe the blouse, but the scarf? No way.

"You look fabulous!" Sebastian said as he strode out of the room.

Thankfully, Lindsay and Kelsey were on my side. As Lindsay was doing my foundation, she "accidentally" got some on the scarf. "Oh dear. We'll have to get rid of that." She untied it with deft fingers and tossed it in the trash can. "That's the best I can do without getting fired."

Kelsey wove fabric scraps identical to the scarf into my Dutch braid, and the results were stunning. I looked like a warrior princess, ready for battle. "If Sebastian gets mad at you, Linds, I'll be your escape goat. He likes me."

Escape goat? Did she mean scapegoat?

Lindsay smiled affectionately and winked at me.

I drank the dregs of my green drink and had to force them down. I shuddered and breathed shallowly through my mouth to try to keep them from coming back up.

This dress was so tight that if I took even a single bite of food, I'd probably burst the seams.

"And for the final touch..." Lindsay handed me a white eye mask. It had a set of wide green eyes with long lashes and smokey mascara printed on it. I glanced at myself in the mirror and laughed—she'd given me the same makeup.

As I went to leave, Kelsey said, "Jenny." I looked back. "May the odds be ever in your favor."

She and Lindsay burst out laughing, and I couldn't help but join in. Glad I wasn't the only one who saw this outfit for what it was. Sebastian had missed his calling in life.

I left my dressing room and nodded to Vince, who'd been standing guard outside the door. I held up the mask next to my eyes, and he chuckled.

"Do you know where Axl and Colby are?"

"Murphy went with them to the communal green room with all the contestants. Axl's quite popular, apparently."

I smiled and made my way to the green room. My security team and Evan's had basically created a schedule and made sure everyone was covered at all times by one of the four of them. Propping myself in the doorway next to the Irishman, I watched Axl make the rounds. Several contestants gave him a high five or a fist bump as he passed. Colby stood in the corner with a group of girls.

He was getting almost as much attention as Axl.

"You got them, Irishman?" I asked.

He smiled his menacing smile. "Yeh."

"Awesome."

Kimball was already at the judges' table when I took my seat.

His critical eye took in my outfit. "I'm not sure about your stylist. When you get your own talk show, you should think about a change, maybe."

"Thanks." I gave him a tight smile, resisting the urge to throw Sebastian under the bus.

Evan climbed the steps to the judges' table with his blindfold in hand.

"Let me see it," I said, nodding to it.

He laughed and sat, then turned toward me and put it on his face. His mask had blue eyes, a little brighter than his, and one was closed in a very Evan-like wink. The brows had that sardonic tilt to them that Evan was known for.

"I showed you mine, now you show me yours." He shot me a mischievous grin.

I laughed and pulled my blindfold over my face.

"Oh, very nice."

I tugged it off, and he leaned forward conspiratorially. "I heard that Lindsay designed them, and that Kimball's is symbolic."

I shot him a questioning look, and he shrugged.

His eyes said, *Guess we'll see.*

Gus and crew quickly wired us for sound and handed us the mandatory earpieces.

Big brother's watching, I mouthed to Evan. He grinned.

Jaryce took the stage, and the audience settled. Jaryce explained the round for the cameras, then had the spotlight pointed toward the judges so we could show the audience our blindfolds.

Before I slid mine over my eyes, I glanced at Kimball's. Both eyes were closed. *Interesting.*

Evan shot me a look that said, *Poetic.*

After we put our blindfolds on, and the audience got a good chuckle, we sat.

"Judges, masks on," Jaryce said. When my mask was firmly in place, he announced the first contest.

It was two male country singers, and wouldn't ya know it, they were singing an Aiden Miller song.

We made it through five contests on day one. Evan and I still had no idea who had been cut and who was still to come—Kimball insisted on it.

After our individual interviews, Kimball brought Evan and me both into the interview room.

"As you know, we'll have our top ten by the end of the day tomorrow," Kimball said. "After that, we go straight into coaching sessions. Traditionally, we bring in two coaches—each one takes five contestants and tries to make them shine."

He gave a small shrug. "But this year's a little different. For our fifteenth season, we're shaking things up."

His gaze flicked between us. "The two of you are our coaches. Together, you'll meet with every contestant to help them select songs and make them their own. Understand?"

I nodded.

I hadn't made enough headway with Evan, so I would have to really up the game. He'd helped me put Axl to bed a total of five times, and each time he'd deflected my questions about raising kids. The last time I'd asked him though, he'd hesitated, like he was thinking about it. I'd been trying to get him to realize that he fit into our lives. He'd shown up earlier and earlier. I'd even cooked—not burnt—him dinner. Now we'd be spending even more time together.

Maybe I'd try to leave him alone with Axl just to see how he handled it. As far as I could tell, he hadn't had any other times where he'd almost slipped and taken drugs. He seemed to be in a good place emotionally. Which meant it was time to turn up the heat.

evan

SPENDING MORE TIME WITH JENNY? Not exactly a hardship.

At the theater for the second day of head-to-heads, production kept us blindfolded while contestants came and went. No spoilers, no whispers about who'd made the cut. Just four walls, bad coffee, and too much time to think.

Axl wandered into my dressing room with his Slash teddy bear tucked under his arm, and Colby popped his head in. "Is he okay in here while I take a quick potty break?"

I raised an eyebrow and grinned.

Colby blushed. "I've been spending too much time around toddlers. Restroom break."

"Go ahead."

Murphy, Vince, and Ryan were all in the hallway, making sure Axl didn't go anywhere unsupervised. I pulled him onto my lap while Sebastian launched into another passionate argument about the leather pants he apparently wanted spray-painted onto my body.

"I have leg hair, Sebastian," I said, "and I'd like to keep it."

I'd already lost a patch yesterday to another pair he'd deemed *perfect for my image.*

"Tighter isn't always better, you know?"

Murphy snorted from the doorway. I grinned.

"Fine." Sebastian pouted, throwing up his hands. "Wear what you want. But don't come crying to me when you star in the *What Not to Wear* spread in *Fashionista*." He stormed out.

I winked at Murphy. "Oh, the shame."

I set Axl on his feet and grabbed the jeans I'd worn in, then went behind the screen to change. "How are things going for you anyway?"

"Mostly good," Murphy said.

"Mostly?" I zipped them up and came out buckling my belt. "You need to talk about something?"

He shrugged, eyes on the floor.

"How's your list coming?" I asked, tugging my T-shirt straight.

"Okay, I guess." He hesitated. "How do you make amends if they're dead?"

That one hit like a sucker punch. I walked Axl to the door and nodded to Colby, who had just walked back up. "You got him?"

"Yup."

Once the door closed, I turned back to Murphy. "That's a tough one. The way I'm doing it with my mom—my real one, not my birth one—is by living the way she'd want me to. Or trying to. I want her to be proud of the life I've got now. And I'm taking care of my dad..." *Finally.* "Because she would've wanted that. It took me too long to see it—thought he was just his own mess. But when I went to Nashville and saw how he was living, it hit me. She needed me to take care of him."

He nodded once. Man of few words, that one.

"You wanna talk about it?" I asked. "Sometimes saying it out loud helps."

He froze, jaw tight.

I waited.

He chewed on his lip for a minute. And I let him stew. Think through what he wanted to share.

He rubbed a hand through his beard and shook his head.

"I know I make jokes, but it really is important to talk to someone. If you don't feel like you can talk to me, you should find someone you can talk to, yeah?"

"K."

As good as I'd get. He needed to start opening up. It was important.

I patted his shoulder and headed toward the theater.

Jenny was opening the show today—singing something she'd been working on. I couldn't wait.

They lined us up: Kimball and me on opposite sides of the table, the lights flaring, the air humming with that just-before-the-show electricity. Then Jaryce called her name.

Jenny walked out carrying a pink glittery guitar. Looked like she'd lost the fight with Sebastian. I really needed to teach her my ways. The art of saying *no*.

"I actually need a backup singer," she said into the mic, scanning the audience. Her gaze found me. Not volunteering. "Evan, thank you for volunteering. Come on up."

I laughed, stood, and jogged to the stage, plucking a mic out of the stagehand's grasp on my way past. The audience whooped like they were in on the joke.

When I reached her, I gave a long, exaggerated curtsy.

She leaned toward the mic. "Umm, Evan? You're a backup singer... Back up."

I'd missed this version of her—the one who threw me curveballs with a smile. I took one big step backward. "Is this enough?"

She glanced over her shoulder. "One more."

I stepped again. "Good enough?"

"Perfect."

"Okay, boss," I said. "What are we singing?"

"I thought you'd never ask." She strummed a few chords. "This is a new one. Couldn't let Evan show me up."

My cheeks actually hurt from smiling. "What's my part?"

"Think you can handle a single word?"

"Depends on how many syllables it's got."

The crowd laughed, but I barely heard them. I was too busy watching her grin.

"Three," she said.

I made a face like I was weighing it. "Might be a stretch, but I'll give it a shot."

"Good enough for me."

She started playing.

> *"You were a wildfire, gone in a flash,*
> *Left me standing in the ash.*
> *I swore an oath, vowed we were through,*
> *But I can't claim my heart back from you."*

My stomach dropped. It was *that* song! The one she'd been writing in Phoenix.

> *"You've got shadows stitched into your skin,*
> *But I've seen the fight you're carrying within."*

She looked my way, looping her chord. "Ready?"

I took a tiny step forward. "Ready."

"*Redemption*—" She sang it, then turned to me. "This is your word."

She sang it again, and this time I joined her. Our voices slid together, hers light and clear, mine rough around the edges.

"Very nice," she said. "Ready to do it for real?"

"Aye, aye, captain."

She grinned and went back into it.

Her lyrics hit harder on the second verse. Every line scraped something raw inside me, but I kept my face neutral, my voice steady.

> *"I've been broken by your fall,*
> *Built my walls, made them tall.*
> *But I see you trying to return,*
> *It makes something deep in me burn.*

Every sinner's got a song to sing,
And yours is a hymn of reckoning."

I kept my emotions in check, but my heart gave a kick at the lyrics. This time, I hit my line without her instruction.

"Redemption—"
"It's more of an apology.
It's the road you walk, the man you choose
     to be."
"Redemption—"
"It's a fire that remakes the stone,
And maybe, just maybe, it leads you home.
Don't tell me with words, don't beg me to
     believe,
Show me with the life you choose to lead.
Every scar can turn into a prayer,
If you prove there's love still living there."

When the last note faded, I stepped forward and slipped an arm around her shoulders.

She leaned into me for half a second, then turned toward the crowd, lifting her mic. "Let's hear it for my backup singer!"

I laughed, but my heart was still hammering. Because that song wasn't just music. It was forgiveness, maybe. Or hope. Or both.

And I wasn't ready for the tidal wave of emotion that had me ready to throw away all my doubts and jump into a relationship headfirst. Axl and all.

CHAPTER FORTY-FIVE

WHEN I WAS all settled at the judges' table with my blindfold on, the next head-to-head started, and I recognized one of the voices. I was about 94.5% sure it was Maisie Grace. The texture of her voice gave it away. And she out-sang her opponent by a landslide.

This girl was something incredibly special.

When it was time to vote, I put her through without hesitation.

Of all the matchups on day two, hers was the only voice I was almost certain of.

When all was said and done, we took our blindfolds off, and Jaryce stood on the stage.

"Are you guys ready to see your top ten?"

The audience cheered.

The contestants rushed onto the stage, jumping and celebrating.

There was one contestant in particular that I wasn't happy to see, but I wasn't surprised. Troy from Jersey had a good voice.

Jaryce stepped up to the camera at the front of the stage and said, "That's it for tonight. Join us next time as the top ten perform live for your votes. Until then, keep singing, keep dreaming, and keep the sensation alive!"

Kimball stood and gave a satisfied smile. "I'll see you two at my top ten party tonight. I've already made sure your assistants have it on your schedule."

Ugh.

I made my way to the dressing room, kicked off my baby blue heels, and peeled myself out of the baby pink balloon dress and yellow tights. Sebastian had dressed me like a walking gender reveal. I almost expected someone to poke me with a pin and explode the dress into a mass of colored confetti. I would've said something, but honestly, I was gathering ammunition against him.

Alli sat on the chaise with her phone out. "Sebastian dropped off a dress for you for the party tonight."

I picked up the see-through piece of fabric. It was a white slip dress.

Alli held up a pair of pink flower-shaped pasties. "He said you should wear these with it."

I gaped. It was pornographic. There would be minors present. That was a big no for me.

"Or, if you want, I took the liberty of calling Fabian." She nodded toward the rack.

A red sheath dress hung at the very end of the rack, with a matching belt and button accents. On the ground beneath it was a pair of silver, strappy sandals with a chunky heel.

"He said if you're feeling self-conscious, there's shapewear in the garment bag behind it, but you don't need it."

"Did he say that I didn't need it? Or you?"

"Both."

I looked down at myself, took the red dress and garment bag behind the curtain, and stepped on the scale.

One hundred fourteen pounds. I'd been drinking that green drink instead of coffee for six weeks, and I was finally down to my pre-*Singing Sensation* weight. It was paying off, but when I looked in the mirror, all I could see were the flaws. The extra weight around my waist just above my hips. Sebastian was right that I needed to lose weight, both back then and now. What else was he right about? *Better body, better life.* His words rang through my head like a mantra.

I'd only had to turn down Evan's coffee offering eighteen times…

Frustrated tears burned the backs of my eyes, and I blinked them away as I wrestled with the shapewear.

"Need help in there?" Alli asked.

I needed to spend more time in the gym, but there didn't seem to be enough hours in the day. And now, with being a judge and a coach, I had no idea how I was going to make it happen. I was already eating a calorie deficit.

"I've got it." I tugged on the shapewear to smooth some of my lumps, then slipped the dress over my head and turned to the side. Fabian knew what he was doing. The belt gave the illusion that my waist was slimmer than it was, and the heels made my calves look toned.

When I came out, Alli whistled. "Very nice. Evan's gonna be tripping over his tongue all night." She stood, grabbed my cup from the vanity table, and handed it to me. "Shall we?"

I took a drink, forcing the green juice down my throat. It was seriously the worst thing I'd ever tasted.

Good things were worth sacrificing for.

"We shall."

KIMBALL'S HOUSE was as obnoxious as he was. I'd been here once before as a contestant when I made the top ten.

Vince walked me to the entrance, then left me with the venue security.

"Call me when you're ready to go. We'll be waiting just down the street."

I shot him a thumbs-up.

The house itself was off-limits to the guests. It was on the beach. The lawn stretched toward the water for a good two hundred feet before the sand took over. Kimball spared no expense to enchant the contestants—ensnare was probably the better word. Maybe it was just the hunger talking...

Strung garden lanterns cast a soft glow, reflecting off the pool. Waiters in tuxedos wove through the partygoers with hors d'oeuvres. Delicious smells wafted through the air, making my mouth water and my stomach growl in protest.

And of course the guest list was the crème de la crème. Directors, musicians, actors, anyone who had licked Kimball's boots was invited.

What did that say about me?

And Evan? Nowhere to be found.

A wooden dance floor had been set up next to the food tent, and a live band played soft background music. I needed to get away from the food before I blacked out and ate everything in reach. I started walking to the far edge of the lawn.

One of the top-ten girls came over and said, "Hi, Jenny! I'm so excited to work with you!"

"Tarry, right?" I continued walking toward the beach, and she kept up.

"I auditioned in Phoenix."

Ah. That was why she didn't stick out in my mind. Phoenix was mostly a blur.

"Remind me what genre you sing." I took a whiff of the air. Still smelled tasty. I wasn't far enough away yet.

"Folk." She started singing, and I nodded. It wasn't the first time, and I was sure it wouldn't be the last, that someone just sang to me unsolicited.

"Oh, yes. I remember your voice. Very pretty." We reached the edge of the lawn, and I balanced on one foot while I pulled my shoe off, then switched sides.

I stepped onto the wet sand.

She followed me without taking off her shoes. "I was wondering if you could give me some advice about making it through the competition?"

The salty air invaded my nose. Sweet relief. "Follow your gut."

Hypocrite! Your gut is literally telling you to eat.

She gave me a confused look.

I clarified. "Don't let them change your style. You have a beautiful voice. You know it better than anyone. You know your range. You know what you're capable of. Push yourself to get better, but trust who you are."

Tarry smiled and retreated to the grass, trying to shake the sand from her shoes. "Thank you."

"Anytime."

Would it really be so bad if I had a few bites? I'd try to stick to protein...

I sneaked barefoot back to the corner of the party and flagged down a waiter with prosciutto-wrapped mozzarella pearls with a leaf of basil skewered to it. I took the entire plate from his hand. "Thanks."

Then I crept back toward the sand.

CHAPTER FORTY-SIX

I WAS PRETTY sure Sebastian was mad at me for blowing off his outfits, because when I showed up to the party wearing the tuxedo he sent for me, my outfit matched the waiters.

The little snake.

I cursed under my breath, yanked off the coat, cummerbund, and bowtie, then unbuttoned my collar and rolled up my sleeves. I ditched the evidence in a bush near Kimball's front walk.

Somewhere inside, I bet Sebastian was sipping champagne and congratulating himself for the fashion revenge. I could practically hear him saying, "Now *zat's* how you blend in."

I meandered through the crowd, waving to people I knew, making small talk, searching for someone in particular. Not just any beautiful woman—a specific one. The one who'd sung a song about me today and made me sing backup.

Just thinking about it made me grin.

A waiter offered me a glass of champagne, and I turned it down without a second thought. I still noticed the way the bubbles caught the light though—old reflex, I guess. Some part of my brain still thought it looked like peace in a glass. But the rest of me knew better.

Where would Jenny be?

She usually thrived in these situations, surrounded by people and lights and noise. But I couldn't find her.

The contestants were clustered around Kimball and Gio—no Jenny.

In the food tent, a bunch of film directors were locked in a pissing contest about box office numbers. Still no Jenny.

Finally, when there were no more places to look, I headed for the one place that made sense—the beach.

And there she was, her silhouette cut against the moonlight, silver on her hair and shoulders.

At the edge of the grass, I kicked off my shoes and peeled off my socks, then rolled my pants to my calves, and stepped onto the cool sand. The tide washed up over her toes with every wave, and I joined her quietly, our shoulders almost touching.

She held a silver tray in her hand, looked over at me, nodded once, then turned her gaze back to the ocean and popped another piece of something in her mouth. I couldn't see well enough to tell what it was. "Want the last one?"

I ate it, and she threw the empty tray like a frisbee toward the grass. "Don't let me forget that."

I laughed, nearly choking on the meaty, cheesy thing. "Okay."

I dug my hand in my pocket and froze when I didn't find my sobriety medallion. That was odd. I hadn't forgotten it...ever.

She took a small step closer and leaned her head against my shoulder.

I stood there, steady for her. Maybe for both of us.

"We have a top ten. It feels surreal. We're literally changing someone's life."

She nodded. "Who do you think is going to win?"

I didn't even have to think for very long. His voice had blown me away from the very first note in Phoenix. "Zane Draven."

Her brow furrowed as she looked up at me.

"Who do you think will win?"

"It's a good year. I'm torn. I think Maisie Grace should win, but I think Katarina Mazarelli's story is more compelling. I think she'll win."

She shifted, laced her fingers with mine, and looked up at me. Her hair caught the moonlight like something out of a dream. After a moment, she spoke, her voice barely louder than the surf.

"Can I ask you something totally off-topic?"

I nodded and tucked a strand behind her ear.

"If you couldn't do music, what would you do?"

"Die."

She laughed and tugged my hand, pulling me a few feet down the beach.

"Seriously though. What would you do?"

I shook my head. "Maybe I'd produce. Write songs. Start my own label—one that doesn't screw artists. You know, easy stuff like that." I glanced sideways at her. "Where is this coming from?"

She squeezed my bicep and snuggled closer. "I don't know..." She sighed. "Music is my life. The talk show was just an idea to give Axl something stable. He needs a mom who's present. A home that doesn't move every week. Friends he can play with."

Her mom had been physically present, but emotionally checked out.

"But you don't really *want* the talk show, do you?"

She shook her head. "I don't know. It seemed like a good idea at the time. But it would kill me to stop singing. I live for it. Still, Kimball won't let me record unless I tour."

"Maybe he'd surprise you?" It felt hollow. We both knew Kimball got what he wanted.

Jenny sighed and looked down, digging her toes into the sand.

"I wish there was a way for you to stay in music but not have to tour."

Her shoulders dropped. "Me too."

The tide came in a little higher, washing around our ankles. Neither of us moved. She didn't let go of my hand, and I didn't want her to.

"You know what's crazy?" I said. "A year ago, if you told me I'd be standing on the beach sober, not tanking my career, talking to the woman I... Uh, talking to you, I'd have said you were out of your damn mind."

She smiled up at me. "And now?"

"Now I'm just trying not to screw it up."

Her laugh was soft, small, but real. It threaded through the sound of the waves and hit something deep in me. For a long moment, we didn't talk. We just stood there, letting the ocean do the talking for us.

I didn't have my medallion tonight, but it didn't matter. Jenny's hand in mine felt like enough proof that I was still holding on.

CHAPTER FORTY-SEVEN

WE MET for our first coaching session the next morning at the studio. Evan hung out in a room they'd converted into my dressing room while Lindsay and Kelsey worked their magic. Sebastian didn't bother to show up, but he did leave an outfit hanging on the rack for me.

I swear the guy couldn't make up his mind.

"Are you actually going to wear that?" Evan said, eyeing the neon monstrosity.

Kelsey wrapped a strand of my hair around the curling wand and held it, her head tilting from side to side. "Do you think he's punishing you because you take him for granite?"

Lindsay laughed; Evan shot me a *What did she just say?* look.

I grinned. "Probably."

When I was all ready, I slid behind the dressing screen and wriggled into the hot-pink leather top and orange leather pants. A lime-green belt cinched around my waist, and bright blue earrings hung from my ears. Oh, this was perfect. Kimball cared about my image as much as I did. I would let Sebastian dig his own grave. He paired it all with white strappy high heels.

As I bent to put them on, the leather squeaked—loud! I burst out laughing.

"What was that?" Lindsay asked, containing her own giggle.

I squelched my way out from behind the dressing screen, straight-faced. "I give you the human embodiment of a whoopie cushion." I almost couldn't get the last words out. I was laughing so hard.

Evan chuckled, then said, "This is what happens when confidence meets polyurethane."

I doubled over, tears leaking from my eyes. "I hope my mascara is waterproof."

"I'm going to pee my pants," Kelsey squeaked. "She has her own built-in sound effects."

Lindsay said between fits of giggles, "You're a walking stress toy."

"I'm a rubber ducky."

When we'd composed ourselves enough, I walked toward the vanity mirror, squeaking the whole way, and we dissolved into giggles again.

Eventually, Evan said, "You can't wear that."

"Oh, I'm wearing it. For the principle of the matter. The editors are going to ream Sebastian for the clothing choice because they have to remove all the stupid sounds. With any luck, he'll get in trouble."

"I hope they make a compilation video," Evan laughed.

Lindsay fixed my makeup, adding another layer of waterproof mascara. "You're sure about this?" she asked, her lips twitching.

I beamed. "Positive. Let's do this."

Evan and I sat in the coaching room, which contained couches, a piano, guitars, and a few other instruments, and was completely mic'd and wired with cameras.

We wore earpieces so the crew could contact us, but we weren't expecting many disruptions to our sessions.

"Do we know who our first session is with?" Evan asked.

I shrugged, which caused a squeak. Evan chuckled.

We had five ninety-minute sessions today and five tomorrow. The contestants had been instructed to bring in two or three songs so we could help narrow it down. They'd rehearse throughout the rest of the week, then on the following Thursday, a week from today, they'd perform.

Eliminations would be Friday, and we'd start all over again with the top nine.

Troy sauntered into the room five minutes late. The show usually provided a pianist, but Evan could play anything they put in front of him—he was a genius with instruments.

Troy raised his arms as if he were on stage in front of an audience. "Let's make it happen!"

Oh goodie.

"Welcome him and get the session started as soon as possible," the director said in my ear. "We're running late."

"Welcome," I said, trying to get us past the awkwardness as soon as possible. I stood, my outfit making all sorts of creaks and groans, and walked to the piano. "What'd you bring to sing for us today?"

Troy's eyebrows almost launched from his face, but he didn't say anything. Evan and I had practiced keeping a straight face, so we couldn't be blamed for the retakes. I hoped they added Troy's reaction to my outfit in the blooper compilation.

Evan sat at the piano. Troy invaded my personal space as he handed the music to Evan. I waited a beat to see if Troy would take a step back, and when he didn't, I creaked and squeaked my way around to the piano bench to sit beside Evan.

Evan held up a piece of sheet music. "Oh, this one's cool. What made you choose 'Butterfly'?"

Troy stroked his chin with his palm as he spoke, reminding me of a ferret. "Yo, like, the chorus is my favorite part, and it hits my register really well, so I can totally belt it."

Evan nodded thoughtfully. "Sweet. Is this the right key then?"

"Yeah."

"Okay, let's start with this, then we'll go through your other choices and decide which one to focus our time on."

Troy raised his hands again. "Let's make it happen!"

I hoped they didn't air my eyeroll.

"Let's just go straight into the chorus then." Evan played the intro, adding his own little spin on it.

And I hated that Troy nailed it.

We played his other two songs, but neither were as good as the first.

And then I got to see Evan in his element.

"How do you feel about a key change before this final verse? And then it'll give the last chorus a more haunted vibe. Put your own spin on it."

I turned into the percussionist and backup singer for Troy, using the guiro to give the song a more playful feel. On the final verse, with the key change, I sang the melody while Troy took the upper harmony. Evan played the new notes flawlessly, without having to rewrite anything.

"How does this work then? Would Jenny sing with me?"

"No, they'll get a backup singer to rehearse with you, then perform when it's time." Evan played a little run on the piano. "Should we go again?"

We went over it again and again until it sounded perfect. The ninety minutes ended, and Troy left.

Evan looked over at me and laughed. "That outfit is so distracting. I doubt they'll be able to get any usable footage from that session at all."

The door opened and one of the PAs entered. "Miss Gentry? We've requested a new outfit for you. Please take this time to change before the next contestant comes."

Evan and I burst into laughter.

"Guess I'll be right back."

I changed into a pair of tan linen pants, a white silk shirt, and wedge sandals. It felt way too neutral to be Sebastian's doing—or he'd gotten in trouble.

When I returned, Evan was playing the piano. I paused outside the door and listened while he sang.

> *"Even when the night feels endless,*
> *Even when the stars fail to shine,*

Every road, every dream, every heartbeat,
Finds me so grateful you're once again mine."

I pushed open the door, and Evan stopped playing abruptly.

"Whatcha workin' on?" I asked lightly.

"Just stuff."

"Does 'Just stuff' have to do with our duet?" I sat on the piano bench beside him and plucked at a couple of keys.

Our eyes met. He smiled at me the way he would have *before.* "Maybe."

I nodded, knowing I wouldn't get anything else out of him. "I look forward to hearing 'Just stuff' later."

evan

WE BROKE FOR LUNCH. Jenny disappeared into her dressing room and came out with one of those swamp-colored green drinks clutched in her hand.

I made a face like a kid caught smelling broccoli. "Why do you drink that stuff? Did you lose a bet?"

She rolled her eyes, plucked a microscopic strip of chicken from the buffet platter, dropped it into her mouth, and made a show of moaning. Then she took a drink of the green sludge. "Mmm."

"You're disgusting."

She smirked over the rim of the cup—slow, confident. She could make drinking pond water look like foreplay, and she knew it.

The afternoon sessions blew by. Jenny had this ridiculous knack for hearing a note that was half a breath off and fixing it without bruising a kid's ego. I mostly just played piano and watched her work.

The way she leaned in when someone hit the right pitch, like she was soaking it up. The way her whole body hummed with the song. She didn't teach music; she *translated* it.

When we wrapped, I trailed her into her dressing room and

dropped onto a chair, kicking my feet up. "Dinner?" I wasn't hungry, just looking for an excuse to be with her.

Fabric rustled behind the dressing screen. Silence. Then a groan. "I'm not hungry. I had a big lunch."

I looked around the dressing room—no takeout boxes, no plates, not even a coffee stir stick. "Are you talking about that tiny piece of chicken?"

She came out in leggings and a sweatshirt and grabbed her green drink. "Besides, I need to spend some time with Axl. I've been gone a lot lately."

Fair. "Okay." I stood, heard something clink and roll. My sobriety medallion. It disappeared under the dressing screen.

Jenny stepped close for a hug, kissed my jaw, and left a ghost of herself behind—perfume, warmth, quiet.

I ducked behind the screen, found my coin, and straightened. That was when I saw the scale.

Curiosity killed the cat, and I guess I was next in line. The number flashed back at me: too low. Way too low. And my stomach turned, not from judgment, but from recognition. Control. The need to feel like you had a say over something when your life had been auctioned off. She starved herself the way I used to feed a craving.

Same disease, different dealer.

Anger surged through me. Jenny didn't need to lose weight. She never had.

I picked up the scale and tucked it under my arm, then stalked past Jenny and through the hallways until I found Sebastian. I showed it to him.

"Is this your doing?"

"Vwat?" he asked, too innocently and not convincing me at all. I threw the glass scale on the ground at his feet, shattering it.

He flinched back and held up his hands like I was about to punch him. Maybe I was.

"If I find out you had anything to do with those stupid diet drinks she's been choking down, I will end you."

Then I stalked away before I did something that would send me to prison.

THE NEXT WEEK WAS A BLUR: coaching, rehearsals, and writing sessions.

Half the time I was running on caffeine and adrenaline, the other half on whatever charge I got from standing too close to her mic. Sometimes she'd hum between takes, not even aware of it, and I'd find myself pretending to check levels just to keep listening. That quiet version of her—unguarded, no audience—was the one that killed me.

By show night, I was wired and raw.

Backstage, I made my rounds, hyping up contestants, pretending I wasn't checking the clock every five seconds for a glimpse of her. Then I saw her. Jenny, toe-to-toe with Gio and Sebastian, her little army of girls behind her, all glitter and nerves.

"...you don't need to sell their bodies to sell their music!" she argued.

Gio's face was doing that thing—arrogant misbelief. "Sex sells, Jenny. It always has. People don't buy songs; they buy fantasy. You think anyone's paying for poetry?"

Her shoulders squared. Her voice dropped to a lethal calm. "Yeah, sex sells—for a minute. But talent lasts. You make them props and, sure, they'll trend. You want careers? Sell *voices*, not cleavage."

Gio bristled. "You'll be hearing from Kimball about this."

"Good!"

Damn. She was fire in heels. Every word out of her mouth landed like a flame on gasoline, and Gio had no idea he was already ash. That was the Jenny that wrecked me from the start. The one who'd rather burn down the room than stay quiet.

But underneath all that spark, she was running on fumes. The green drinks, the skipped meals, the hollowed-out look when she thought nobody saw.

It was like watching somebody save everyone else from

drowning while refusing the damn life raft themselves. And it hurt, because she deserved to believe in her own gospel.

How did I tell her that without making it sound like a lecture? She didn't need a pep talk. She needed someone who saw *her*. Not the brand. Not the act.

I wanted to tell her she didn't have to earn her worth. That the world was already lucky to hear her sing. But that kind of truth was too heavy for a hallway argument, so I just stood there in the dark, listening, trying to memorize the sound of her courage.

And for the first time, I wanted to be the mirror that showed her something beautiful. Not the guy who'd broken her. Not the addict. Just the man lucky enough to stand in her orbit and watch her fight for everyone but herself. Because when the lights came up and the music started, I knew one thing for sure: she didn't just save other people. She saved me too.

And she needed someone to save her from herself.

CHAPTER FORTY-NINE

I FELT him there before I even turned around. His footsteps were quiet but deliberate, like he didn't want to startle me.

"Jenny," Evan said, gentle, careful. But I wasn't ready to be gentle back.

"What?"

He took my elbow and guided me to a private room and closed the door. It was a costume storage closet. I spun on him and glared.

"I heard what you were saying back there," he said. "And you were right. Every word. But—"

I cut him off. "But what?" I snapped, even though my voice sounded small in my own ears.

"Don't you see? You're letting them do the same to you."

My anger surged.

"You're fighting for those girls, but you won't fight for yourself. The green drinks. You've been barely eating. The scale in your dressing room." He ran a hand through his hair, agitation clear on his face. When he spoke again, his voice had a pleading edge. "You don't have to sell your body either. You're the music. You're the one they'll remember."

He didn't get it. He couldn't. Men didn't have the same pressures on them to look good. He could put on a T-shirt and jeans every day, and no one would say a word.

"You don't understand," I said. "You don't know what it's like to have everything riding on being perfect, to have them tell you who you're supposed to be...who you're allowed to be."

Evan didn't answer. He just watched me, quiet, letting me spill it all out.

He'd never had to deal with his image splashed across headlines: "Jenny Gentry's Voluptuous New Look" or "See how Jenny Gentry is Rocking Her New Curves."

The pressure to be perfect. To lose weight. To wear the latest fashion. To be the perfect mom. To eat healthy. To count calories. To cut out coffee.

And then, my emotions a tornado in my mind, I said, "Better body, better life."

The words had left my lips before I realized it.

Even as I spoke, a part of me recoiled. Not just because of Sebastian, but because it echoed all the other lies I'd been living —the ones saying I had to be perfect, to smile, to give, to please, to be everything to everyone just so no one would hurt me.

Part of me still wanted it to be true. The part that believed if I could just shape myself into someone else's ideal—someone controllable, agreeable, marketable—maybe the fear, the anxiety, the loneliness...would all vanish.

My lip trembled. My hands shook. Tears broke their barriers and tracked down my cheeks, and I dashed them away with angry movements.

And yet. And yet. Even as I hated myself for thinking it, I couldn't push the thoughts away. Change. Control. Survival. *Better body, better life. Be everything, give everything, don't let them see the cracks.* It was a lie and a truth all at once, and I didn't know which part scared me more.

I felt Evan watching, and I wanted to tell him to step back. To not see this side of me. But I couldn't make the words come out. He didn't get it. He couldn't. Not the constant balancing act, the armor I built just to survive, the way every choice felt like a test I couldn't fail.

Evan's jaw tightened, just a little, like he was trying not to snap. His eyes were wide, and...it wasn't anger. Not really. It was something heavier—hurt, maybe, or disbelief. Or both.

"Jenny..." His voice was soft, careful, like he was stepping around broken glass. "I hear you. I hear what they've told you. But that...that's not you talking. That's Sebastian. You're more than that. You always have been."

"Just go," I finally said. "You couldn't possibly understand."

He sighed, heavy and soul-deep, then left.

Maisie Grace caught my arm on my way back to the stage. "Thank you for what you said back there. My daddy would just die of humiliation if I went on stage in one of those short skirts. And they're not really me anyway."

I gave her a tight smile, feeling like the worst possible person to give her any sort of advice. "Be true to you."

My insides felt like they'd been clawed out, scraped raw.

I walked away.

I envied her. Envied that she had the guts to stick to her values.

But I had nothing left to stick to.

CHAPTER FIFTY

I FOUND SEBASTIAN BACKSTAGE, curled my hand into a fist, and had an out-of-body experience as I punched him square in the jaw.

He went down like his body rage-quit.

It didn't feel as good as I'd hoped. I shook out my hand and left him in a pile of tulle and lace.

I expected to hear about it from Kimball, but he stayed suspiciously silent. Maybe Sebastian hadn't told anyone to save face? That didn't seem like him. He was the type to roll over on his mother if it would advance his career.

THAT NIGHT, Jenny came to my apartment to write. She'd been distant all week—two feet away, but emotionally somewhere near Pluto. I'd said some things she needed to hear, but she wasn't ready to hear them.

Better body, better life.

Still couldn't believe she'd said it. Then, not even an hour later, she was choking down that green sludge like penance.

It was her body. She could do what she wanted, but she'd

been coerced into losing weight. And I was livid that they'd talked her into thinking she was anything other than perfect.

The bastards.

She couldn't see how beautiful she was, no filters, no fixes, no kale smoothies required.

Jenny drifted toward the wall, eyeing the guitars hanging there. She gave a small nod, like she was grading an art exhibit. "It's a good start."

That was the warmest thing she'd said to me all week.

I cleared my throat and joined her. "Hey. I need to apologize."

"No. You don't."

I opened my mouth, but she shot me that look. The one that could stop traffic.

A beat later, she sighed. The fight went out of her shoulders. "I don't want to talk about it."

I still owed her an apology, but the second she gave me another warning glance, my mouth shut itself.

"I've been working on something for the finale," I said, sliding behind the piano. "It's what you caught me singing the other day. Feel free to improve on it."

I played the intro, then the first verse, rough, then drifted into the bridge.

When I stopped, she grabbed her notebook, scribbling like a woman possessed, then set the lyrics in front of me.

> *"Every thought pulls you nearer,*
> *Every heartbeat is calling your name.*
> *I'm seeing everything clearer,*
> *Let's put every thought into restoring love's*
>   *flame."*

Her cheeks flushed. She stayed focused on her notebook, not me.

"That was good," I said.

We sat there, close enough that I could feel her warmth, but the space between us might as well have been a canyon.

"Well," she said briskly, standing, "we should do this again sometime."

Before I could respond, she was halfway to the door.

I followed her, ready to at least walk her out, but the door swung open first.

Murphy stood there, eyes wild. "I need you."

Jenny used the distraction like an Olympic sport—slipped right past both of us and was gone.

Murphy's voice cracked. "I need to... I dunno. I need to go somewhere."

He looked in no state to drive.

"Go get in my Charger." I pointed to the garage, like he didn't know where the cars were parked. My heart pounded and my stomach coiled in knots. "I'll tell Ryan we're leaving."

I found him in the security room, glued to the monitors. "Everything okay?"

"Murphy's off. I'm taking him for a drive. Gonna call Kellan to meet us."

Ryan gave a quick nod. "You got your insert in?"

"Yeah." The GPS trackers in my shoe soles. Always the rock star babysitting protocols.

Murphy was already in the passenger seat when I hit the garage. Rocking. Muttering. Not good.

"Murphy?"

He blinked at me.

"You good?"

"For a minute," he said, and that was enough honesty to tell me that, no, he wasn't.

I texted Kellan on the way out.

> Me: Something's going on with Murphy. Might need your help. Meet us at Bicentennial Park, basketball courts.

The drive was quiet except for the sound of Murphy's knee bouncing off the dash every three seconds. I didn't push. Sometimes silence did more good than a lecture.

When we pulled into the lot, he cracked. Reached into his hoodie pocket and pulled out two prescription bottles. My heart hit my throat.

"Shit, Murph," I said, keeping my voice level. "You brought them with you?"

He stared at them like they were a treasure. "Bought them this morning. Wasn't gonna tell ya. But…it's been eatin' me alive."

I leaned back, exhaling slowly. "All right. First off, you did the right thing saying it out loud. Secrets'll kill you faster than the addiction will."

He tightened his grip on the bottles. "It's right here, man. All I have to do is take one pill—just one—and it'll stop hurtin' for a bit."

"Yeah, I know. That's your addict brain talking. Selling you twenty minutes of peace, then an all-night hate-yourself marathon. Play the tape, Murphy. You use those pills? You know how it ends. You've seen the credits roll before."

He swallowed hard, eyes still on the bottles. "I don't know if I'm strong enough."

"You don't have to be strong forever. Just tonight. Just this hour. One step, one breath, one heartbeat. That's it."

His hands trembled, still clutching the bottles.

"Look at me." He did. "That pill isn't your friend. It's a liar. It doesn't care if you burn your life down. But I do. The guys do. Kellan does. Hell, you care too—you wouldn't be here if you didn't."

He blinked, tears threatening. "I'm so bloody tired, Ev."

"I know," I said quietly. "Let me carry it for a while."

A long second passed before he dropped the bottles into my palm, like they weighed a ton.

"Good," I said. "Now we walk. Clear your head. When you wake up clean tomorrow, you'll thank yourself for not giving in tonight."

Murphy nodded, silent, then he stepped out of the car. I slipped the bottles into my glovebox before he could see where they went. My heart didn't like it. Neither did my sobriety medallion. But what was I supposed to do—stash narcotics in a public park where kids could find them?

We stepped out into the cold night air. He stayed beside me. For now, that was enough.

We walked the cracked sidewalk that wrapped around the park. The streetlights buzzed overhead, half of them flickering. Murphy kicked a pebble so hard it skittered across the asphalt and pinged off a dumpster. Neither of us spoke for a while.

Kellan's car pulled into the lot. He parked it crooked and nearly ran to join us.

"Knew you'd show up," I said.

His eyes went to Murphy, scanning him from head to toe. "You okay, man?"

Murphy rubbed his arms. "Been better."

Kellan nodded once, not pushing. "Good thing is, 'better' starts with 'still here.' You guys wanna go for a walk?"

Murphy groaned. "We've been walkin'."

"Then keep walking," Kellan said. "Sweat the poison out before it gets comfy again."

I barked a short laugh. "Inspirational as always."

Kellan smirked. "That's why they don't let me run group therapy."

We walked another loop around the park—three men, trying to out-stubborn their own ghosts. Murphy's shoulders started to loosen. The tremor in his voice faded. By the time we reached the Charger, he was breathing normal, hands steady.

He wiped his face with his sleeve. "Sorry, lads. Didn't mean ta drag ya out."

Kellan clapped him on the shoulder. "You didn't drag us. You called before it got worse. That's the work."

Murphy nodded, eyes glassy but clear. "Yeh. Thanks."

"Why don't I drive you home?"

Kellan led Murphy to his car, and I waited until they pulled away. The lot went quiet except for the hum of the streetlights.

I leaned against my car and stared at the glovebox. Funny thing about addiction: it never knocked first. It just showed up, asked to crash on your couch, and then the next thing you knew, it had the lease in its name.

CHAPTER FIFTY-ONE

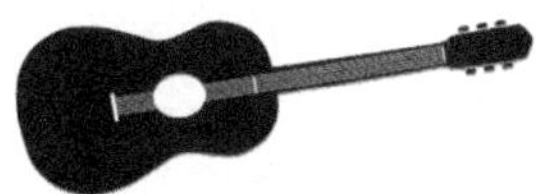

I PULLED the earpiece from my ear after filming and tossed it to Gus on my way past. I had to get out of this dress. Two scraps of fabric connected by nothing but mesh. That was it.

Don't get me wrong, I looked good.

When I made it to the hallway outside the dressing rooms, I got lightheaded and had to brace my hand against the hallway wall to keep from passing out.

As soon as I felt steady, I went into my dressing room and behind the dressing screen. I stepped onto the scale: 107. It was working. The green drinks and the calorie deficits were doing their job.

I slid the dress over my head and hung it over the short wall. When I had my green romper back on and cinched the belt, it was on the tightest notch.

And Sebastian hadn't made a single comment about my weight today.

Alli came in as I was fluffing my hair. "Top eight! How are you feeling?"

I shrugged. "Good." *Hungry.* But I would never voice that. My stomach only growled occasionally these days.

"Tomorrow, you have the girls, Saturday the boys. Starting at eight, they want you at Titan at five for hair and makeup."

I yawned and glanced at the clock on the wall over the door. If I left now, I could get Axl to bed and get a workout in before I collapsed from exhaustion.

The next morning, I woke up Colby with a pancake with a candle lit on top. I sang him Happy Birthday and made him blow it out.

"Sorry to wake you up so early, but I have no idea when I'll be home, so I wanted to wish you a happy birthday. You can go back to bed now. My guilt is assuaged."

After I gathered all of Axl's essentials, I made my breakfast.

I lifted the glass, its green liquid glowing in the morning light, and took a careful sniff. Kale, celery, ginger...maybe a hint of something exotic I didn't recognize. I sipped. Bitter. Earthy. Like swallowing self-discipline. My lips puckered, my stomach churned, but I didn't gag.

I sipped again, slower this time, letting it coat my throat, telling myself it was armor, proof that I wasn't weak, that I could hold it together when everyone else expected me to crumble. And maybe, somewhere deep down, I even believed it.

Vince carried Axl to the car. I'd gotten permission to bring him to the coaching session today so Colby could have his birthday off. Plus, it helped me feel better when I could spend time with him.

When we got to Titan, I took Axl to the rehearsal room, left him with Vince, then headed to get ready.

In the dressing room, Kelsey yawned behind me while Lindsay blended my contour. "A little birdie told me Sebastian was coming in to dress you today."

I groaned. "What did I do to deserve that?"

He'd been punishing me since the squeaky "vegan" leather incident. He'd even gone so far as to say if I weren't so big, my thighs wouldn't have rubbed together. He wouldn't be able to say that now. I had a freaking thigh gap.

Take that, Sebastian, you French sadist. For the first time in a long time, I was happy with where my body was. Nothing he said could change that.

The door opened, and Sebastian strutted in, holding up a sequined mini-dress like it was the crown jewel of the fashion world. "Try zis."

It didn't look *so* bad, so I didn't complain. As soon as Kelsey and Lindsay gave me the okay, I took the dress and underthings behind the dressing screen.

I pulled the sheer panties on, then the strapless bra. "Umm."

"What is it?" Sebastian came around the screen without asking. "Your breasts are too small."

They hadn't been. It was just a natural part of losing weight. "I need a smaller size."

I never thought Sebastian would complain about those words coming out of my mouth, but he gave me a look like I had destroyed all his plans. "Zis won't do."

What was the big deal? It was a bra size.

He snatched the dress from my hand, then left me standing there in oversized underclothes.

I peeked my head around the screen. "Where did he go?"

Lindsay and Kelsey shrugged.

"Is he coming back?"

Another shrug.

I changed back into my own clothes, which were significantly more comfortable and less camera-ready, grabbed my green drink, and barely made it out in time to start filming the coaching sessions.

The tune to Chopsticks floated through the hallway as I approached the coaching room, and I paused at the door to watch. Evan sat at the piano with Axl perched on his lap, tiny hands reaching for the keys. Evan laughed softly, his voice gentle, patient, coaxing Axl's clumsy little fingers to land on the right notes.

My chest loosened just a fraction. The sight made something inside me ache in a good way, the kind of ache that made me want to crawl into the moment and never leave.

Axl's giggle echoed through the room, pure and unselfconscious, and Evan leaned down, brushing a lock of hair from Axl's face. The way he looked at my son—*our* son—like he was the most precious thing in the world caught me off guard. I'd been bracing myself for tension, for defensiveness. Instead, I felt warmth, small and stubborn, spreading through me.

Even after all the fights, the lectures, all the things I hadn't wanted to hear about myself... I was still drawn to him. The pull hadn't faded; it had just shifted, softened. Seeing him with Axl, seeing him *be good*, made me notice the way my chest lifted, the way my stomach flipped, the way I...still cared.

And then Evan's head tilted, just slightly, as if he'd sensed me before I moved. His eyes met mine. "Hey." His voice carried that same gentle lilt that always made my stomach tighten. Not a question, not a challenge—just a quiet acknowledgement.

I swallowed, forcing a smile. "Hi."

He gave a little nod, returning his attention to Axl, but I could feel it, the subtle pull, the unspoken understanding. I was still seeing him the way I always had, even after everything. And for the first time that day, standing in the doorway, I didn't fight it. I let myself feel it: warmth, longing, and that stubborn hope that maybe this—*us*—wasn't over yet.

Axl laughed, Evan's hand brushing over his tiny fingers, and I felt a softening in my chest I hadn't realized I needed. I stepped forward, closing the distance, and in that small movement, I felt the first threads of something fragile but alive: trust, comfort, a feeling that maybe, just maybe, we could find our way back.

Katarina rolled into the room on a knee scooter. "Am I interrupting?"

evan

THE NIGHT of eliminations started with shouting.

Never a good sign.

Sharp voices ricochetted off the green room walls like someone had decided backstage needed a little domestic warfare. I pushed through the door and froze.

Jenny faced off with Sebastian like a mother lion guarding her cub, jaw tight, eyes blazing. The cub was Maisie Grace, currently crying into a denim jacket and trying to become one with the wall.

Sebastian, in all his self-proclaimed creative-genius glory, waved a scrap of black fabric that might've qualified as clothing in another galaxy.

"Zis will do," he declared, all hand gestures and arrogance. "It's edgy, it's sexy—it's what ze audience wants."

Yeah. Nothing said cutting-edge artistry like "minimal coverage and maximum lawsuits."

Jenny planted her hands on her hips, that dangerous calm settling over her. The kind of calm that made me rethink my life choices. "Do not—under any circumstances—make her wear that." Her voice was cool enough to freeze lava.

Sebastian blinked. "Jenny, it's just a dress—"

"It's not *just* a dress." Her voice dropped a note lower. "It's a statement. About what we value. About how we treat these girls. And I will *not* let you make her feel unsafe—or ashamed—on my watch."

Maisie Grace didn't look up, but I saw the tiniest flicker of relief in her eyes. Somebody was finally in her corner.

Sebastian tried to salvage some dignity, muttered something in French, and slunk off to the racks. Jenny stood there, fierce and blazing, the kind of beautiful that was half wildfire, half warrior.

And I just stood there in the doorway, watching her defend the world one mini-dress at a time.

I was about to back away when Lindsay breezed past, holding a garment bag. "Jenny, I have your outfit."

Great. Her turn for the gladiator ring.

TEN MINUTES LATER, Jenny strolled toward the judges' table wearing something that could be generously described as *a whisper of fabric.* The color was "nude illusion," which was stylist code for "everyone's going to think you forgot your clothes."

I jumped from my seat, shrugged out of my leather jacket, and draped it over her shoulders. She gave me a look that was half gratitude, half *don't start.*

"You look naked," I muttered. My jacket was longer than the dress.

Her eyes narrowed, but I'd already grabbed her by the shoulders and steered her off the stage and down the hallway. "You just told off Sebastian for trying to shove Maisie into something she didn't want to wear, and now you show up in this?"

She bristled instantly. Defiance: Jenny's default setting. Chin up, eyes sharp enough to draw blood. I could practically hear the argument loading in the chamber.

But then...something cracked. Just for a second.

Her shoulders sagged beneath my hands, and I saw it—the flicker of realization. Shame. Her eyes dropped to the lace clinging to her body. She ran a hand down the fabric, slow, like she was seeing it clearly for the first time. Not a look. Not empowerment. Just...exposure.

It hit her all at once. I watched the emotions flash through her—anger, disbelief, a little heartbreak—and then, finally, something quieter. Resolve.

"You're right," she whispered.

And I swear, my chest actually ached. Because Jenny never gave ground easily. Not to me. Not to anyone. This wasn't me winning; this was her reclaiming something.

She straightened. Nodded once. "I'll change."

I let her go carefully, like I was holding glass. She turned for the dressing room, and for the first time in a long time, I saw her walk away without armor.

Just herself.

Free.

And damn if that didn't make me fall a little harder.

CHAPTER FIFTY-THREE

I STIFFENED my spine for what was to come as I walked to the interview room, at Kimball's request. Alli and my attorney had been doing some research for me, and I had a little wiggle room in my contract, so I was going to confront the problem head-on. It might backfire, but I was sticking to my guns. And the best way to do it was with a preemptive strike.

I threw my shoulders back and opened the door in my emerald-green sheath dress. Sebastian was pacing like a madman and spun to glare at me when I walked in. Kimball, calm as ever, lounged in a director's chair in front of the row of cameras.

"Hello, boys," I said. "Here's how it's gonna go. I checked both my contract and the contracts of the contestants. It doesn't name a specific stylist, just that I must use one, so from this moment forward, I—and any other contestants who want to—will no longer be styled by Sebastian."

Sebastian gaped.

Kimball's eyes gleamed, and a proud smile ticked up one side of his mouth. "And who will their stylist be?"

"Fabian," I said. Kimball was familiar with him.

"Very well. And who will be paying Fabian's salary? We

already have a stylist on staff." He looked at his nails as if he were bored with this conversation and wanted to move on already.

Well, I hadn't thought that one all the way through, but I'd come this far—in for a penny, in for a pound. "Me."

"All right." Kimball conceded.

"All right?" Sebastian wailed.

I spun on my heels and left.

EVAN WAITED for me by my dressing room door. "I have a surprise for you. I'm taking you to dinner."

My stomach cramped just thinking about food. I hated that I was so dumb, but I'd been turning it over in my mind since my argument with Evan, and especially today after he'd used his jacket to cover my "dress." He was right. I had let them treat me like my body was a better asset than my voice—while standing up for the girls on the show. It made no sense.

"Oh?" I leaned in, gazing up into his sexy blue eyes.

He looked down at me, his hair falling into his face. "Do you trust me?"

I pinched my lips together, thinking. "That depends on what we're talking about..."

His gaze flashed with mischief. "Railway Cafe!"

I laughed. "Deal."

Three months after I won *Singing Sensation*, we were being hounded by the paparazzi. We couldn't go anywhere without them following our every move. So, we'd devised a plan—which apparently he wanted to enact *right now*.

Evan took my hand and tugged me into my dressing room. Kelsey, Lindsay, Fabian, and a man I didn't recognize all stood by, waiting to help.

"I'm glad you said yes. It took a lot to get this together."

For the next ninety minutes, they worked together to turn us into completely different people. For Evan, it was brown contacts, a fake mustache, and a Roman nose piece. For me, it was a blonde wig, blue contacts, and a nose that would've made anyone uncomfortable to stare at for too long. I didn't even recognize myself!

Fabian dressed us in ill-fitting clothes, and when we were ready, we slipped into a white equipment van driven by Vince, and escaped the venue completely unnoticed.

"Let's agree right now," Evan said as we buckled in, "that we have to talk with ridiculous accents."

I chuckled but immediately used my best British accent. "Of course, dahling."

"Ve don't vant anyvone to vrecognize us," Evan said, in an accent I couldn't decipher.

"I can't take you seriously with that nose," I said through a laugh.

"*My* nose? You should see *your* nose!"

My voice squeaked as I said, "I *can* see it," and went cross-eyed.

We dissolved into laughter, and it felt good to just be carefree. Not worry about what pictures were being taken of us.

We arrived at Railway Cafe, a retired train car-turned-restaurant. Vince went in first and sat at the booth beside us.

The smell of fried food and seasonings wafted through the air. My mouth watered.

Our bored-looking waitress trudged over and held her pad in front of her face as she took our order.

"I'll have ze fried chickzen sandvich wiz steak fries and a Coke."

I almost lost it when he looked up at her and sucked on his tooth.

She didn't blink twice, just turned to me. "And for you?"

"Yes, I'll have the chicken noodle soup with a water." My accent sounded fine, cultured with long vowels, until I got to the word water, then all I could think of was "wah-uh" in that Cockney-esque accent I'd heard in videos.

Evan snorted a laugh and tried to cover it with a cough.

She gave him a dead stare. "I'll have it out shortly."

As she walked away, we both burst out laughing. We were

probably the strangest customers she'd ever had. Vince sent us an amused look but otherwise kept his head on a swivel and ignored our antics.

When she dropped our food off, Evan said, "Zank you, zis looks very delizous."

I laughed into my cup.

Steam rose from my soup and the soft roll beside it. It was the kind they made from scratch every day, and the smell alone had my mouth watering and my stomach begging for a taste. For a brief moment, I hesitated, Sebastian's words repeating through my head: *Better body, better life.* I exhaled and put my hands on the table in front of me.

Evan had no such reservations and popped a fry into his mouth. "You okay?"

"You forgot your accent, dahling."

He raised a brow.

My attempt to deflect didn't work, so I said, "I haven't eaten carbs in seven weeks. I'm worried."

"Start slow."

I took a shaky breath and picked up the roll. Evan stared at me with that soft look in his eyes.

"It's weird seeing you with brown eyes." I took a nibble of the roll, then a spoonful of broth. My eyes dropped closed as the flavors exploded on my tongue. "Mmm."

"Good?"

I took another bite, this one with carrot and onion. "Delicious."

He reached across the table and grabbed my hand. "I'm glad. I've been worried about you."

I affected my accent again. "We do recover."

He chuckled. "We do recover."

When I went to take my third bite, my gigantic prosthetic nose dipped into the spoonful of soup, and Evan nearly spit out his mouthful of Coke. We laughed until my sides ached and my eyes watered. I gently dabbed at the prosthetic nose with a napkin.

"That's the funniest thing I've ever seen."

"Funnier than the time you walked into the glass sliding door in front of a dozen paparazzi?"

His forehead had been red for twenty minutes afterward, but his ego was still a little bruised. The photos had been all over the internet—still were.

"Way funnier."

We shared a look and a private smile.

We ate in silence for a few minutes, and I couldn't help but think about what a future with Evan would look like.

"Hey. I hope this doesn't start an argument..." I abandoned my accent and leaned my elbows on the table, watching his brown eyes for his reaction. "We've been getting...closer."

He nodded, matching my posture. "Uh huh." A small smile played on his lips.

"And I just wanted to know if you still had the same reservations about having kids as you did before."

He put his napkin down and folded his hands in front of him on the table. "Axl is a great kid," he said, and I could already sense the "but" coming. "But I don't know how to be a good role model." He wouldn't look at me. His gaze trained on his linked fingers. Cheeks stained red.

That wasn't a no. In conversations in the past, he'd always had a firm rejection. This was an improvement. I couldn't help the hope that fluttered in my chest. "Why not?"

Something shifted in his eyes, like armor going on. Walls going up. "Because I've screwed up my life beyond all recognition. I can't bring someone into this mess. Especially a kid."

My throat burned and I nodded, even though he didn't look up at me to see it.

I had to help him see he was wrong. He was a good role model *because* of what he'd been through. I had to work up the nerve to tell him about Axl. The more I saw them together, the easier it was to picture the three of us together as a family.

As long as he forgave me for hiding it from him for so long.

MONDAY, between coaching sessions, the door burst open. Alli skidded into the room, eyes darting from Evan to me. "I'm so sorry to interrupt." Her gaze locked on mine, and something in her face went sharp. *Bad. Really bad.*

My stomach dropped. "What is it? Axl? Colby? Dylan and Aiden?"

"It's all over the news. Last night, they caught the men who busted out of your dad's house—the ones who totaled your car in Phoenix."

I shot to my feet, my body going instantly numb. "And?"

"They said he owed them two million dollars in gambling debt."

The words hollowed me out. My knees gave, and I sank back onto the piano bench, the world tilting sideways. "What?"

Evan's arm slipped around me, steadying me, pulling me into his side before I could fall.

"There's more," Alli whispered.

Evan's voice was hard. "How much more?"

She hesitated, her lips pressing together like she wished she could swallow the words.

"Tell me," I rasped.

"Your dad was staging his own kidnapping to con you for money. They arrested him. If you hadn't shown up when you did…" She exhaled shakily. "You would've gotten a ransom note. They were going to demand the full amount from you."

The room blurred. A sound tore out of me, muffled only when I buried my face in Evan's chest. His hand cradled the back of my head as if he could shield me from it all.

Alli's voice wavered. "It's been picked up by all the news outlets. It's everywhere. I'm supposed to ask if you have a comment."

I shook my head, unable to speak. My gaze met Evan's, my eyes pleading with him to voice the words I couldn't.

Evan's answer was steel. "No. She has no comment."

My father's face flashed in my mind—his crooked smile, the way he called me *pumpkin*. How good he was with Axl, his little buckaroo. I couldn't even wrap my mind around an addiction so strong he was willing to throw his own grandson's future to the wind. Every memory warped, cracked. All the lies I'd swallowed without question curdled in my chest until they felt poisonous.

He hadn't just gambled away money. He had gambled away *me*.

And he'd lost.

When Bonnie showed up for her coaching session a few minutes later, Evan took point while I sat in the corner and rage wrote.

> *I was just a daughter wanting to believe,*
> *But you folded with an ace up your sleeve.*
> *Every bet you placed built another wall,*
> *And I was left with nothing at all.*
> *Nothing at all.*

A tear hit the page, but I ignored it and kept going. Writing always helped me process my feelings.

You gambled us away on a fleeting high,
Burned every bridge for another lie.
You played with fire, and the cost was trust,
Now the table's empty—it's ashes and dust.
And I'll never forget the day...
You gambled us away.

Javi approached with two coffee cups in his hands and an uncertain expression.

"Evan asked me to get you these, but don't shoot the messenger if you don't want them..." He held out the cups like they might explode—or like *I* might explode, more accurately. "This one is your usual." He raised one cup. "And this one is a grande skinny vanilla latte, no whip. I asked the barista what she'd recommend. Evan wanted me to tell you that you don't need a lower calorie drink, but this one only has 120."

Okay, as far as calories went, that wasn't bad at all. Especially compared to my usual drink that was 400+. I took the lower calorie option and sipped it cautiously, letting the first taste of coffee in nearly eight weeks touch my tongue.

"Mmm." The sound came from somewhere deep within my soul—or my stomach.

He watched me with a wary expression. "Good?"

"It's excellent. Thank you."

CHAPTER FIFTY-FIVE

AFTER FILMING, Jenny and I rode together back to her apartment.

We were hoping to get the song completed tonight and rehearse it a few times to learn our parts.

It was after ten, so Axl should've been in bed, but when we walked in the door, he perked up on the manny's lap and ran toward us.

He hugged my legs as I patted his head.

Colby was bleary-eyed. "Sorry. He won't go to sleep."

"He can hang out with us for a bit," I offered, as Axl reached his squashy hands up to me. "Get some sleep."

"Hi, Van. Hold you."

I lifted him, and Axl laid his head on my shoulder as Colby staggered into his bedroom and shut the door.

Jenny took my notebook from my hand and put it on the coffee table as I sat and positioned Axl on my lap.

She took a fresh sheet of paper and carefully wrote out all three verses, the bridge, the pre-chorus, and the two choruses.

Axl was fully asleep now, cuddled deep in my chest.

Jenny got up, grinning, and gestured for me to follow her. She tiptoed across the tile like a sleep-deprived tooth fairy on a mission. I carried Axl to his room and laid him in a child-sized bed.

And then, as I laid him down, he stirred and mumbled two words that rewired my entire nervous system.

"Stay, Van."

Just that. Soft. Half-asleep. Probably nothing. Probably everything.

I glanced at Jenny, but she hadn't heard.

We crept out of the room like normal people—like my whole world hadn't just shifted on its axis—and shut the door behind us. Because I wanted to. I wanted to stay. But I couldn't. I couldn't want this. I didn't trust myself not to destroy it like I had everything else in my life.

Jenny sank cross-legged onto the floor with her notebook, hair falling out of its bun, and for a second, I forgot how to breathe. She looked...happy. Comfortable. *Home.* And I tried not to think about how badly I wanted to stay right there.

I picked up her guitar, pretended to focus on the frets. Distraction via six strings and denial. My specialty.

And just for a few minutes, I let myself have it. Just the music. The laughter. Her voice humming along while she nudged toy cars out of the way like she'd been juggling motherhood and melodies her whole life.

It was perfect. Which meant, obviously, it was dangerous.

Because perfect never stuck.

Not for me.

I could already feel the other shoe hovering in the sky, waiting for gravity. Once she realized how unstable I was, she'd leave. She'd done it before. She had her reasons, sure, but the fact was, when things got hard, she walked. My mom had too. Same song, different verse. If I'd been enough, she would've stayed clean. Instead, she chose the easy way out.

My thoughts lingered on Jenny's dad too. How long had he stayed away from the casinos before he relapsed? Years. He'd built himself a good life. A steady business. Yet it still wasn't enough. How long before Jenny made the connection between her dad's addiction and mine? How long before she realized my relapse potential was too big of a risk.

And me? I was the kind of guy who made it easy for people to go. I burned things down, ruined trust, relapsed, said the wrong things, choked when it mattered. Pattern recognized, never corrected.

Now Jenny had a kid. A whole *life*. She didn't need a recovering addict orbiting too close, dragging ghosts behind him like luggage.

So yeah, tonight felt good. Too good. And that was the problem. Because part of me wanted to reach for it—her, Axl, all of it —and the other part knew better. Knew that if I let myself have it, I'd lose it. And I didn't know if I could survive being left again.

"I should go," I said, before my heart did something stupid.

By Saturday, the good feeling had curdled. With only five contestants left, we consolidated song selection sessions into one long day. Translation: a lot of forced smiles and thinly veiled tension.

Jenny could feel it too. I could tell by the way she constantly studied me. The air between us was off. I shoved my hands in my pockets and thumbed my sobriety medallion until the edges dug into my skin. *Stay strong.*

It wasn't even cravings anymore. It was shame. The kind that sat heavy in your chest. Axl deserved someone solid. Jenny deserved someone who wasn't perpetually one bad day from an implosion. Even sober, I was still the guy who burned his whole life to the ground.

Never enough. Not for them. Not for anyone.

Jenny flitted around the rehearsal room barefoot, wearing flowy pants and a silk shirt that looked too soft for a world this sharp. Hair up, strands escaping, completely unaware that she was the most distracting person in any room.

Zane was already tuning his electric, professional as hell, like he'd been born with perfect pitch. He rarely needed us for anything beyond song selection.

The first song he played was "Friday Freak" by JC Doran. Catchy. Pop-rock candy.

Then, he played "Break the Silence."

Jenny lit up like someone plugged her in. "This is the one!" she said, looking to me for confirmation.

"I like 'Friday Freak' better."

Her eyebrows shot up. "No. Don't get me wrong, it's a great song, but it doesn't showcase his range. That chorus sits too low in his register. He's not hitting the notes."

"But 'Friday Freak' is a more well-known song," I countered. "People vote for songs they recognize. Nostalgia sells."

The fire in her eyes flared. "Why are you arguing with me right now? You *know* I'm right. If he did a stripped-down version of 'Break the Silence,' it would blow up the charts. That song is begging to be slowed down."

Zane looked between us like a kid caught in a custody battle. "Can we try the stripped-down version? That sounds cool."

"Yes," Jenny said.

"No," I said.

She pointed toward the hallway. "Outside."

I didn't argue. Just walked out, let the door swing shut behind me, and kept walking—right past her, out the doors, into the parking lot.

Sometimes distance was the only way to breathe.

CHAPTER FIFTY-SIX

WHAT IN THE hell was Evan's problem? I stayed outside the room for a few minutes—enough time to regain control of my temper and make it seem like we'd had a rational conversation, even though he stormed away without a backward glance—then I went back in.

"Sorry, Zane. Let's try the stripped-down version, shall we? Evan will be back in a bit. He needed to get some air."

Zane chewed his bottom lip but took his electric guitar off and swapped it for an acoustic. He was about twenty, light brown hair that fell to his nose that he kept tossing out of his face, and dark lashes that made his brown eyes pop. The female fanbase would vote for him.

"Hear me out. What if instead of doing it in C major, you sang it in C minor?"

His eyes widened. "Oh my gosh, that would sound so eerie."

For the rest of the session, we worked on tempo, vocal delivery, and instrumentation. I sang the harmony half a key down for the final chorus, and Zane and I stared at each other as the final note faded out.

"That was amazing!" He held his hand up for a high-five. I laughed and slapped it. It felt good to work with someone with so much natural talent. In less than a day, we'd turned this song into a hit.

"Are you allowed to sing the backup vocal? That would be like a dream come true."

I laughed. "Unfortunately, no. We'll get you a backup singer who can do it justice though. I promise."

When he left, I went to see if I could find Evan. He sat at the far end of the parking lot, in the shade of the hedge that blocked the lot from the street. His hand was open, and his sobriety coin sat in his palm.

I sat on the cement parking barrier beside him. This was almost where I'd been sitting when we met.

Silence stretched between us for a full minute—I counted each of the seconds.

He let out a breath and pocketed his sobriety medallion, turned to me. "I owe you an apology. I've been feeling off, and I took it out on you."

I tilted my head, studying him. "Yeah, what's your deal? Things were going so well, and then you just...shut down."

Evan ran a hand through his hair, mussing it. His jaw worked as he stared out over the parking lot, like debating how much to say. "It's just that the longer I spend with you, the more I realize I'm not good enough for you."

A lump crawled up my throat. I shook my head, denying his words. "I get to make that decision, not you."

He pulled a pack of gum from his pocket and popped a piece in his mouth. "How long was your dad in recovery? Then he relapsed and tried to steal all that money from you. What if I relapse? What if I hurt you and Axl?"

I swallowed, my eyes filling with tears. I wished he could see himself through my eyes. "That's a risk I'm willing to take. You know how much it hurt you when your birth mom did that to you. Would you do that to my son?"

"Of course not. But the addiction... What if it...takes control of me?"

I wouldn't let it. Plain and simple. "You are *not* your mom.

And you are *not* my dad," I said fiercely. "I believe in you. We'll work through it together, just like we did in Nashville."

He grabbed my hand, linking our fingers together. His shook. He brought my hand to his lips, kissed my knuckles. "I want so much to believe it's true," he rasped.

I turned toward him until he looked at me, until our gazes locked, so he could see the sincerity in my eyes. "I have faith in you. Now you just need to have faith in yourself."

Evan hugged me to his chest, placed a kiss on my forehead. Held me until he stopped shaking.

Finally, he said, "You were right about the song choice."

I wanted to lighten his mood. "I usually am."

He nudged my shoulder with his. "I came in and listened to the end. It was really good. Seriously. You've got such an ear for music." He swallowed, scratched the scruff on his face.

"So do you. Zane wasn't even on my radar. You picked him to win."

Evan shook his head. "It was a hunch. He reminded me a lot of me."

"He does have your same rasp. He'll make a good lead singer or solo artist." Just like Evan.

So much amazing talent would be cast aside after the show ended. Yes, they would be picked up by smaller labels, or even strike out on their own, but they deserved better. Only the winner got a recording contract with Titan.

"After Zane's session, I'm feeling really bad for Katarina and Maisie. They're both incredible, but I'm not sure they can beat him."

He smiled.

"What?"

"Nothing. It's just interesting to watch your maternal instinct stretch beyond Axl."

I shrugged and clasped my hands in front of me. "I almost feel like we're using them. And it's not a good feeling."

He nodded, and we sat in silence again. My thoughts swirled around, names, faces, songs, arrangements. I could only do so much for these kids. They were all bright-eyed and had their whole futures ahead of them. I couldn't stand that we were just going to send them back to their own lives to try to figure things out.

But how could I help?

"We need a contingency plan," I said.

Evan smirked. "Contingency plan? Sounds ominous."

"It's not ominous. It's...practical." I fiddled with the silk end of my blouse. "Let's be real—three of the five remaining contestants will probably never do anything big with music after this."

He sat up, folded his arms. "Harsh."

"Realistic," I corrected. "And I don't want to just pat their backs and say 'better luck next time.' These kids are good, Evan. Too good to disappear after a TV show decides they're not shiny enough."

His smirk faded into something more raw, more interested. "So what's your big plan, Jenny Rose?"

We were back to Jenny Rose. I sighed, relieved that things between us seemed to be a little better, but I felt a flicker of nerves, like maybe I was overstepping. I pushed through. "We help them. Even if they don't win. We find ways to get them gigs, studio time, maybe even pair them with directors we know. Just... something. A next step. So they don't feel like the rug got yanked out from under them."

He studied me, tapping his fingers against his arms. "That almost sounds like...infrastructure."

I narrowed my eyes. "Don't make it sound corporate."

"I'm not. I'm saying"—he leaned in now, grin tugging his lips —"you're talking about more than hand-holding. You're talking about...building something for them."

I shrugged, feigning casualness when my chest buzzed with something I couldn't name. "Maybe. I just...I don't want them to feel thrown away."

"Contingency plan," he repeated, as if testing how the words felt in his mouth. Then he nodded slowly. "Yeah. I like it."

AFTER ELIMINATIONS, I stood backstage with Jenny as she held a crying Katarina, and for a minute the world narrowed to two women and one broken moment.

"This isn't the end for you or your career. I promise," Jenny whispered, hugging her tight. Tears shimmered in Jenny's eyes, but her spine was steel. I admired the hell out of her.

Usually, the first thing I did after filming was yank my earpiece out like it was contagious. Not tonight. Whoever was in my ear hadn't switched off the mic, and I was getting the world's most toxic encore. I reached up to fish it out when Kimball's voice floated through—slick, certain, like he ate the truth for breakfast. "What did I tell you?"

Another voice answered, softer, garbled, but unmistakable French. Sebastian. I couldn't make out his words, but that was definitely his cackle. I drifted away from the crying contestants, away from the comforting hugs, away from the relief radiating off the people who'd been spared.

"Next week, we'll cut Maisie."

"Zey should 'ave lizened," Sebastian sneered. "Zat amateur Fabian zinks he's so chic."

Kimball laughed, the sound hollow and practiced.

My stomach went cold. The truth slammed into me. They were cutting girls who'd switched stylists. They were rigging the bracket. They were choosing winners.

The feed fuzzed out. I waited, stupidly hopeful for another line, but all I got was static and the muffled chatter of people doing their best to look human. I finally yanked the earpiece out. How was I supposed to tell Jenny about this? That the competition she'd poured herself into was a setup? That her so-called mentor had fixed the game?

And worse—what if he'd done the same for her season?

She'd ask herself that, and I couldn't stomach the idea of her questioning the one thing she'd earned with every ounce of her soul.

By the time I got to my dressing room, Javi and Murphy were already there. I ducked behind the changing screen and ripped off my vest.

"What's up, *amigo*?" Javi asked.

"I overheard something, and I don't know what to do with it."

"What kind of something?" Murphy's voice was all business.

"Katarina got cut because she switched stylists. Kimball and Sebastian rigged the damn show." I ran a hand through my hair and tugged hard.

"*Cac naofa,*" Murphy muttered, and even without a translation, I knew it was bad.

"Are you gonna tell her?" Javi asked carefully.

"Do I have to?" I turned to them, hoping someone would tell me no.

Murphy didn't hesitate. "No. It'll only wound her. She'll blame herself for talkin' the girls into changin' stylists. You put that in her head, and she'll carry it as if it were her own doing."

He was right. Probably. But it didn't make me feel any better.

The idea of keeping something like this from her made my chest hurt. But the idea of watching her doubt herself? That was worse.

Still, the thought of Kimball—untouchable Kimball—gloating about it made me want to break something.

"I have to say something," I muttered.

"*Amigo*," Javi warned, but it was too late.

I marched to the door and threw it open.

"Where are you goin'?" Javi called.

"To give Kimball a piece of my mind."

"This is a bad idea—"

"Noted."

I didn't knock. I just shoved Kimball's dressing room door open. Gio shot to his feet like I'd fired a gun, but I ignored him.

"Kimball," I barked.

Kimball stepped out from behind the dressing screen, adjusting his tie like I was a minor inconvenience between him and a mirror. "What can I do for you?"

"I heard your conversation with Sebastian."

He raised a brow, calm as someone always in control. "What conversation?"

"The one where you bragged about fixing the competition. Where you said you cut Katarina for switching stylists—and Maisie is next."

A muscle ticked in his jaw, just once. "You must have misheard. If you check the tapes, you'll see I predicted Maisie would win." He stepped closer, eyes cold. "And if I were you, I'd think twice before biting the hand that signs your paychecks, Evan."

His voice was soft, but the tone beneath it was steel.

Every instinct I had screamed to swing, to wipe that smug look off his face. But I didn't. Because I knew how this game worked—and men like Kimball Stone made sure the people who swung first lost everything.

"Go ahead," he taunted. "Take a swing like you did at Sebastian. See how far that gets you."

So Sebastian had told him. I unclenched my fists, turned, and stalked out.

Back in the hallway, the lights were too bright. Laughter spilled from the green room. Nobody else knew the show was rigged; the whole world kept spinning, shiny and fake.

And I kept walking, jaw tight, carrying the weight of the truth like a current under my skin.

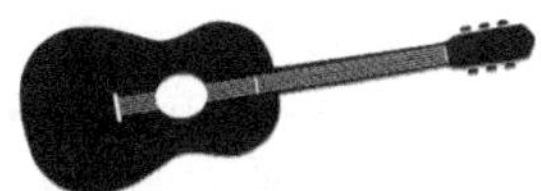

I COULDN'T BELIEVE we'd reached the semi-finals.

The four contestants met with us on Saturday, and we worked on their arrangements, giving advice and making tweaks until they were beautiful.

When Zane walked into the studio, he dropped his guitar and wrapped me in a hug. "Thank you," he whispered.

Evan raised a brow at the piano but didn't do much else.

"You're welcome. That's my job."

"I know, but this is different. I have a number one song, and it's all because of you." He beamed and bounced on his toes. "I can't believe it. I keep pinching myself, and it's still real!"

Zane was a good kid...and I hated that Kimball was going to screw him up.

"Do you have some song ideas for next week? You're one performance away from the finale." Evan played a couple chord progressions on the piano.

"So, I was thinking of doing the same thing I did last week, only the opposite. I want to take a stripped song and make it a rock song. I've been playing with one in particular, and I hope you guys can tell me if I'm on the right track or if I should go another direction."

"What song?" I asked.

"'Echoes of Yesterday' by Heidi Harrow. Before you say anything, let me just play you a couple lines..." Zane plugged his guitar into the amp—he really needed to go wireless—and played the first chord, his eyes closed, his whole body feeling the music.

When he sang the opening line, with his growl and the edgy emotion, chills spread over my body. I held up my arms to show him. He grinned.

Evan nodded enthusiastically. "Yes! This is awesome." He abandoned the piano and went to the drums—that was new—and found the rhythm like it was second nature.

I had no choice. I grabbed my guitar and tried to play along, though I wasn't nearly as good as Evan.

We jammed out for our entire session. Evan had some excellent advice about tone and delivery that he was uniquely qualified to give. And watching him in his element had something in my chest going all gooey.

As we were wrapping up for the night, I packed my guitar in its case and looked up to find Evan staring at me with a soft look in his eyes, standing very close. I got to my feet and faced him, our toes touching.

"Hi," he said.

I bit my lip and glanced at his mouth. "Hey."

He smiled, and my breath caught.

His hand gently brushed the hair from my face, then traced a torturously slow line down my cheek, my jaw, his eyes tracking the movement. He swallowed and our gazes met.

This man who, months ago, had been the last person I wanted to see, had quickly become everything. He cupped the back of my head, his gaze touching my every feature: eyes, nose, cheeks, lips, chin. Lips again.

My stomach swooped. My whole body gravitated toward him. His smile dropped, and he tried to pull away, but I dragged his face down and leaned up on tiptoes to meet him.

Our other kisses had been full of passion, fire, and desire. This kiss, this soft brush of lips, this slow tasting, testing, was like a promise. A future dawning behind my closed eyelids.

I clutched his arms, drawing him closer, and he moaned softly against my lips, the sound rumbling in my chest.

When he pulled back, he rested his forehead on mine, breath short. His eyes remained closed, so I leaned up and kissed his lips, a soft peck.

He smiled and brought our lips together again, this time with more fervor. He wrapped his arms around my waist and lifted me from the ground, and like I had done a thousand times before, I wound my legs around him.

Evan pulled back again, but he didn't put me down. He stared into my eyes, his expression open and happier than I'd seen in... well, years. "I've missed you," he said.

"I've missed you too," I whispered, emotions suddenly making it hard to speak.

And I was transported back in time to Axl's birth. My mom had been there, trying to help in her own way. Dylan wasn't, for obvious reasons—she couldn't walk out of her own wedding. But I couldn't help but wish that Evan had seen my water break and that he had come with me. That I was holding *his* hand through the contractions.

That he was there to cut the umbilical cord. To hold our son.

And when Axl was finally born, I had written the name on the birth certificate: Axl Noah.

CHAPTER FIFTY-NINE

MAISIE GRACE WAS CUT, leaving our top three: Troy Maddox, Zane Draven, and Bonnie Flynn.

Jenny and I hugged Maisie as she cried. "What did I do wrong?" she kept asking, and I wanted to scream that she'd done *everything* right. Except getting on Kimball's bad side.

Jenny held her until her sobs turned to hiccups. When the girl finally walked off, Jenny stayed by my side, her arms looped around my waist as we watched the others leave.

It felt weirdly like being parents—our kids off in the great big world.

"She'll land on her feet, Jenny Rose. Too much talent not to."

She nodded, shoulders slumping as we headed toward the dressing rooms.

We changed fast, then went back to my place to rehearse our duet and eat a late dinner. The show would be over in a week. And then what? No more excuses to see her every day. No more late nights in her living room pretending we were just writing songs.

I didn't want to think about it.

I sent Ryan and Murphy to bed and Javi home for the night.

We wandered into the kitchen and opened the takeout boxes.

Silence settled between us as we scarfed down our respective meals. Jenny had gone more sensible, but it was more food than I'd seen her eat in at least two months.

When she finished, I asked, "Shall we get started?"

She wiped her mouth and put her garbage in the trash. "I've been thinking..."

That sentence never meant good things.

"Oh?" I folded up my takeout container and added it to hers in the garbage can.

She pulled her knees to her chest and wrapped her arms around her legs. "Not that it matters, but I'm shocked that Troy made it through. He butchered rehearsals, and Maisie was clearly the better performer..."

That made me blink. "Okay..." Better than where I thought she was going with an intro like that.

Her lip caught between her teeth, eyes distant, like she was somewhere miles away. "I don't want a talk show. Coaching the contestants these last few weeks reminded me how much I love music. I can't just sit behind a desk pretending to care about celebrity gossip. I want to create."

I exhaled, bracing myself. "I overheard something."

Her eyes narrowed. "What something?"

"Kimball and Sebastian rigged the votes."

Her laugh was sharp and humorless. She put her feet down and threw her arms up. "Of course they did."

"I wanted to tell you sooner, but..." I shrugged. "Timing's never been my strong suit."

She muttered something that sounded like "cheese and crackers."

"There's more. I talked to my agent, and he said that Kimball put enough wiggle room in our contracts that he could avoid giving you your talk show and me my solo contract. I've had a little bit of time to think about it, and even if he doesn't follow through, I'm done with Chapel of Dust."

She blinked. "But you love your music. You'd really break up the band?"

The hope in her eyes nearly undid me. Could I do this? Could I walk away from the band without the safety net of a solo contract? I studied Jenny's face. The hope in her eyes. "Yeah. I would. With or without the music, I can't be part of their lifestyle."

She laughed, then shook her head, tears glittering in her eyes. "I guess part of me still worried you weren't serious about staying clean. But hearing you say that... Wow. I'm proud of you. I'm sorry I doubted you."

I crossed the room and pulled her into my arms. I breathed into her hair, inhaling the intoxicating scent of her, and in that moment I knew. I *could* do this. I could be the support Jenny needed. I could step in as a father to her son. I could do all of it if Jenny was by my side. "I'm serious. About staying clean. About wanting you."

She kissed me softly, no fireworks, no dramatics, just *real*. The kind of quiet you didn't get in my world. "And Axl?" she asked, hope in her eyes.

I couldn't deny that the kid had embedded himself in my life, that I liked being around him. Holding him. I wanted to try.

"Yeah, with Axl too. Want to run an errand with me?"

Her brow crinkled.

"I just need to pop over to the Parkland house and tell them."

"Right now?"

"Why not?"

She smiled. "I'm proud of you."

That smile could've enticed men to build empires.

We snuck out to my Charger like teenagers. She laughed as I held my keys out of reach and told her she couldn't drive. "Not a chance."

Her laugh faded into silence as we hit the open road. Three minutes in, my neck stiffened—migraine incoming. Of course. Perfect timing.

Maybe I should've turned around. But the way she looked at me when I said I wanted to go talk to the band tonight... I couldn't back out now. I wanted her to see I was serious. That I could *show up*.

By the time we reached the neighborhood and went through the first gate, my vision shimmered like heat waves.

"You're awfully quiet," she said.

"Just driving," I muttered, trying to sound normal while the pain clawed through the base of my skull. Each street light made it worse.

She hesitated. "Are you having second thoughts?"

I shook my head. Mistake! Knives exploded behind my eyes.

Before I could answer, she said softly, "I have to tell you something."

Perfect. Anything to distract me from the throbbing in my skull.

"I've wanted to for a long time now. I've been trying to find a way, to find the right moment." She fiddled with the tassels on her sleeve and nervously chewed her lip. "I was too scared until... you said you'd break from your band. Maybe the time is finally right."

Pushing back the mounting pain in my neck, I reached for her hand. It trembled in mine. "What is it? You can tell me anything."

At last, she met my gaze. "It's about Axl's father."

I frowned.

She bit her lip, her eyes trained out the window. Hesitating.

"What?"

She didn't reply. Her bottom lip trembled. She looked at me meaningfully, as if hoping I'd infer her meaning without her having to tell me.

It's about Axl's father.

Memories flashed through my mind like a kaleidoscope. Murphy seeing Axl for the first time: *He looks just like you.* Carl during house renovations. *Are you sure he isn't yours?* Jenny on *Couple's Cruise,* walking out on me because I wouldn't change my mind about having kids.

"Axl is my son." My voice broke.

evan

AXL WAS MY SON.

My throat closed. And the car accelerated as every muscle in my body tightened. I let off the gas and slammed on the brakes.

She stared out the windshield. Her hand covered her mouth, her eyes welling with tears.

"Is he?" I asked, my voice jagged.

She wouldn't even look at me.

"Yes." Her voice broke.

A heaviness settled in my chest where my heart used to beat. My hands were blocks of ice, gripping the wheel.

Why hadn't she told me?

Look at your track record, a dark voice taunted inside my mind.

I'd missed his whole life.

You would've missed it anyway. I was probably high while he was taking his first breath. Drunk when he said his first words. Stoned when he was taking his first steps.

A lump lodged in my throat, and no matter how much I swallowed, it wouldn't budge.

It was official. I was just as bad as my birth mom. I'd had a son for four whole years, and I'd been too drugged to notice.

But the difference was my mom knew about me. I didn't even have a chance to know Axl.

Jenny had lied. She'd hidden it. My voice shook. "Seriously?"

"Evan, I—" She cut herself off. Nothing she said would make it better.

"You what?" I rasped, my head throbbing. "You lied to me. You didn't think I was good enough to be a father."

"That's not it." A choked sob tore from her throat. She curled her knees up to her chest, her head shaking from side to side. "I called you the day after he was born."

"No, you didn't."

"I did. I told you about Axl." Her eyes begged me, pleaded with me to believe her.

"Bullshit." I pulled up to the gate in front of Parkland house and scanned the key.

Jenny waited for the window to roll back up before she continued. "You called me a liar. Accused me of cheating on you. You said I was despicable. That I couldn't keep my legs closed. Then you ended the call by telling me you had a vasectomy."

She dashed tears from her eyes, her shoulders straightening, her body shifting to face me fully. "Then three months later, I saw you all over the news. Drugs and alcohol! I thought you were lashing out at me. That you were trying to show me how over us you were."

Her words hit like a slap. I recoiled and threw the car in park in the driveway. Loud music from the house vibrated my chest and attacked my skull. No wonder she'd been so mad at me.

"When Aiden told me you didn't remember, I made him promise not to tell you. Not until I was sure you were ready to hear it. We made a deal that I'd tell you when you were clean for a year."

My headache pounded, my chest ached. I was an asshole. An absolute and complete jerk. And Aiden... He was dead to me. He'd kept a secret for how long? While claiming to be my best friend.

I opened my door, ready to get out, needing some fresh air to process this new information. Self-loathing and I had been acquaintances before, but now he was my new best friend.

Jenny grabbed my arm. I jerked away, looked back at her.

Her chin quivered, but steel replaced the hurt in her eyes. "You weren't ready. I thought you were now. Guess I was wrong."

We both were. "Stay here," I barked. "We can continue this *discussion* when I finish breaking up my band." I got out and slammed the door, then stalked into the house. I could barely see through the pain in my head and the tunneling in my vision. I wasn't mad at her as much as I was angry at myself, at the situation, at Aiden for betraying me. At life for dealing me the shittiest hand of all.

I entered the house, the music nearly knocking me off my feet.

Beckett shouted, "Evan!" and the guys all cheered from the living room, already drunk and high.

I lifted a half-hearted hand in greeting. "I need migraine medicine."

Beckett jumped to his feet and jogged over, the cloying scent of weed and alcohol clinging to him. "I think Trish has some. C'mon."

His girlfriend had supplied me with some triptan on tour before, when I'd left mine at the hotel. I followed him up the stairs. I needed quiet. "Any chance you can bring it to me in the music room?"

The room was soundproof, and I definitely needed to silence the loud music. Too bad it couldn't silence the noise in my mind.

"I can trust you, yeah?" I rubbed my temples, breathing through my mouth to keep the nausea at bay.

"Of course."

"Nothing's official yet, but the band should start looking for a new frontman."

His brow furrowed. "You're leaving us?"

I managed a shrug. "I've got a solo offer coming my way."

Beckett didn't respond.

We split at the top of the stairs, and I headed to the music room. I closed the door behind me, shutting out the thump of the bass, the high-pitched screech of the guitars. A deep, ugly hunger started in my gut and spread to my limbs, like something feral clawing its way out of me.

My hands clenched so tight around my sobriety medallion that it cut into my palm. *Breathe.*

There was no way Axl could love me after everything I'd missed. Four entire years. His first steps, first words... Too many firsts to count, and I hadn't been there. I'd been somewhere else.

The worst part was Jenny wasn't wrong to keep Axl away. I couldn't blame her at all for protecting her—*our*—son.

How much different would my life have been had I known? Just one more thing the drugs had taken from me.

I looked down at the coin in my hand, then threw it at the wall with a shout. What was the point? If it didn't change the way people looked at me, what did it matter?

A few minutes later, Beckett came in and closed the door behind him, a pill bottle in each hand. He held one out. "You sure you don't want the good stuff?"

I stared at the bottle of colorful pills. Every cell in my body begged me to reach out. To take them. It would be so easy. This crushing weight would disappear.

Then I glanced at my sobriety coin on the carpet by my feet. What would Jenny think? What about Axl?

I swiped the other bottle with Trish's name on it.

"This is triptan?"

"Of course, man."

I dumped the last two tablets into my hand and tossed them in my mouth. Beckett pulled a water bottle from his back pocket and gave it to me. I drank deeply, trying to drown this feeling, this ache, this need.

I closed my eyes and laid my head on the back of the couch. Beckett cleared his throat, a smirk etched across his lips. "Those'll cheer you right up. I've got more if you need 'em." He winked and left the room.

Within seconds, everything went dark.

CHAPTER SIXTY-ONE

DID he have any idea how long I'd been working up the nerve to tell him? I almost told him a hundred different times throughout the day, but I was trying to be patient, find the right time.

And then he left me sitting here in the dark.

I never should have told him.

I crawled over the center console and got into the driver's seat of his precious car, shoved it in gear...and the engine died.

"Are you kidding me?" I yelled at the windshield, every curse word I wouldn't say in front of Axl spilling out.

He'd taken the stupid key fob.

I needed to move. Needed air. I slammed the door and stormed toward the sidewalk. The walk-through gate was padlocked. Great. I waved my arms, jumped, shouted like an idiot —but the gate only opened if you had the keycard.

I stood at the edge of the driveway, arms hugging myself like that could hold me together. I'd ruined it. Again. There was just no winning with Evan. I wasn't wrong though. He wasn't ready to be a father back then. After his reaction, I wasn't sure if he was ready to be a father now.

I should go in there and demand answers—or just hop the fence and walk away. Forever. Both options felt unbearable.

The porch lights threw a soft glow over the lawn. The grass looked greener than I remembered, the maple leaves whispering secrets I'd just spilled. Honeysuckle floated on the air—sweet and heavy, mocking the pit in my stomach.

Evan had never looked at me with that much venom. He might hate me now—or worse, feel nothing at all. My nails dug into my palms.

I took a step toward the porch, then stopped. My body wanted to move; my chest screamed to run. I'd already detonated everything. Why twist the knife? Heavy music poured out of an open window near the front of the house, so I headed toward the backyard. To the solace.

A hive of bees buzzed low in my gut. I should just go in there and make him talk. How could he order me to *stay* like I was some obedient dog? I thought I was here for moral support, not to be abandoned in the driveway.

I stalked along the fence line, glaring at the perfectly trimmed hedge. Add that to my impossible dream-house list.

Dang it. Even my dream house had Evan in it—because I'd told him about my happy place to calm him on that flight. He'd tainted that too.

And while he was angry about my omission, he didn't give me any indication about how he felt about having a son. Just his knuckles white on the steering wheel.

Fine. I'd go in there.

Halfway to the porch, I stopped again. He was breaking up with his band. He said we could talk later. I was losing my mind over here.

I was still arguing with myself beside the pool gate when I heard the front door slam open. Finally. I checked my phone— twenty minutes. That was fast.

Laughter spilled out. Drunken, sloppy. Had he changed his mind? They wouldn't be happy after he told them he was out...

Then came the smell.

Smoke.

I rounded the corner to the front of the house. And froze.

Nolan, Jimmy, Beckett, and Derek were piled on the grass, laughing, pointing at the flames roaring out the living room window.

I scanned the grass, the window, and when I got close enough, the drunken faces of his bandmates. "Where's Evan?"

"Shit. Evan," Jimmy said, and they laughed harder.

I ran. The heat hit me before I reached the porch. Opening the door would be suicide.

"Call 911!" I yelled, already sprinting toward the back.

The sliding glass door was locked. *No, no, nonono.* I grabbed a patio chair with trembling hands and hurled it. It bounced. The second time, I swung it like a hammer, and the glass cracked.

My heart pounded in my chest, and adrenaline coursed through my body. *Breathe, Jenny. You can't help him if you don't stay calm.*

Two more hits and there was a hole big enough for my arm. I reached through and flipped the lock.

Fire had eaten the front of the house.

"Evan!" My throat burned. The fire drowned out my voice. "Evan!"

He couldn't die. Not like this.

I tore through the first floor—empty.

The stairs glowed orange in the flickering flame. Smoke thickened, black and choking. My eyes stung. My lungs screamed for clean air.

I yanked my shirt over my nose and took the stairs two at a time, crawling under the smoke. The main bedroom was empty. My eyes burned, and I left bloody handprints on the carpet in the hallway—I must've cut myself when I reached through the broken glass.

He had to be here. Please.

I threw open the door to the music room, and smoke immediately poured in through the open door. Evan lay on the couch, lips blue, an empty pill bottle on the table beside him.

No.

Sound vanished. Everything tunneled.

I shook him. *No!*

"Evan!" My voice shook, my whole body trembled.

Nothing. No breathing. No chest movement. Just stillness.

Move, Jenny.

I grabbed his arms and dragged him off the couch. He was heavy, deadweight heavy, but adrenaline surged through me. Thank heavens I'd been working out.

Live. Please, live.

The hallway felt endless. Each breath scraped my lungs raw. I couldn't control the tremor in my hands, my core, but I didn't stop, easing him down the hallway.

I can't do this. We're going to die. I can't breathe. I can't see.

When we hit the stairs, I pulled him down, step by step. Something in his arm popped, and a broken sob ripped from my throat. *I'm sorry, Evan. Just hold on.*

By the time we reached the bottom, the fire had swallowed the living room. The heat blistered the skin on my arm, and an otherworldly surge of strength bolstered me. I kept pulling. We got so close to the fire that Evan's pant leg caught, and as soon as I had him in the kitchen, I smothered it with my hands. My palms were raw, bloody, but I couldn't stop. Not yet. I kept pulling through the smoke, out the back door, until the grass hit my knees and cool air filled my lungs.

I collapsed beside him. Clutched his face.

"Evan, please—don't do this. Not now. Not after everything."

CHAPTER SIXTY-TWO

"EVAN?" My voice rasped, shredded. "Wake up, please."

Nothing.

I laced my fingers and started chest compressions—when I took the CPR training after Axl was born, I hoped to never have to use it.

"Help!" The word ripped from my throat. He couldn't die. Not here. Not now.

Stayin' Alive. I forced the rhythm through my head, counting the beats, pushing down hard enough to make his chest rise. *Stay alive. Please.*

Where was everyone? Why wasn't anyone helping?

My tears dripped onto his shirt, mixing with the blood from my arm.

Sirens wailed in the distance. Relief hit like a sob. Someone had called. Help was coming.

"Help!" I screamed again, my voice cracking into nothing. My body shook, but I didn't stop. Too many people had vanished from my life—walked away, disappeared, or only returned when they needed something. I couldn't lose him too. I couldn't survive a world without Evan.

The gate clanged open. Flashing lights flooded the yard. "Help," I croaked, barely a whisper.

My lungs burned. My hands trembled. *Please, Evan.*

A uniformed officer rounded the corner.

"I need Narcan!" My voice came out broken, strangled. "He overdosed."

The officer barked orders, knelt, and jammed a small device into Evan's nostril. Another responder pushed me aside, taking over compressions with a brisk precision.

"What's his name?" someone shouted.

"Evan." My body folded over. "His name is Evan."

He couldn't die. He wasn't allowed. We were supposed to be a family.

A woman crouched beside me. "What's your name?"

I must've been in bad shape if she didn't recognize me. "Jenny."

"I'm Kayla. Where are you hurt?"

I lifted my arms. My left arm had burns from wrist to elbow, and the right had bloody gashes. I stared, unseeing. Disconnected.

They gave Evan a second dose of Narcan.

Tears blurred everything.

At some point, someone put an oxygen mask over my face and they wrapped my arms, but when they tried to lift me to my feet, I pulled away.

I stared at Evan.

"We need to get you to the hospital, Jenny," Kayla said.

I shook my head. Couldn't move. Couldn't blink. Evan's skin was the color of ash.

Third dose of Narcan.

Kayla's arm anchored me upright. My breath came in staccato bursts through the mask.

Fourth dose.

Evan's body jerked. Then they moved fast. IV line. Board. Stretcher. One medic straddled him, still pumping his chest as they rolled him toward the ambulance.

My vision tunneled. The world tilted.

My eyes felt like sandpaper.

My hands hurt.

My head.

My arm.

Me.

Kayla's voice broke through the noise. "We've got you. Can you stand?"

I nodded weakly, though the motion sent stars spinning above my head. She looped her arm around me, guiding me toward the flashing red lights. I stumbled, my legs giving out.

Then everything went dark.

CHAPTER SIXTY-THREE

THE WORLD CAME BACK in fragments.

Beeping. A hiss of air. Something plastic tickling my nose.

Pain. So much pain.

I cracked open one eye. White ceiling tiles. Too bright. The world screamed in fluorescent tones. My elbow flared with pain and my left leg felt like it had auditioned for "Great Chicago Fire: The Musical."

I coughed—bad move. My throat felt like I'd swallowed a cactus. Excellent. Zero out of ten. Did not recommend.

"Hey, you're awake. Just stay still for me, okay?"

I turned my head, regretted it instantly. A redheaded pixie wearing green scrubs hovered over me with a clipboard and too much cheer for someone in a room that smelled like antiseptic and despair.

"I'm Nurse Amber. I've been watching out for you."

"Congrats," I rasped. "Hell of a show."

She laughed, a tinkling sound. I coughed, phlegmy and rattling.

"What happened?"

Amber tilted the bed just enough to stop me from choking on my own lungs. "Jenny Gentry dragged you unconscious from a burning house and gave you CPR until paramedics arrived. You're very lucky to be alive."

I blinked, then looked down. My arm in a sling, leg bandaged like a mummy. Every inch of me hurt.

Then her words hit in delayed replay. *Jenny. CPR. Fire.*

My brain short-circuited. "Come again?"

"She saved your life."

I stared at her, waiting for the punchline.

"She dragged you out," Amber added. "You overdosed, were unconscious in a burning building, and dislocated your elbow during the rescue. Honestly...you're a medical miracle."

My head felt like it had been split open and baked in an oven. Pain radiated from every direction, my stomach and muscles staging their own revolt. I didn't remember taking the pills.

Then it hit me. The bone-deep, clawing, nausea-twisting, sweat-drenching *withdrawal feeling*. Oh, of course. Because why not compound smoke inhalation, dragging injuries, and overdosing with a full-on Narcan crash?

"No..." I rasped. "I've been clean. Fourteen months. I—" I stopped because my brain kept trying to make words while my stomach tried to murder me. "I wouldn't have just thrown it all away." With my left arm, I patted where my pocket should have been, in search of my sobriety medallion, but of course I had on one of those bougie hospital gowns and no sobriety medallion.

"Well, between the overdose and the five doses of Narcan it took to bring you back, I'm sure you're not feeling great."

Five. Holy cow. I wanted to laugh, then vomit, then laugh while vomiting. My elbow and lungs all agreed I could only pick two.

"But you're safe now," she said, misinterpreting my reaction.

Safe. Sure. I had a pulse. I had oxygen. I hadn't burnt to a crisp yet, but I'd just survived the perfect storm of bad decisions, heroic women, and chemical warfare in my own veins.

"Jenny... She's okay?" My voice cracked. Not from fear, though fear was there. From sheer disbelief that someone could be a saint and a masochist in the same act.

Amber's eyes softened. "She will be. I can't say much more, but she's alive, and so are you, thanks to her."

I exhaled as the tension in my stomach uncoiled. Then, to lighten the mood, I let out a bitter chuckle. "Well, that's one way to start the weekend."

She checked a monitor on her waistband. "I've gotta get this. Your call button is right there by your hand. If you need me, you know what to do." She did a couple of things with my IV, then said, "That should help you sleep for a while."

Sleep? I didn't want to sleep. My blinks got longer, my pain easing, my head swimming and floating at the same time. I opened my mouth to protest but nothing came out.

CHAPTER SIXTY-FOUR

I WAS BEING TREATED for shock, second-degree burns, cuts on my right arm, and severe smoke inhalation, but that wasn't what I was actually suffering from.

No one at the hospital would give me an update on Evan's status. They said it was against HIPAA. I whispered a voice text to Javi.

Me: Is he alive?

The phone vibrated a reply almost immediately.

Javi: Yes! Thanks to you, amiga!

Tears pricked my eyes, and I slouched back against the hospital bed. *He's alive.*

The TV played in the background, and various clips of the Parkland house burning to the ground ran throughout the day yesterday, along with variants of this script:

"This is what remains of Chapel of Dust frontman Evan Black's house in Beverly Hills. Details are still forthcoming, but here's what we know. Friday night, a 911 call was placed around eleven p.m. When authorities arrived on scene, the house was engulfed in flames. The cause of the fire is still under investigation, and Evan Black and Jenny Gentry, judges for *Singing Sensation* season 15, were both taken to the hospital."

The respiratory therapist that Kimball had hired also visited twice yesterday and once this morning, with a nebulizer and strict instructions not to talk unless necessary, and to wear my oxygen mask for the next two days. I could only remove it to sip water and eat—I'd taken in a lot of smoke.

But none of that mattered. What if Evan didn't make it? What if he was in a coma and never came out? What if I didn't get to him soon enough?

My hands and left arm were burned. Each one of my fingers was individually and completely wrapped except the fingertip of my ring finger on my right hand. They kept my arms elevated, and the bandages felt hot, but that was normal apparently.

Vince sat quietly in the corner, arms folded, brooding silently that we'd gone anywhere without security. I did a lot of staring. Out windows. At walls. At nothing.

And a lot of sleeping.

I hit the call button. The nurse came in a few minutes later.

"How can I help?"

I swallowed, glanced at Vince. "Is there any way I can go visit Evan?" I had to whisper, and my voice was muffled by the oxygen mask on my face.

Vince sat up.

"I think so. Let me check with his nurse. If they're okay with it, I'll bring a wheelchair in and we'll take you."

I nodded.

Vince came over and stood at the foot of my bed. "Are you sure about this?"

I quirked a brow in lieu of answering because it hurt less.

"We don't know what kind of shape he's in. We don't know how long he's been using. We don't know if he's been lying to you this whole time. As your bodyguard, it's my job to protect your body, but as your friend, it's my obligation to protect your heart."

It was too late for that.

I looked pointedly from one hand to the other.

He ran a hand through his hair, paced two steps one way and two steps back. "I'll support whatever you decide, but I think you should wait for all the facts before you run headlong into a relationship."

If only he knew.

I nodded anyway.

The nurse came back in with a wheelchair and a bright smile. "She said you can visit him, but he's currently resting."

Maybe that was better. My thoughts were reflected on Vince's face and the way the tension eased from his shoulders.

She helped drape a second hospital gown around behind me before easing me into the wheelchair. Then she transferred my IV to the pole attached to the wheelchair, positioned a portable oxygen tank on the back of the chair and hooked me up to it.

I felt like such an invalid not being able to do any of it for myself, but if I moved my fingers, even just a little, it felt like the skin was tearing, and it hurt. I was supposed to start occupational therapy tomorrow.

Vince stomped behind us like a raging bull, glaring in everyone's direction as we passed them on the way to the elevator. I hadn't even looked in a mirror to see if my hair was a mess or if I had any makeup left—or soot, for that matter.

We went down to the ICU floor, and my chest squeezed. Intensive care. I said another quick prayer that he would be okay. The nurse had said he was resting, not that he was unconscious. That had to be a good sign.

Evan's nurse met us at the elevator and escorted us to his room. Vince stood outside while the two women wheeled me in.

"Just let us know when you're done. You can press the call button right here on the bed."

I nodded. "Thank you."

Then they moved and I got my first look at Evan since the fire. He was asleep—or close to it. The monitors hummed, a slow rhythm of green lights and soft beeps. His left arm was strapped to his chest, wrapped so tightly it looked fragile. I tried to hold back my whimpering cry, hold back the pain tearing through my chest.

What if I hadn't been there? What if he had died? What if I had never told him about Axl? What if we'd just stayed home?

Beneath the blanket, I could see the thick dressing on his leg, the faint outline where the burns ended just below his knee.

He's alive. That's what matters. He can heal. But my heart ached because he had to go through this at all. All this pain, all this suffering, all the worry and the hurt.

I hadn't been ready for this.

Friday night, as we'd worked on our song, he'd been alive in a way that filled every corner of a room. Now, his skin looked too pale against the white sheets.

I wasn't supposed to talk. The respiratory therapist had repeated it every time he'd checked my oxygen.

"Your voice needs to rest," he'd said. Like silence could heal everything. That if I didn't rest my voice it would be damaged forever, and my career in music could be over. Evan's career could be over. One drug-fueled mistake could change the course of our lives forever.

Still, I found myself, breath caught behind my mask, wondering what words would even come if I broke the rule.

I leaned closer, careful not to bump the IV stand with my bandaged hands. The gauze made everything clumsy. I couldn't even tuck a loose strand of hair behind my ear.

He didn't stir. His chest rose and fell, shallow but steady.

A part of me wanted to touch him—just to prove to myself he was really here, still breathing—but my arms ached, and my palms couldn't bear even the thought of pressure. So I just sat there, watching the slow pulse on the monitor, the proof that he hadn't slipped away.

Then I let my thoughts touch on the one thing that I kept pushing away. He overdosed. Relapsed. He'd been trying to deal with the bomb I'd dropped about Axl. Maybe he'd been trying to forget. The thoughts looped like static in my head.

Would he relapse every time life got hard?

Was this what life with Evan would be like?

I leaned forward and pressed a kiss to the back of his hand, near the IV line that pumped fluids into him. Then I hit the call button with the back of a knuckle and had the nurses take me back to my room.

CHAPTER SIXTY-FIVE

NURSE AMBER TAPPED on the door like she was afraid I'd flatline if she knocked too hard. "Evan?"

"Still breathing," I croaked.

Javi chuckled from the corner. "With a voice like that, you don't sound like it, *amigo*."

I flipped him off.

Amber cleared her throat like she was waiting for naughty children to behave. "You have a visitor."

Carl walked in.

"Dad," I rasped, because it was either that or sob, and my throat was already on fire.

He didn't say a word, just crossed the room and folded me into one of those full-body, rib-crushing hugs that Hallmark would call "healing" and I'd call "a tactical mistake." My elbow screamed bloody murder, and my cannula popped out of my nose and poked me in the eye. But I figured he needed the hug more than I needed working lungs.

"I thought I'd lost you," he whispered, voice cracking in a way I hadn't heard since Mom's funeral.

I tried to find my usual brand of levity, but my voice sounded like a garbage disposal. "Takes more than fire and a few drugs to kill me."

He hiccupped a sob.

"Too soon?"

"Yeah," he said, still pressed against me.

When he finally pulled back, he wiped his eyes, embarrassed, like crying was a rookie move.

I adjusted my cannula with my good arm. "You here because you decided you can't live without me?"

He laughed, shaking his head. "More like I can't trust you not to set yourself on fire again. Your mom would haunt me if I didn't help you. So, yeah. I'm here. We'll figure it out. Sell the house in Nashville. Rent it. Whatever."

Amber popped her head in again. "The police are here to speak with you, if you're feeling up for it."

I glanced at my dad. He nodded. I shrugged. "Sure. Send them in."

Javi sat up. "Should we get your lawyer here?"

"Why? I have nothing to hide."

Two cops entered. One tall and wiry with a notepad, the other built like a refrigerator.

They stared at Javi and my dad until the latter stood. "I'll just go check what the cafeteria is serving for lunch."

"I'm not going anywhere," Javi announced, stubborn Puerto Rican that he was.

The cops turned their attention back to me.

"Mr. Black?" Notepad asked.

"That's what the bracelet says." I lifted my wrist. "Though it makes me sound like I'm seventy-five and getting my meds mixed up."

Neither laughed. Tough crowd.

"We just need to ask you a few questions about the other night."

"Sure. Nothing I love more than a police interrogation while I'm marinating in morphine."

I tried to rewind the tape in my mind. Static. Smoke. Jenny. Two pills. A white horse galloping down a hallway. So, just your average night. "Triptan. I had a killer migraine."

Notepad's eyes did the full skeptic salute. "So you don't remember taking fentanyl?"

The air rushed from my lungs. "I've been clean for fourteen months. I wasn't looking to break the streak." Or was I? Everything was a blur after I slumped onto that couch, except the cravings. I remembered those as clearly as this very second. Had I given in? Had Jenny's bomb been more than I could handle?

Fridgeman put a hand on his hip—which also happened to be on his gun. "Do you know how the fire started?"

"I don't remember," I whispered. "The last thing I remember was going up to the music room to go somewhere quiet and ride out my migraine."

The craving hit then, sharp and sudden, like someone whispering from the back of my skull: *just one line, one time.* My hands trembled. I bit the inside of my cheek hard enough to taste copper.

Notepad didn't notice. "So, you're saying you don't know."

"I'm saying maybe interrogate the guy who wasn't literally on fire."

He ignored that one. "One more question, and I hope you'll be honest this time..."

My guard snapped up. "You're batting zero so far, champ, but go ahead."

"What can you tell us about the two prescription bottles we found in your car's glovebox? They didn't have your name on them."

Oh, for f— Yeah, that one hurt.

"So they're yours?"

As a celebrity, I could get away with it. People expected the worst of me—of people who lived my lifestyle. Murphy on the other hand, a retired cop, would get dragged through the mud.

I nodded, because what was I gonna do? Rat out the guy I was supposed to be sponsoring? Might as well light his whole life on fire again.

Notepad scribbled. "We'll add that to your charges."

"Terrific," I muttered. "Maybe you can engrave it on the headstone too."

They left. I stared at the ceiling, half expecting tabloid photographers to burst through the vent like paparazzi ninjas.

Ten minutes later, the band stormed in like a pack of golden retrievers that had found a tennis ball.

"Evan!" Jimmy yelled, arms wide. "The guy with nine lives!"

Derek went for a high five, saw my sling, slapped his own hand instead. "Dude, the house is gone. Nothing left."

"If it destroyed your hideous Nickelback shirt, it was worth it."

The guys jeered and teased Derek.

Nolan dropped into the recliner. "Bro, my favorite guitar was in there."

"My drums are toast," Derek said. "Hope your insurance is baller."

Beckett chuckled. "I'm just glad Evan's alive."

"Barely," I rasped. *Thanks to Jenny.* Just thinking her name made my chest ache.

Beckett sat on the edge of the bed. "So, what happened?"

I sifted through the mental static. Two pills. Smoke. A gremlin. Nothing coherent. "No clue."

Derek, lacking both tact and volume control, blurted, "So you don't remember why you tried to kill yourself?"

Beckett smacked him.

"He didn't try to kill himself," Nolan said, glaring.

I rolled my eyes, but the words stuck like barbs.

Beckett leaned back. "You gotta miss it though, right? The rush?"

Jimmy smacked him this time. "Dude. Seriously?"

I didn't answer. Because yeah, maybe.

They stayed a bit longer—noise, jokes, the smell of burnt coffee. It should've grounded me, but when they left and the room went quiet again, the real noise started. The craving. The guilt. The whisper that promised peace if I'd just give in.

It'll pass.

It didn't.

Maybe that was what happened at Parkland house. Maybe I'd gone looking for silence. And found the loudest kind there was.

CHAPTER SIXTY-SIX

SOMEONE KNOCKED ON THE DOOR, and Vince leapt up. Two police officers stepped inside, calm, professional, like they did this every day.

"Miss Gentry, are you okay if we ask you some questions about the fire?"

I glanced at Vince for help. He pressed his lips together. "Does Miss Gentry need her lawyer?"

"Of course not," the bigger of the two men said. Barrel-chested, square-jawed, solid. If I ever read *barrel-chested* in a book again, I'd picture this man.

"Miss Gentry's voice is her career," Vince said coolly. "She's supposed to be resting it. Please keep it brief."

"Understood." The officer turned to me. "Can you tell me what time you got to the house on Parkland Drive?"

I hated that they were here. Hated that I had to talk. My throat burned, raw and tight. I pushed my oxygen mask aside just long enough to sip some room-temperature water—metallic from the paper cup—before settling it back in place.

I held up both hands, all fingers raised.

"Ten?"

I dropped two fingers, leaving three—pain shot through my hands, my skin tight and burning. I winced.

"Ten-thirty?"

I nodded.

"And you didn't get out of the car, is that correct?"

I shook my head. My voice rasped as I forced it out. "I got out. I didn't go inside until after the fire started."

"What time was that?" the shorter officer asked, notepad ready.

"Eleven," I whispered, because it hurt less than moving my fingers around.

"Then what happened?"

I glanced at Vince, silent apology in my eyes. Another sip of water. My voice came out like hushed gravel. "I ran to the front door, but I could already feel the heat, so I went around back. The door was locked, so I broke the glass and reached in." I lifted my arm, the one wrapped thick in bandages, the memory searing hotter than the burns. "I looked through the first floor, then ran upstairs. The smoke was thick. I found Evan in the music room."

I didn't have to close my eyes to see it—it was branded there. The blue of his lips. The empty prescription bottle beside him. The pills. The smell of smoke. The fire.

"Did you see what the prescription was for?" Notebook Cop asked.

I shook my head.

"Go on."

"I dragged him out through the backyard and started CPR."

After I'd put out the fire on his pant leg with my bare hands.

"Where was the band? Did anyone offer to help?"

I shook my head again. "They were high and drunk." The words tasted bitter.

Barrel-Chest's tone softened. "We have to ask this question because it's our job to explore all possibilities. Is there any reason Evan might want to take his own life? Was he upset about anything? How did he seem when he went into the house?"

My blood went cold. Goosebumps rippled over my bandaged arms, each one an echo of pain.

Was this my fault?

I'd dropped the biggest truth of our lives in his lap. Told him about Axl. And then what? He'd walked into that house alone.

"Jenny?" the officer prompted gently.

No. No, he wouldn't do that. He wouldn't use again. He'd been *so proud* of that stupid coin. Fourteen months clean. He rubbed it between his fingers like a prayer. "He was getting a migraine when we got there," I said. "He needed quiet."

I was grasping at straws, and we both knew it.

"Do you know what he took for migraines?"

"Triptan."

The two officers exchanged a glance. Shook their heads.

Something in my chest cracked open. "What does that mean?"

Barrel-Chest hesitated. "Do you know if anyone in the band would've wished him harm?"

I shook my head, but it was a lie. He was breaking up the band. Had he had a chance to do that yet? They could've all been in on it as far as I knew.

Notebook Cop scribbled something down.

Barrel-Chest rolled closer on his stool. His voice was careful now, almost kind. "Miss Gentry... What can you tell me about the narcotics found in the glovebox of Evan's Charger?"

My body went still. My heart stopped. "What?"

He repeated it slowly. "We found two bottles of narcotics in the glovebox. Neither of them had his name on it."

I blinked, waiting for the words to make sense. They didn't. They just hung there, heavy and impossible.

Evan wouldn't. He *wouldn't.*

Unless...

How long was your dad in recovery? Then he relapsed and tried to steal all that money from you. What if I relapse? What if I hurt you and Axl?

And I'd stupidly told him I was willing to take the risk.

I turned to Vince, my throat closing. "I didn't know," I whispered. And it was true. I hadn't known. Or maybe I hadn't wanted to.

All this time, I'd told myself I was protecting Evan—keeping Axl secret because I didn't want him growing up with a father who might relapse. Because Evan hadn't wanted kids anyway. Because I wanted to keep my son safe.

But now all I could think was that maybe, if I'd told him sooner...if I'd given him a reason to keep fighting...maybe he wouldn't have been alone in that house.

Tears burned my eyes. What a fool I was. I'd let my fear of the past write our ending.

I'd believed the medallion meant something. I'd believed *he* meant something.

I had to get out of this room. Out of this hospital. Away from these questions that scraped me raw.

"That's all the questions we have for you," Barrel-Chest said quietly.

But it wasn't. Not for me.

Not even close.

CHAPTER SIXTY-SEVEN

ON THE THIRD day in the hospital, they finally moved me out of the ICU and onto what they called a "regular floor." Regular, as in *you survived but still look like hell.*

The doctor came in with a smile that didn't quite make it past his Botox. Guy was probably in his forties, but his forehead hadn't gotten the memo.

"Evan, let's talk about pain management."

I nodded, because what else was I gonna do?

"We've been using opioids," he said, like he was confessing a sin, "but with your history, I feel very strongly we should move to something less addictive sooner rather than later. If it's too painful, we'll go back to the stronger stuff for another day or two, okay?"

"Okay."

"Excellent." He typed something on the computer, probably noting *Patient compliant, delusional, still moderately attractive despite burns.* "Amber will transfer you down to the PCU. We'd like to move one of your nurses with you, to help with the transition and protect your privacy. Would she be a good option?"

"Yeah, the pixie's good."

He cracked a smile. "Great. If you keep progressing like this, I think we can release you in four days or so. Sound good?"

"Yup."

"How's respiratory therapy been? You like your therapist?"

I nodded again. I was basically a bobblehead with a pulse.

"Good. Any questions?"

So many, but none he had the answers to. "Nope."

"Perfect. Let's change that bandage one last time."

He rewashed his hands just as Amber walked in—the only nurse I could stand. They started peeling the bandage off my leg.

And by *peeling*, I meant *ripping out every hair one by one while my soul left my body.*

Honestly, it hurt more than the burn itself.

When the bandage finally came off, I got my first real look at the damage. "Look" being generous.

My leg was...a horror show. A patchwork of pinks and browns and angry reds, like some deranged artist had tried to paint emotion and then set it on fire. The burns ran from my ankle to my knee—a roadmap straight to hell.

Amber had said "mostly second-degree," which I now understood to mean *medium-rare human.* I'd never look at a steak again without flinching.

The skin had a strange waxy sheen, like someone poured hot caramel over me and dropped a grenade on top for fun. My stomach twisted. My head spun. I looked like a science experiment gone wrong, and not even the cool kind.

Once they'd mummified me again, I let out a breath that could've been mistaken for gratitude.

Amber and another nurse wheeled me toward the elevators. A couple people in the hallway snapped pictures, because apparently "charred rock star on a gurney" was trending material now. I tried not to look as dead as I felt.

My new room had a stunning view of a rooftop AC unit and the corner of the parking lot. Five stars.

Amber dimmed the lights. "You should get some rest."

Since the *incident*—if that was what we were calling it—I'd done nothing *but* sleep. Still, my eyelids drooped. "Am I allowed to go see Jenny when I wake up?"

She hesitated. "I'll see what I can do."

Translation: *Probably not, but I don't want you to cry again.*

She turned on the TV, muted the volume, flipped through channels. Every headline had my name in it: *Evan Black Overdoses, Drugs Found in Car, House Fire Mystery.*

She turned the TV off fast. "Maybe just try to sleep."

Yeah. Sleep sounded great. Forgetting sounded better.

I woke up to a knock.

Before I could answer, Kimball and Gio strode in.

Gio carried a massive bouquet of flowers, because nothing says *Sorry you almost died* like pollen and a tacky ribbon.

"Hey, Evan," Kimball said, expression hovering somewhere adjacent to genuine concern. "How are you feeling?"

I lifted my elbow a few inches, pain lancing through my ribs. "I've been better." My voice was hoarse, scratchy. I coughed to prove my point.

He took the doctor's chair and wheeled closer. "Save your voice. I'll just ask yes-or-no questions. Jenny has severe smoke inhalation and inflammation in her trachea. We're pausing the show for three weeks, but that's as far as we can push it. She's got a respiratory therapist seeing her twice a day. Singing is out for now."

I nodded.

"Do you think you can find someone to sing your part of the song in the finale?"

"Like a friend?" I could probably get Aiden to do it, but it would be weird with his twang.

"Someone from the top ten—Colton, Joey, Milo. Let me know by the end of the week."

I croaked, "How's Jenny?"

He froze, glanced at Gio. "She flew back to Montana yesterday. I haven't seen her."

My chest tightened—not from smoke this time.

She left.

I tried not to react, to stay positive. But why would she leave without saying goodbye? Without checking on me?

"Get me your pick by the end of the week." He left before I could process that my heart had just been quietly sawed in half.

Jenny had run. Again. And this time, I wasn't sure I blamed her.

I stared at the wall, the beeping monitor, the blank spot where my life used to be.

She'd taken Axl too—our son. The family I hadn't gotten a chance to fight for.

I didn't remember what happened that night. Everything after she told me the truth was a blur—static in my brain. I'd gone to the house. Let myself in. A migraine. Then...nothing.

Why would I take drugs? Why would I risk losing her and him after fighting so hard to stay clean?

I needed answers.

I pulled out my phone, searched for her name on Google.

There she was. Everywhere.

Jenny, her face streaked with soot and tears. Jenny, crying as they wheeled me out. Jenny in an ambulance, oxygen mask on. Jenny, boarding a plane, her eyes puffy and red.

I called her.

Voicemail.

Called again.

Voicemail.

Texted.

> Me: How's Montana? We should talk. Can you call me?

Nothing.

I texted Kellan.

I stared at the blank spot where three dots should be. They never came. And the room felt smaller than it was.

THE DOOR OPENED, and the band shuffled in—Beckett, Nolan, Jimmy, and Derek. The tension came in with them, thick enough to taste.

Beckett spoke first. "How you doing?"

I gave him a thumbs-up, studying their faces. Nolan stood apart from him, arms crossed.

"We were all pretty high that night," Beckett said.

Well, there's a headline.

Nolan's tone was sharp. "Yeah, it was a wild night."

There was something in Beckett's eyes: desperation. And in Nolan's: disgust.

"I'm just saying things happened by accident," Beckett muttered.

"Like the fire?" Nolan asked.

My stomach tightened. The air between them crackled.

I whispered, "What's going on?"

Derek stepped forward like a human shield. Nolan pointed at Beckett. "Tell him. Tell him what's going on."

Beckett's jaw flexed. "It was an accident."

Nolan laughed—cold and humorless. "I heard you on the phone with Trish. It wasn't an accident."

My blood went cold. "What?"

Before Nolan could answer, Beckett lunged at him.

Chaos exploded, fists flying, the nurse-call button mashed, Derek tackling Beckett, Jimmy shouting, Nolan bleeding from the mouth.

Amber and Murphy burst in just in time to hear Nolan spit, "He told Trish you were leaving the band, so he took matters into his own hands. He said something about how dead rock stars sold more albums and how the band would be notorious after this..."

Amber gasped and ran for help.

Beckett shoved Derek into me, sending white-hot pain ripping through every inch of my body. I screamed.

Murphy grabbed Beckett and put him on the ground, forcefully.

Security arrived, looking like they'd just jogged from a retirement home. Ryan stormed in behind them, and within seconds, Beckett was cuffed and screaming.

Then they were gone—Murphy and Ryan making sure they left. The room was quiet again, except for the beeping monitors and my pulse pounding in my ears.

Amber reappeared, eyes wide. "Are you okay?"

I shook my head. My newly wrapped leg had blood and pus oozing out of the bandages.

She sighed, eyeing it. "I'll grab the doctor."

When she left, the silence pressed down.

Beckett had tried to kill me.

And all I could think was: *Of course he did.* Because that was what happened when people got to know me. I was wholly unworthy of love.

A ghost of a memory flickered—Beckett handing me a bottle of pills. His voice, oddly gentle. I'd thought he was trying to be kind. Turned out, he was just making murder cozy.

A hollow opened inside me, familiar, endless. The same one left by every person who'd decided I wasn't worth the trouble.

Jenny. My birth mother. My band.

I'd fought so damn hard to stay clean. To be better. To be the man Jenny and Axl deserved. And what did it get me? A near-death experience and another lesson in disappointment.

Would I ever be enough? Would anyone ever stay?

I hit the call button. Amber came back. "Are you okay? The doctor did say I could give you the good stuff if you needed it."

The good stuff.

Man, I wanted it.

I could almost taste it. That floating, untethered feeling where everything went quiet. No pain. No guilt. No voices whispering that I wasn't enough.

One word and I could have peace.

Just one.

Then Axl's face flashed through my mind and the craving ebbed.

"No, thanks."

CHAPTER SIXTY-EIGHT

THE MORNING after we arrived at my house in Montana, Axl cried and tugged on my shirt. "Hold you," he sobbed again and again.

I looked down at my bandaged hands and swallowed the ache rising in my throat. I wanted to hold him. I wanted to hold him more than I needed air. But I couldn't. Having him this close and still being unable to touch him—to feel the weight of him, the warmth of his cheek pressed against mine—hurt in a way no doctor could treat.

I couldn't even explain why. Couldn't whisper a single word to soothe him.

Dylan rushed from the bathroom, drying her hands. "Hey, Axl, come see Auntie Bean." Dylan and Aiden flew in the same day I did, and Dylan had been here helping with Axl.

She scooped him up, his tiny hands still reaching for me, and held him to her chest. The sight of it split something inside my body.

An ocean of inadequacy crashed through me, pulling me under before I could take a breath. I couldn't do anything. What kind of mother couldn't take care of her own child?

The front door burst open. Mom stumbled in, tears streaking her face.

"Jenny! I just ran into Beverly Dixon at the grocers, and she showed me this story on social media…" She held out her phone, crying, and scrolled to a video. I leaned closer despite myself.

It was about me. News of Evan's band breaking up had hit the news waves.

The comments burned into my brain, one by one:

She's bad for Evan Black.

He wouldn't have relapsed if she'd just stayed away.

If he'd died, it would've been her fault.

Someone even threatened to hunt me down and make me pay. Thousands of people had liked the comment.

They were calling me *Yoko 2.0*.

Alli and my PR team had kept these headlines from me for a reason. Because now that I'd seen it, I couldn't unsee it.

I jerked back like I'd been slapped. Pain tore through my arms, tugging at the stitches and burns until I gasped and tears streamed down my cheeks.

"What's wrong?" Mom asked, startled.

I shook my head. Put a trembling hand to my mouth to try to hold back the anguish.

Of course it was my fault. He'd been sober for nearly fourteen months. After three months with me, he relapsed. What did that say about me? About the kind of chaos I brought into people's lives?

She kept talking, but I couldn't hear her. My ears were ringing. I turned and ran upstairs, kicking my bedroom door closed behind me.

I didn't need to be liked—but maybe I had liked it. Maybe I'd built my entire life on the soft hum of approval. Knowing that my songs had meant something to someone. Knowing that I could take care of my mom, my dad, Axl, my employees, my band… I'd done everything I could to make their lives better.

But this? This was a different kind of spotlight. This was fire.

Did people actually hate me? Wish me harm?

I lowered myself carefully onto the bed, every motion a slow negotiation with pain. I couldn't even flop dramatically like a normal person.

I felt so helpless.

Who was I really? The woman who had "ruined" Evan Black. The daughter who'd been conned by her own father. A walking cautionary tale.

A loser.

I screamed—loud, guttural, animal. The sound ripped my throat raw before I choked it off and buried my face in the pillow. The pain was so sharp it felt like punishment.

Footsteps thundered up the stairs. Vince burst through the door like he was ready for a fight. "Jenny! What happened?"

I couldn't answer. The sobs came out broken, half-whimpers, half-gasps.

He crossed the room and sat beside me, easing me upright, careful of the bandages. His arm came around my shoulders, solid and warm. "Hey, hey. It's okay. You're okay." He pressed his temple to mine, gentle as a prayer. "You'll recover. You'll be as good as new."

I shook my head, tears soaking through his shirt.

What did that even mean? *Good as new.* Was the old Jenny even good enough? I'd let everyone down.

He kept rocking me, murmuring words I barely heard.

But all I could think was—what if I didn't recover? What if I'd destroyed my voice for good? What if I never sang again? Never stood under the lights, never lost myself in music, never hummed a lullaby to Axl in the dark?

I cried harder.

What if I never saw Evan again? What if I never kissed him again? Felt his touch? What if it really was my fault he turned to drugs? Again.

"The pain won't last forever," Vince whispered.

But some pains didn't heal—they just became part of you.

CHAPTER SIXTY-NINE

"I'M CHECKING OUT," I rasped at Amber. My voice sounded like I'd gargled sandpaper.

She didn't even blink. "You can't."

I yanked the IV out of my arm and flung it toward the stand. "Watch me."

She laughed but then gave me the nurse look—the one that said she'd dealt with a thousand idiots just like me, and I was still her favorite brand of trouble. She grabbed a packet from a drawer and handed it to me. "Evan, you're getting blood everywhere. It's important you listen to the doctors. I know I don't look like it, but I'm a fan of your music. I'd like you to keep those pipes for a while."

"Yeah, me too." I took the gauze packet from her hand and opened it, applying pressure to the crook of my arm where a small geyser of blood was erupting. Then I gulped a long drink of water to keep from coughing up a lung.

But I couldn't stay. Not here. Not when every beep and sterile whiff of antiseptic made my skin itch for an escape hatch.

"Give me the painkillers," I said.

Her brow lifted. "Bad idea."

"Yup. But if you don't let me leave, I'll request them and no one will ever hear me sing again."

Now both eyebrows went up, twin question marks of disbelief. "Are you blackmailing me so I'll let you leave?"

I grinned. "Yes, ma'am. Where are my clothes?"

Amber sighed, like she'd been hoping I wouldn't ask that question and pulled a white hospital bag from under the bed.

The shirt that used to be gray was now soot-black. The pants looked like they'd been through a barbecue and lost. Especially the left leg, which had apparently volunteered as kindling.

I dug into the pocket and came up empty. My sobriety medallion was gone. My hands shook like I'd just come off stage. "It's gone."

"What is?"

"My sobriety medallion."

While I sat there trying to remember how to breathe, Amber wordlessly started wrapping my arm in blue coban. Then she went to the sink, came back with a damp cloth, and gently wiped the soot off my hands.

It was such a small thing, but it hit me hard—that simple act of care. The smell of ash, the sting of air, the reminder that I was still here. Still breathing. Because of Jenny. Because of her love. Because of Axl. They were my sobriety medallion. They were what I would hold onto.

I clung to *Stay, Van* and *Hold you.* I clung to the memory of Jenny's lips on mine. The signed guitar she'd gifted me. The belief she'd shown in me.

Amber was just finishing when the door opened, and Kellan came in like a man on a mission.

And I lost it.

Just—gone. Tears, snot, the whole pathetic waterfall.

He didn't say a word, just hauled me into a hug.

"Ow," I mumbled into his shoulder.

He huffed a laugh that was mostly pain. "I've been off grid for a week. Just heard. I'm sorry I wasn't here sooner. You've been through hell, man."

I nodded, still choking on everything I couldn't say.

He crouched so we were eye-level, one hand gripping the back of my neck. "You okay? Hanging in there?"

I shook my head. Not even close.

"You're stronger than you think," he said quietly. "This—this is a moment. One minute at a time. And listen to me: you didn't relapse. You didn't *choose* it. Ryan said someone slipped that crap to you."

Yeah, but tell that to the cravings screaming in my bloodstream. Fourteen months clean and suddenly my body was begging for another hit. Like all the work I'd done didn't mean jack.

My hands trembled. Pain spiked up my arm.

HE SOFTENED. "EVAN. LOOK AT ME."

I didn't want to. Didn't want him to see the mess. But I finally dragged my eyes up.

"You. Are. Enough," he said. That hit like a punch to the ribs. I flinched, the nasal cannula tugging. "You've got people who care about you. I'm one of them. And I hope you'll be one too."

My throat closed up. I swallowed and nodded.

He stuck out his hand, and I shook it.

"Now," he said, squeezing once, "let's figure out how to fix this."

"Okay," I croaked.

"Okay," he echoed, like that word could hold up the world.

Amber got a new IV kit from the cupboard. "Let's get you hooked back up, shall we?"

"CAN I get some paper and a pen?" I asked Javi later.

While he was gone, Ryan settled into the seat across the room.

"Where's Murphy?"

"Around," Ryan said.

I nodded.

When Javi returned, Ryan gave me a nod and left the room. As the door closed, I saw him settling into a chair across the hall.

Writing was how I bled without making a mess. How I processed everything that happened to me. I stared at the blank page. All I could see was darkness. Smoke. Silence so sharp it could cut skin. I remembered thinking—*this is it. This is how it ends*. With ashes.

I started to write:

> *I don't remember the flame, just the dark,*
> *The weight in my chest, the silence sharp.*
> *I thought that was it, no one left to care,*
> *Just smoke in my lungs, just ashes and air.*

Ashes and air.

That was what it came down to.

But I wanted this to be a thank you. A breath-for-breath kind of gratitude. Jenny had given me CPR. She'd dragged me out of the fire and back into life—even after everything I'd done.

I wrote:

> *But you pulled me out when I was already*
>   *gone,*
> *Gave me breath I could never deserve to*
>   *breathe on.*
> *I'm still here because you were there,*
> *Ashes and air...ashes and air.*

Every word hurt, but in a good way. The kind of ache that meant healing was possible.

Then came the bridge. I didn't want this song to trap her in some guilt trip. She didn't owe me anything. She had Axl. She had a life. I just wanted her to know I knew the score.

> *I'm not begging you to believe in me.*

I won't deceive. I am what you see.
I'm just saying this breath is borrowed
from you.
And every beat of my heart says it's true.

I stared at the page. My elbow throbbed. No guitar. No way to test the melody.

"Dammit," I muttered.

Guess I needed backup.

CHAPTER SEVENTY

ZANE SHOWED up the next day, bright-eyed and over-caffeinated, like a puppy that could also shred on guitar.

I'd put *Ashes and Air* to music, but I needed to hear it out loud to know if it actually worked—or if I'd just written something that should be set on fire along with my house.

He perched on the rolling stool and started picking through my notes, humming softly. The kid hit the chorus, paused, changed a chord, changed a word, and somehow made it *better*. Disgusting. Truly offensive levels of talent.

I nodded along while making edits one-handed, pretending it didn't bother me that a twenty-year-old was casually rewriting my emotional trauma into a chart-topper.

When he stopped to take a drink, he leaned on his guitar and met my eye. "Can I sing this for the finale?"

My gut said yes, but I shook my head.

"Why not?"

"Kimball." That one word explained everything from global warming to why musicians drank.

Zane grinned. "If I can get Kimball to approve it?"

Kid had guts. I nodded.

He stayed for hours—through physical therapy, breathing

treatments, a nurse shift change, and one very awkward sponge bath—for me, not him. By the time he finally packed up, the song was perfect. Too perfect.

It didn't feel like *my* song anymore. I'd written the bones, but he'd given it soul. The kind of soul that reminded me why I used to love music before it tried to kill me.

DAD CAME by the next morning, holding a clipboard like it was a weapon. "I'm going to start the insurance process with your house, okay?"

"Sounds good." My throat was feeling a little better, but I was still supposed to speak sparingly.

"Do you want to rebuild, or...what's your plan?"

What *was* my plan? Jenny's face flashed in my mind—her Pinterest board of dream houses, the way she lit up when she talked about space for Axl to run. "I need an architect," I said.

"I can handle that. We can make it just like it was."

I shook my head.

"No?"

Shake again.

He studied me. "Okay. I'll get you an architect. You have a plan?"

I nodded.

He smiled, like he thought that meant "logical blueprint." It didn't. It meant *Jenny*.

AMBER CRIED when they discharged me. We took pictures, I signed autographs for her sons, and she gave me the kind of look nurses gave idiots they'd grown fond of despite their better judgment. My arm was still in a sling, there were bandages on my leg, but I could hobble around without blacking out from the pain, and that was good enough for me.

"Take care of yourself, Evan—and that girl you love."

I froze.

She smirked. "Please. I've been watching *Singing Sensation*. You're not subtle."

Busted.

I hugged her one last time before she insisted on treating me like an invalid, forcing me into a wheelchair and pushing me through the automatic doors into a wall of paparazzi flashbulbs. I smiled, but it felt forced. I raised my good arm in a wave.

Murphy and Ryan flanked me like bodyguards with anger issues.

"Good to see you alive," a reporter shouted.

"Good to *be* alive," I croaked, sounding like an eighty-year-old smoker as I gingerly climbed into the SUV.

Murphy got in beside me, staring holes into the side of my head. "Got a minute to talk when we get back?"

I nodded. He'd been basically avoiding me in the hospital, only coming in when he absolutely had to.

"Good. I've got a lot to say."

I nodded again. Communication level: mime.

"Can we drive past the Parkland house?" I asked.

Ryan met my eyes in the mirror. "Absolutely."

The guys talked on the drive, but when the gate opened and the wreckage came into view, the car went dead quiet.

The lawn was too perfect. The hedges trimmed within an inch of their lives. And in the middle of it—rubble wrapped in yellow tape, a crime scene from a life I'd burned to the ground.

I stepped out alone. The others hung back, letting me haunt the place in peace.

The pool was black, a layer of ash and debris floating on top. The patio—where they'd done CPR on me—looked eerily normal.

I glanced at the tree where I'd first told Jenny I loved her all those years ago. Still standing. Thank heavens.

I could picture it—Axl's treehouse up there. A pirate ship with a rope bridge. A swing. Maybe a gazebo with a hot tub where Axl would sneak his first girlfriend and I'd pretend I didn't notice.

Hope, dangerous and stupid, warmed my chest. Kellan said my worth wasn't tied to other people—but he was wrong. Jenny was the one person it *did* depend on.

If she could see this house—this life—I wanted to build for her, maybe she'd see *me* too.

I plucked a leaf from the tree, held it like a promise, and walked back to the SUV.

WHEN WE GOT HOME, Murphy followed me into the kitchen. He hovered like a nervous dad about to give "the talk."

"You shouldn't've done that," he started. "Takin' the blame for my pills in your glovebox."

I raised my good hand. "Stop."

"I mean it, lad. 'Tisn't right, and ya know it."

I shrugged my good shoulder. Translation: too late. Deal with it. "I like having you around. This was the only way to keep you."

He chuckled, half laugh, half sob. "I appreciate ya more than you'll ever know."

I smiled at him—my version of *you're welcome. Now shut up before we both cry.*

This was what friends did. We covered for each other. If it meant taking a fine for Murphy so he didn't go to jail or relapse, then so be it. The paperwork could list my name; the guilt didn't.

I held out my hand. Murphy took it. A silent promise passed between us—brothers in bad decisions and good intentions.

BACK HOME IN my music room, Jenny's guitar waited. The one she'd given me when she still believed I could be someone worth believing in.

I ran a hand down the neck, the way you touched something sacred. She'd trusted me with her heart—and with Axl's. I'd dropped both. But maybe I could rebuild.

I sat at the piano, fingers hovering. "Every Thought" sat on the stand, sheet creased, notes smudged. I played through it one-handed. It needed a verse for her.

Javi came in mid-song and dropped onto the couch. "Your dad invited the architect. Twenty minutes."

I gave him a thumbs-up.

He frowned. "I know you're not supposed to talk very much, but you're *really* quiet. You okay?"

I smiled. "I'm okay," I rasped. Lie-adjacent.

I ran one more chord and looked around the room. Every instrument, every lyric, every mistake—pieces of me I was still trying to glue together.

Time to build Jenny her happy place.

I wasn't an artist—at least not one whose stick figures didn't look like crime scenes—but when the architect arrived, I showed him everything I'd been imagining. Jenny's dream house. Axl's treehouse. The pirate ship, the hot tub gazebo, the wildflowers, and definitely a coffee bar where she could make whatever kind of sludge made her heart happy.

It was a flurry of nods and scribbles and pointing. I tried to explain the kind of place where happiness could maybe, possibly, live again.

When he left, he promised to design something "she'd love."

I nodded, pretending not to notice the ache in my chest when he said *she*.

Because that was the problem.

I didn't just want her to love the house.

I wanted her to love the man who came with it.

CHAPTER SEVENTY-ONE

THE MATTRESS DIPPED BESIDE ME, and Alli whispered, "Jenny?"

I cracked open my eyes.

Then her phone was in my face.

I blinked, trying to get my sleepy eyes to focus.

The headline hit me first: *Beckett Jones, bassist for Chapel of Dust arrested for the attempted murder of lead singer, Evan Black.*

I blinked hard, reading the smaller print, the words swimming and reforming. *The band alleges Jones intentionally substituted fentanyl for triptan, nearly killing frontman Evan Black.*

Chills crawled up my skin, like every nerve had woken up all at once. My throat burned, eyes stung. I took the phone from her with ginger, shaking fingers, careful not to tug the cannula from my nose as I pushed myself upright.

What?

My brain tried to piece it together. It meant Evan hadn't intentionally relapsed. He hadn't been running from being a father. He'd just been trying to treat a headache.

A sob clawed up, small but sharp. But then—why the prescriptions in his glovebox?

My head shook. Relief tangled with suspicion, refusing to

settle. This changed everything and nothing. He hadn't tried to relapse—but the drugs were still there. It meant he would've used, sooner or later.

A memory flashed, too vivid, too cruel. Evan sprawled unconscious on the couch, flames casting ominous shadows across his face and an empty pill bottle on the carpet beside him. I felt that same drop in my gut now—the helplessness, the ache of loving someone you couldn't save.

I CHOSE Maisie to sing "Every Thought." Her tone carried that ache I could never fake. And she deserved a second chance.

Colby picked her up from the airport. She walked into my house like it was a museum—wide eyes, open mouth, touching things like they might break. The platinum records, the awards, the ghosts of all the things I'd done right and wrong.

We went into the music room. She sat at the piano, fingers hovering before she began to play, humming softly along.

"This is a duet?" she asked.

I nodded, pointed to the first verse, then to her. Second— shook my head. Third—nodded again.

"So, first and third for me?"

Another nod.

She started to sing, her voice spilling into the air like it belonged there. But even as she filled the space, I heard the absence—the missing weight of a male voice.

Then Axl came tearing in, tiny feet thumping against hardwood, Colby chasing behind him.

"Colby!" I called, or tried to, my voice a whisper of its former self.

He looked over, and I nodded toward the piano.

Maisie grinned. "I think she wants you to sing the tenor parts."

I nodded, wanting to clap, but stopped myself before I tore

anything in my still-healing hands. The OT said I was improving, but every motion still came with a warning flare of pain.

Colby leaned over the piano and started to sing. It took about ten seconds for my heart to forget how to beat properly. I hadn't heard him sing since he was a kid, voice still changing—and now it was warm and strong and heartbreakingly good.

By the time they hit the last verse together, I was wrecked. Maisie's harmony lifted under his, and something inside me just... split open.

Maisie turned to him, eyes wide. "My goodness! You're so good! Why didn't you audition for *Singing Sensation?* You're way better than Troy."

Colby's smile tightened. "I'm not cut out for that life."

She looked to me, incredulous.

They sang again. I hit record on his phone without telling him and sent it to Dylan. Her heart-eyed smiley face reply came quick.

I sat back, Axl climbing into my lap, his little hand pointing to my arm. "Mommy's owies?"

I nodded.

He kissed it, soft and serious. My throat caught. I pressed my lips to the top of his head and breathed him in—baby shampoo, applesauce, sunshine.

Alli opened the door. One look at her face, and my heart dropped. She jerked her chin toward the hallway.

Vince stood outside, arms folded, jaw tight.

Alli pressed her palm over the receiver of her phone. "It's your dad."

My stomach turned. I took the phone; it stung to hold it.

Vince's voice softened. "You're not supposed to talk. I'll take it."

I shook my head.

He hesitated, then said, "I'll only say what you want me to."

Alli slipped out, bless her.

I studied Vince's face—steady, patient, no judgment—and finally handed him the phone.

He put it on speaker. "Hey, David. Jenny can't talk. What do you want?"

"What makes you think I want anything?"

Vince cut me a look. I gave a tiny shrug.

"What can I do for you then?" His tone was pure steel.

"They set my bail at two hundred thousand. Thought maybe she could help me out. Just this once."

Vince's knuckles went white. "You're joking."

"This is the last time. I promise."

Vince's voice cracked open, sharp and controlled. "So you're calling—not to ask if she's alive, not to check if she's okay—but for money? To bail you out, after *you* tried to defraud her? That's what you're doing?"

The words hit like a slap. Hearing them spoken made the truth in them hurt worse. My father wasn't calling about *me*. He never had.

Heat rose behind my eyes, shame mixing with fury. Vince had seen me bend myself into knots for years—trying to be the good daughter, the good artist, the good everything. He'd never said much, but he'd seen it. And now I saw it too.

Evan was right. I didn't need to keep twisting myself to fit other people's needs. Perfection was a myth, and I'd bled myself dry chasing it.

"Hello?" Dad said. "You there?"

"No," I whispered.

He laughed. "What do you mean, no? You're there."

"She means," Vince said evenly, "she's not giving you a cent."

I took the phone back. My hands trembled, my throat scorched, but my voice—what was left of it—held steady.

"You have an addiction," I rasped. "And the only way past it is through it. Deal with the consequences."

"Evan Black had an addiction," he shot back. "And you gave *him* a second chance."

A guard's voice echoed in the background. "One minute warning, inmate."

My pulse hammered. How dare he compare himself to Evan?

Evan had fought. He'd owned his damage. My father only weaponized his.

I looked at Vince. His eyes told me what I already knew.

I pressed the phone to my ear. "Dad," I said, voice raw but sure. "I'm cutting you off. Don't call me again."

Then I hung up.

The silence that followed was almost holy. I pressed a trembling hand to my mouth. My body shook, but it wasn't fear—it was release. The weight that had sat on me since childhood was gone.

I wasn't just *saying* I was done this time. I *was*.

Vince left me in the hallway, and I stood, thinking about Dad's addiction, about Evan's, about the fire. About my life and all the mistakes I'd made. Evan had been right about me. About how I'd stood up for Katarina and Maisie while letting them degrade me. If I hadn't eaten a big meal that night, if I'd still been starving myself, would I have even had the energy and muscles to pull Evan out of the fire?

This body, this wonderful, scarred, imperfect body had saved the man I loved. Had saved me. It would never look the same again, but dang it, it had given me all I'd ever needed. I'd probably never pose in a bikini on the cover of *Fashionista* or do another Dior commercial. My burned skin would be considered ugly by the entertainment industry. But if given the chance, I'd run into a burning building again to save him.

evan

HAPPY PLACE, *happy place. Go to your happy place, Evan.*

Rain pounded the airplane windows like the universe was personally offended by my existence.

This was it. My own personal hell.

The plane lurched, the metal bird equivalent of a drunken albatross with vertigo. I gripped the armrest tight enough to convince myself I was in control. *Which, let's be honest, was adorable.*

Breathe.

The blueprints rattled in the tube beside me, bumping my leg like they were mocking me. *The happy place I'm going to build for Jenny. Assuming I survive long enough to pour a damn foundation.*

Another jolt. Murphy swore in Gaelic—or possibly summoned Satan, hard to tell with the accent—and clutched his seat like a man auditioning for an ejector test.

We were gonna die. No question.

I closed my eyes. *Jenny.*

Her name hit first—clean, solid. A single note cutting through static. I clung to it. Tried to picture her face, and the panic dimmed around the edges.

Her laugh. That low hum she made when she was happy, like

a secret melody she didn't know she was singing. The world outside could fall apart, and Jenny would still find the right note. She always did.

I matched my breathing to that rhythm—her hum, not the engines. Hers was steady. Theirs...not so much.

"Notebook," I said, reaching under the seat.

Murphy grabbed the bag. "What d'ye need?"

"Notebook."

He found it and slapped it into my lap. I pulled the pen from the spine, flipped it open. My hands shook hard enough to make the words stutter.

A verse. A bridge. Something to trick my brain into thinking it was somewhere safer.

When the world crashes, I find my peace—

Nope. Scribble, scribble. *Find alternative.* Probably shouldn't tempt fate with "crashes" at twenty thousand feet.

When the world— Blank. Damn, my head hurt. *I still find peace.* Or perhaps, *In your arms I can make the insanity cease.*

Jenny's hand, the one that held mine after everything fell apart. That tether back to reality. I wrote faster.

You are my harbor, my home, my space.

A picture rose—her head in my lap, Axl playing in his treehouse, sunlight flickering through leaves. My chest tightened.

My heart has settled—this is my happy place.

A smile tugged at my mouth. It wasn't perfect, but close. Close enough to survive on.

I thought of the photos—her getting on the plane, bandages on her arm. Guilt sliced through the calm I'd just built. I scribbled again.

Through every scar, through every fire,
You're the calm, my heart's desire.
No. Too much Hallmark, not enough *me*. I
    crossed it out.
Through every scar, through every fight,
You're the calm that brings me light.

Better. Less like a poem, more like truth.

I lost myself, but now I see,
I'm exactly where I'm meant to be.

My chin trembled. I wanted to sing it to her. Or hand it to her. Something. Anything. What if she didn't believe me? What if she said no? What if she looked me in the eye and told me I couldn't be in Axl's life?

That thought hollowed me out from the inside.

My mind went to the blueprints. The architect had labeled everything like it was already ours. *Axl's treehouse. Axl's music room. Axl's fireman pole. Axl's pirate ship.*

Each one a promise. Each one a maybe.

Another burst of turbulence hit, and I gritted my teeth, forced the air out slow.

Breathe, Evan.

If we went down, at least I'd die doing what I did best—writing bad poetry under extreme stress.

CHAPTER SEVENTY-THREE

ALLI BROUGHT me the form to add Evan to Axl's birth certificate this morning, and I'd been staring at it ever since. Technically, I wasn't filling it out. Alli would have to do that for me, but the decision still felt like mine alone.

Yes, Evan had been drugged. That part wasn't in question. But the prescriptions in his glovebox... That was the part that stuck in my throat. The part that whispered, *Don't be stupid twice, Jenny.*

I sat on the fence so long it started to hurt.

The same rationalization from the night of the overdose crept back in. *Maybe this gesture will help him find courage. Maybe it's the thing that finally tips the scale.*

Thunder grumbled low outside, a sound that settled somewhere behind my ribs. The rain was relentless, streaming down the window so hard it blurred the garden into a watercolor smear. Poor Alli. I shouldn't have sent her out in this weather.

Still, storms always had this strange pull on me. They destroyed, but then they gave the world back, washed clean. Afterward, everything felt new. Grass glistening, puddles pooling in flowerbeds, the air smelling like rebirth. Montana air after a storm was the closest thing I had to religion.

The intercom buzzed. I ignored it. Probably one of the medical staff coming to check my bandages again. My arm had started to itch, which I told myself was a good sign—healing always itched before it hurt again.

Thirty-seven stitches on the outside. I didn't ask about the inside ones.

I flexed my fingers, touching thumb to fingertip, one by one—slow, careful, like I was defusing a bomb. My OT always made me close my eyes when she changed the bandages, which told me everything I needed to know about what lay underneath. If I couldn't look, I probably didn't want to. One glimpse of my left arm had been enough to not even question her.

Humility. That was what this was supposed to teach me. I'd been the caretaker for so long, the one who had it together. And now? I couldn't brush my teeth. Couldn't button a shirt. Couldn't... *Well, let's just say independence had left the building.* I'd never realized how much pride I carried in silence until I had to ask my mother to help me put on socks.

The door creaked open behind me.

I turned, half expecting Alli. But it wasn't her.

Evan stood in the doorway, rain dripping from his hair, eyes locking on mine like a punch to the chest. Every emotion I'd spent days trying to bury came roaring back to life. His gaze flicked from my face to my arms, to my bandaged hands, then back up again. His eyes were glassy, wet. He shook his head once, like he was trying to shake off the sight of me.

And heaven help me, all I wanted was to go to him—to step into that broken, familiar space and let him hold me together again.

He must've seen the hesitation on my face, because he said, voice hoarse, "The prescriptions in the glovebox weren't mine. Murphy almost slipped, and as his sponsor, he came to me. I took them from him and stuck them in the glovebox and forgot they were there."

Hope hit me so fast it hurt. My heart jumped into my throat. That sounded like *him*. Like the man I knew.

"Beckett," he said, voice breaking on the name. He cleared his throat, shook his head hard. "Nolan heard him telling Trish he'd slipped me fentanyl."

My eyes filled instantly. My chest clenched like it was trying to protect something precious and fragile. How could anyone try to break him like that?

He dragged a hand through his hair—it fell right back into his eyes. "I'm still clean, Jenny. When I was in the hospital and they offered me something stronger, it was the thought of you that kept me from saying yes. I want this life. I want you. I want Axl. The picket fence, the tire swing, the whole shebang. I want it all."

I let out a watery laugh, lifting my bandaged hands between us—proof of how broken I was. The strong, independent woman who couldn't even open a jar of peanut butter. Who was being spoon-fed humility three times a day.

"In sickness and in health," he said softly.

My breath caught. He said it like a vow. Like he meant it.

"I also owe you an apology. Nothing I can ever say will make up for the names I called you when you called to tell me about Axl."

I shook my head. He didn't need to apologize. He'd just lost his mom. I understood he was in a bad place.

"Yes. I do. I am so sorry. I don't deserve your forgiveness."

I nodded. He did deserve it, and I owed him an apology of my own. "I'm sorry too," I whispered.

Tears gathered in his eyes. He shook his head. "Please, don't. Your poor voice. Oh, Jenny." The tears fell now, his chin quivering. "You saved me. Time and again, you've saved me."

I stepped forward before I could stop myself. He wrapped his good arm around me, pulling me tight to his side. His body shook with quiet sobs, his lips pressing into my hair. For a long moment, I just stood there, breathing him in—soap, rain, jet fuel, home.

When I finally pulled back, we stared at each other like maybe we'd both dreamed this moment and didn't trust it to be real.

Then I nodded toward the desk. The form. My decision.

He followed my gaze, brow furrowed. When he saw what it was, he blinked. Once. Twice.

"You're putting me on Axl's birth certificate?"

I nodded.

He cupped my face with his good hand, thumb tracing my jaw in a worshipful caress. He kissed me, soft and shaky. "Thank you." He pressed his forehead to mine. "I have one more thing for you."

He crossed to the door, picked up a long tube, and came back, balancing it between his knees as he pulled papers free single-handedly. The clear sheet at the top caught the light, a glint of promise.

"I had this made for you."

He unrolled the papers across my desk. At the top, in bold letters, it read "Jenny's Happy Place."

I gasped, staring at the large papers. They were blueprints. House plans. With words like "Axl's bedroom" and "Axl's tree-house" written in tiny print.

"For us?" I whispered.

Evan nodded and I threw my arms—what was left of them—gently around his neck. Pain be damned.

"It's going to be built where the Parkland house was," he said, his grin breaking through the tears. "I made sure to include this." He pointed to a spot in the kitchen labeled "Jenny's Coffee Bar."

I laughed and nodded. The coffee. Oh, how he'd fought for that coffee. And I was so glad he hadn't given up after that first time when I'd thrown it in the garbage.

He flipped the back page forward. The second drawing showed the front of the house—Victorian trim, a tower, every little detail I'd ever babbled to him about in passing. It was perfect. My tears dripped onto the paper, tiny dark circles of proof.

"I can make any changes you want," he said, then pulled the transparent sheet free. "But I'm hoping you'll agree to this one."

He laid it over the blueprint, aligning it carefully. Where it had said "Jenny's Bedroom," it now read "Jenny and Evan's Bedroom."

I looked up at him. Hope fluttered to life in my chest, small and terrified.

"Please," he whispered. His eyes were raw.

And I nodded.

CHAPTER SEVENTY-FOUR

"CAN I SEE AXL?"

I'd waited as long as I could. Jenny first, then Axl—that was the deal I'd made with myself. I'd done my penance, said my apologies, and now I just needed to see him.

Jenny's eyes glittered like she was holding back a flood. She pressed her lips together and nodded. Hooked her bandaged arm through mine and led me down the hall.

Halfway there, I stopped. My ribs protested, but that wasn't the pain making me hesitate. "Are you okay if I tell him who I am?"

Her eyes softened. "Yes," she rasped.

I cupped her cheek with my right hand, thumb catching her tears. "Thank you," I said quietly. "I keep saying it, but I need you to know how grateful I am. For everything. For keeping him. For knowing I wasn't ready for him back then." My voice cracked. "I am now."

A single tear slipped free. I kissed it away before it could fall.

"I'm going to try like hell to be the kind of man he can look up to. The kind of dad who doesn't just show up when things are good."

Jenny pressed her lips together, nodding hard.

And guilt—good old reliable guilt—clawed its way back in. If I hadn't been in that house, she wouldn't have gone in after me. Wouldn't have been hurt. "I'm so sorry, Jenny Rose."

She stood on tiptoe and kissed me, soft and quick, like we were both made of glass. Then she linked our arms again and tugged me along.

Upstairs looked like Willy Wonka had gone into the childcare business. The playroom dropped into a lower level—ball pit, slide, rock wall, fireman pole, built-in swings. There was even a hammock reading nook. It was more than I'd designed for the house, and I made a mental note to remind Jenny she could sneak in any upgrades she wanted.

And then I saw him.

Axl.

In the hammock with his manny, a picture book open on his lap.

That's my son.

The thought hit so hard it actually hurt. My chest went tight, vision blurred. I had to swipe the back of my hand across my eyes just to see him properly.

He looked up, saw me, and grinned—wide and bright, just like his mother's.

"Van!" he shouted, waving like I was a rock star.

Jenny laughed beside me, wiping tears with the back of her bandaged hands. That sound—her laugh—was the closest thing to sunlight I'd ever heard.

Axl wriggled free and launched into a full-on sprint, arms flapping like he was trying to take flight. I didn't even pretend to act cool; I took the slide down into the ball pit like an overgrown child, wincing as my elbow and leg reminded me I wasn't built for acrobatics anymore.

He squealed, diving into the balls. I caught him one-armed, protecting my elbow like a fragile antique.

"Van! Play with me!"

My heart nearly burst. "Always."

He grabbed a ball and chucked it straight at my forehead. Direct hit. Future baseball star, apparently.

"Careful, Axl," the manny said, laughing. "Van's hurt."

My leg and arm both throbbed, but I wouldn't have traded that moment for all the painkillers in the world.

"Axl," I said, "is it okay if I come play more often?"

"Yeah!" He hurled another ball for emphasis.

I looked at Jenny. She smiled through tears and nodded.

"Axl," I said softly, "I'm your dad."

He was four—old enough to know the word, but maybe not what it meant. I didn't expect tears or fanfare. But he just looked at me for a long moment, then jumped into my arms and wrapped his tiny arms around my neck.

"Squeeze!" he demanded, voice muffled against my collarbone.

I did. I held on like my life depended on it.

AIDEN AND DYLAN came by the next day. The kitchen smelled like coffee and antiseptic and new beginnings. Dylan sat at the island, filling out the affidavit of paternity, while Jenny leaned against her shoulder like she'd finally let herself rest.

Axl sat on the floor by the fridge, pushing a toy car back and forth, making those sound effects only toddlers and grown men in denial could get away with.

Aiden and I made peace. I understood why they'd kept it a secret, and I told him so. My gaze kept flicking back to Axl every five seconds. My son. I still couldn't say it in my head without tearing up.

Then Dylan gasped. Pointed at something on the form. Jenny lifted her head, met her gaze. Dylan gestured toward me, eyebrows raised.

Jenny smiled and nodded.

"Evan," Dylan said, "do you know what Axl's middle name is?"

I frowned, trying to remember. Jenny had never said his full name. "Rose?" I guessed.

Dylan snorted. "Not that I'm one to talk, but that'd be a tough name for a little boy. It's Noah."

The air left my lungs. I turned to Jenny. She watched me, calm, proud, eyes shining.

"Really?" I whispered.

"Bruh," Dylan said, grinning, "I wouldn't lie to you."

Jenny laughed softly, a tear slipping down her cheek. I walked around the island and wiped it away with my thumb. "Is this a happy tear?"

She nodded. "I'm happy," she whispered.

I kissed her—slow, reverent, like a promise. Like we'd both crawled through fire to get back here.

"Get a room!" Aiden called.

Dylan smirked. "You guys are freakin' adorable."

Aiden grinned at his wife, the way only a man who'd found his person could. "We have something to tell you."

Jenny gasped and pointed to Dylan's stomach.

Dylan laughed. "No, I'm not pregnant."

Aiden's arm tightened around her. "We had some tests done. The doctors think the chemo made it impossible for Dylan to get pregnant."

"Oh, sh—oot. I'm sorry," I said.

Dylan waved it off. "It's okay. We've got good news."

Aiden looked straight at me. "We're adopting. We just got approved to foster—and we're hoping to adopt a teenage boy."

Jenny's hand found my waist, tugging me closer.

"Why?" I asked before I could stop myself. "I mean, most people want...you know, smaller models."

Aiden's gaze softened. "Because one of the strongest, most resilient men we know just needed a chance. Someone to believe in him. When I looked at the pictures of those teens in foster care, I saw the same potential Tracy and Carl saw in you."

The words hit like a punch to the sternum. I swallowed hard, blinked fast, then grabbed his hand and shook it like it was a life-line. "Thank you," I croaked.

Dylan grinned. "You're gonna be an uncle."

An uncle.

I let the words settle. For the first time in a long time, the future didn't scare me. It felt like something I could actually reach for.

CHAPTER SEVENTY-FIVE

EVEN IN OUR little blissful haze, life didn't pause for us. The clock kept ticking down—a week and a half until the finale.

We still had to prep Maisie and Joey for the big night. Joey was the only singer who'd been cut from the top ten whose voice even faintly resembled mine, which is how he ended up as my pick. The show had flown Joey out to Montana, which sounded fancy, but right now it just meant my living room looked like a musical triage unit.

Evan sat at the piano, playing one-handed. I was on the couch, trying to ignore the deep, crawling itch in my palms and arm that meant the skin was knitting back together. Axl played at my feet, cars and blocks scattered in a cheerful mess. Colby sat beside him, doing his best to keep him quiet while the two rehearsed.

Joey coughed for a minute, then said, "Can I take a quick break?"

Evan nodded and stretched his back. He walked over to us as Joey left the room. "He'll get it."

Maisie stood by the piano, plucking out the harmony as she sang the melody.

After a little whispered encouragement from Colby, Axl

wandered to the piano. Colby followed behind him, using Axl as his wingman.

"Want me to?" he offered, sitting at the piano.

"Sure."

Evan took the seat beside me on the couch. "That was smooth."

Then Colby started singing. Evan's eyes widened and his gaze shot to me. Colby's fingers moved with easy grace, and the room changed. His tone was rich, effortless. Maisie sang her part of the third verse while Colby filled in the male vocal, and it *worked*.

Evan's jaw practically hit the floor.

"I had no idea," he whispered. He shook his head slowly. "Can we get rid of Joey?"

Maisie didn't even glance away from Colby.

I smiled, shaking my head. "Kimball would have kittens."

"Damn."

Evan reached for my right hand, gently turning it over so he could see the cuts along my wrist. His breath caught. The stitches were almost gone now, but the twin scars stood out—two nearly parallel lines that had missed the major arteries by fractions of an inch.

It was the first time I'd gone without a bandage during the day. It made me feel both braver and strangely exposed. And my other scars were going to be even worse.

He lifted my arm and brushed a kiss over the thin red lines. "I owe you so much."

I shook my head. *No.* It was the other way around. Without him, I wouldn't have Axl. I wouldn't have this life, this *peace*.

I whispered, "You would've done the same thing."

His eyes softened. "I would."

Axl, who'd wandered back over to us, suddenly dropped his Slash bear and barreled toward Evan, arms outstretched.

Evan scooped him up with his good arm, and Axl burrowed in, giggling when Evan kissed the top of his head.

Watching them, something settled inside me. Love wasn't a feeling—it was a foundation. A steady heartbeat. I'd spent so long trying to build a stable life for Axl that I hadn't seen what real stability looked like until now.

It was this. Evan's arm around our son. The quiet laughter between takes. The sound of home breathing between piano notes.

Axl didn't just need *a* father.

He needed *Evan*.

And so did I.

THE SHOW SENT a camera crew a week before the finale.

The directors sat me down in Jenny's office for an interview. The same room that still smelled faintly like her shampoo and coffee. Not distracting at all.

They asked about the fire, about the OD, about the drugs in my car. I told the truth about the first two and a soft-focus version of the third.

"They were just in my glovebox from when I used," I said, keeping my face open and my voice steady. "Didn't realize they were there. I'm just grateful I didn't find them when I was trying to get clean."

The director smiled and nodded like he'd just witnessed a redemption arc in real time.

Then he flipped a cue card.

"How does it feel to find out you're the father of Jenny Gentry's son?"

I couldn't help the grin that spread across my face.

"It feels pretty dam— Dang good," I said, catching myself before I slipped. "Still getting used to the language you have to use around a toddler. He's all the best parts of Jenny. Haven't seen much of me in him yet, but maybe that's a good thing."

"So, are you and Jenny back together?"

My hand drifted to my pocket, fingers finding the ring that had replaced my sobriety medallion. A different kind of promise I wasn't ready to cash in yet.

"We haven't really defined it," I said. "But I love her with everything I am. I don't deserve her—but I'll spend the rest of my life trying to be worthy of her."

"Cut."

I stood, shook the director's hand, and nodded toward the door. "Be easy on Jenny. She's not supposed to talk much yet."

"You got it."

Back in the music room, Jenny brushed a kiss across my lips before heading to her own interview. Her touch still managed to ignite my entire system. I sat behind one of the cameras, pretending to watch the monitors instead of missing her.

Joey held a mug of tea in one hand and a tissue in the other as he sang his part. His voice was more nasally than usual.

"Joey, are you getting sick?" I took a shallow breath like breathing less air could keep me from catching it.

"I'm fine,"

"Take five, man. Go get some air."

The kid all but sprinted out.

"Poor guy," the cameraman said.

I nodded. "Yeah."

Two days before the finale, we flew back to L.A.—on a *real* airplane this time.

I held Axl on my lap the entire flight, which was probably the only thing keeping me from clawing through the fuselage. My body stayed calm because his was pressed against mine, warm and steady. His head smelled like sugar and shampoo. My son.

The ring in my pocket dug into my thigh, but I didn't move. Didn't dare wake him.

When we landed, Ryan and my dad were waiting on the

tarmac. Seeing Dad climb out of that car felt like the world tilted back into place.

His eyes went straight to Axl. "There's my grandson."

Jenny smiled, the picture of grace even with bandages still peeking out from her sleeves.

Dad's throat bobbed. He crouched down to Axl's level, hand out like he was greeting royalty. "Hey, Axl. Remember me? I'm Grandpa."

"Papa," Axl said solemnly.

Dad blinked fast and nodded. "That's right. Papa." His voice broke clean in half.

Axl hugged him, small arms around my dad's neck, and the man just—crumbled. Shoulders shaking, soft sob muffled in Axl's hair.

When he finally pulled back, he insisted on buckling Axl into the car seat himself. I watched him fumble with the straps, tears streaking his face.

Then he turned to Jenny and hugged her too. "Thank you for believing in my son. For giving me a grandbaby. He's perfect."

Jenny caught my gaze over his shoulder and winked. "You're welcome."

CHAPTER SEVENTY-SEVEN

"YOUR POOR VOICE," Lindsay murmured the night of the final performances, already pulling out her brushes. "Let's get your makeup done so you can feel your best. I hear Fabian will be here soon. He said he has an outfit that's going to make you feel *absolutely beautiful.* He called it a statement piece."

Kelsey began curling my hair.

Lindsay worked moisturizer into my skin, gentle as rain. "Tell me about the fire," she said softly.

"Non-disclosure, right?" I rasped.

"For sure," Kelsey said.

At the same time, Lindsay added, "Of course."

I gave them just enough to satisfy curiosity, keeping my tone low and even. I wanted to save what was left of my voice for the contestants. Bonnie, Troy, Zane—they deserved a judge who could still speak with warmth, not croak through a half-lost voice.

"Can we see your hands?" Lindsay asked after a moment.

I shook my head. "It hurts to have the bandages off. But you can see the cuts on my wrists."

The mesh netting over my bandages itched and tugged against healing skin. The stitches had come out last week, but the scars still looked angry—tight, shiny, red-pink. Skin that didn't quite belong to me yet.

Lindsay winced. "Holy Moses, that looks painful."

I'd seen Evan's leg. It looked terrible. If my hands looked like that—I didn't even want to think about it. He could walk though. I still needed help with nearly everything. My poor nurse hadn't had a full night's sleep since the fire.

Kelsey spritzed my hair one last time and gave it a satisfied pat. "All done."

Fabian waltzed in a few minutes later, all drama and perfume, two garment bags slung over one arm. As soon as he put them down, he caught me in a gentle hug.

"How are you feeling, you warrior goddess?"

I grinned and squeezed him as tight as my injuries allowed. "Extra crispy."

He laughed, and when he pulled back, he wiped a tear from his eye. "Are you ready to see your dresses?"

"Plural?" I teased, pretending to rub my hands together.

"Plural." His grin was pure theater. "One for tonight, one for tomorrow."

He hung the bags on the dressing screen and unzipped the first with a flourish.

The gown inside was black and impossibly elegant—lace half-sleeves, off-the-shoulder neckline, a trail of buttons marching up the spine. It looked like mourning and strength sewn together.

"This one's for the final performances tonight," Fabian said, reverent. "I spoke with your nurse. We'll use a loose pair of black lace gloves—like coal or ashes."

He unzipped the next bag. My breath hitched. The second gown shimmered like flame—black lace overlay, orange-red underlay, every thread flickering like it was alive.

"And this one is for the final eliminations tomorrow."

I held my hands to my mouth, careful not to touch anything. "They're stunning."

"I thought so too." Fabian's smile softened. "Let's get you into this black one."

BACKSTAGE, the sound of the crowd pulsed through the floor like a heartbeat. When Evan saw me, his jaw actually dropped.

"You look stunning."

"Thank you," I whispered. My throat ached, so I didn't dare use more than a few words. I needed them later.

Gus came to wire me for sound.

Evan walked over gingerly, flexed his left arm. I gasped. "You're out of your sling!"

"It's stiff," he said, rotating it carefully. "Can't straighten it all the way, but my PT says I'll get full range of motion back."

I let out a slow breath. "No permanent damage then?"

He laughed. "Well, this giant scar on my leg probably won't go away."

"Probably not. We're both permanently scarred."

He tilted his head, smirking. "You have no idea."

I laughed—quietly, but for real this time.

Then Jaryce introduced me, and the world tilted.

The roar of the crowd hit like a tidal wave—deafening, relentless. I waved my bandaged and gloved hands, mimed blowing kisses. The lights blurred, and I blinked fast to keep the tears from spilling.

I climbed the stairs carefully, each movement a negotiation between pain and pride. Kimball already sat on the judges' dais.

Evan's welcome was even louder. He stood on the stage edge, tears shining under the lights. When he mouthed *thank you* and put a hand over his heart, I felt mine swell in response.

Jaryce waited for the cheers to fade. "We're so glad you're both okay," he said. "We here at *Singing Sensation* have kept you both in our hearts and prayers."

The crowd erupted again, and this time, I didn't stop the tears. One slipped free.

"Let's get this show on the road! Please welcome Troy Maddox!" Jaryce stepped aside.

The big screen came alive with Troy's journey—from the audition line to his best rehearsal moments.

Troy's performance was strong. Confident. His tone had grown smoother since the start, and I found myself smiling despite the ache in my throat. And how much I disliked him.

Then came Bonnie Flynn. Her montage was all sunshine— sweet and funny, ending with a moment of laughter between her and Zane. And then, in the middle of her song, she stumbled. Forgot the words. My heart cracked.

When it was my turn to give feedback, I leaned close to the mic and focused on her strengths—the control in her chorus, the beauty in that last verse. Because sometimes that was all a person needed: to be reminded of what still worked.

Zane's montage rolled next.

"Singing *Ashes and Air* by Evan Black," the announcer said. "Please welcome Zane Draven."

My head snapped toward Evan. "What song is this?"

He didn't look at me, eyes locked on the stage, but a slow, knowing smile curved his mouth. "It's new."

My pulse kicked. "Is this—?"

He pointed toward the stage, still smiling. "Just listen."

So I did.

Zane strummed the first chords, low and hollow. The screen behind him flickered to life. Flames. Smoke. My stomach knotted.

Then he sang.

> *"I don't remember the flame, just the dark,*
> *The weight in my chest, the silence sharp.*
> *I thought that was it, no one left to care,*
> *Just smoke in my lungs, just ashes and air."*

My throat closed. My chest hurt. Oh no.

Don't cry, Jenny. You'll ruin your makeup. You'll set off the mic. You'll make this about you.

Didn't matter. Tears still welled.

> *"But you pulled me out when I was already*
> *gone,*
> *Gave me breath I could never deserve to*
> *breathe on.*
> *I'm still here because you were there,*
> *Ashes and air...ashes and air."*

On screen, a fire raged behind him. My lungs filled with phantom smoke. My hands tingled with remembered heat. My breath hitched, and I swallowed hard on a small sob.

> *"I don't know why you walked through the*
> *fire,*
> *Carried me down when the flames climbed*
> *higher.*
> *You saved me from death with the strength of*
> *your hand,*
> *You gave me a life—I still don't understand."*

Evan's hand found my knee under the table—steady, grounding. His thumb drew soft circles, and something in my chest cracked open. I turned toward him. Tears glimmered in his eyes too.

He was remembering it, same as me. The fear. The silence. The moment the fire went out, and everything else went quiet.

> *"'Cause you pulled me out when I was already*
> *gone,*
> *Gave me breath I could never deserve to*
> *breathe on.*
> *I'm still here because you were there,*
> *Ashes and air...ashes and air."*

I sniffled, completely undone. The song wasn't just beautiful

—it was raw. Holy. Like Evan had written down the parts of our story we'd never said out loud.

> *"I'm not begging you to believe in me,*
> *I won't deceive. I am what you see.*
> *I'm just saying this breath is borrowed*
> > *from you,*
> *And every beat of my heart says it's true."*

I remembered giving Evan chest compressions, my voice shouting for help that couldn't come fast enough. Tears streamed down my face, and I dabbed at them with the back of my bandaged hands.

> *"You pulled me out when I was already gone,*
> *Gave me breath I could never deserve to*
> > *lean on.*
> *I'm still here because you were there,*
> *Ashes and air...*
> *Ashes and air."*

The final frame froze on the charred skeleton of Evan's house, the morning fog curling around it like smoke refusing to die.

Then silence. Then thunder. The audience rose to their feet, applause crashing like surf.

I stood too, wiping tears from under my eyes with the backs of my bandaged hands.

Evan rose beside me and pulled me into his arms, pressing a kiss to my forehead. The world blurred.

"Thank you," he whispered, just for me. His voice trembled. "I hadn't seen the footage they were going to use. I'm a little shaken."

I nodded against his chest, the fabric of his jacket rough against my cheek. "Me too," I tried to say, but it came out as a quiet sound, half sob, half breath.

Jaryce stepped back onto the stage, voice booming over the cheers.

"That's it for tonight! Remember to vote for your favorite performance! Call or text the numbers on your screen. Keep singing, keep dreaming, and keep the sensation alive!"

The lights dimmed, applause still echoing as security ushered us backstage.

The contestants waited just off the wings, faces flushed from the lights and adrenaline. I moved through them one by one, hugging each in turn.

"Great job tonight," I rasped, my voice barely holding. When I got to Bonnie, she tried to smile, but tears streaked her mascara.

"I'm so sorry that happened," I whispered.

She shook her head. "I kept struggling with that one part. I should've practiced more."

"Sometimes that's just the way the chips fall," I told her.

She gave a small nod, as if trying to believe me.

A director appeared with a man in a charcoal suit and a Titan Records badge clipped to his lapel.

"Evan, Jenny," the director said, "this is McKay Steele, chairman of the board."

He shook Evan's hand, then hesitated when he looked at my bandages. His hand twitched like he wanted to shake hands but thought better of it.

"Can we talk somewhere private?" he asked Evan.

Evan shot me a quick look, checking in, and I nodded. *Go.*

"Sure," he said.

And as they walked away, I let out a shaky breath, my throat raw, my heart still thrumming with the rhythm of the song. *Ashes and air... Ashes and air.*

CHAPTER SEVENTY-EIGHT

JENNY'S REACTION to my song was perfect. The kind of perfect that made my chest ache. I wanted nothing more than to pull her close, tell her I loved her, and mean it without sounding like an apology.

But the suit wanted a word, and while I wasn't exactly known for keeping the peace, I had no idea where my career stood after this circus.

He led me into a private dressing room that still smelled like Kimball's cologne—expensive confidence and ego.

"Evan, first I want to extend my deepest apologies for what happened with your band. We had no idea Beckett was...well, unhinged. We intend to work fully with authorities to make sure he's punished to the full extent of the law."

"Thank you, Mr. Steele."

"Please, call me McKay."

I nodded, pretending I wasn't halfway to the door already. "I appreciate the apology."

If I could just make it back to Jenny before the adrenaline wore off, maybe I could tell her what the song hadn't.

"There's one more thing..."

Of course there was.

I raised an eyebrow.

"It hasn't been announced yet, but this is Kimball's last season with *Singing Sensation.* We've been very impressed with you—your insight, the way you work with contestants. We think you have a director's instinct. We'd like you to interview for his position."

My mouth fell open. My brain scattered like marbles on tile. Of all the things I thought he'd say, this wasn't on the list.

"You don't have to answer today," McKay added. "Just think about it. We'd like your answer by tomorrow after the finale."

"Right. Sure. I'll...think about it."

We shook hands, and I walked out in a fog thick enough to choke on.

What the hell had just happened?

Jenny's dressing room was down the hall, and my feet carried me there before my brain caught up. She came out from behind the screen in jeans and a T-shirt, hair loose, face soft. Home. Her nurse left the room with a silent nod.

"What was that about?" she asked.

"The suit asked me to interview for Kimball's job here on *Singing Sensation.*"

Her eyes went wide. Then she squealed—actually squealed—and threw her arms around my neck. "Congratulations! You'd be amazing! Would you be the head judge on *Singing Sensation?*"

An idea started clawing at the back of my brain. "I have an alternate option."

"I'm listening."

We sat on the chaise, her knee touching mine, and I let the thought unspool.

"Black Rose Records."

Her brows pulled together. "What?"

"We start our own label. Our contracts are both up. Why not build something that's ours?"

Jenny gasped. "And we could sign Katarina and Maisie! And make it about the music—not the image. We sell voices over vanity."

"That's the slogan right there," I said, grinning. "'For the voices, not the vanity.'"

For the first time in a long time, the future didn't feel like a threat. It felt like a possibility.

THE NEXT DAY, I sat in the back of the theater, waiting for Joey to show up for final rehearsals as Colby sat at the piano flirting with Maisie Grace.

Javi rushed over and perched on the seat beside me. "I just got a text from Joey. He's got bronchitis. He's out."

I clapped my hands, startling Colby and Maisie's gaze my way. "Joey's sick. Congratulations, Colby, you're in."

Colby twisted around on the piano bench. "You can't be serious."

"Dead serious. This is your shot."

"I don't want a shot. If I wanted to be a singer, I have a very famous sister and brother-in-law I could ask."

Fair point. I stood and started hobbling toward the stage. "Okay, then here's the deal. This song matters to me. I need someone who won't ruin it. Do it for me—for Jenny."

He sighed, fingers dragging through his hair. "Fine. For Jenny."

I raised my hands in victory. "Perfect."

I climbed the steps and sat on the bench beside him. "I've got a favor to ask though."

He groaned. "Of course you do."

"It's small," I said. And for once, I actually meant it.

THE FIRE DRESS WAS...WELL, fire. It hugged me in all the right places and shimmered every time I moved, like it had its own heartbeat.

Kelsey and Lindsay chattered around me—lip gloss, camera angles, curls—and their voices blurred into background noise. My mind was still stuck on what Evan had said yesterday.

Our own record label.

It sounded insane. Like jumping off a cliff and hoping the ground rose up to meet you.

But it also felt *right.*

It would let me stay home with Axl. Give him roots. Stability. And I'd still get to create, to pour into new artists, to shape something good out of the chaos we'd survived. I could even decide when and how to tour—one show a year or one hundred, or none at all if I wanted. The idea of having that kind of control was... intoxicating.

"You're glowing," Lindsay said, tilting her head like she'd just discovered a new species.

I couldn't help but grin. "I'm happy."

Alli poked her head in. "They want you backstage in two minutes."

My stomach flipped. Two minutes. The end of a chapter.

It had all gone so fast—and yet somehow it felt like I'd been living inside this season for a lifetime.

Tonight, we'd crown the winner.

Zane probably had an edge with Evan's song and, well, the *rescue* drama that had practically gone viral by now. The memory still lived under my skin—the smoke, the fear, the sound of the flames destroying the past.

But I wasn't the same woman who'd run into that fire.

I'd learned something about myself.

I wasn't flight. I was fight.

And I'd fight for all of it—for Evan, for Axl, for every artist who deserved better than what Kimball had built.

My agent was already wrangling lawyers to set up the label, and Evan's dad—sweet, steady Carl—had agreed to handle our finances. Evan said it'd be good for him. Healing even. Maybe it'd be good for them both.

By the time I reached the stage, my heartbeat had steadied into something sure and strong.

Vince and Colby had Axl in the front row, his little head bouncing as he waved both arms. I found them easily—Vince's familiar grin, Axl's curls catching the light—but Colby's seat was empty. Odd.

Evan slipped into the seat beside me just as the lights dimmed. The two of us stood and waved as the crowd roared, the sound so loud it buzzed in my bones.

Jaryce stepped forward, his smile bright beneath the stage lights. "Now, as you know, our judges usually perform a duet they've written together. But with Jenny recovering from smoke inhalation, we've made a few changes. Singing 'Every Thought' by Jenny Gentry and Evan Black, please welcome Maisie Grace and Colby Kennedy."

I gasped, turning toward Evan. He just smiled.

"You rat," I hissed, half laughing.

He only laughed harder.

Colby took his seat at the piano, dressed head-to-toe in black.

Maisie sat on top in a white gown that glowed under the lights—shadow and light, perfectly balanced.

Colby's fingers brushed the keys, and the first notes rose, gentle and haunting. Then Maisie's voice carried through the room—pure, effortless, the kind of tone that could stop time.

> *"We fit together, like mountain and sky,*
> *But our love held a poison we tried to deny.*
> *At first truly happy, then merely brave faces,*
> *Our flaws took us both to such different*
> *   places."*
> Colby's voice came next, smooth and
> *   steady.*
> *"How long will your memory haunt me?*
> *The pain of your absence is taking its toll.*
> *Will I find a way I can break free,*
> *From the image of you that's burned into my*
> *   soul?"*

Then the chorus, their voices intertwining.

> *"Every thought pulls me under,*
> *Every step takes me farther from you.*
> *Yet every thought makes me wonder,*
> *With every thought do you think of me too?"*

The audience hushed, as if the whole room had forgotten to breathe.

Colby sang the next verse, and I felt my chest tighten.

> *"I've buried us in a place deep below,*
> *A spot in my memory where I never go.*
> *Yet every day you're escaping, it seems.*
> *Pulling me back to us in my thoughts and my*
> *   dreams."*

They built the harmonies, trading lines like a conversation between heartbreak and healing.

By the time Maisie began singing the bridge, I could feel tears prick behind my eyes.

> *"Even when the night feels endless,*
> *Even when the stars fail to shine..."*

The song wasn't just music anymore. It was *us*.

A crew member crouch-crawled over to us and handed Evan a microphone. My heart stuttered.

The lights dimmed until everything but a single spotlight was gone. It found him—Evan, standing there beside me with that crooked half-smile that undid me every single time.

"Jenny," he said softly, "I wrote one more verse for you."

The crowd cheered. My mouth hung open, my heart galloping.

Then he sang.

> *"When the world crashes, I still find peace,*
> *In your arms, I can make the insanity cease.*
> *You are my harbor, my home, my space,*
> *My heart has settled—this is my happy place."*

He pointed between himself and me.

> *"Through every scar, through every fight,*
> *You're the calm that brings me light.*
> *I lost myself, but now I see,*
> *I'm exactly where I'm meant to be."*

His voice cracked on the last line, raw and unguarded.

Then, with nothing but the sound of his breath to guide him, he sang the final chorus a cappella.

> *"Every thought pulls you nearer,*

Every heartbeat is calling your name.
I'm seeing everything clearer,
Let's put every thought to restoring love's
flame."

Silence stretched after the last note. The kind that filled every corner of the room. Then the room erupted in applause. Ovaries burst, and manly men cried.

Evan reached out and cupped my cheek, thumb catching my tears. I pressed a kiss to his palm, unable to find words big enough for what I felt.

This moment...couldn't be more perfect.

Then a small hand tugged on his sleeve.

Axl.

Evan scooped him up without missing a beat, settling him on his hip just as the lights came back up. Vince's panicked search found us, and I waved him off with a laugh.

The audience laughed too, warmth rippling through the room.

Evan's arm came around my shoulders, steady and sure.

Now it was perfect.

evan

NO ONE GASPED when Bonnie Flynn got cut. We'd all seen it coming from miles away. Still didn't stop the tears. She took it like a pro, bowed out with that trembling smile people wore when their heart was breaking, but they were determined not to show it.

The final two stood under the lights, side by side, their whole futures sweating under the glare. The screen behind them played the standard montage—hotel footage, bloopers, snippets of us pretending to know what we were talking about. I sat there with Axl on my lap, waiting for the inevitable.

Jaryce milked the pause like a man who got paid by the second.

"Kimball, Jenny, Evan, do any of you have a prediction?"

Jenny leaned into her mic, graceful as ever. "I think there's no wrong choice here. Both of these boys are talented singers, and either way, I think we'll hear both of them on the radio. They're phenomenal."

Of course she said that. She could find the silver lining in a hurricane.

Jaryce turned to me. "Evan?"

I shifted Axl higher on my lap, pried his fingers off the microphone. The audience collectively melted. "If I were a betting man," I said, "I'd put my money on Zane."

That was the kind of off-script honesty that made Kimball twitch.

"Kimball?" Jaryce asked.

He leaned back in his seat and gave a satisfied nod. "I agree with my judges. There is no wrong choice. Let's hear what America had to say."

"The season fifteen winner of *Singing Sensation* is…" Jaryce paused for drama that could've lasted a lifetime. "Zane Draven!"

Confetti. Balloons. Screaming. The whole circus.

Zane took the mic, launched into his victory song, while the crowd roared and the cameras ate it up. Kimball, Jenny, Axl, and I climbed onto the stage, hugged Troy, whispered the usual "so proud of you" lines that no one ever remembered but everyone needed to hear.

Then Zane's family stormed the stage—like thirty people deep—and swallowed him whole. We waved to the audience and the cameras until the red lights blinked off.

After the chaos died down, I carried Axl backstage, Jenny's arm looped through mine. My chest felt full, and not the scary kind of full. The good kind.

Outside the dressing room, I stopped. "Go on in. Axl and I have man-to-man stuff to discuss."

She laughed, then she disappeared behind the door.

I crouched in front of Axl, the kid already fiddling with the hem of his tiny jacket. "Hey, buddy," I said softly, "I love your mommy very much. You know that, right?"

He gave a shy nod, fingers going straight to his mouth.

"You're the man of the house," I told him. "So I need your permission to ask her to marry me. That okay with you?"

He blinked those big eyes at me.

"Is it okay if I live in your house and be your daddy all the time?"

Another small nod.

I smiled and pulled him close, pressing a kiss to his curls as I lifted him into my arms. "I love you, little dude."

Right on cue, McKay Steele appeared, like a jump scare in a suit.

"Evan," he said, all business. "Have you given any thought to our offer?"

I shifted Axl to my hip. "Yeah. I appreciate it, but I'm gonna pass."

His face fell about an inch. "I'm sorry to hear that. We'll reach out to your agent about renewing your contract."

"Sure thing." I'd drop that bomb later. For now, I had a woman to make happy.

We shook hands, and I watched him walk away—one door closing, another one waiting somewhere else. I wasn't scared of what came next. Not anymore.

But my stomach still did a few backflips. Not fear—just nerves. Proposal jitters. I didn't have fireworks or a string quartet. No ocean backdrop. No cameras rolling. Just a dressing room that still smelled like hair spray and fishy crackers.

And somehow, that felt right.

I knocked.

"Come in," Jenny called.

I opened the door, set Axl on his feet. My hand found my pocket automatically. The ring was there—where my sobriety medallion used to be. Fitting.

For years, I thought I stayed sober *instead* of loving people. Turned out, I stayed sober *so I could.*

"You okay?" she asked, eyes soft.

I blinked back to her. "I'm perfect."

"Want to get takeout and go back to your place?"

I shook my head. "Our place."

Her eyebrows lifted—then I pulled out the ring.

It hung on a platinum chain. Her hands were still bandaged, and I didn't want to make her struggle. "Jenny," I said, voice rougher than I intended, "I want forever with you. Will you marry me?"

She gasped, then laughed when she saw the chain. "Yes!"

The word hit like a melody I never wanted to end.

She threw herself at me, and we tumbled to the floor, laughing. Axl jumped on top of us, a giggling pile of limbs and love.

"Oof!"

Not exactly cinematic—but it was ours.

And it was perfect.

ONE YEAR LATER

EVAN BLINDFOLDED Axl and I for the drive. I had a sneaky suspicion I knew where we were going, but his excitement was contagious, so I played along.

We'd had a small Montana wedding two weeks after *Singing Sensation* wrapped, and then announced the launch of Black Rose Records a month later.

I could hardly believe this was real life. I worked myself to the bone every day, but I was home each night, satisfied and happy in the life we'd built. Some nights I cooked, some Evan did—we'd both been taking lessons. And Axl had started kindergarten in the fall. It was surreal.

The car slowed, and the window rolled down, letting in the cool autumn air. I'd been banned from the Parkland property for nearly a year while the house was built. Part of me still worried seeing it would send me back to that night, when I'd almost lost my whole world.

We pulled through the gate and into the driveway.

"Can I take it off yet?" I asked, my voice nearly whole.

I could feel Axl bouncing in his booster seat beside me.

"Almost," Evan said.

The car stopped, and Evan jumped out. Axl's seatbelt unbuckled, but I waited patiently. A few seconds later, my car door opened, and Evan's hand found mine. I hid the wince at the contact, because the pleasure of his touch far outweighed the pain. After the fire, my hands were sensitive. Occasionally, a spark would zing beneath my skin, like now.

Evan released me and put a hand on the small of my back, guiding me to the lawn. I inhaled, almost expecting the acrid smell of smoke. Instead, I got honeysuckle and hope. Axl's hand wrapped around the pointer finger on my right hand—one of the least injured.

"Ready?" Evan breathed.

"Ready," Axl and I said in unison.

Evan's hands found the knot at the back of my head and fumbled for a second before he gave up and just lifted the blindfold. "Take them off."

My eyes took a second to adjust to the sun, but I heard Axl's delighted squeal as he took off toward the trees in the side yard.

The house rose from the lot like it had always been there. A Victorian—tall and proud, all gables and grace. Gingerbread trim curled along the eaves, lace cut from wood. Fresh white paint caught the sun, warm and clean and new.

And still...

My chest tightened.

This was the lot.

I could see it even now: the columns of smoke, the way the heat had flattened me, the exact path of the ground where I'd dragged Evan, counting breaths I wasn't sure he'd keep. I half expected the memory to rush me, to blot out everything else like it sometimes did.

I took a step, then another. And another, bracing for the acrid smell of smoke, the phantom burn of heat on my skin.

Nothing came.

The yard was green and wide, sunlight spilling across the grass. A maple tree shaded the side yard, its branches holding Axl's impossible and wonderful pirate ship treehouse. Vince stood behind Axl as he climbed a rope ladder that had been mounted to the tree. A black pirate flag snapped in the breeze.

I laughed before I could stop myself. The sound felt unfamiliar —too light, too easy after what had happened on these hallowed grounds.

The house didn't flinch. The ground didn't remember.

I crossed the yard and ran my fingers along a porch rail. The wood was smooth and warm beneath my hand. New. Solid. Real. No heat. No ghosts.

The fear I'd carried with me loosened, strand by strand.

This house didn't ask me to relive anything. It didn't demand I carry the past through its doors.

"It's perfect," I said.

Evan linked our arms and led me to the front door.

"Ready, Mrs. Black?" He sent me that smile that melted my core every time.

I laughed. "I'm ready." He brought my hand to his lips and placed a soft kiss on the back of it.

"I love you," he said.

"I love you too."

He opened the door, scooped me into his arms, and carried me across the threshold.

"Welcome home, Jenny Rose."

BLACK ROSE RECORDS formed a month after *Singing Sensation* ended. This label was something different. Built from the ashes, held together by calloused hands and second chances.

Movement caught my eye through the window. Maisie Grace.

Without conscious thought, a smile tugged my lips.

She breezed through the front doors like she owned the light around her, shoulders back, chin high—the kind of confidence that had made America fall in love with her. My stomach did a slow, traitorous turn. She stopped at the front desk, all sleek lines and composure—until she saw me.

Her face lit up, and she waved with zero chill. I waved back with equal excitement. She'd mentioned her recording session was today when we had lunch together this afternoon.

She checked her invisible watch, then mouthed, *Are you almost done?*

I held up a finger and turned back to Rafe, the engineer, at the console.

The control room hummed quietly, alive in that way only studios were—fans whispering, monitors pulsing, a low bass thrum that settled into my bones. I could feel her gaze on the side of my face.

Evan's voice poured through the speakers—unpolished, honest. Jenny followed, her harmony wrapping around his—her voice only holding a whisper of the damage she'd sustained in the fire.

Rafe leaned forward, fingertips dancing over the board. The man mixed like he was coaxing a ghost to stay—barely breathing, all focus. A millimeter on a fader, a flick of the mouse, the quiet reverence of someone who understood how fragile a perfect moment could be.

The waveforms scrolled across the screen—tiny earthquakes, heartbeats in neon blue—this job was invisible. No one would applaud Rafe for getting the levels right, but he'd make sure the world heard the truth.

That was enough for me.

Even though I used to dream about being a rockstar, I'd seen what publicity did to a relationship. After my sister married Aiden "Freaking" Miller, the paparazzi had followed Dylan through her cancer treatments like a horde of rabid zombies. My high school had begged me to finish senior year online because the vultures had tried every tactic imaginable to get to me. To ask how I was coping with the "tragedy."

Which was why a relationship with Maisie wouldn't work, no matter what my heart said. I dealt with enough just being her friend. If she was the spotlight, I was the shadows. I wanted no part of that.

I glanced toward the foyer again. Maisie in her cowboy boots strolled slowly down the hallway, past my door, and toward the second booth. My pulse didn't get the memo that she was off limits.

Rafe hit the talkback. "That's the one," he said. "Let's punch it from the chorus."

Through the glass, Jenny flexed her hands—still stiff but healing—and nodded. Evan gave her that small, private half-smile that never made it to camera.

Rafe rolled it back and started the recording.

Jenny came in soft, uncertain for a beat, then sure. Evan

followed, low and rough-edged, like gravel under velvet. Together, they filled the air. I felt it in my ribs. It amazed me how two people could pour everything they were into a microphone and leave something real behind. Something that outlasted the applause.

Rafe lifted his hand at the final note. The silence that followed was heavy, like the air after a storm.

"Got it," he murmured, saving the take.

On the screen, the new file appeared—two names, one moment. Just a few seconds of sound linked eternally.

I leaned back, heartbeat steadying. *Yeah. This. This is what I want to do.*

Even if nobody ever knew my name.

I slipped out the door and into the hallway. Maisie met me there, a giant smile on her beautiful face. Her green eyes sparked with humor.

She looked up and down the hall to make sure we were alone, then whispered, "I earned the Golden Microphone."

A grin stole across my face. "What'd you do?"

We'd implemented the Golden Microphone award after the *Singing Sensation* finale. I went to leave the stage after our performance and slipped on stray confetti. Luckily, the cameras had missed me trying to regain my balance and ripping an entire row of black stage curtains from their hooks—though they did catch the flash of chaos right beforehand.

Maisie and Katarina both witnessed it, and the Golden Microphone award was born. The girls had gotten together and spray painted an old microphone gold, then glued it to a miniature mic stand and had a plaque made.

"Have you checked the group chat? Katarina has been laughin' about it all afternoon."

I shook my head. "Not yet. I've been deciding my destiny." I nodded back toward the booth. "Sound engineer sounds like a pretty cool gig."

After the wedding, Jenny and Dylan staged an intervention and told me I had to do something with my life besides being

Axl's nanny. Since then, I'd been exploring various music-related jobs.

"You're goin' to school to be a sound engineer?" She squealed and threw herself into my arms, her warm-sugar scent invading my nose and almost killing my resolve to just be friends. "Congratulations."

"Thanks, now tell me what embarrassing thing you did to earn the Golden Microphone."

She stepped out of my arms and ran a hand over her red hair, tucking it back in place. "You know how after lunch, Katarina and I were runnin' to the coffee shop? Well, I ordered a sweet tea, and after I got it, I wasn't watching where I was going and went to take a sip. I tripped over one of those wrought-iron chairs and went down, boots over britches. I spilled the whole thing all over me. It's probably all over the Internet by now."

I laughed and pulled my phone from my back pocket and clicked on my socials. I found the video within seconds, Maisie pressing against my arm as she watched it over my shoulder.

As her boots flew into the air and sweet tea exploded all over the restaurant on my screen, she yanked the phone from my hands, laughing so hard she could barely contain herself. She rewound it and played that part again and again, until she collapsed onto the floor in a fit of giggles.

Ladies and Gentlemen, the woman I was trying not to fall in love with.

I was screwed.

It takes a village to raise a child. It takes a special sort of village to help you raise a book baby. I have the best village behind me. (Please excuse the length of this section, as I am exceedingly grateful!)

When this book was a few short months from publication, I did something every author fears—I deleted the manuscript. It was gone with a capital G. I cried. But I also found the will to continue writing, because these characters mean so much to me. And because my village inspires me.

Thank you to God, for inspiring me. For seeing what I can't. For the words to tell the stories.

Thank you to my husband, Daniel, for turning into a superhero. For taking the kids to after-school activities and jumping in to save the day. Thank you for telling me to remove the brain matter—you may hate fiction, but you have a story brain without even knowing it.

Thank you to my amazing writing group, the Sisters Prim and Grimm. You held me up. You sustained me. Kelsey Larson, Allison Anderson, Kayla Tillotson, Amber Mae Weston, Marci Johnson, Tarry Parry, H.R. Boyd, Natalie Kraus, Bonnie Jo Pierson, and Lindsay Hiller.

Lindsay, you get your own paragraph. You are wonderful. You saw the potential in this book before I even knew all the characters. And you listened to me ramble about it and wrote the outline as I paced at a writing conference and dreamed of getting it done. The Lord knew I needed you in my life, and I will forever be grateful that you are my friend. Thank you for your encouragement, for the phone calls, the brainstorming sessions, and for somehow shaping this into something worthy of public consumption.

Alli, you have such a fantastic story brain! Thank you for pushing me to be better, for challenging my thinking, and for helping me figure out what wasn't working. You are one of my favorite humans. I trust you.

Kelsey, you inspire me to overcome. Thank you for the "Kelsey Edit." You wrote almost as many words telling me how to fix my book as I did creating it. Genius Count: 1,000.

The Draft Pack: Alli, Lindsay, and Marci, you kept me on track and didn't let me fall. I can never thank you enough for encouraging me to finish this book.

Thank you to Tanya Anne Crosby and Oliver-Heber Books for believing in my stories. Thank you to my wonderful editor, Christy. You are brilliant.

Thank you to the recovering addicts who let me pick their brains about all things addiction. Thank you for sharing your stories with me. Your heartaches and your triumphs. I am inspired by you all! Mandy Lynn Carter, Gavin Monteath, and Lindsay Riggs-Young.

Thank you to my BFF Chat: Neeley Wolfe, Kim Rosqvist, and Rachel Correa. Your friendship and support has meant the world to me. Thank you for always being there to share in my triumphs and my sorrows.

And lastly, thank you to Dr. Pepper for fueling my sleep-deprived dreams and giving me the extra oomph I needed to get them in this book. You will forever be The Drink of Queens! (Long live the queen!)

Sally O'Keef was born in Canada, but moved to the US when she was a wee babe. She's been married to the love of her life for twenty years, and has six wonderful children and a huge dog who snores in the background as she writes. When she's not writing, she loves reading, volleyball, and watching her children achieve their dreams.

You can connect with me on:
booksbysally.com
Subscribe to my newsletter:

A small press bound by the belief that every voice matters.

Sign up for our newsletter to learn about new releases and more.
https://oliver-heberbooks.com/subscribe/

Follow us on social media:

facebook.com/oliverheberbooks
instagram.com/oliverheberbooks
amazon.com/oliverheberbooks
youtube.com/@OliverHeberBooksPublisher